ecstasy club

ecstasy club

club

a novel

DOUGLAS RUSHKOFF

Harper*Edge*
An Imprint of HarperSanFrancisco

ECSTASY CLUB: *A Novel.* Copyright © 1997 by Douglas Rushkoff. All rights reserved. Printed in the United States of America. No part of this book may be used or reproduced in any manner whatsoever without written permission except in the case of brief quotations embodied in critical articles and reviews. For information address HarperCollins Publishers, 10 East 53rd Street, New York, NY 10022.

Harper*Edge* Web Site:
http://www.harpercollins.com/harperedge

HarperCollins®, ♣ ®, HarperSanFrancisco™, and HarperEdge™ are trademarks of HarperCollins Publishers Inc.

FIRST EDITION

Library of Congress Cataloging-in-Publication Data
Rushkoff, Douglas.
Ecstasy Club : a novel / Douglas Rushkoff. — 1st ed.
ISBN 0–06–017309–2 (cloth)
1. Title.
PS3568.U737E28 1997
813'.54—dc21   97–3442

97 98 99 00 01 ❖ RRDH 10 9 8 7 6 5 4 3 2 1

1.

The space looked huge the first time we saw it.

"This is a great place for a party," Lauren shouted, spreading her arms and twirling around in the colossal concrete room. She said what we were all thinking, which saved each of us the embarrassment of having to express what had amounted to a cliché for our posse. Even if it was true. And we did have fantastic parties there. Outrageous. Brilliant, as Duncan would call them.

George Thomas Duncan was Lauren's boyfriend at the time, and kind of our leader. He was from England. He went to either Oxford or Cambridge and talked like it most of the time, but when he'd get angry at Lauren or one of us or the cops or society or the universe, his accent dropped into East London, granting him instant street cred.

Duncan had been through tough enough times. He ran away from home and squatted with heroin-addict punk rockers when he was still only fourteen. Somehow he got himself into college and learned more about philosophy and cultural history than the rest of us did put together. He really seemed to *know* stuff—at least he talked like he did.

That's probably why none of us agreed out loud with Lauren. We all did think it was a great space, but if Duncan didn't, we'd be subjected to a lecture on why it was *so* wrong and he'd be even less likely to listen to our opinions in the future. It was just easier to let him decide first because he was going to get his way, anyway.

Duncan just walked around the space with his lips closed, wearing the new Doc Martens Lauren had bought him. They creaked and looked odd on his feet even though he probably deserved to wear them more than any of us. He was really from England, after all. He'd hosted tons of raves there and tripped far more and far harder than we ever had. Plus, he had that whole working-class-British thing about him. Those are the people who wore Doc Martens in the first place—before the punkers and then the ravers decided they were so cool.

But on Duncan they really did look odd. His reddish hair was neatly cropped in a modified bowl-cut, like a BBC Prince Hal's—some girl who designs clothes did it for him in the bathroom of a club one night—and his posture was just too straight and stiff, like he was about to answer a question in boarding school, for the down-and-dirty grunge of black boots to suit him.

Oblivious to the incongruities in his style, Duncan pivoted confidently on the concrete, his head tilted back to the forty-foot sheet-metal ceiling above, taking in what would, hopefully, become our new digs.

I guess the first thing people would want to know is how one decides to join a cult at all. Or, as in our case, to start one from scratch. I suppose for Moonies and Krishnas it's something one just falls into. You're bored or lonely or hungry—things basically suck in one way or another—and the cult can relieve the pain. You construct a religion around the idea of suffering.

But for us it wasn't so much about pain as pleasure. A conscious effort toward sustained bliss, enacted willfully. That was the whole point. Self-determination. Will over matter. Directed evolution. Renaissance.

At the beginning, though, it was more about finding a place to live and throw parties. Duncan and Lauren were about to get evicted from their apartment in the Lower Haight; the tuition check Lauren's dad sent her had about run out, and after he found out she hadn't even registered for classes he had cut her off completely. The fact that Duncan stayed with her even after her money was gone reassured a lot of us that he really did love her—even if his highest priority was to touch the next dimension.

So when we heard about this old abandoned piano factory in the warehouse district of Oakland it seemed like the perfect answer. We could make money by throwing the same sorts of parties we had been organizing sporadically for the past few months, without having to worry about copping a new location every time. We'd also have a giant studio where we could do some art, conduct social experiments, collect cool technology, and live our own version of the ideal life—the communal live-in workshop everybody talks about creating while they're still in college but no one ever actually does after graduation because the pressures of "real life" start to seem too real.

Homeless people had been living in the factory off and on since the late eighties, but eventually the skate kids found a way in and so much graffiti went up that *Spin* magazine came and did an article about it. Brooks, a wiry guy from Chicago who did promotion for our parties, heard about the article before it came out and started telling people that we were already planning a big party in the Piano Factory. This way, if anyone else got the idea to do it we would have first claim, at least in gesture. The propaganda staked our turf.

None of us had physically seen the place before, but as we packed into my Ford Escort to check it out, Duncan started talking about the PF as if we were all going to live there. That's how we knew we probably would.

"A party, isolated in time and space from other similar events, never reaches critical mass," Duncan explained from the front passenger seat. The DJ on Live 105 was taking listener calls about Jerry Garcia's death. Duncan popped in a trip-hop cassette, cutting off the litany midstream. "We need to create one resonant field—an ongoing pagan mass—always initiated from the same location, at regular intervals. We keep hitting it, again and again. Each party is a beat of the drum."

"And in each beat, the thousands of individual beats of music," I added. I was into fractals at the time. Everything self-similar to everything else, all on different levels, all working at the same time.

"That's right, Zach," he said for everyone to hear. Duncan was tired of me using chaos math to explain everything, but he was trying to get on a roll and every bit of enthusiasm, even if he saw it as tangential to his Great Message, was worth incorporating.

Looking at it all more cynically, which I guess I can do now, Duncan's habit was to determine his personal needs and then retrofit the rest of the cosmos to match. I doubt that this was a conscious manipulation, but Duncan had a way of making everything and everyone conform to his personal vision. By the time we got to the PF for the first time, it was all of us wanting to move in there and Duncan acting like we had to convince *him*. Still, however much it may have helped Duncan out of his housing jam, taking over the PF did turn out to be a great idea.

And once we were all actually in the space, staring in awe at its forty-foot ceiling and twenty-thousand-square-foot floor, Duncan didn't take long to join in our enthusiasm. He pointed to a ledge that held an old winch of some kind, and said the words that decided our fate: "We'll put the DJ booth up there."

2.

Of course we used my car to move everything in. I spent about eight hours going back and forth across the Bay Bridge with mattresses and bookshelves and speakers tied to the roof. It wasn't supposed to work out that way. Henry—this old friend of Duncan's from Britain who came to SF to DJ our last party and never left—owned a van, for chrissakes. I hate to be all suburban-Jew about it, but I take care of my stuff and didn't want my car getting three years' wear in one weekend. Everyone would get pissed off when I got "proprietary" about my car or computer or tape deck, but that was the reason my stuff always worked and theirs didn't. Originally, we were to use Henry's van for the move but, characteristically it turns out, he drove to LA to score some raging dope from a dealer friend of his before it got cut with whatever crap they mix it with when it hits the streets.

So instead we used my tiny hatchback to cart four apartments' furnishings out to Oakland in at least two dozen separate trips (and twenty-four bucks of bridge tolls). I wasn't in the habit of letting anyone else drive my car—yet—which meant I was the lucky one who got to load everyone's crap. Serves me right for telling Lauren how I had been working out so much. Duncan got out of the whole ordeal by staying at the PF to envision a suitable ground plan. That much did make sense. And then to save room in my car, which for some strange reason was a priority everyone except me put first, only one person could fit along with me. I had suggested dropping everyone off at their own houses and taking them back, with their belongings, one at a time, but Duncan called my plan "inefficient" and assigned me one helper for the whole day.

That meant Brooks, the only guy left. I guess we operated with some lingering chauvinism. But Brooks, the weasel, only helped with the biggest items like bed frames, which aren't even so heavy.

The rest of the time he just stood in the street chatting with club kids and handing out invites for our first party.

"PF" is all they said, in puffy 3-D letters with surfaces like concrete on three-inch-square glossy cardstock. Not even a map point. Just the date, 11.4.95. It was only two weeks away, but Duncan loved the way the numbers added up to twenty, which, in numerology, becomes a two. He was thinking of the PF like a biosphere. Pre-Fab. The second world creation, planned consciously by humans. Us. Maybe a second life for the SF rave scene, too. Post-Francisco. No more saints.

Brooks didn't use any of these explanations, though. He made up his own. Brooks had become the best and most respected club promoter in the city (which in itself should have been enough to make me question the whole scene). He could look people over and guess their affiliations instantly. Then, somehow, he managed to come up with a name for the party that fit what they would want to do. He told the jungle kids that the letters stood for Planet Forest. Black kids he told it was Pumping Funk. Obvious SF Art students got "Pomo Factory," and seventies-retro kids got "PF Flyers." He told some Beavis-types it was Party Farty, and explained to the Goths that it was Pandora's Fox. Gay guys weren't even told a name. Brooks just glanced at them and smiled like they should know what it meant already. No one asked.

I learned a lot about Brooks that day. He had no morals, just tactics—for which you almost had to admire him. On our third trip back into the City, he asked me to pull over at a Mail Boxes Etc. on Powell so he could check his box. He came back to the car puffing a cigarette and holding a stack of about fifty envelopes. He looked like one of those guys who hang around the Offtrack Betting stores, with his hair in a greasy mess and a dirty trench coat over clothes that hadn't been washed in weeks. My mom probably would have put a towel on the car seat to protect the upholstery before he got in.

"Come on, Zach, let's go."

I stared at him for a second. He seemed nervous.

"What?!" he asked.

"What've you got there?"

"A bunch of letters. Never mind."

I knew I had him on something, so I used my leverage to bum another cigarette before starting the car and pulling out. I watched him out of the side of my eye as he carefully opened the envelopes. Inside each was a check and another envelope. He removed the checks and put them in his wallet. There were a lot of them, but I couldn't make out the amounts. He collected up all the outer envelopes and chucked them out the window. Then he took out the letters from the inner envelopes, crumpled them all up and threw them out the window too. Last, he sorted the inner envelopes in an order I couldn't determine, wrapped a rubber band around them, and shoved the stack into his bag.

"What gives, Brooks?" He knew I was dumbfounded.

"Business, my friend. Business."

"Okay, okay. What kind?"

"It's called 'break the chain.' It's a service company."

"Come on, Brooks, what's the scam?" I widened my eyes to make him think I'd be impressed if he told me.

"Imagine you're a lonely old superstitious woman, all right?"

"Okay, okay. I'm a lonely old superstitious woman."

"And what could happen to really ruin your day?"

"I don't know. A black cat could jump on me. A mirror could crack. Come on . . ."

"You're not listening."

"I hate games."

"The name of the business?"

"Oh, um . . . Break the chain? Chains?" Then it hit me. "Chain letters!"

"Right you are, Zachary. Take a look." He pulled out a *Weekly World News* from his bag and, sure enough, back in the classifieds was an ad that read:

Break the Chain! Have you been sent a dangerous chain letter and don't know what to do? Have you been told you will get sick or even die if you don't pass it on? Don't magnify its spell by sending it on to 25 others! Send the letter to us—in its original envelope—and we will destroy it in an ancient ritual guaranteed to neutralize its evil power! Money-back guarantee! Send the letter, envelope, and a check or money order for $25 to . . .

"Isn't that mail fraud?"

"No way, man. It's a service."

"But how can you prove there's any magic in the letter? Or in your ritual?"

"You can't. That's why no one will ever get the money-back guarantee!"

Someone once said you can never go broke underestimating the intelligence of the American public.

"So you must have, what? Like five hundred bucks' worth of superstition there?"

"Five hundred and twenty-five. One off. You're a good bean counter."

It felt like he was making an ethnic crack but I let it go.

"And why do you want the original envelopes?"

"That's a recent innovation," he told me, crossing his legs and putting his feet out the window. All I could think of was that Michael Caine movie where the guy gets his hand chopped off by a passing truck. Maybe I was feeling a little aggressive. "Business started out great—maybe thirty, forty letters a week up to a high of about a hundred."

"God—that's twenty-five hundred bucks a week!"

"I do a lot of coke, okay?" He had a weird defensive first strike of slamming himself faster and harder than anyone else could. "But just as I was getting used to the big bucks, business started to drop."

"Was there competition?"

"No. Demand decreased. I think too many people were sending the chain letters they received to me instead of copying them twenty-five times and passing them on, so the whole circulation died down."

Brooks had altered the entire dynamical system of chain mail. Incredible. "So what'd you do?" I asked.

"The envelopes, Zach. They're the most valuable part of the business."

"Mailing lists? Of superstitious people?" I thought I was catching on.

"Sure, I sell the names. The list is worth something. But when money is really low, you know what I do?"

I had no idea.

He smiled and continued conspiratorially. "I create customers."

"How?"

"I send chain letters to all the people on the list!"

Vintage Brooks. I had to laugh.

"Don't give me shit," he said. "I dropped out of AA and I've only got a four-inch dick, fully erect, okay?"

I didn't say anything else until we pulled up at Duncan's place off Haight.

"This is a prime location," Brooks said. "I'll do some handouts. Get me for the big stuff."

Duncan's apartment was only half-packed. All of Lauren's things were in labeled boxes. Duncan's were all over the place. I had to admire the way she maintained her own orderly lifestyle in the midst of Duncan's chaos. Still, she was a bit passive-aggressive about it. Even the medicine cabinet was empty of her stuff, and half-filled with Duncan's herbal asthma remedies and herpes creams. I remember wondering if Duncan used condoms—I didn't see any around—or if Lauren had maybe already caught herpes. That would be a pity, I thought. She didn't deserve herpes. Not that anyone does—it's just that Lauren was so open and trusting.

I wasn't the only one worried that Duncan might take advantage of her caring nature. She had gone into urban planning at Berkeley because she honestly believed she could create environments that minimize anxiety and violence. She once worked on a ground plan for an elementary school without corners to make it impossible for a child to feel spatially excluded. We knew she saw Duncan as needy, even if he believed he didn't need anything or anyone at all. Maybe that's what she thought he needed to get over.

Packing people's stuff, however temporarily humiliating, offers you an intimate window to their lives. Duncan's was made up of promotional T-shirts from indie ambient labels, tons of twelve-inch dance remixes, fringe philosophy books, weird drawings given to him by junkies in coffee shops, and lots of candles, amulets, and herbal remedies. I couldn't find his real drugs and I know he always had some, so he must have taken those with him.

The only boxes of Lauren's that weren't sealed held the remnants of her stalled academic career. Books and papers on urban planning, architecture, and fêng shui philosophy that based home design on the I Ching. One box contained meticulously constructed models of little houses and an apartment complex. In another, she had packed one of those rubber things with a tube used for enemas or douching, I think. Maybe I was being a little nosy but, shit, I was practically their servant at this point.

It was while packing Duncan's many possessions that I first realized I wasn't cut out to be a follower. I started my task quite respectfully, keeping his twelve-inches in their alphabetical order and carefully wrapping his little bottles of medicinal herbs in wads of newspaper. But the more I thought about how Duncan had probably assumed I would be this diligent about wrapping his stuff, the less I felt like doing it. I began dumping stuff into pillowcases and just rolling his T-shirts into little balls instead of folding them up. Major revolt.

When I got downstairs to recruit Brooks for "the big stuff," I found him pitching the first PF rave to a cluster of Deadheads. Haight Street has never been the same since Jerry's death, but in these first few weeks after the news broke, there was a palpable dismay. You'd see swarms of crusty kids walking around in a haze. They came to San Francisco from all over the country, not knowing what else to do or where else to go. The Haight was already inundated by punks and self-proclaimed homeless kids with guitars, all panhandling for loose change and loose joints. This newest lost generation of orphaned Deadheads gave the whole neighborhood a spaced-out, tweaky, aggro vibe.

Brooks was explaining to the Deadheads that PF stood for Prana Festival, but they weren't buying it. His cons always worked on the level of aspiration or desperation, but these kids were in a state of pure limbo and no matter how Brooks tried, he couldn't find any leverage in any direction.

"You've got to celebrate Jerry's ascension," Brooks offered.

"The band says they may still tour together," said one of the kids—a tall longhair in an army jacket and utter denial.

"Then come to focus that energy. There'll be a lot of fans there. You can network."

Brooks sounded too eager, and he knew it. I figured he had snorted a couple of lines while I was packing and spying. He kept fidgeting with the handouts, compulsively stabbing the pads of his fingers with the sharp corners of cardstock.

"Look," asked this little guy in a tie-dyed shirt, peacoat, and blue shades, "you got any money? We're really hungry."

I had a ton of change in my pocket collected throughout the day from the backs of drawers and the corners of closets. I was looking at the group, deciding which one to give it to when I saw her. She had long brown hair and a sweet, calm face. She was just looking down as if the whole ordeal—club promotion and panhandling alike—was dirty business.

"Hey," I said to her. When she looked up, I noticed she had a little silver ring through the flair of one of her nostrils. Normally I'd have been a little repulsed by it, but on Kirsten (that turned out to be her name) it served as the only hard thing on an otherwise completely soft person. She wore one of those flowing gauze skirts and a knit Mexican sweater-poncho hybrid. She brushed the hair away from her eyes with her finger—she had really clean hair for a Deadhead—and smiled at me.

As if by instinct, I analyzed the possible relationships between her and the other two Deadheads based on their body language. The tall army-jacketed guy looked too disinterested to be her boyfriend; she didn't look like the type who would go out with an insensitive stoner. The little guy seemed too weird. He was really flashy for a Deadhead, and looked more like a crystal meth dealer (usually impotent) than a lover. Then, the way Kirsten glanced down to her feet again, half-embarrassed and half-coy, convinced me that she was available. I could feel hormones being released into my blood, as they must have for my most ancient ancestors on encountering attractive females from a neighboring tribe. *Spread the code,* they told me.

"I got a bunch of change," I said, producing a bounty of quarters and dimes (I don't reach into dust-bunny colonies for nickels and pennies). A few of them fell to the ground, and the little guy bent to pick them up.

We all stared at the overflowing pile of metal in my palm. It must have been eight or ten bucks' worth. I used both hands to offer it to Kirsten. Perhaps I was trying too hard.

"Is this, like, trick or treat?" she asked. "You want us to pick one each?" I was surprised by her edge. But challenged. Amused. Turned on.

"No. Take it all."

"Cool!" said the little guy as he gathered the change from me and put it in his peacoat pocket.

"We gotta put some gas in the van first," said the army-jacket guy in one of his few sentences of the day.

Maybe I was still charged from having come across some of Lauren's garters and lacy silk nightclothes while rifling through her stuff (did I forget to mention that?), or maybe the possibility of a larger vehicle and a few extra hands spoke to my aching shoulders.

"You can crash at our new place, if you like." This was pretty forward, for me. I felt like I had said, "You want to fuck me tonight?"

To my surprise, they agreed. I gave them all the change and then bought them some gas. We loaded Duncan's, Lauren's, Brooks's, and Henry's stuff into the Deadheads' van and they followed us out to Oakland. The whole way Brooks was checking the rearview mirror, to make sure they weren't going to run off with his junk.

"This isn't like you at all," he told me. "Very irresponsible."

I put on my best holier-than-thou tone. "You can't be so paranoid," I told him.

My own stuff was in the Escort with us.

3.

It was supposed to start with just Duncan, Lauren, Brooks, Henry (when he got back), and me living there full-time.

Lauren and I had actually met months before Duncan ever showed up. I had just gotten my master's in psychology and had decided to take a year off to figure out what to do with it. I worked as an SAT tutor during the day and went to clubs at night, rationalizing that I was involved in social research. Lauren and I kept recognizing each other as fellow discontents at those bad, commercial raves South of Market. We'd get in for free (the doorpeople knew us) and then just stand around complaining about the event, the yuppie crowd, and how we wouldn't even feel comfortable taking E there. If we had, it might well have been me instead of Duncan going out with her. We met Duncan together at one of those awful parties, and he challenged us to quit complaining and do something about it. With him. Maybe he had us pegged from the beginning.

Duncan conceived the grandest rave events—"one-offs" we called them, with themes like Kali, Tantric Sex, and Japanimation—and then Lauren and I would do most of the work putting them together. We hired Brooks, still just a doorperson at the time, to hand out flyers, and his quick mouth and wily ways soon made him an indispensable member of the gang. I think Brooks would have preferred me to be in charge, but after Duncan moved in with Lauren and then imported his old British pal Henry (using club funds), he naturally rose to the position of patriarch.

To be fair I have to admit that, more than anything else, what secured Duncan his place at the center of our posse was his special ability to unify our events. Whenever a party was getting sketchy, Duncan would bring it back into harmony. Sometimes this was just by changing the lasers or coaching the DJ, but at other times it seemed entirely mystical.

At our third party together, for example, a whole lot of people were tripping on a variety of drugs. We had been busted two weeks earlier (we threw that party illegally in the VISA Headquarters parking structure in Foster City) and didn't want to make the same mistake again, so we held the party on a remote, abandoned pier down in Santa Cruz. We were unfamiliar with the local crowd, and there weren't enough SF regulars to tip the vibe in our favor. Conflict and confusion were in the air, and we drew some weird energies toward us. Out of nowhere, a few dozen black kids from San Jose drove their cars right out onto the pier, flashing their headlights and threatening to run us down or push us off into the water.

Our friendliest ravers tried to appease them by inviting them to mix in, but they weren't responding. A few guys got out of their cars and scared the younger girls by pretending to be tough inner-city gang-bangers—which for all I knew they may have been. This was a bad trip, both in the real world and in the magnified terror-sphere of LSD in an uncontrolled setting. I was close to freaking out, even though I knew my perceptions were colored and intensified by the drug. In a hallucination based on fact, I could see the energy of everyone around me emanating from their bodies as jagged, broken lines—like in a chaotic Keith Haring painting. I beheld the battle for control of the space occurring as colored lines colliding angrily in the air between the people.

Just when I sensed that physical violence was about to break out, I felt something warm beaming at me from one side. I turned toward the heat and saw Duncan, at least thirty feet away, sitting in a chair and wearing a satin robe. There was a girl—one of the young ones that the intruders had frightened—kneeling at his feet. Duncan held her head in his hands and whispered something to her as she cried. I noticed all around me that people were turning toward the same thing. I saw smooth, rounded lines of energy—waves—appearing to emanate from Duncan's body as he stroked the girl's hair and smiled down at her benevolently. In an expanding circle, more and more of the crowd turned to face Duncan, and as they did their energy, too, changed from jagged, broken lines to Duncan's smooth round curves.

Then I was somehow able to hear what he was whispering to her. "All is bliss. All is bliss." It was an almost silent whisper, but it seemed to come from inside my own head. I could have resisted. I could have shrugged off Duncan's smooth lines and maintained my own identity—my own jagged lines. But it felt good to give in, and I knew it would benefit everyone there. The more of us who supported and amplified Duncan's peaceful carrier wave, the stronger the benevolent vibe would become.

I watched as the black kids with the cars struggled to understand what was happening to them. They started to laugh—at us, I think, sarcastically but also a bit frightened. Duncan gently laughed too, repeating "All is bliss. All is bliss." Then we all laughed with him, as if it were a responsive reading in church, and their tension dissolved into the smooth lines around them. People began swaying in the waves of energy, gently embracing one another as the intruding kids became indistinguishable from the rest of the crowd.

Not many people I knew had the ability to pull off stunts like this. He had used the classic hypnosis techniques of pacing and leading, but he had done it to a group of several hundred sketched-out people, without their ever even knowing it.

Later, none of us mentioned Duncan's role in the event, only that it was so great how the black kids got into our vibe. Maybe no one else saw what I saw, or maybe it didn't really occur that way at all. Perhaps I just happened to be looking at Duncan when the energy on the pier changed. I was too embarrassed and a little too frightened to admit to anyone what I had seen—but I silently credited Duncan with conjuring us into safety and trusted him to do so in the future.

Acknowledged or not, these precarious trips had rendered us intimate enough to live together, and tolerant enough to give Duncan the space and strokes he needed to do his brand of subtle magic. That's why we all agreed not to let anyone move in without Duncan's permission—so nothing would get out of balance.

But I had told Kirsten and her friends they could stay for a few nights, and then Peter, a friend from JFK (the college for consciousness research where I got my master's the year before), took my description of the commune as an invitation to join, too. When I pulled in with Kirsten and the others, Peter was already there, standing in the loading dock with his knapsacks, getting grilled by Duncan on Psychedelic Ethics 101.

He was conducting a fucking entrance exam, and I would have stopped him if the Deadheads hadn't been getting such a kick out of watching (and if I hadn't felt so responsible for having foisted Peter on everyone in the first place).

"We're all here with a common purpose," Duncan explained.

"I know, man, Zach told me," Peter answered. "It's what I've been working toward for a long time."

Peter really had paid his dues. Back at JFK he'd conducted a series of highly involved experiments on himself and a friend of his using electronics and psychedelics. It was far beyond any of the research they taught us to do on pigeons and mice. Peter and his friend did all the experimentation on themselves, and it wasn't just so that they could dose on pharmaceutical-grade chemicals. The work they did was so intense, in fact, that Peter's friend ended up in a coma and eventually died in a hospital. You'd think this would have made us afraid to have Peter live with us, but dedication and sacrifice, even with disastrous results, served as the best credentials. Peter looked something like Christ, mostly because of his gray, intensely bright eyes (that I've-seen-God-face-to-face look you get from smoking DMT), but he also had a beard and long hair, and liked to tell stories with definite parabolic value. Duncan preferred to be the only messiah in a crowd, so he wanted to make sure Peter would value the needs of the group (meaning Duncan's needs) over his own.

"We're creating a vibration here, and it's essential that we don't dilute that energy with other interests, at least not at the outset."

Peter looked hurt, which turned out to be the best response he could have mustered. Duncan took it as a sign of Peter's weakness and his own alpha-male supremacy.

"It's going to be a lot of work. Not just in the traditional sense of hammers and nails, but, bottom line, it will come down to spiritual warriorship. This is a revolution. A declaration of independence from status quo reality. We are attempting to intensify the overall level of novelty in the extant cultural organism, in order to change it. Mutate it."

In all fairness, Duncan was using this impromptu interview less as an assertion of his will than as an opportunity to clarify his own vision for the PF, which he needed to do. Duncan never did his best thinking alone. It always had to be in the context of an argument. He couldn't drum up the will to articulate anything unless it was to persuade someone else to accept his own line of thinking. This is why he never feared brainwashers or public relations. He used to say that in the act of appealing to the public appetite, the marketers and programmers were twisting their own intentions to match the appetites of their constituencies. The programmers have nothing to express until they find a group they want to express it to. Duncan, in the guise of reviewing a tenant application, was merely learning about himself. However dominating he looked, Duncan was simply incorporating Peter's worldview into the mix. Exchanging memes and mutating both parties in the process. That was his job.

I'm not sure exactly how it happened, but by nightfall Kirsten's two friends had departed in the van, leaving her behind. We all got really stoned in the afternoon once everything was unloaded, and just sat among our possessions, giddy with thoughts of the life that awaited us. I was too busy staring at Kirsten to notice when or why her friends left. Maybe that had something to do with their departure.

I don't understand how I managed to be so forward about my intentions. I remember we were sitting in a circle, passing around this joint of wickedly powerful dope that Peter had gotten from a *New York Times* reporter who was doing a story about government-grown hemp. This particular strain was called G-13, and it was quite a score. Apparently, the feds built these secret, giant greenhouses in Arlington, Virginia, where they cultivated mutant cannabis using state-of-the-art hydroponics and fertilizers. Needless to say, G-13 (I never did find out how it got the name) packed a wallop. A total THC high, without all the munchies, paranoia, and bakedness of regular pot.

So I was pretty wasted. I hate to use that word. "I'm so wasted" and "I'm fried" are terrible ways to describe being high. They connote brain damage, and I'm probably not the first to wonder just who it was that passed off these words on pot smokers. For all practical pursuits, I was definitely baked past the ability to make any useful contribution, but for my purposes at the time—musing on the possibilities of the PF and getting Kirsten to have sex with me—it was the perfect altered state. You don't ask a meditating Buddhist monk to operate heavy machinery, now, do you?

We were sitting in a big circle. We hadn't found the electricity yet, so Lauren carefully arranged dozens of Mexican votive-candles-in-glasses all over the space. She was wearing a lime-green vinyl outfit that, along with her short blonde hair and little Kewpie nose, made her look like an alien fairy off *Lost in Space*. She kept checking to see how each candle contributed to the total illumination, no doubt attempting to create the homiest ambiance possible. I remember musing on how almost everything we owned was either rustic Mexican handiwork or shiny, plastic, and electronic.

Once the male Deadheads had gone, Peter went off on a conspiracy riff about the Grateful Dead. He was saying something about how the Merry Pranksters got their acid from a CIA-funded scientist named Gregory Bateson, who was at Palo Alto VA Hospital testing LSD on old soldiers.

"Even the words *Grateful Dead* were part of the campaign to convince the American public of the benefits of eugenics and race war," Peter argued, peppering his sentences with names and dates. "Darwin based his evolutionary theories on the writings of Reverend Thomas Malthus, who believed that populations will keep increasing geometrically and eventually eat themselves out of existence if an elite group overseeing them doesn't manage their expansion."

"The Dead were a rock band," said Kirsten. I was glad she said "were." It proved she was through the mourning period.

"So they would have you believe," continued Peter, confidently. "Malthusianism gave rise to racist forms of socialism. Call it what you like: social Darwinism, national socialism—which is just a nice way of saying Nazi—and even corporate capitalism, which is merely a form of international socialism masked as competing free markets. All our social and economic systems are based in race war. Then the Nazis came to the U.S. in an effort called Operation Paperclip. Look it up. They started the allopathic and genetic models of medicine. Treatment as battle. Superior and inferior genes."

"But aren't Deadheads into homeopathic stuff?" I offered. I guess I *was* pretty fried.

"The other side was equally co-opted," Peter explained. "Who do you think did the publicity for the Merry Pranksters?"

"They had publicists back then? How about that Realist guy, Paul Krassner?" Lauren guessed, giggling like that seventies' TV cereal character Quisp.

"It was Hubert Strand. Massachusetts Media Center. *Whole World Quarterly.* Get the picture? Ever wonder why Jack Harlow, cyberspace advocate and devout Republican, was one of their lyricists? Because the guys at these elite institutions were taking Bateson and Malthus at their word. The globe can't support all these people, so some are going to have to be killed, or at least allowed to die."

"Oh, I get it," said Brooks. "They were marketing cultural code: the death meme. Grateful Dead."

"Exactly. Listen to the lyrics. Smoke the herb. Why do you think Samuel Clearwater's first big psychedelics manual was based on the Tibetan Book of the Dead? And the whole environmental movement that came out of the sixties? It's based on the incorrect notion that we've depleted the planet's resources, and that someone's going to have to die, somewhere."

"But haven't we destroyed the planet?" Kirsten asked. As the Dead's only spokesperson, she probably felt obligated to muster a defense. She lit a cigarette while all eyes rested on her. "Look at the Brazilian rain forest. We destroy thousands of acres a day for grazing land so we can all eat Big Macs."

Peter liked a debate. "You care about the rain forest?"

"It's the lungs of our planet. We need it to breathe, and we are destroying it for the less than 10 percent of the world that can afford meat."

"How can you sit there and tell someone else to save the planet's lungs while you pollute your own with a cigarette?" His syllogism stopped Kirsten dead, so to speak. We were all waiting for her to fight back or make a joke. Her long hair just hung down, framing her soft face. She cared about the world and the people in it, but somehow this grad student had made her efforts seem like the result of social programming perpetrated by the most evil covert operatives. She pulled the sleeves of her sweater over her hands, and then something came out of my mouth.

"You're about the most beautiful girl I've ever seen."

What? You don't just tell a girl she's beautiful. Not like that. I looked over at Lauren (our best social barometer) to gauge her reaction to my faux pas. She had a weird, knowing smile—she saw me as cute and stoned, and not nearly as lecherous as I felt. When I looked back at Kirsten, she was staring straight at me with her clear vegetarian eyes.

"Thanks," she said. Her one-word response confirmed that I had taken a real action, set something in motion that would have to play out one way or another.

Duncan took this opportunity to offer his conclusions on the Malthusian conspiracy's influence on the social agenda of the Grateful Dead.

"Just because the Pranksters' memes were co-opted by the Malthusian elite doesn't invalidate their fundamental premise," he explained. "In death comes rebirth, and the Pranksters understood that for culture, for civilization itself to move on, we would have to cast away our obsolete, ego-based images of ourselves and be reborn as a fully conscious, unified whole."

"But they were exploiting this philosophy to justify genocide," argued Peter earnestly, still unaccustomed to the fact that Duncan's point of view would eventually win out.

"And to that purpose, merely extended the truer ideals of the Tibetan Buddhists, Samuel Clearwater, and psychedelics users everywhere," Duncan responded coolly. I smiled again at Kirsten. This was the kind of intellectual repartee I had moved here for in the first place. "So what if the original subtitle of Darwin's *Origin of Species* was actually *The Preservation of the Favored Races in the Struggle for Life?* Which of his memes ultimately survived?" Duncan probably knew more specifics of conspiracy theory than even Peter. And he used the word *ultimately* a lot. "What the Pranksters and Grateful Dead proved, regardless of who might have been supporting their efforts, was that the cultural mindset and, thus, reality itself can be irrevocably altered through propaganda alone. But these adjustments only stick when there is a cultural propensity toward that change in the first place. That's the bottom line here. They can market the 'death' meme all they want, but it will be incorporated only if it appeals to the underlying societal appetite."

"But if we aren't vigilant about what we accept, we can get led down a wrong path," Peter pressed earnestly.

"Have you considered that your compunction for vigilance is precisely the programming that has been inflicted on you against your will?" Duncan was great at folding a person's entire essence into the core of his own argument. "On the one hand you are telling us that the past century of social pessimism, culminating in the death memes of the elite-sponsored Grateful Dead, is the result of an insidious attempt at manufacturing consent for ignorance and genocide, but on the other hand you argue against the unrestricted consumption and evaluation of ideas in a free marketplace by the same Malthusian logic. So do we need an educated elite to censor out the bad information, or are we evolved enough to accept or discard prescriptions for change using nothing other than our intuition? Maybe it's *you* who are unduly afraid of the dominance of favored, state-sponsored memes. If we accept the basic premise that our mindset extends, eventually, to the reality we inhabit, then wouldn't your attribution of the psychedelic revolution to a fear-mongering elite and subsequent admission of your own powerlessness in the face of such adversity ultimately result in the full manifestation of the very forces you hope to quash?"

I always wanted to have a tape recorder around at moments like these. I'm sure Duncan said it even better than that, and that's partly why we all respected him so much. He had the social theory down cold, but, more than that, could always bring us back—however far into paranoia we'd get—to the essential truth that the way we thought and felt was the most important thing. That's why he became, for lack of a better word, our leader. We were all allowed to express doubt in our proposition that our goals should be joy and bliss. We were all free to question whether our deepest desire was really to evolve toward higher states of consciousness and social organization, or if this was even a good thing. All of us, that is, except Duncan; for the privilege of calling the shots, he had to maintain the belief twenty-four/seven. All is bliss. If he got egotistical, inconsiderate, or even downright nasty, it was a small price for us to pay. Ultimately, to use Duncan's word, he did show us the way.

God, I was so enthusiastic sitting there absolutely stoned, listening to my peers talking about issues that really mattered to me. All those breathy cyber-books of the early nineties tried to explain the notion of "designer reality," but we were really going to live it. Call it a battle for religious freedom, except in this case, our new, self-styled belief system would change the perfectly designed little world we lived in and, eventually, through our parties and media events, the consensus reality as well. Maybe we were no better than the Malthusians or the Media Center, but I think we were. It wasn't about extending our power base, however much it may have looked like that sometimes. We had created a pure space unpolluted by the petty concerns of the mundane world—where we could improvise a new reality. We had lost our sense of allegiance to the hollow goals, war taxes, and suburban rewards of the consumer culture. I was supposed to be in med school by then studying to be a psychiatrist. Instead, I was going to enact global therapy.

But global therapy would wait until tomorrow. Tonight I wanted Kirsten. By the time we were all unpacking our bedding and piling it on scattered mattresses, futons, and foam pads, it became clear that getting close to her wasn't going to require much more effort on my part. Kirsten had her own little woven Navajo blanket that she unrolled next to my queen-size mattress. I offered to share my mattress if she'd share her blanket. Combined resources against the elements, I think I called it.

We were all pretty cold—there wasn't any heat at the PF yet—so we wore our clothes as we settled into our scattered temporary campsites. Duncan and Lauren slept in separate sleeping bags—odd, I thought; Peter kept fumbling around with his stuff, trying to read a book or something by the light of a candle; and Brooks picked a spot awfully close to Kirsten and me. Too close, but I wasn't going to let that bother me. This was communal living.

Kirsten squirmed around like a little girl as she got under the blanket. She snuggled against me, front to front, all her clean-smelling hair in my face. She touched one of the buttons on my shirt—not so much to undo it but just to feel its hard little surface with her thumbnail. Somehow this little gesture got me quite excited. It hadn't been that many weeks since I'd gotten laid, but it had been a long time since I'd slept with a girl I was this attracted to.

I was going to caress her but I saw Brooks staring right at us. I threw him a cold glance and he averted his gaze but began humming some stupid tune. I think it was the incidental music from *My Three Sons.* Then Kirsten nuzzled her nose against my neck, and I just plain didn't care about anything or anyone else. I could feel that little piece of cold metal dangling from her nostril, but it only heightened the sensation of her warm, wet breath. Before we even kissed, our hands were on each other's waists, zippers, and drawstrings. Most of this was going on right through our clothes. She had my pants open and I had her big skirt up, the distance between us increasing with the amount of material accumulating at our chests. She pulled me against her, reaching under the waistband of my shorts when—

SCREEECH! The piercing sound of metal against concrete and a loud, hacking cough from somewhere in the darkest corner of the room. Then, suddenly we could see it, running toward us, waving a plank of wood in its hand, screaming a wordless stream of vowels. Brooks shot up and screamed back. Before the monster had time to swing its plank, Duncan was standing in its path, smiling benevolently.

"Thank heavens you're here," Duncan said, taking the creature—who by this point was clearly a man—by surprise. He stopped dead in his tracks and stared at Duncan for a long while, cocking his confused head to the side. The man had a beard and looked about fifty. He wore a tattered, gray, tight-fitting suit and huge clown shoes stuffed with newspapers. The fingers on one of his hands were all brown.

"We were having trouble finding the electrical power," Duncan said in his most upper-crust Queen's English. "They told us you knew how to get it on." It wasn't a tactic I would have thought to use, but it worked like a charm. The plank went down and the man motioned for Duncan to follow him toward a panel in the far wall. He had some bruises on his face that Duncan correctly surmised were the result of fights with the skateboard kids.

"You won't be having any more trouble with those wheel-goblins now that we're here," Duncan assured him. "The Palace is yours again."

Kirsten and I quickly reassembled our clothes and emerged from the bed as everyone sat up to watch Duncan tame the indigenous population of one. Duncan later explained to me that in a panic situation most people are merely desperate for a definite role to play. The poor bum was less afraid of us and our presence than the fact that he couldn't determine his relationship to us. His attack was an expression of an identity crisis. Duncan had instantaneously—and through sheer confidence of will—created a social context for us to live in harmony with this schizoid old vet, whose name, we soon learned, was Tyrone.

We all took Duncan's cue to treat Tyrone as our servile master. It was an ambiguous role, but Tyrone was an ambiguous fellow. Pretty soon, we were all playing the game: this was his Palace and he was our King, but we were noble, magical people, unaccustomed to the ways of this new world and completely dependent on him for hospitality and guidance.

"The way to light wears sad metal," Tyrone proclaimed as he opened the rusty old fuse box and flipped an ancient, uninsulated circuit breaker.

"Sad, sir?" Duncan asked, respectfully.

"The metal has seen pain," he said, bowing his head. "I have been inside it."

Tyrone opened his arms as a long, low buzzing filled the air. Moments later, huge sodium lights hanging from the ceiling sparked to a glow, then slowly increased in intensity until they overwhelmed Lauren's little candles, bathing the entire space in bright, yellow light—the same color as Tyrone's crooked smile.

"The subject is at the coordinates now!" he said happily. "I can see it clearly."

"Can you orient us to the grid?" Duncan asked, effortlessly adapting to Tyrone's shift in nomenclature.

"With precision, sir," Tyrone said, jerking to attention and leading us on a tour of the facility. He opened a large sliding metal door that we had thought led to a lot in back of the building, but instead revealed an entirely unexplored section of building. All sorts of little machine rooms and passages could be accessed through metal trapdoors in the floor and walls.

Finally, he took us into his own chamber—a large janitor's closet with sink in the floor and a long ladder leading to a skylight, maybe fifty feet above. The room was decorated with hundreds of tiny wax sculptures he had made of monsters and elves with little guns, bent and contorted as if they were melting. They were awfully good, and Brooks whispered to me that he could probably sell them to novelty stores in town.

"They aren't for sale," Tyrone eyed Brooks suspiciously.

"I wasn't—I-I-I mean," Brooks stammered.

"Who do they represent?" Duncan interjected.

Tyrone picked up one of his miniature monsters proudly.

"The creatures first came to me in Vietnam. We were deep in enemy territory. I was wounded. Right here."

He showed us a scar on his neck.

"Too far from camp to get back. They left me and went on. Waited for three nights, I did. That's when they would attack me. Alone, in the jungle." He got tense, and squeezed the figurine angrily.

"They followed me back home. The doctors put me in a chair and made me tell stories about the little beasts. About where they were, what they were doing. The little elves. You look at one and you know where the rest are." He stopped himself short. "I can't tell you more."

"It's okay," Lauren told him. "You're safe now."

He laughed. "You don't know. Every city I go, the monsters find me. Here was safe. In this place. But they came back—with little wheels on their feet." He picked up a sculpture of a skateboarder. "You will be my allies now. Will you?"

"Yes," Brooks said. "We're your allies. Of course we are."

"I am glad then."

I guess he was relieved to have found anyone willing to support him in his three-decade struggle against the demons and, as a welcoming ritual, offered us some of his tobacco—a plastic bag filled with recycled cigarette butts that he emptied and rolled into new ones using the extra newspaper sticking out of his shoes.

We sat around in the main space smoking the tobacco with our new friend as Lauren, ever our Martha Stewart, dug into one of her boxes and presented Tyrone with a package of blue clay that she used for her architectural models. He loved it—especially the fact that, as Lauren explained, the clay would never dry.

For my part, once Tyrone no longer represented an immediate threat, all I could think about was what had happened with Kirsten in the bed. As Tyrone told his versions of war stories and we all politely listened, I kept brushing up against Kirsten, trying to make sure we would pick up exactly where we'd left off. Even Tyrone noticed, and looked over at us once and grunted his approval of our coupling. In an odd way, the native King's seal of approval made it a blessed event.

The night ended with Tyrone practically tucking us into our beds and turning off the lights. Duncan slept with Lauren this time—I'm not sure what made the difference: his achievement? Tyrone's presence? Kirsten and me? Brooks knew to keep his distance now, and Peter was tired enough to put his latest reading down and go to sleep.

As Kirsten and I began to kiss silently in our bed, warm enough with the power on to peel off each other's clothes and feel our skin make contact, Tyrone sat up on the concrete ledge, fashioning tiny blue sculptures of each of us.

4.

I wonder where the Pilgrims slept that first night at Plymouth Rock. Did they go back into the boat or did they camp out on the beach? Did a scary native attack and then befriend them? Could they have possibly felt as secure as we did that first night?

I whispered these musings into Kirsten's ear the next morning as we lay together watching everyone else wake up and look for water. Brooks brushed his teeth with his finger, and Peter sat near the center of the space doing yoga. Maybe I'm seeing it all through nostalgic eyes, but our first days at the PF were the most innocently genuine I've ever lived. We were a fledgling society, living off the land.

The two weeks before the first PF rave must have looked like the time-lapse footage in an artsy documentary as we developed from a primitive campsite into a full-fledged colony. Somehow Duncan coerced two architecture students into taking on the Piano Factory as a thesis project and then enlisted a few out-of-work theater technicians to erect their design: a maze of platforms, staircases, and walls that served to turn the cavernous space into a freestanding anthill of chambers and passageways.

It stood in the shape of a big U opening to the freight doors, leaving most of the original concrete floor clear for a dance space, and giving us plenty of rails on which to hang lights and projectors that could point down onto the walls. I pitched in a thousand dollars (compared to everyone else's one or two hundred) that I had saved from my tutoring job for lumber, bolts, and the rental of power tools, but most of the wood was recycled from old theater sets, making the entire structure look like a stack of Chekhovian drawing rooms patched together with unfinished pine.

A main staircase at the center led up to a big living area—what came to be known as the mezzanine. It was maybe thirty feet across and furnished with mismatching upholstered couches, car seats, and sixties-style coffee tables. A big Formica table, chairs, and appliances against the far wall of the platform constituted our kitchen. Branching off to the right and swinging around to the front of the space were a series of lofts overlooking the dance floor. These were supposed to be our offices, studios, and workspaces. To the left of the mezzanine were our living quarters. We built about twelve of these rooms, really just platforms at different heights separated by railings, each with an electrical outlet and a space for some storage. We pilfered most of the wires and hardware late at night from the construction site for a new geology building at Berkeley.

My room was quite big compared with most of the others— maybe eight by fifteen feet, but it was more of a hallway than a room. Most of the bedrooms had only one entrance, but because mine was one of the first platforms off the mezzanine it had two doorways. Anyone going up to Duncan's room or to the catwalk leading to the DJ perch had to come right through it. Still, in my role as COO to Duncan's CEO, the location allowed me to keep abreast of almost everything going on and gave me instant access to Duncan in a crisis. No rest for the compulsive.

Duncan's room wasn't the biggest at all but by far the most impressive. It hooked out from a staircase coming from my room all the way back over the dance floor. It was positioned almost at the apex of the roof of the building, and had a large Plexiglas window in the floor so that Duncan could look down directly at the center of the dance floor from above. His whole room was in the shape of a pyramid, and it appeared to be suspended over the space when you walked into the building. Very dramatic.

We decided to use the series of rooms that Tyrone had shown us—the ones on ground level off the main space—as theme rooms for the parties. One was going to be made into a mind gym with brain machines; another would be the herbal pharmacy and smart bar; and another would sell official PF merchandise, like T-shirts and artwork.

I was content with leaving the construction for everyone else and worked instead on getting a DBA, federal ID number, and checking account. I was the only PF member who actually left the building to conduct real-world business, and I think it gave me a lot more objectivity than everyone else. At the beginning, though, I hated to break the magic spell of communal living and cross the bridge into a city filled with bureaucracy.

As I got into my Escort one morning for a long, lonely day of banking business and SAT tutoring (I had retained a few of my best students, both for the money and out of guilt), Kirsten came running out with a cup of coffee in a big clay mug that she and Tyrone had fashioned for me. It was a bizarrely domestic scene, but I loved it. I got out of the car to thank her and she pressed me against the door and kissed me for a long time. I saw Duncan out of the corner of my eye, practically scowling at our traditional, quasi-marital style. *That's his problem,* I thought.

Mornings like that, ones that left me so charged that I could smell Kirsten on me for the rest of the day, gave me enough fortitude to face the cars, noise, tolls, parking meters, and panhandlers of the urban world. The city, state, and federal buildings were the worst, though. After spending an hour fighting one-way signs and finding a parking spot, I stood in one line for another hour just to find out that the name The Piano Factory was already being used by a real piano factory in Orange County. The lady behind the counter adjusted her wig as if it were a hat and told me to give her an alternate name right then and there or I'd have to start the application process all over again.

"But you know me," I pleaded, more on principle than anything else. "You've seen me in here every day for the past week. You'd really make me start over?"

"If you don't have a name I can't process your application," she said plainly, like a machine.

"I'll come up with a name—that's not the point," I told her. This meant so much to me. "The point is you know who I am. I'm a human being in relationship with you. You don't even say hello."

"There are other people in line, sir," she said, tightening her face. I could tell she was resisting her own humanity. She wanted to break free but couldn't. "Please write your alternate name selection on the line provided by the form."

"I'd sacrifice my application and start all over again if you'd just acknowledge you know me." She stared at me a moment and then frowned. She pitied me.

"Do you really want to start over, Mr. Levi?" she asked.

"That's good enough," I told her. We had connected. I think. I took the pen to write in a new name for the business. I asked her name, hoping I'd be able to work it into the name of the business and impress upon her our meaningful exchange as well as my own ability to turn a phrase. She just smiled sarcastically and pointed to her badge that read MS. ROBERTS in big letters.

Here I was, giving her a hard time for not connecting with me, yet I had never even thought to look at her name tag. I flushed with guilt, and wished I was back at the PF with my friends. What was happening here wasn't my fault. It was the fault of a mechanized, bureaucratic world. How could I be expected to behave consciously and compassionately in this setting? I wanted to be on ecstasy, with my own posse, away from all this real-life friction.

I quickly scrawled the name that came to me on the line provided by the form: The Ecstasy Club.

Later that afternoon, I mused on the dehumanizing effects of institutional structures as I stared out the bay windows in the living room of one of my richest students, Melanie, while she worked on a geometry practice drill. Across the water, I thought, at the foot of those hills in Oakland, was my beautiful Kirsten, working industriously and harmoniously with the other PF members while I was here in town, helping the rich maintain their stranglehold over American culture by giving their kids an unfair advantage on college entrance exams.

"Zach is getting laid," Melanie giggled from the huge oak table where she was working.

"Huh?" I was stunned back into the room.

"You're getting laid, aren't you?" she asked, almost seductively chewing on the eraser of her number two pencil.

"Why do you say that?" I asked, stalling.

"You stand different than you used to, Zach," she said. "Your posture is changing. You put your hands on your hips a lot. And your face looks so, I don't know . . . relaxed."

She was right. I had never had so much sex before. I felt more centered, and more aware of that half of my body below the belt when I stood or walked. I had started using my arms differently, and habitually let my wrists go limp unafraid of looking like a fag for doing so. Kirsten was pretty insatiable. She was only nineteen to my twenty-six, which doesn't sound like a whole lot now, but it made a difference. She was satisfiable, but insatiable. Kirsten was always ready, which kept me at constant, pleasant, half-mast hard-on. I felt alive.

Just thinking about her right there, and hearing how she had noticeably changed the way I held my body, got me excited. I was afraid to turn around and face Melanie. When I did, she gave me a look so knowing that I blushed. It was as if Melanie and the whole world were in on something I was just discovering. But the love they had in the outside world was tainted by competition and so-cial mores. Melanie would go on to an Ivy League college (thanks to my costly tutelage) and find out the truth.

As I crossed back over the Bay Bridge toward the PF, I nearly swerved into a truck as I hid my SAT teaching materials in my knapsack. I hadn't told anyone that I was still teaching, and didn't see any reason for them to know I was still earning money. Not that I wasn't allowed to teach—it's just that they would have seen it as a tie to the status quo workaday mentality that we had all, presumably, shed. I knew they'd be thankful if we ever needed more cash.

When I got back to the PF and saw the now-completed infra-structure, I started to feel a little guilty about how hard everyone was working while I was just standing in lines and drinking servant-prepared iced tea while teaching math to rich seventeen-year-olds. Brooks and Henry (who had finally got back from his dope run) were struggling with a giant piece of plywood so I dropped my bag and helped them lower it onto its waiting frame.

When Duncan saw me, though, he shouted for me to stop what I was doing.

"That's not your job, Zach," he said, smiling. "Let's go up to the kitchen so you can brief me on what you've accomplished." I didn't look at Brooks and Henry as I traded their grunt work for my own executive duties.

Duncan and I sat on the steps overlooking the workers.

"I couldn't use the name we agreed on," I confessed quickly.

Duncan nodded and swallowed. He could tell I had picked a name myself, but pretended he didn't know this yet.

"So we have to find a new name, then?" he asked.

"Well, there was a lot of pressure to figure one out on the spot. I would have had to start the application process all over again if I didn't."

"I see," he said plainly.

"So, at least for legal purposes, our official, business title is The Ecstasy Club."

"You should have consulted me first," he said.

"I'm sorry. It was a tough call." I made a tactical retreat.

"That's why we need to make these decisions together," Duncan said.

I was getting pissed off. He didn't know how to make decisions with other people. He meant that *he* should be the only one to make important decisions.

"Look, Duncan, I've paid for the whole first set of applications out-of-pocket—"

"You'll be reimbursed. That's not the issue."

"We don't even have any legal rights to this space, and it's my name going on all the paperwork," I said, getting louder. He motioned for me to keep my voice down. "We're flying by the seat of our pants here. According to City Hall, whoever owns this place went into foreclosure and gave the property to the city. It's slated for an urban renewal project next year for low-cost artists' lofts."

"Well then, we're just accelerating that process," Duncan said. "It's no reason to make rash decisions or to get agitated."

"I'm not agitated!" I shouted.

Just then, Kirsten came floating down the stairs to greet me. Her face changed instantly when she saw my state. I was pretty agitated.

"What's wrong, baby?" she asked, putting her hands on my shoulders and kissing the top of my head.

"Nothing." I should have stopped there but I didn't. "I had to come up with a name for the club and Duncan doesn't like it."

"That's not what's happening at all, Zach," Duncan said calmly. "It has nothing to do with the name you chose. And you're not making this any better right now." He meant that my challenging his authority was bad enough; bringing Kirsten into it was a crime against the spirit of the club.

"Well," Kirsten said, trying to diffuse things, "what's the name?"

"The Ecstasy Club," I answered meekly.

"That's a great name, Zach," she said. "Don't you like it, Duncan?" She was so straightforward. So direct.

"Yes I do, Kirsten," he said. I could tell he hated her. "I like it very much. 'Ecstasy Club' might have been better than '*The* Ecstasy Club,' but you picked a good name, Zach. I don't know if we could have thought of a better one as a group, but I would have liked us to have had the opportunity to do so."

"I'm sorry the situation didn't allow for that," I said. "I really am."

"Come on up, Zach," Kirsten broke the mood. "I want to show you what I did to the room." She took off up the stairs for me to follow. I rose, but then lagged behind for a moment.

"I really am sorry, Duncan. For everything. It's just so tough out there and I didn't want to have to go back, you know?"

"You have the most challenging job in many ways, Zach," he said. "But that's why I want you to be the one to do it."

I felt no urge to defend myself any longer, and I wanted to get back to Kirsten, so I just smiled, said "thanks," and went up to my room.

"Wow! It looks great!" I told her as I stepped onto the slightly skewed platform that we lived on. She did do a fantastic job of turning the piece of plywood into a home. She'd found some wallpaper and put it up on the closet and our one real wall. It must have been for a kid's room because it had little airplanes all over it. She knew I treasured privacy so she hung a set of Mighty Mouse sheets as curtains over the railing. On the floor, she had arranged carpet scraps into a seamless, wall-to-wall mosaic.

"It's really amazing!" I repeated. "Especially the Mighty Mouse curtains! How'd you know he was my favorite?"

"He is? Funny. Lauren had a set she'd been using since she was a kid but Duncan said they were bourgeois. She was going to throw them out."

"Well, I'm glad she didn't." It was an odd moment. "Thanks for saving them."

"No big deal."

"And thanks for saving me, too. Down there with Duncan before."

"Like I said, no biggie."

"I love you, Kirsten," I said to her.

"You love to make love to me, Zach," she said. "There's a difference."

She didn't express a trace of resentment—just truth. Then we started to make love. I hadn't been using rubbers because at some point before I entered her she would usually say something like "It's all right," meaning she was covered.

At least it meant that to me. This time, though, against everything my body was telling me I asked her, "Exactly what do you mean by 'it's all right'?"

"That it's okay, baby," she said. "I'm ready."

"What about birth control, Kirsten?" I asked somewhat horrified. "I'm not wearing a condom, you know."

"It's okay, Zach," she said, pulling me down toward her. "I know my body. It's safe now."

I was going to get up and rifle through my stuff for a condom but, no matter how responsible I was in my head, my body just went ahead and made love to her, anyway. She was a Pisces. They know their bodies. Somehow this was my rationalization. Besides, there was no way to say no to her. I'm not sure if it's that I was afraid to lose her, afraid to insult her, or afraid to miss out on any opportunity to be touching her soft, water-creature body. I made a mental note to store some condoms right under my mattress, and returned to the heavenly being beneath me.

Kirsten turned out to be much more of a grounded homebody than I would have expected. I had originally pegged her as a vagabond, following the Dead from town to town. In reality, even though she frequently listened to concert tapes, she had only seen about twenty shows. Her parents lived up in Humboldt Bay, raised her on a houseboat where they still lived, and ran a ski shop. She had been home for a few months after getting "cut" from the University of Washington's acting program for "an inability to find neutral" or some shit. I remember her saying to me, "What's neutral, anyway? Every person has a character. How can a person be neutral? They'd have to be a corpse." She had traveled down to San Francisco with some die-hard Dead fans on the news of Jerry's death, more as an experience to put in her journal and a way to sort out her own life than as a proper shiva call.

By nightfall we decided to get out of bed and see what was going on downstairs. We must have been asleep for a while, because I could see tracks of sand from where someone had walked through our room. I bent down and inspected the grains as if I were a detective.

"It was Brooks," she said. "He kept coming through."

"God damn it," I cursed. "While we were doing it?"

"No. While you were asleep."

"This sucks." It really did. We had a beautiful carpet and a beautiful relationship and everybody just trampled right through them.

"I'll get a plastic runner tonight," she said. "We're doing a dive. Wanna come?"

5.

Kirsten was the only one of us to genuinely befriend Tyrone, and he used to take her out on Dumpster dives at night, teaching her the lay of the land. Mondays and Wednesdays were food nights. The bagel shops and bakeries would just dump big garbage bags full of day-old breads out onto the sidewalk at closing time. Thursdays the Salvation Army dumped the furniture that even they couldn't use—they'd gotten pretty picky because everyone was giving them useless shit for tax deductions—and anything with a broken leg or loose stuffing would get rejected.

Kirsten had no fear of Dumpsters. One night on a dive behind a K mart that was being transformed into a Wal-Mart, I watched as Tyrone held Kirsten by the ankles so that she could go digging, head first, into a big Dumpster filled with stuff the demolition crew had ripped out of the old store. She kept coming up with fluorescent light fixtures, ceiling speakers ("Attention, K mart shoppers"), and those blue lightbulbs they used to announce specials. She also found a case of pink and black pantyhose that had been cut open improperly so that each pair had a razor slice down one leg.

By the time Henry finally got back to Oakland with his van and all those hits of heroin, Kirsten was leading dives herself, recruiting the rest of us to help load the big stuff into the van. We got two refrigerators, an old electric stove, a bunch of couches, and a couple of those big wooden spools that the phone company uses for wire but everyone else uses for coffee tables.

As the PF got more and more livable, it seemed like everyone in town wanted to move in. I was glad Duncan took it upon himself to evaluate potential tenants. He only accepted people who were going to be able to make "a significant positive contribution" to the first party or our initial setup. As a test of their dedication, new members had to build their own rooms off the existing rooms and staircases. Duncan liked the way this promoted "organismic architecture" as more and more little additions grew out of what we had already built. It also maintained the power base of the original core group, because the new tenants' rooms orbited ours.

One of the most valuable new members was a Stanford robotics grad who called himself Pig. The day he moved in he began wiring up the entire PF with phone lines he diverted from a junction box on a pole across the street. He hacked into Pacific Bell's computers to upgrade the lines to high-speed ISDN connections, too. Pig was about thirty, had a neck beard and potbelly, and always wore oversized T-shirts he got free at computer conventions, with slogans like DIGIMAX: CONNECTIVITY FOR ALL MACS or GET AN A WITH C++. He had worked on a few award-winning computer games, and gave talks at places such as MIT about how to control machines over the Internet. He had a big scar on his forehead that he'd earned while working with the guys at Survival Research Laboratories building robots that fired lasers and blew up things. He had been a member of a huge cult called Cosmotology when he was in college, so we figured he must have had some spiritual inclinations, too.

He was amazingly patient with those of us who knew less about computers than he did, and was always willing to explain how something worked or, as he put it, functioned. ("The word *work* refers only to the movement of a mass over a specified distance," he liked to remind us.) The easiest way to win him over was to approach him looking for an "elegant" solution to a problem rather than just a quick fix. Pig was well connected in the hacker underground, too, and enlisted his cohorts to help him make a telephone junction box and to divert the ISDN lines to each of our rooms.

The night before the first PF party, Pig's cadre of self-styled phone technicians was perched on beams throughout the building, running wires and testing signal strength as the rest of us tended to decorations, details, and Duncan. He was nervously pacing the mezzanine, trying to use a phone that Pig's helpers kept accidentally disconnecting. The platform that was supposed to be the living room area was crowded with as-yet-uninstalled appliances, impeding his anxious padding through the space. From what I could overhear, he was attempting to convince Dr. Samuel Clearwater, the infamous former Yale psychedelics hero from the sixties, to come up to the PF from Los Angeles and make an appearance at our opening. He had me include Clearwater's name on our press release, using the Prankster logic that if you assume something will happen, it will.

But Clearwater was already sick of raves and the computer revolution, and well into another trip by now. Plus, he didn't want to risk more exposure to attacks that he was just piggybacking onto the cyber meme for easy publicity. Duncan finally got Clearwater himself on the phone and told him that the whole party had been orchestrated to celebrate the publication of the doctor's new comic-book novel that we would be selling in the PF store. But Clearwater's assistants cut in and told Duncan that "Sammy" only made appearances for three thousand dollars or more, and Duncan hung up in disgust.

Then a guy with a tool belt who said he was from the electric company showed up wondering who we were and why we thought we were entitled to so much free current. Duncan called me over to talk to the man, and I convinced him that we were on the city's tab and had been given the space on a temporary basis as part of a neighborhood reclamation effort. Luckily it was Friday evening and the guy wouldn't be able to check my story until Monday at the earliest.

Lauren was freaked out because Duncan was so freaked out. He kept throwing tantrums at everyone because the lasers weren't bright enough, the bass speakers weren't loud enough, the smoke machine was too loud, the turntables had the wrong cartridges, the projectors' images were distorted, no one had ordered the wrist stamp from Kinko's, and there was no mention yet of the party on the Web.

Brooks, oblivious to the mayhem, settled in a clearing on the mezzanine to do lines of coke and shots of tequila with his new business guru, a tall albino with red sunglasses named Parrot. As

Brooks told it, Parrot was some sort of economics genius who won an award for his theory that money was "social grease" and who had connections at Merrill Lynch capable of getting Ecstasy Club listed on the NASDAQ exchange. That was enough to earn Duncan's approval of Parrot's tenant application at the time, but now no matter how politely Duncan asked them to get up and work on setting up a cash booth, they just nodded and did more lines.

Kirsten was busy painting the kitchen appliances in Day-Glo colors, so, defenseless against Duncan's escalating wrath, I retreated to Henry's room to hang out and see what heroin was all about. I figured it would be an escape.

Henry almost never wore a shirt, and as he sat cross-legged in the center of his little room preparing his syringes, I got my first close look at the tattoos all over his arms and torso. They were nothing more than black lines drawn over his own veins—like a road map of his circulatory system. He certainly never needed to hunt for a spot to inject himself. I had never seen anyone shoot up before, and once Henry had found a vein, drawn out his own blood, and then injected the blood-heroin mixture back into his arm, I decided I would definitely be a snorter, not a shooter. I wasn't at all concerned about becoming an addict. I made a promise that I would only do it once, no matter what, and I was good at sticking to my silent resolutions. All I wanted was to try the stuff. Heroin is the mother of all drugs, the last hurdle—the blackest, deepest, darkest high. When you've done heroin, you've acquired the biggest "been there, done that" of all.

Henry had prepared two fat lines (about ten dollars' worth) of the fine brown powder for me ahead of time, knowing that after he shot up he'd fall into his hazy stupor and wouldn't be able to help me. I rolled up a dollar bill and snorted about two-thirds of one line, thinking that Henry's estimation of a single dose, at his level of tolerance, was going to be twice mine. Besides, I wanted to start slow and take more if I needed it.

It went up my nose smooth as silk but after about five seconds it burned intensely. I should have split it between the two nostrils.

My whole left sinus felt like it had been plunged with Drano. Once the pain passed, nothing happened. I looked around, stood up, sat down, but my state would not alter.

"You hardly did any, mate," Henry said in a Cockney drawl. As I snorted the other line-and-a-third with my right nostril, I felt the first hit coming on but it was too late to undo the second portion. I'd just have to ride it out. But riding out a physical drug like heroin is very different from coping with the psychological roller coaster of acid or even speedy ecstasy. Mind games can't bridle the white pony.

At first the high was euphoric. Well, not euphoric exactly, but insulated and safe. Objects seemed to contain themselves within their own volumes with astonishing precision. The ashtray was an ashtray. The floor was just the floor, and nothing else. Duncan's voice, harassing someone about something, was just a sound. It had nothing to do with me. I stared at the sodium lights above and they refused to glare at me. There were no beams of light, just illuminated glass globes, holding their own. I understood why people in the ghetto take this stuff. Nothing threatens you. It was like being drunk but without the distortion and gregarious overflow. There was no need to make jokes. Who gives a shit about humor and self-reflection? On smack there is no irony. There's no need for distance since everything sits exactly where it is, apart from you and minding its own fucking business.

Henry's head was bobbing up and down—then I realized this was because my head was bobbing up and down. He looked up at me and gave a weak smile. I tried to stop my head from moving for a second and that's when the trouble began. See, the room needed my head to be bobbing up and down. Once I stopped my head from moving, the pressure of the entire volume of the room was exerted on me and my head. The room couldn't bob without me, and forcibly compelled me to comply. I finally gave in, but it was too late. My mouth got really dry, and then this hot sensation started to rise from my thighs, up through my hips, stomach, chest, and neck. All of a sudden I doubled over and heaved into a bucket that Henry kicked in front of me just in time. But however much I heaved, nothing came out. If I had been on acid I would have been worried about fucking up Henry's trip with my display, but I knew that if Henry was half as self-contained as I was (and he looked a hell of a lot more self-contained than that), he wouldn't be fazed by whatever I did. I could have shot him and he wouldn't have cared.

I must have gone on like this for ten or fifteen minutes before something—why didn't I eat lunch that day?—came out. God, did that feel good. For a second or so. Once I was completely emptied I leaned all the way back, but I wasn't in a chair or on a cushion so I hit the floor. Under normal circumstances, my head would have hurt from the impact. All I felt was a distant thud. I had this to be thankful for.

As I lay there, trying to decide whether to fight this drug or let it pass over me, I started to feel a vibration. The floor seemed to rumble beneath me, and I heard a grinding, machine sound—a buzz like the sound some people say they hear on DMT. But this was heroin, I told myself. People don't hear buzzes on heroin. Whatever I told myself, the noise got louder and louder until I could feel my body vibrating with sound. Just when I had gotten myself used to the shaking, feeling my whole body resonating with the noise, I felt a sharp, burning sensation in my calf. I yanked my leg away but it was stuck on something. A long metal drill had burst through the floor and was ripping up the leg of my jeans.

"Oh shit!" I could hear Pig shout from underneath me as I managed to extricate my leg from the revolving metal spike. Blood came from between my fingers as I clutched my calf and tried to fight off the spins from having sat up so quickly. I puked into the bucket again as Kirsten and Lauren came to my aid, wrapping towels around my leg and telling me it was "just a scratch." I couldn't feel anything anyway. Just nausea.

They set me down on a couch in the mezzanine and put gauze and tape over my wound. Everyone that passed by just looked at me. I really didn't give a shit what they were thinking. Pig kept coming up and apologizing, but I didn't have the strength or particular desire to let him know that my injury was not the reason I was decked out like this. Duncan came through a few times and, to my surprise, didn't scold me at all. He knelt down next to the couch, touched my forehead with his hand, and looked into my eyes with concern.

"Just relax, Zach," he said. "Everything's under control. Take it easy, friend. We're going to need you tomorrow." He gave me slack and support when he had the power to ream me. I was more dedicated to him than ever before.

6.

I didn't wake up until about eight the next night, when people were already arriving for the party. I was in my own bed, with no idea how I'd gotten there. I felt like shit, but not as shitty as I could have. Kirsten had left a big glass of water and a bucket next to the bed, bless her heart, and as I gulped down the water I could feel my cells soaking it in. She had also tacked a long clear plastic runner along the floor connecting the room's two doorways. There was a lot of dirt tracked on it, from which I surmised that a lot of traffic had passed through while I was out.

Through a crack in the Mighty Mouse curtains I could see that DJ Sparky was already spinning some ambient tunes, and Parrot had set up a ticket booth in front of the main doors. Assigning an economics Ph.D. to take the money might be considered overkill, but Duncan had accepted Parrot to the PF for a reason. Brooks was just a scammer with good rap. For Parrot, money was a religion. "The lubricant of all human interaction," he called it. For him to pocket any of the proceeds—as every other doorperson in town, including Brooks, was likely to do—would have been sacrilege. Next to him in the booth sat a PowerBook that Pig had connected to a cash drawer. Parrot entered the approximate age and affiliation of each attendee, in case we ever decided to do market research with the results. The computer also held our complete guest list, five or six hundred names by the time everyone had typed in their friends' names in spite of Duncan's protests.

So far only kids had shown up—seventeen-year-olds in last year's rave gear and hip-hop outfits. The boys were in oversized T-shirts and baggy jeans. A few of them had big clunky medallions hanging around their necks. The girls were more assorted: a couple were dressed in skater clothes like the boys, a few were in flannel grungewear, and others were wearing thrift-store clashing seventies' polyester prints. It seemed there was no dominant style anymore, just a mix of looks that had worked well in whatever scene they were involved in before ours.

It's hard to look cool when there are only a dozen people in a club, so the kids stayed mostly by the door in little clumps as if they were waiting for more of their friends. Two boys had cans of spray paint in their bags, and Brooks was telling them to put it back in their cars. Duncan had decided not to have any official security; if we expected no trouble, there would be no trouble. Bouncers would only inspire people to do something that required bouncers. Besides, once everyone was tripping, bouncers would dampen the vibe.

I managed to get myself up and into the shower. We had two stalls set up back behind the kitchen, and although we hadn't worked out the hot-water details yet, the cold spray revitalized me. I remember walking back to my room with a towel around my waist as Lauren emerged from her and Duncan's pyramid in a pink plastic blouse and miniskirt she had made from shower curtains. She looked so alive and sharp. Crisp and intelligent, like some benevolent anime girl. It was easy to see why Duncan had picked her.

"Tonight's the night!" she said, excited.

"Yeah. Sorry about yesterday."

"And today," she laughed.

"*What* today?"

"Exactly." She had a way of scolding and nurturing at the same time. "Don't take it so seriously, Zach. None of this would be happening if it weren't for you."

"Thanks, but—"

"Really, Zach. You're a treasure and we all know it."

"You mean that?" I must have sounded like I was fishing for a compliment, but I was honestly surprised.

"Yeah. And Duncan does, too. He was yelling at everybody all day to be quiet when they walked through your room."

"He did?"

"Don't look so surprised, Zach," she said, cocking her head sweetly to one side.

I felt the water dripping off my body onto the floor. I was so naked before her.

"I better . . ."

"Go get dressed and promise to dance with me later, okay?"

"I promise." She made me feel like I belonged.

She scooted past me down the stairs, then suddenly turned around.

"You're looking ripped!" she said, pinching my shoulder gently.

I thought she was telling me how stoned I appeared, but by the time she had vanished I realized she was referring to my muscles. Those pull-ups on the railing were not wasted.

I combed my hair to the subtle rhythm of the ambient music, and started to get psyched for the party awaiting me. We had done it: created a perfect space, an industrial utopia where people could have some deep, meaningful fun. Tonight was the beginning of something that had no boundaries other than the limits of our own imaginations. I was selecting the evening's outfit, a pair of new black jeans and a shiny blue button-down shirt I'd never worn before, when Duncan's voice squawked from a little speaker Pig had installed next to my door.

"Zachary. Can you come to my room, please?" After my performance the night before and absence throughout the day, I decided not to overreact to being summoned like a valet. Besides, Lauren's words had convinced me that Duncan valued me more than his manner indicated. I was big enough to play to his ego.

Duncan's room had been fixed up quite a bit since I was in there last. Lauren probably did most of it, and it was amazing—a cross between a Persian tent and a Zen prayer room, with ornate tapestries hanging on all the walls and nothing but a futon and a few low tables on the floor. Duncan was sitting on a small meditation cushion planted directly on top of the triangular Plexiglas window overlooking the giant space below. In front of him on a Japanese tea table were three petri dishes, each containing powders—two white and one beige.

"Tonight's a very important night," he told me. "We're lighting a fuse, and it has to be done properly. We are setting something in motion that won't be in our control for very long."

Behind him was a deck of tarot cards and an I Ching book open to the hexagram "Gathering."

"It's going to be fine," I told him, not really having any evidence to support my claim.

"I want each of us to do the same drugs tonight, and at the same time," Duncan said. "This way we should be able to direct the peak together."

I wasn't particularly looking forward to more drugs—especially not ecstasy, which tends to drain your energy in the long run. I didn't have a lot of energy to spare.

"That sounds good," I said before adding, "but we should probably wait until later so we don't go over the top too soon."

"I've laid out some amino acids for you, Zach," Duncan said, motioning to the petri dishes. "This one's phenylalanine, this is l-tyrosine, and here's some l-glutamine to help you stay alert."

What a gesture, I thought. Here I was—the trusted colleague on whom Duncan's dream was depending—barely able to walk a staircase or construct a two-part sentence. I had let him down, yet he was nursing me compassionately.

"Just mix them with some juice and take a few vitamins if you have them," Duncan said. A moment later, Peter came in with a glass of juice and a spoon. Duncan must have told him to get them for me. *How kind,* I thought. It was a weird moment in status establishment. Peter had to serve me so that I could better serve Duncan. And I was feeling so honored about it all. That's how cults get started.

Duncan's concoctions replenished me almost immediately, and before long I was downstairs helping with the herbal pharmacy and smart bar. Nomie, whom Duncan had hired to run PF's smart-drinks franchise, was San Francisco's preeminent club girl. In New York she would have been called an "it girl," but I doubt that she would have earned her reputation if she had had to compete with the East Coast's professional party girls. She was known less for any of her achievements than for the fact that she attended every important Bay Area event. If Nomie didn't show up at your party, it meant you were doing something wrong. Nomie had recorded some weird sex music, too, but her tapes were only available in San Francisco because no major label felt like distributing the sounds of her genuine orgasms. I often wondered what she would have done for a living if she hadn't had a fat trust fund, courtesy of her Fortune 500 daddy.

Nomie had parked her station wagon—the Fantasy Ride, she called it—at the side entrance of the PF, next to the herbal bar and lounge. This was one of the building's original concrete-walled rooms, so it would be shielded from the noise of the dance floor. She had two blond, blue-eyed boys helping her, Adam and Andy, a young gay couple who made most of their money performing live, softcore sex shows downtown. They even had a videotape out for a while where one of them is said to have fist-fucked the other. No one I know ever actually saw the tape, though.

Nomie had milk crates filled with bottles of juice, plastic bags containing herbal potions, and cans of pyramid-scheme commercial smart powders (speedy herbs like ephedra and amino acids) in the back of her wagon, and I helped load the stuff in. Ostensibly to keep my shirt from getting soiled, I took it off and put it on the back of a chair in the herbal lounge before lifting the crates. I may have been hoping to impress Nomie with my physique as I had Lauren just minutes before. But Nomie didn't really look at guys as sex objects. Her male friends were all boyish, gay, and nonthreatening. She was beautiful in a witchy kind of way, with long black hair that she had shaved on the sides near her temples like the first Queen Elizabeth used to do. She wore long shiny robes and effortlessly mixed pagan and techno aesthetics. Nomie was the kind of girl you liked to imagine having sex with, and then leave it at that. But at the time I wasn't even sure if she knew my name, and I wanted, at least, to be noticed.

I was lifting crates two at a time to make sure my biceps were flexing fully when one of the gay guys, I think it was Andy, asked me, "Are you gay?" Just like that.

"I usually go out with girls," I said. Usually? Like sometimes I go out with guys? I guess I was desperate for acceptance.

"Oh," Andy (I think) said, straightening his little green satin neckerchief (Adam's was pink) and heading out to the Fantasy Ride.

Then Nomie herself peeked up from behind the bar and asked me, conspiratorially, "So, you like Astral Andrew?"

"Huh?"

"Astral Andrew, the Boy Wonder? Don't you think he's cute?"

"Yeah, he's a really nice guy."

"And what's your name again, darling?" Great. She doesn't know my name and she's treating me like I'm gay.

"My name's Zach, Nomie," I said flatly.

"Zero-Gravity Zach, how 'bout that!"

The bar itself was built out of old pieces of colored Lucite epoxied together and fitted with flashing lights. We had a library in the herbal lounge, too, filled with books and handouts about how to use smart drugs, and detailing why U.S. pharmaceutical laws and the FDA make them so hard to get. Someone had built a little stage in a corner of the room, for spoken word and other solo performances. Above us hung those pink pantyhose Kirsten dove for. They were filled with Styrofoam peanuts, making it look like a hundred pink women had been thrust into the ceiling all the way to their waists. I wondered what they would have looked like from upstairs.

Next door, in the mind gym, Brooks was trying to con the guy we had invited to demonstrate his products into letting him have a free brain machine if he promised to use it to get new distributors. The poor brain machine guy was just sitting in an underdecorated room with wires and headsets in a big tangle all around him. He was already so low on his own totem pole of distributors that the last thing he needed was more competition from within the psychedelic youth community. Brooks explained that this outlook was what was killing his business, but the guy didn't want to hear anything about it. I grabbed Brooks and took him out to the dance floor, much to the brain machine guy's relief.

By now, about eleven, the place was starting to fill up. People were really excited, and their expectations for the evening were high. Sparky was playing a mix of hardcore techno music and trance-dance stuff, but he was clearly holding back something, coming just short of letting the music reach a peak before pulling back. Sparky was a master shaman, and the entire crowd was drawn into his spell. We were all thinking the same thing: it's going to happen tonight. He was just making sure we were all going to be there together when it did. Whenever some new people came in, Sparky would take the whole group down, and then draw the newcomers up to the same level as everyone else. It was like being brought up almost to the level of orgasm and then let down again. Each time we went up, it was with more people and greater anticipation.

Brooks was particularly pleased with himself. He kept pointing at customers he remembered from his canvassing on the street and repeating the PF explanation he had used to convince each one to come.

"The marketing is the message," he told me, twisting the famous McLuhan quote. "Everyone has come here expecting something different, but in the end they all want the same thing. To be appealed to directly and sold a bill of goods that they believe their own desire has generated. But all we're doing is selling these people back to themselves. We are delivering unto them their own higher selves. And that's why they pay for it. It's beautiful."

"If you build it they will come?" I asked, sarcastically.

"Don't you see it? We're just telling them that they can have a good time here. Nothing else. And then they are the ones who have to make the good time."

"But we have a DJ, and lights, and a mind gym, and an herbal bar. We are supplying them with something, too. We created the space—the setting." I hated the idea that we were just taking money for doing nothing. "We've been doing a lot of work here."

"Sure we have," Brooks answered, "but it's all just to give them an excuse to feel good. About who they are, and what they really like." It sounded like an est course, where people decide to "get it" simply because they've blown a few hundred bucks.

"Look at that guy over there," Brooks said, pointing to a boy, an obvious nerd, dancing with his elbows out like a chicken. "He feels really cool right now. We all know he's dancing like a total geek, but he's happy dancing like a geek because he feels cool doing it, so he *is* cool."

I understood his point and had my own ways of justifying it, but I preferred to force Brooks to defend himself.

"So last year he felt cool for buying a Nirvana jersey and going to Lollapalooza, and this year he feels cool for knowing to come to our party. What's the difference?"

"It's totally different," Brooks said. "The T-shirt made him cool by an association. He liked something outside himself—some hero. That's why rock and roll is so over."

"It's hardly over," I told him. "There are still supergroups. How about Pearl Jam?"

"Pearl Jam is the number-one group only because someone has to be the number-one group. They're not a cultural icon like Zeppelin or the Stones or the Beatles were. Pearl Jam is just the best rock has left to offer people who still want to worship some long-haired guys on a stage. This is homemade music, recorded by kids in their garages, then DJ'd by other kids just like them. We're showing people how to worship themselves. The fact that they're willing to pay for it just confirms its value. The marketing itself, and the acceptance of that marketing, is the product. There is no agenda."

Brooks had already taken his hit of ecstasy, so his ability to feel great about himself and his schemes was no doubt enhanced, but his underlying, overexpressed point was valid. All we were trying to do was create a space for the thing to happen. If we ended up a few thousand dollars richer as a result, we wouldn't complain.

Brooks had so thoroughly convinced himself of the party's merits that he couldn't help but dance his way into the crowd and become part of the teeming mass of bodies. There were gay kids and straight kids, cool kids and nerds, boys, girls, and transvestites, all dancing with one another. Hardly anyone ever danced in pairs—too organized and restrictive. This was group revelry, and most of these kids had been to enough raves in the past few years to know how to behave. This was a retro-rave. A self-consciously styled event, based on an already self-conscious medium. Meta-

meta. A few guys beneath the DJ perch were trying to start a mosh pit, but some girls from the old hardcore rave crowd kept dancing among them to break it up. This was a clash or a mating of social hybrids, attempting to form a new one. Freeform social engineering. We were mutating the club scene under our own roof.

I was still a bit too weary to get into the dance myself, and stayed on the periphery monitoring the action. Feeling like an usher at a wedding, or a Secret Service agent at a campaign dinner, I was getting off on my role as caretaker and conceptualizer. This was a brand-new form of pagan ritual, and I was one of the high priests.

I finally found Kirsten, who was at the door explaining to Parrot that her Deadhead friends were supposed to be on the list and should get their money back. But Parrot was willing to field these pleas only until he had put someone's money in the drawer. Once it had been registered, the money was gone.

"It's a unidirectional cash flow," Parrot was telling her as I got over there to smooth things out. "The energy has been exchanged."

"But they came from all the way upstate," Kirsten pleaded. "I told them they were comped. You've got hundreds of names on that list. These are the only two I'm asking for."

"It's okay, Kirsten," I said. "We'll take care of it later."

"But they've already paid and they're going back in the morning. It's a lot of money to them!" I hadn't seen Kirsten this adamant about anything before. Her hands were in little fists, like a Marxist or someone.

"It's okay," I said. "Where are they?"

Kirsten let out an angry sigh and led me to them. I could tell she thought I was going to try to talk my way out of it. But when we got over to the guys I pulled out my wallet, still filled with tutoring cash, and handed them each a ten-dollar bill.

"Sorry they took your money," I said. "I'll work it out with him later."

As the Deadheads took my money, Kirsten folded her arms angrily. Wasn't this satisfactory? Wasn't I being a sport about things? I was the one taking the risk of not being reimbursed. This is where Kirsten and I really differed. To her, it was the principle of the thing. Her friends should have been welcomed, officially, and let in for free. Giving them money after the fact was dirty. Sinister. A payoff. *Fuck her,* I thought, and it must have shown on my face.

"Come on, guys," she said, turning her Deadhead-houseboat-dwelling back on my suburban-upper-middle-class front and leading her friends up the stairs toward the kitchen. "I'll get you something to eat." *Fine.*

For security reasons we had all agreed that no one was to go up the stairs tonight except those of us who lived there or were working the party, but I wasn't about to reiterate this to Kirsten. I saw Lauren manning the stairs and thought, for once, to let something be someone else's problem.

Besides, duty called elsewhere. Peter was at the entrance to the mind gym, waving me over. Duncan was inside, giving an interview to a reporter from the *Bay Area Guardian.* No sooner was I in the room that Duncan incorporated me into his media event.

"Zach here, for example, got his Ph.D. in mass psychology at JFK," he bragged. (It was actually a master's in clinical psychology. I don't think there's such a thing as a degree in mass psychology—not since the Nuremberg rallies, anyway.) "Together, we are forming the first node in the new colonial human organism. The herbs, smart drugs, mind gym, music, lights, lasers, and whatever psychedelics people have ingested all combine to create a group awareness. A common resonant frequency. The party itself serves as a remote high-leverage point that, if it's successful, will iterate throughout the rest of the social system as these kids go home and share their experience with others."

The thirty-something woman from the *Guardian* looked more like a stringer for the indie rock scene than an electronic music listener. She gave Duncan that tired, "been there" eye roll that Summer of Love casualties like to throw the way of anyone who believes what he is doing may have an effect on the culture at large. But she wasn't old enough to have been through the sixties.

She was just a bitch. Duncan adopted his working-class accent and took another tack.

"We're here illegally, you know."

The woman perked up.

"This is a confiscation of public space by a consortium of like-minded individuals."

He had her hooked. She began scribbling on her notepad. Just tell them what they want to write, and then they'll attribute it to you.

"By establishing ourselves here, we are in the face of the logic that says you have to have a nine-to-five job in order to get by. Or that you need a mortgage from a lending institution to occupy property. It's a defiance of the concept of property altogether, and the taxes that the government levies for the privilege of standing on a piece of the earth." Ideology on demand.

Once he had her engaged, Duncan tried to bring her around to his rave philosophy again. "By rejecting the consensus material reality—," he began, but she was done. She had her story and wanted nothing more than to get out of there. She closed her notebook, thanked Duncan, congratulated me on my doctorate, and took off.

Duncan checked his wrist but he wasn't wearing a watch. From my own I could see it was just after midnight, but before I could tell him, he put up his hand for me to be quiet and sniffed at the air as if for a sign.

"Have you dropped yet?" he asked me.

"No, not yet. Have you?"

"No. It's time."

Duncan produced a small plastic bag containing a few dozen clear capsules filled with brown crystal. This was special ecstasy he had gotten from an old Detroit techno music promoter. It was made solely from the brown residue left over after a batch of E is cooked, which ends up being much purer than the regular white powder. He took two capsules for himself and handed me the bag. I took one and together we swallowed them.

"You might want to do another soon," Duncan advised in that authoritarian way he had when he was dispensing drugs. "Why don't you distribute the rest now?"

This was both an honor and an easy way to make new friends. There were only enough doses for official Ecstasy Club members to have two each, but since when was it my obligation to make sure people knew they were entitled to two? I'd let people take what they wanted and then see what was left.

Parrot refused to be relieved at the door but he took a hit, anyway. I found Brooks on the dance floor, coming on to a very pretty high-school girl wearing a fairy dress with hundreds of little stars pinned to it. He took one capsule for himself and gave one to her. Henry was standing on one of the bass speakers, shirtless, like a go-go dancer. He had been to more raves in his time than anyone, even Duncan. He used to tell stories about those seminal raves in Ibiza. From his high makeshift platform, he led the entire dance with his own furiously intense movements. He danced like his tattoos—smooth but fierce. I didn't think he was aware enough of his surroundings to see me, but he smiled and gave me a thumbs-up, so I tossed him a capsule that he deftly caught and then flung into his mouth without missing a beat.

Nomie was in the herbal lounge telling some girls how one of her concoctions really feels like taking E—"It's way better than that Herbal Ecstasy crap." But she knew the limits of her own products and discreetly shoved two of my capsules in her mouth before making a weird, almost sexy biting gesture at me. Her two boys were over on the stage, one sitting on the other's shoulders trying to reach up to touch the pink legs hanging from the ceiling. I didn't want to see what they'd be like on E, so I slipped out before they noticed my roving dispensary.

Lauren was on the main stairs smiling gleefully at the crowd dancing before her. When she saw me with the bag she just leaned her head back and opened her mouth like a little girl. I dropped one pill in her mouth and she swallowed. Then she leaned her head back again for a second dose. I playfully tossed it in her mouth.

We stood a moment, enjoying the jubilance of our revelers.

"I think it's working," she said.

"Already?"

"No, not the E," she laughed. "The party. I think we really have something here."

"Yeah." It occurred to me that she might be high, so I spoke carefully, keeping my words and thoughts between the white lines of social decorum.

"I can't believe a guy like you would want to do this," she said.

I felt almost insulted. What did she mean? I wasn't cool enough for the Ecstasy Club? I *named* the place.

"I'm not a total geek, you know."

"Of course not," she said. "I mean, you could be doing anything you want to. You could have a real job."

"Right. Tutoring kids on their SATs."

"Come on, it took a lot for you to come here. We're lucky."

"That's sweet of you to say, Lauren. But I'm the lucky one."

"Good, then," she said, patting my butt. "You're so pious about all this."

"Too pious, you mean?"

"No, not at all," she said. "It's endearing. Keep thinking that way and maybe it'll be contagious."

I smiled at her, not quite sure what she meant, and went up the stairs to the mezzanine where Kirsten was sitting, smoking hand-rolled cigarettes with her friends. The guys asked me to sit down but Kirsten still seemed distant. I thought I'd make up for it with the bag of E.

"It's supposed to be for the people who live here," I said, dropping the bag on the table, "but there's enough for you guys, too, if you want some."

Kirsten took it all wrong, again. "That's a nice way to offer something, Zach."

My E was starting to hit, so I could empathize with her point. If I was going to give something I should just give it. To announce my graciousness was the least gracious thing I could have done. But it was a small infraction, and the E helped me see that too. If Kirsten was going to bug out on some Maoist trip, that was her problem. Nothing to do with me, at least not right then. I left three caps on the table, shook hands with one of the guys, and headed up to the studios.

That's the great thing about E, I remember thinking. You get the insight without the pain. You see how things are but, unlike with acid, the knowledge doesn't spin you into the drug's control. The only way to have a bad E trip is to be afraid to look. You can't shut down the process. Just look, love, laugh. That's the Rule of E. You can always deal with it in the morning.

I got lost in the complex of studios. I had barely been on that side of the building at all. I kept coming to the same place, some-how—the studio that was supposed to be mine, although I hadn't done anything to it yet. I looked at the bare room—the symbol of work not done—and laughed. *Deal with it in the morning.* I could see my bedroom across the floor, the Mighty Mouse curtains hanging from the little tacks that Kirsten had used to put them up. I thought of her sweet hands pushing each one in while I was in the city tutoring. I ached for her. She was so lovely. She could see through me, and knew how to demand better of me. Why was I being such an asshole about her friends? *Morning will come,* I reminded myself.

I followed the sound of voices up to Pig's studio, where he, a smelly hacker friend of his, and Peter were sitting on the floor passing around a bong made from glued-together Legos attached by rubber tubing to a nitrous tank. I threw down the bag of E and took a hit off the bong.

"But Steven never came back at all," Peter was telling them. "Once we got out there, he either liked it too much or couldn't nav-igate his way back."

"That's why we'll use the computer," Pig said, pointing up to the giant Sun workstation on the table. "Simulate the entire trip using the real feedback from the cortex. That way we can pull the plug at any time. I've had significant experience with these devices."

I had no idea what they were talking about doing. The smelly hacker just shook his head.

Then he passed me the bong. *What the fuck*, I figured, I can't get much higher anyway. May as well be social. Just as I filled the main chamber with smoke, Pig opened a little spigot on the rubber tubing and a rush of nitrous oxide pushed the pot smoke into my lungs, then made room for itself. My diaphragm had been forcibly expanded to its limit. I looked at Peter and something made sense before I forgot what it was. Above our heads, on the desks in the studio, fractal screensavers pulsed with color. It made me remember once more what had made sense, but then I forgot it again.

As I came down from the nitrous hit, I realized something was tense in Pig's room. I sensed Pig and his friend were pressuring Peter somehow, and I didn't want to be there to watch. Maybe it was just that hacker kid's odor. I made sure everyone had all the E they wanted, then made my way to the door. Peter came with me, and I got the feeling he was relieved to have an excuse to get out of there.

"They want to try using the computer to re-create my JFK project," Peter said.

"Oh. The one where your friend died?" He just nodded. I didn't want to get too far into it. I knew I was the one who had invited him into the PF and I felt guilty that I had hardly spent any time with him at all, but I wasn't in the mood to hear his whole story and the lesson that would come with it. I had a terrific buzz on.

We took the catwalk over to the DJ perch, where Sparky was spinning and Duncan was shouting orders over the din. He looked like Napoleon directing his troops.

"More tribal! And increase the bass!"

Sparky may or may not have complied. He was deep in the DJ trance, one with his crowd, feeding back to them and amplifying their own energy. Peter and I looked down at the dancing mass. Its thousand hands pumped in the strobe light. It pulsed up and down in time with the music. Like a sea creature, it waved its tentacles back and forth, revealing patterns. The movement could emanate from anywhere, then resonate throughout the rest of the mass. It made sounds, too, and shouted with glee from hundreds of little mouths at once.

"We made this thing!" I shouted to Peter. This creature was alive, breathing, thinking, feeling. We had made it, yet we were part of it, too.

"That's a dangerous way to think," Peter said. He stared at me with his huge, globelike eyes. "We're not God, you know."

But I was already onto something else. Kirsten was dancing near the center of the crowd. She looked so happy. Free. Her hair was flying all over the place and her arms were straight above her. I wish I had a picture of her just like that. Sweat on her forehead. Eyes closed in bliss. So happy.

I had to be near her. *Now,* a voice told me. I grabbed onto one of the lighting pipes attached to the catwalk and swung myself down over the dance floor. Some heads looked up so I let myself go. As I fell toward them I felt my blood move up my body, and the wind against my skin. I got nearer and nearer to waiting hands, and the warmth of the colonial being emanated up toward me. I made myself limp, and the hands accepted me into the wet, warm, throbbing walls of flesh. I had been born in reverse.

I danced through the crowd. Brooks was there, and beautiful little Lauren spinning in circles like a futuristic dervish. Nomie, Adam, and Andy formed a multiarmed goddess that glided across the floor. We, the core members, all saw one another, and smiled in communion. We were the Ecstasy Club. The framework holding it all together. The tiny individual nodes within the greater body. Resonating fibers. This was the moment. Synchronicity.

Kirsten opened her eyes to find me dancing right in front of her. She hit me once on the chest with both hands as final, self-consciously enacted, stylized punishment for my earlier gaffs, but then she laughed and in seconds her anger changed to acceptance. She framed her feelings in play and they all went away. We danced and danced as, at our feet, in the very center of the floor, directly beneath Duncan's pyramid, Tyrone sat holding his tiny figurines of us all, squeezing them together.

7.

I had already gone up to bed with Kirsten before all the shit went down. Kirsten was still really flying on the E while I was starting to come down. I loved being with her, but I was in that cuddly, warm-and-fuzzy state at the end of the trip where all I wanted to do was feel her perfect, loving body next to mine. E can screw with your sex drive but I didn't mind, as long as she was there filling in that gaping hole I'd get without her flesh against me tight. Something about the sudden serotonin release while you're high makes you feel pretty pathetic when it wears off. The only thing that helps is the secure comfort of another human body. But Kirsten kept trying to take my clothes off and I started to feel like if I didn't do something she'd get the wrong idea or leave, so I decided to work up a hard-on and have sex with her anyway. When it was over, I'd have her the way I wanted her: still.

It shouldn't have been a problem. Kirsten was beautiful, and as hot for me as I could ever wish a girl to be. After she went down on me awhile—and she usually didn't even have to do that—I was ready and she got on top and drove for a while. With all the drugs in me, though, I kept tripping out. It was all sensation. Non-human. We were ivy, wrapping around itself. I started to get into the image of our plant-selves melting into each other but, lovely as that was, it made me feel all soft and had a corresponding effect on my body. Kirsten was still moving and moaning anyway, pretty oblivious to the moment-to-moment ebb and flow of my excitement, actually, so I got on top—the better not to fall out of her altogether—and decided to focus on more active, sexual imagery. And that's when Kirsten became Lauren.

It only lasted for a second and it plunged me into a whirl of guilt, but following my "Rule of E" I figured I might as well press through the image, so I let myself pretend it was Lauren beneath me, and it worked so well it almost scared me. I had fantasized about Lauren a few times in the distant past but always suppressed the image because it felt like a betrayal of my friendship with Duncan and especially with her. Our bond depended on my self-vigilance. Even if I were just alone masturbating, she was a zone of thought I strictly forbade myself to enter. But now, with the E still in me and my growing resentment of the way Kirsten was ignoring my whole being even during this most intimate moment, I figured it wouldn't do any harm to let my thoughts wander where they wanted to. Dr. Ruth would have approved.

So I made sure not to say Lauren's name or anything, and let the image take over. I focused on her short blonde hair and her slender little body—the little ledge that her butt made when she stood up straight, and her upper lip that perked out like a Kewpie doll's, making me want to pull at it with my teeth.

I found myself getting more excited than I could contain. I pulled her legs up onto my shoulders and went for broke. I could see Lauren's soft face beneath me. A fairy from another dimension. Her brilliant, caring eyes staring into mine. Her delicate limbs.

But wait—the legs on my shoulders were strong and large. Not Lauren's little Tinker Bell legs at all, but Kirsten's! When the image broke I stopped cold. I thought maybe I'd fake an orgasm somehow by clenching my buttocks and just rolling over, but I didn't know if I'd get away with it. Kirsten pulled me down with her legs, trying to get me to keep moving, and scraped my shoulder with the stubble on her thigh.

I winced in pain, then laughed, as if that was what had broken the moment. I was still inside her, and mumbled something about why can't we just stay exactly like this and go to sleep. She knew something was up and rolled over on her stomach. I tried to get her to spoon with me but she just sighed and brushed her hair away from her face. The music was still throbbing on pretty loud so we couldn't really talk, but I knew we had turned a corner.

I was the first one up in the morning except for Parrot, who must have stayed awake all night counting the money and putting it in neat little piles. Twelve thousand dollars. Pretty impressive, but takes of this size were not unheard of in the club scene, and after the lasers, sound system, and promotion were paid for, there would be only about eight. I was feeling pretty good physically, probably because I had slept the entire day before, and made my way downstairs to avoid having to face Kirsten when she woke.

I found a mop and started to clean up what, in the dim morning light, looked to me like puddles of dried blood.

In my loose, post-E state, I had a vague memory of my father telling me how much my mother bled when I was born. "You weren't a long labor," he'd said. "Just bloody." My dad's dad was a Levite—one of the tribes of Israel—which made my dad a Levite and then me, too, as soon as I was bar mitzvahed. Yeah, I did one of those. Zachary Meyer Levi. The Levites were an important group. While the Kohanes (where they got the name Cohen from) were boss rabbis in charge of conducting the sacrifice, the Levites were the ones who cleaned up the blood afterward. If you look in Leviticus, you'll see all these rules for how the blood is supposed to be drained and how many cubits tall the altar should be.

I thought about all this as Parrot sorted money and explained to me the origins of the dried red fluid on the floor.

"That child Brooks was wooing last night?" Parrot asked me in the manner of a law professor.

"Yes?" I managed.

"Cute, but bipolar it seems. On prescription Prozac and lithium. Brooks gave her a full hit of your 'superecstasy' and she flipped."

"It wasn't my ecstasy, exactly . . ."

"Well, it wasn't a good idea, exactly, either. She began screaming that everybody was sucking her into a pit of pure evil and that she intended not to lose her soul to us."

"She said all that?" I asked.

"That was the gist of it, yes. And then she tried to run away but Brooks took hold of her arm, at which point she fell to the ground. Right about where you're standing, Zach."

I looked down at the dried puddle of blood.

"It must have been some fall, then."

"Oh, it was. Quite dramatic, truly," Parrot slid his red glasses down to the end of his nose and peered over them. His eyes were pink. "Remember those little silver stars she had pinned all over her dress? It seems she managed to stab herself on almost every single one."

"But still, all this blood?"

"It gets better. Rather than simply pulling out the pins, she went into a panic. Brooks did, too. They began desperately ripping the dress off her body, tearing her skin all over. Thus . . ."

"These puddles of dried blood," I finished for him, "mixed in with the beer, smart drinks, and all the other crap."

"Happy mopping."

"Thanks."

"Oh, and Zach?" Parrot smiled. "I almost forgot." He reached into his shirt pocket and pulled out a piece of pink paper. "At about 7:12 A.M., an officer of the law came to visit. The girl in question, one Carrie Miller from Larkspur Landing, was indeed underage. When she got home her parents phoned the police. The public servant who called on us threatened to break up the party but it was already waning anyway, and I convinced him that our soiree had been cleared with the Oakland Police Department and that we'd take care of everything on Monday morning. There's an address on the back of the summons."

More mopping for Zach.

By about four in the afternoon everyone else was moving around. Duncan said not to worry about the summons. (Easy for him. It was my name on all our paperwork.) He said these obstacles simply provided friction. Footholds in our climb. Gravity is what gives you the impetus to take off. We simply needed to stay alert and skillfully handle any obstacles that arose, without projecting our own emotional needs onto them. They were tests of our determination.

Lauren helped me clean up, but I had a hard time looking at her. I had done something to her she didn't know about. Kirsten came down and gave me a kiss. She said she was sorry about last night. I said "That's okay" and tried to act as normal as possible, but it was already clear that we were foreign to each other. She was like a stranger now. Alien in her rigid social values. Not of the tribe. Our days together were numbered and we both knew it but had no immediate reason to say so.

Lauren and I found a couple of kids sleeping in the mind gym and gave them some juice before sending them on their way. They said they wanted to live in the PF and be "just like you guys." We had fans. Pig and the smelly hacker came downstairs together, arguing the merits of some HTML protocol. They were sitting at the table eating bagel chips when Duncan walked over with a pot of coffee.

"Would you like a cup?" Duncan asked the hygienically challenged hacker. He was an outsider, and smelly, and we all wanted him to leave.

"No, thanks," he said, taking the cue. "I better be heading out."

I looked over to Kirsten, who was glaring at me. *What?* I thought. But I knew what she meant. Duncan had a way of getting rid of someone so politely that they'd think they were being asked to stay. I wasn't as good a host. But it was my job to be worried about stuff. Besides, how is it better to mask social rejection in fake acceptance? Or maybe that was Kirsten's point. I didn't really want to find out.

Once everyone but residents was gone, Duncan called us together for a meeting. It was all very official. He had printed out charts and everything.

"I've made a schedule for our next events. I think we should take maximum advantage of the space and alternate parties on different nights of the week."

He outlined a plan that would begin a week from Monday. Monday and Wednesday would be gay party nights. There were more gay people in the Bay Area than anything else, so we might as well capitalize on that. Brooks would be in charge, but Adam and Andy should be the publicized hosts. Tuesday we'd either do or sponsor performances. Kirsten, with her theater background, would be in charge of arranging the talent and play selections.

Thursday would be Goth night—Henry could DJ if he wanted, and Lauren would find out where to canvass for that crowd. Friday would be a trance-dance night for younger rave kids, straight and gay, white and, hopefully, black. Saturday night would be the big weekly PF trip-hop/spiritual party, and each one would boast special guests or cool equipment like VR gear and amusement-park rides. Sunday afternoons would be Peter's "ambient chill-out," with live acid jazz and hundreds of beanbag chairs spread out all over the place. He would be free to schedule lectures by gurus and pop geniuses.

Lauren was to design and Pig was to program an Ecstasy Club Web site to announce our party schedule, publicize our philosophy, and invite discussion. I was supposed to find out if ecstasy-club.com could be registered as our URL.

To me it sounded like a lot of work, but everyone was so pleased with their individual assignments that no one saw the big picture: we were going to have a club going on in our home every night of the week. Even the Levites only had to deal with sacrifices on Saturdays.

8.

I held the paper bag filled with twenties and drove as Parrot smoked a cigarette in the passenger seat. We had met with the Community Affairs officer in Oakland, who scolded us for a while, but after Parrot told him we had taken in five grand on Saturday night (a lie), the desk cop instructed us to pay a visit to the PBA in San Francisco to consider making a donation. He would call and let them know we were on the way. (Gee, thanks.)

Parrot knew exactly what was going on. We were making a pay-off. He figured about a third of our take would go to the cops in exchange for their cooperation—namely, a promise not to bust us. Business as usual in post–Bill Grant San Francisco. Grant used to exercise absolute authority over the Bay Area music scene. It seemed as if an event wasn't "Bill Grant Invites . . ." (meaning half of gross receipts for Ticketmaster distribution and a dozen untrained kids in "security" T-shirts), then it couldn't pull in more than about a thousand bucks before the cops mysteriously showed up. Now that Grant was dead and his whole organization was in disarray, the cops had decided to take charge of the club scene themselves before any organized crime families moved in on the lucrative turf. At least it was better than New York; here in San Francisco you knew who to pay off, and didn't have to choose between competing protection rackets.

Officer Phil Laruso's office was in a high-rise downtown near the Transamerica pyramid. I couldn't believe we were actually going to the police to make a payoff. I had finally reached that age where seeing a cop car made me feel safe rather than paranoid (except in LA), but this was a whole new game. We were being exploited—extorted by a gang of thugs with the power of government behind them. I worked myself into such a state of righteous indignation that I passed the entrance to the underground parking structure twice before Parrot just took the wheel and steered me down into the bowels of the evil empire.

"Don't worry, we'll get it validated," Parrot said as I pulled off the paper tongue the ticket machine stuck out at me with a menacing buzz. I wanted to just crash through the fucking wooden arm. Brooks had given me a hit of Dexedrine before I left the P.F. He said it instills confidence. Fuck, yeah. It instilled me with the Schwarzenegger urge. The eighteen hundred bucks on my thigh practically gave me a hard-on, too.

As we went up in the elevator, Parrot reviewed our strategy. I was to stay quiet and act like the boss. I'd hold the money, and Parrot would hold the folder of paperwork with our DBA certificate and do all the talking. He didn't have any real-life experience in business or extortion, but Parrot loved the thought of how the ordeal was an extension of free enterprise, and took a certain delight in getting to play along. He cracked his knuckles and sucked some air through his teeth as if he were about to be served a plate of ribs. I would have liked to feel secure at his side, but with my name on the signature line of every document in his folder, I felt more like I imagine my dad did that time he got audited, when a woman from the IRS took a tour of our house and checked the labels under the rugs.

Laruso had us wait in his outer office for about twenty minutes before he would see us. We sat on an oversized Naugahyde couch so low to the ground that our knees were as high as our chins.

"It's a psyche-out," Parrot whispered to me as the secretary eyed us suspiciously. "I read about it in Michael Korda's book *Power*. 'Make them wait. Make them feel like little kids.' Don't let it affect you. Remember, if he needs to use a cheap technique like this, it's because he feels impotent without it."

I didn't buy that logic. Just because the U.S. has atomic bombs doesn't mean we close Radio Martí. Besides, the technique was working. By the time Laruso intercommed his secretary to let us in, I was flashing on the time Mrs. Turner sent me to the principal's office for practicing judo moves with Marty Kasdin.

The secretary opened the door to reveal Laruso behind his desk, smiling. He held his hand out over the framed pictures of cop funerals, and Parrot didn't miss a beat. He extended his hand to take Laruso's but simultaneously checked the watch on his other wrist. A handshake with no eye contact.

"We've got another appointment in fifteen minutes," Parrot said apologetically. "I shouldn't have scheduled it so close."

I just shook Laruso's hand and said "hi."

Laruso sat there grinning. I want Brian Dennehy to play him in the movie. Parrot sat down and motioned for me to do the same.

"Terrible about that Miller girl," Laruso opened. He perused a folder supposedly containing some sort of case file.

"Yeah. We could use some pointers on spotting fake IDs," my albino advocate countered. "Do you know if any literature is available through the department?"

"I can give you a number to call," Laruso said.

"Thanks so much. And we've been having some problems with traffic and parking. I thought we could get an officer or two to help on busier nights."

"I'm sure there are a few off-duty patrolmen who could use the extra money," Laruso said. He was already looking at my paper bag. I casually moved it to my other knee just to watch his eyes follow.

"But badged officers would lend so much more respectability," Parrot said as he played with a plastic windup policeman on Laruso's desk. He let go, and the little cop marched across the blotter toward Laruso.

"I'll see what I can do," Laruso offered. "But we're not here to talk about business, gentlemen, are we?"

We had made it to the second level.

"No indeed," Parrot said. "We were hoping to show our appreciation for the police force, as well as firmly establish our place in the Oakland community by becoming supporters of the PBA. Officer Denby in Oakland thought you might be able to accept a regular contribution from us."

"We'd be delighted, of course." Laruso opened a drawer and pulled out a form. They had a form for this! "Now what size donations were you planning to make?"

"Well, we hope to take in about five large each weekend and, since your department has been so successful in weeding out the corruption that accounted for as much as a quarter of receipts off the top, we thought we'd just pass that share of the money directly on to you."

"Well, twelve-fifty wouldn't qualify you as sponsors, I'm sorry to say. We could accept the donation, of course, but I couldn't give you decals for the car or any other special privileges." Laruso knew that Graham would have taken half, and he had every reason to suspect that Parrot was lying about our gross.

"Gee," Parrot said, disappointed. "Everyone was hoping for one of those little shields. They're so superstitious they think it'll prevent them from getting traffic tickets!"

Laruso and Parrot laughed long and loud. I was lost, but smiled along with them.

Parrot got very serious all of a sudden.

"If I advise Mr. Levi to give you the eighteen hundred cash he's holding right now, plus an additional eighteen every week, and we implement wristbands for drinking and a fake metal detector at the door, you have to guarantee us no crashes until at least 3:00 A.M., warning phone calls, and two uniforms from eleven to two."

Laruso put his hand out for the bag. "You realize those uniforms know how to count cars, Mr. Levi."

I had to say something. I couldn't be as cool as Parrot. "If we start getting larger crowds, I'm sure our ability to support the PBA will increase accordingly." I handed him the bag and said "thank you." I was thanking the guy who was ripping me off. Thank you, sir, may I please have another?

Was our Ecstasy Club based on a foundation of graft and shame? Was the next evolutionary level of the human species to be fertilized by the most corrupt mutation of the obsolete organism?

"Shit makes the best fertilizer, Zach," Parrot told me as we drove home sharing a celebratory joint. I felt even guiltier for not being paranoid about smoking the joint in my car with the windows open. Hell, the cops were on our side now.

"How can you escape the moral implications of all this?" I asked him. "You treated them like you were a customer buying a service! And they took it. What made you think you'd get away with it?" My speed had totally worn off. The world was glaring. I wanted to be back in the dark, isolated cavern I called home.

"You felt abused by them?" Parrot asked. "Persecuted?"

"Sure did. And then I felt even worse when you turned it around on them."

"And this would have paralyzed your own ability to negotiate from a position of strength?"

I nodded.

"Fascinating," Parrot said, licking his fingers and using the spit to extinguish the joint before putting it in his pocket. "Even the people who sold the world on the idea of money have never been able to grasp its higher purpose as a pure form."

"Huh?"

"What do you think money is?" Parrot asked in his econ prof tone.

"Grease. You told me that."

"It functions as grease, but it isn't really. Money is just a metaphor. A metaphor for time." We turned onto I-80 as Parrot, without a hint of malice, recounted what he believed were the sins of my ancestors.

"Money was invented so people wouldn't have to trade goods for services. If I put up a fence for you, I wouldn't have to accept six chickens as pay. I could take money from you instead and, in effect, store my labor over time. I could buy your chickens, or someone else's for that matter, whenever I wanted to. Money is pure potential energy and retains its value over time."

"But it doesn't," I said. "Inflation and interest rates make it lose its value." I had unwittingly stumbled into Parrot's trap.

"The only reason money loses value is because the moneylenders started charging interest on it. That's what Christ got so upset about when he walked into the temple and saw all the money changers. He didn't care that they were selling stuff. The temple had always been used as a marketplace. What pissed him off was that his fellow Jews were blaspheming the sacred metaphor."

"Surely Jews weren't the first people to charge interest on loans," I argued.

"Well, they were certainly the first people to be remembered for it, Zach."

"But if they were lending money, they deserved some interest, didn't they? It was their money, right?"

"Not at all. They weren't providing anything at all. They weren't conducting a labor. They simply had the official right to make the coins, a privilege bestowed on them by the Pharisees. To charge interest on it puts a drag on the system. Money is supposed to ease the engine of commerce. Grease the parts of the engine so it doesn't overheat. It makes time more flexible so that you can cash in on your productivity when you want to. By charging interest on money the Jews altered its viscosity over time. They positioned themselves in the places where they could get the grease to build up, and then siphoned off whatever they could. This was a crime punishable by death in a lot of places."

"But if the grease is building up, why not take some off? Even a mechanic gets some oil on his hands." I was defending the Jews as a reflex. What did I care? I wasn't a banker and Parrot was clearly a racist. Maybe he hated all races because he had no pigment of his own.

"A mechanic fixes a car and gets grease on his hands as a by-product. A moneylender stimulates an artificial buildup or depletion of capital wherever he may have decided to position himself in order to drain off as much as he can. It's very different. It's an external manipulation of the money supply—macroeconomic heresy. Toying with metasupply and metademand. You become an agent of commerce itself. A middleman, constantly in the role of convincing people not to trust one another. You must justify your very existence by making other people feel like strangers."

"But the Jews were wanderers. Social outcasts. Historically, they tended to facilitate communication between different cultures because they wandered from empire to empire with no home of their own."

"They couldn't own land so they needed to invent a way to create something out of nothing. The Jews went 'meta' and practiced commerce. They pretended to be facilitators but actually generated demand for their services by fomenting fear and conflict. That's why the Spanish and Romans hated the Moors so much. The Jews made them out to be slave traders, but that was pure propaganda formulated to instill paranoia in the Europeans and fortify the Jews' place as intermediaries. Why do you think the Spanish kicked all the Jews out in 1492? Some insane racial bias? Come on."

"The Inquisition was insanity. You can't—"

"Which is more probable? That an entire nation went insane and started killing people who were essentially no different from themselves, or that a nation that had adopted an invention from a foreign people that ultimately reduced them to economic slavery finally got wise and fought to take over the banks themselves? Even if Isabella and Ferdinand were simply hoping to usurp the Jewish role in moneylending, they were only perpetuating the intrinsically countercultural system that the Jews had initiated in the first place."

I looked at him a moment and realized I didn't have the ammunition to fight back.

"The modern Jewish posture of guilt and persecution is just spin control on having been exposed as the enemies of open commerce. And it's an attitude that'll kill your ability to do business."

I think that, deep down, Parrot was a Nazi.

9.

The Piano Factory turned into the Party Factory overnight, with everyone competing to secure our limited resources for their own events. Kirsten was the most self-reliant of the bunch. You had to respect her for that. She was going to use the herbal lounge with its built-in stage as her theater to avoid conflicts with other parties using the main space, and she went Dumpster diving for her sets and props instead of asking for money. She recruited some theater students from SF State to be in her company, The Performance Front, and they went into rehearsals for Kirsten's first play, a silent piece (no lines to learn) called *Hand to Mouth,* that week. Kirsten started sleeping in the theater some nights, saying that she really needed to "feel" the quality of the space. I got a different message. The "really bad cramps" she complained of on the nights we did sleep together communicated something, too.

Everyone else focused almost entirely on the graphic design of their handouts (what else really characterizes a party?), and this meant going through Duncan. All materials coming out of PF— T-shirts, flyers, stickers—had to be approved by Duncan. To Duncan approval meant creation, since he only approved of the things that he himself had designed.

The individual club managers signed up for time with Duncan when they could sit with him as he conceptualized their flyers at the Sun workstation. Pig did all the actual work. He was like a cyborg: one with the machine. Operating Pig was like operating a Macintosh. He served as the user-friendly interface to some pretty daunting technology.

"Make the letters stand out more. It should have a 3-D effect," Duncan instructed Pig while Henry scoured the cover art on CDs by Renn A. Sanz, his British Industrial music idol, for inspirational images. The Goth-Industrial scene was largely about the reclamation of language, sex, magic, and symbology, so the flyer for

Henry's party, Pandora's Fix (a variant on Brooks's Pandora's Fox), had to do that too. Everything we produced was "meta."

They were working with two-toned 3-D letters, so that if you looked at the words *Pandora's Fix* in that fuzzy, Magic-Eye way, you'd see the words *True Will* emerge from underneath them—an oblique reference to Aleister Crowley's idea that finding your true will and following it, no matter what, is the path to power and bliss.

"Do what thou wilt shall be the whole of the law," Henry read off one of the albums. "Cool."

I was troubled by the phrase. "What if 'thou wilt' is to shoot people? Or take advantage of them?"

"Why would I want to do that, mate?" Henry asked, deeply perplexed by my question. "My wilt would be for more sex and drugs. And better sex and drugs, mind you."

"Thy will be done," I said sarcastically.

Duncan looked up from the computer screen, annoyed to have been drawn from his trance.

"The ultimate point," Duncan began, using his favorite word again, "of rave, Goth, Industrial, even performance, is just that. To enact your true will. The real challenge is to find it. Break the social codes and external programming in order to become one's own programmer. It's very Samuel Clearwater, really. Use whatever you can—drugs, music, ideas—to break down the old programs and replace them with new ones."

"You know there's bookstores that carry the Satanic Bible," Henry announced out of context, "but not Crowley or RAS [short for Renn A. Sanz]. They're scared of them." Scared of them not selling any copies, most likely.

The Goth scene was decidedly more warlike than the puffy rave world I was used to. The kids pierced themselves all over, wore tattoos, and conducted dark magical rituals they thought would restore the personal power that had been usurped by authorities and societal programming. They talked a lot about following their bliss, but they didn't mean delighting in good sex or a summer day. Each piercing or tattoo was a reclamation of territory. Their skin, bodies, and minds were part of the battleground. They liked almost anything dark or satanic or just plain horrifying because it went against the grain—and the grain itself had been imposed by kings and popes and secret societies dedicated to dominating and stifling popular will. Goth kids saw the appropriation of their will as an act of war.

"It's a metapropaganda war," Duncan explained. "They control the imagery in our media—both electronic and otherwise—in order to maintain control of language, symbols, and the magic they contain. They want to render us afraid of ritual, ashamed of sex, and ignorant of our natural power."

"And that's why we focus on the bliss," I tried to contribute, steering the conversation toward a somewhat brighter philosophical outlook, "because it brings each person closer to his individual will."

"Right." Duncan went on as Pig continued to shade and reshade the letters on the computer. "We use the bliss, the music, and the trance to retrain ourselves to believe that what feels good *is* good—which goes right in the face of conventional Western, puritanical thought. Bliss itself is the great attractor. It's what pulls life through time. To monopolize and divert that evolutionary pull—that Gaian motion toward complexity and consciousness—is the only true sin. The buying and selling of time, first documented in the New Testament, was akin to the invention of slavery."

Not this again. The "Jewish" problem. I felt I had to defend myself.

"You don't believe in that power elite stuff, though, do you?" I asked rhetorically.

"It's as old as the stones in the Tower of London," Henry said. "Older even." The British had a better sense of oppression.

"To believe in their power gives them their power," Duncan said. "But they're out there, irrefutably." When Duncan used words like *irrefutably*, we took it on faith that he could prove his point. Language as control. "The British East India trading company was a cover for eighteenth-century British intelligence. The trade meant less to them than the espionage. These were master empire builders. Trade led to intelligence, cultural subversion, and, eventually, colonization."

"But we live in a democracy now," my reflexes took over.

"Do you realize how deeply programmed you are, Zach?" Duncan asked, half-amused and half-appalled. "You think the American Revolution really liberated you? Just take a look at *Plugged* magazine, or the International Business Society behind them. They advise businesses and governments about cyberspace and new media the way that Margaret Mead used to advise Roosevelt on the Japanese or South Pacific peoples. Cultural anthropologists in the empire's service. Look at Massachusetts Media Center for that matter, and the British Intelligence behind them. These concerns grew directly out of the Anglo-Dutch slave-trading industry and, later, World War II intelligence operations. It carries right through to today's media empires and movie-star cults like Cosmotology. The direct lineage can be drawn."

"It's as old as the stones in the Tower of . . ." Henry said, trailing off. Maybe he remembered that he had said this before.

"Watch what they do when they catch wind of what we're up to," Duncan smiled. He was gearing up for battle. The revolution would be fought from the PF, and it would look like a rave.

In one of those odd synchronicities that would soon become the rule rather than the exception at the Ecstasy Club, Peter burst in. He was terribly agitated.

"The Pacific Gas and Electric guys are here," he said. "They're pulling out the power."

Another job for Zach.

10.

The electric company didn't care so much that we were squatting—only that without a lease on the space, we couldn't be billed for the power. They needed a "legitimate titleholder." We spent about a week repeatedly losing and then taking back our power. They'd come with a truck, disconnect the line, and put a big cap over the relays at the pole across the street. Then Pig would climb up (well, we'd hoist him up with a lot of ropes and pulleys) and tap back in. They never called the cops on us—at least not to our knowledge. I think the power guys appreciated our spirit and determination.

Tyrone would start screaming every time the power went off, and the surges were wreaking havoc on the computers, so I came up with a better solution: make our own power. We spent three thousand dollars on four used gas-powered Honda generators and set them up just behind the building. We ran cables in through a grate under the mezzanine platform. Ironically, the bums who lived out in the lot behind the PF started tapping into *our* power. Every night at around midnight we'd lose a quarter of our circuits as the bums replaced our leads with one that they used for a few small lamps and a black-and-white TV. We decided to be better hosts than the power company and ran them their own little line so they wouldn't keep yanking ours out.

As long as we conducted our business with cash, no one asked any questions. Buying gasoline was easy once we found a station that let us fill up our nonstandard cans. We used about thirty gallons a day on average, but once the parties started and all the lights and sound went on, we had to get two more generators and the daily cost went up to about seventy bucks. Pig made sure everything was installed safely. We didn't need a generator fire to add to our problems.

On Monday afternoon, the day of our first gay party, PooF, Lauren came back from canvassing Berkeley carrying two potted bonsai trees and waving a fresh copy of the *Bay Area Guardian*.

"We made the front page!" she shouted as she ran up the stairs to the kitchen where Duncan, Peter, Brooks, Parrot, and I had been sitting drinking coffee and prattling on about our own events. She plopped the paper down on the table in front of Duncan. "Isn't it great!"

Duncan said nothing.

The headline read: LOOK MA, NO MORTGAGE! YOUNG OAKLAND SQUATTERS TAKE A STAND.

It was a neo-Marxist interpretation of the PF that analyzed the ethics of landownership and tenancy. Apparently *squatting* used to mean staying somewhere and literally shitting there to make it your own. We had certainly taken our share of dumps at the PF. The writer was impressed by how we took over the space, but she said nothing about the party, or our higher intentions.

Lauren just stood there waiting for Duncan to say something. She was wearing a brand-new tight neon-green dress and a tight, expectant smile to match. I prayed for Duncan not to break her heart, then prayed for him to just do it and get it over with so I could pick up the pieces. Adam and Andy were downstairs using a staple gun to run streamers across the space. *Ke-bap. Ke-bap.*

"It's preposterous," Duncan said, scanning through the article.

"That's what we get for stooping to their level," I said, committing the unpardonable sin of making a judgment before Duncan had finished and, worse, condemning him in the process.

"I only mentioned the squatting aspect to get her attention," Duncan said, more to himself than anyone else. "It was a calculated change of tack. I had no reason to suspect that the media here were so unsophisticated." What Duncan couldn't admit was that he had *mis*calculated. Mr. Media Hacker had been caught in his own game. The reporter drew out of him the story she wanted to tell, and had Duncan's quotes to prove it. All that stuff about the "confiscation of public space by a consortium of like-minded individuals" was in there, verbatim.

"I bet the cops are going to want more money now," I said, almost relishing Duncan's despair.

Lauren, a far better person than I, tried to console him instead. "Well, it's only one paper. Let's just throw it out."

Duncan kept scowling at the headline. She tried to change the subject.

"Look at the bonsai I got!" she said, putting one of the mutant trees on the table.

"How much did you spend on those?" Duncan asked accusatorily.

"They gave them to me for free when I told them what it was for," she said, stroking his hair. "The manager of the store wants to come and take pictures of the garden when it's done."

"So now you want to position the PF as a fêng shui project?" Duncan asked.

Lauren had been cultivating a Zen garden on the roof since we moved in. It was the only personal expression she had left since being folded into Duncan's empire, and it meant so much to her that she didn't want any of us to see it until she was finished. Watching Duncan ridicule her work made me want to hit him.

"Don't let this article upset you, honey," she said, reverting to the midwestern accent I imagined her mom probably had. "Come on, Duncan. Cheer up. Look at the new dress I got on Telegraph!" She twirled around for Duncan. It was a pretty cute dress, and cut in at her waist just right to make her little butt stick out.

Duncan watched Lauren parading in the dress for a moment, and then he let her have it. "Everything in this country is so garish. You'd never see something like that in London. Not even on a poser in Chelsea."

I felt a sympathetic adrenal discharge. Fight or flight on her behalf. But I just sat there, letting it surge through my veins unused.

Thankfully, Lauren didn't look to me for defense but just stared at Duncan, uncomprehending of his cruelty. Surely she had taken worse from him over the months they had been together. She bit that upper lip of hers and slowly walked up to the pyramid. I wished Kirsten had been there to see the way other guys treat their girlfriends.

Duncan pretended that nothing had happened—or maybe he really was so wrapped up in the media gaff that he didn't realize what he had done. He went back through the article, pulling quotes and repeating how the American media were so stupid and how we had to come up with an overall media strategy so "they don't do it for us. There's no margin for error."

"But the *Bay Area Guardian* is basically on our side," Peter said. "Aren't they our allies—at least compared to *Plugged* or the *Chronicle?*"

"Liberal sympathy is more dangerous than overt attacks from the controllers," Duncan explained, getting back on his comfortably high horse. "It's insidious because it takes the form of praise, but it misdirects you if you take it seriously and let it affect your purpose. We don't do things because they're 'right.' That's the whole point."

"Why do we do things, then?" I asked, less antagonistically than to help Duncan formulate his argument into a coherent whole. That's the job of a lieutenant intellectual, after all.

"We're creating a new civilization," Duncan answered immediately. "We're going to push evolution forward by touching another dimension. We are going to break time altogether, and to do that we need to maintain a pure environment, uncontaminated by the agenda of the *Bay Area Guardian* or anyone else."

"But do the kids coming to our parties know that?" I asked. "They get high, get off on the group vibe, but how are they different the next day?" Duncan knew I meant to coax and not confront.

"We've got to make them understand what they're here for," Duncan said, thinking out loud. "They can't be trusted to be their own programmers."

We were all stunned by Duncan's admission. Can't be trusted? He quickly corrected himself.

"I mean, yet. In their current condition, they are unprepared. Ignorant. The PF can alter that. Liberate them from their current set so they can find a new one."

"One that we provide for them?" I offered half-incredulously.

"We can show them a direction," Duncan said.

And thus the Nine Points were born.

While the gay kids poured in downstairs, Duncan and I sat up in his pyramid writing what would become the first PF press release: The Ecstasy Club's Nine Points. Duncan was going to use eight, based on the eight noble truths in Buddhism, but I suggested we bump it up to nine, seeing as how we were the next evolutionary level—the next great age of humankind.

I felt more like a hired scribe than Thomas Jefferson. Yes, the original draft would be in my handwriting, but pretty much a direct transcription of what came out of Duncan's mouth. It took nearly the entire night of arguing back and forth with everyone who came up to see what we were doing and register their own votes. Peter sarcastically suggested that we use the rules they came up with in *Animal Farm* as a template. By the time we were done it sounded like ideological rave babble, but a lot of work had gone into it, and it accurately represented where we were at.

In the end, the press release went like this:

The Ecstasy Club is an open collective dedicated to peace, harmony, and understanding. Through group bliss, music, and ritual, we hope to direct ourselves toward the following ultimate goals:

1. To become more than human. [We ripped this off from Crowley.]
2. To evolve consciously and purposefully within a single lifetime.
3. To deprogram the social set designed to trap us in mundane thought structures.
4. To reprogram that set as individuals and as a collective.
5. To disconnect from personal habit, character, and ego.
6. To reframe and disengage from mundane attachments through ritual and ceremony.
7. To synchronize ourselves into a metaorganism: no one more important than any other.
8. To increase the frequency of this organism, making it capable of rising above matter.

9. To rebirth ourselves as pure consciousness, breaking through time itself.

Welcome to the next phase. Peace Love Unity.

Around the edges of the document we repeated the main verbs of each goal, become–evolve–deprogram–reprogram–disconnect–reframe–synchronize–increase–rebirth. That framing became our letterhead. It balanced our high ideals in some good, old-fashioned rave lovey-dovey cliché. There wasn't a whole lot of slacker-irony in it, but by being unabashedly idealistic we were taking a stand.

Once we'd finished the whole press release, including the Nine Points, a schedule of upcoming parties, and a list of the celebrities we hoped would be there, Duncan called for Brooks and Kirsten to print out a bunch of copies and stuff envelopes. Brooks had a mailing list of all the music journalists in town, so he was a logical candidate for this important but menial labor. As for Kirsten, well, I guess the Ecstasy Club was still pretty sexist. When it came to getting someone to do something for him, Duncan always seemed more comfortable asking a girl than a guy.

Lauren and Pig were to post the Nine Points on ecstasy-club.com, which was looking pretty good—especially considering that it was optimized for the old, pre-tables version of Netscape. The site had a clickable map of the PF that Lauren had created in Photoshop, an archive of scanned-in photos from parties, a database of all our upcoming events, and pointers to other rave and psychedelic sites on the Web. Peter had lobbied for us to include links to conspiracy sites, too, but none of us saw the logic in doing so. Yet.

When everyone came up and got their marching orders from Duncan, I had assumed I would be stuffing envelopes too, or at least helping update the site. But Duncan just put his arm around me and said, "Let me buy you a drink, Zach." It felt weird to leave them all working like that while I was going down to the party—like we were in Plato's Republic, with the gold- and silver-blooded people writing the important documents while the bronze-bloods stuff envelopes.

The bigger the Ecstasy Club got, the more I felt privileged to delegate such duties to others. Duncan encouraged this attitude because it prevented me from criticizing him for doing the same. Buying me the drink—well, actually telling the bartender to pour us complimentary drinks against our club policy—was a final confirmation of my complicity. The Levites and the Kohanes. Big cats at the sacrifice.

The party was jammed with boys. I saw one girl standing alone at the bar and, while Duncan scolded poor Adam about the way he was abusing the lasers ("the patterns are much too predictable!"), I thought I'd chat her up. I was feeling pretty confident, having firmly established my role as a cocreator of the Ecstasy Club, and with Kirsten unavailable in more ways than one, I figured I might as well put in some options for the future.

Danielle had delicate features but wore a large collection of gaudy jewelry. Frankly, up close she wasn't the babe I thought I had seen from across the room, but I had returned her smile and approached her with such a swagger that I was committed to exchange a few words. I bought her a refill for her drink—well, actually, I used my rank to get another illegal comp, which looked even better. She had a joint of some really strong skunk, so we smoked it and chatted about the PF. Danielle was already a convert, which made my status all the more relevant.

"They say we're all going to mutate soon," she said, a little too enthusiastically but with appealing, naive sincerity.

"It could happen," I said. "That's why these gay parties are so interesting." I wanted her to know I wasn't here for the boys. "We're evolving past sexuality into a new human being. A postsexual form. On some level, gay people realize this already."

"I never thought of it that way," she said, sipping her drink. "It's such an enlightened outlook."

A stool opened up behind hers, so I picked it up with one arm and scooted it under myself in one motion.

"You have really strong arms," she said, touching my shoulder and buying my biceps trick better than anyone had ever done before. I smiled and checked out her legs. Then she added, "I bet you're a bottom, aren't you?"

So she was actually a he. I can only imagine what it's like for those guys on *Ricki Lake* who have sex and get married to a transvestite before finding out.

Duncan's move to the dance floor gave me an excuse to part company—which I did pretty discourteously considering my earlier gestures, but I reasoned Danielle was used to that.

I followed Duncan out into the pack of dancing boys. About half their shirts were off, and they had physiques that made me look like Woody Allen. Some of them had whistles tied around their necks which they blew during the drum breaks. They all danced with their arms up in the air, and Duncan and I did too.

The pot was coming on strong—not heady, but very physical. My whole body was tingling and I could feel my heart pounding. Duncan was, for once, absolutely happy. He was finally accepting me as an equal, so I decided to enjoy the moment. Men dancing with men. It's what the Hassids do, and it felt good. No pressures of looking cool or attracting anyone in particular. It was pure dance. Pure flesh. Sweaty skin, sculpted torsos, waving arms, and bouncing hair. We were Greek gods. I could appreciate the beauty of the moment.

Duncan got near the center of the floor and did that weird, choppy dance of his. He looked like a young boy figuring out how to dance for the first time. Awkward little movements, made on the oddest selection of beats. He was a strange man. Domineering, controlling, almost fascistic in his thinking, but brilliant nonetheless. Underneath it all was this awkward little kid, trying to make sense of the world, tear down the crusty old bullshit around him, and make a better place for all of us in the process.

I loved Duncan at that moment. I don't know if it was the pot, the atmosphere, or some recessive homosexual gene, but I could see him as a beautiful being. Even his flaws just made him more human. I didn't love only Duncan, though. He was just the focus of devotion. It extended outward from him until I loved everyone on the dance floor. Every guy there was beautiful in his own way. This was a perfect, unified world. One dancing male creature with hundreds of heads. Giving itself pleasure. The perfect physical gratification—just boys getting themselves off. I felt I knew what it was to be gay. There is no "other."

Women, I thought as I got into bed with Kirsten later that night, are so different from us. They are a separate species. Why did it have to be that way? Why couldn't I just connect with her like we used to? The Ecstasy Club would change all this somehow. Make us all just human beings in collective.

I stroked her hair for a while. We were both naked. I don't think we had really talked for a few days, other than business or trivialities. As we lay there, I tried to envision everything working out for us. I'd meet her parents up in Humboldt. They'd like me. Parents always do. I'm an Ivy League graduate. We could have kids together. Kirsten could run a theater in San Francisco and I could run a national organization of Ecstasy Clubs, with its own record label.

Kirsten turned around and faced me, then reached down to take me in her hand. She smiled at me—a half-smile that I couldn't interpret—and started to stroke me. I got excited fast—despite or maybe because of the fact that the bond between us was gone. We were two separate people. We both knew that "us" was over—but in that separation was a certain freedom. A deep otherness. I moved to get on top of her but she put her other hand on my hip to keep me still.

"It's okay, baby," she whispered to me. "I know. It's okay."

What did she know? Why did she want to touch me like this?

But her hand felt so good. So foreign. Not a trace of anger or resentment. I felt myself breathing harder. Closing my eyes. And then I came. *Totally exposed.* She just stayed there, holding me as I softened. I knew it was the last time we would be together like this. For some reason, I started to cry. Hot tears streamed down my face. I was learning a lesson, but I wasn't sure what it was.

Kirsten put her other hand on the back of my head and held me to her breast.

"Yes, baby. It's okay. It's going to be okay. It's okay, baby."

11.

I must have been asleep for less than half an hour. I was in that postorgasm stupor—the one where all the endorphins hit, making you roll over and go to sleep. I never got that from real sex. In real sex there's an energy exchange, not just a release. It can invigorate you as much as it tires you out. But this time with Kirsten wasn't an energy exchange at all. I was all alone; I just happened to be with another person.

I didn't sleep the rest of the night. I know this as a fact because I specifically remember looking at my alarm clock each time the digits were the same: 1:11, 2:22, 3:33, 4:44. How odd, I thought, that the landmarks on a digital clock are different from those on one with hands. Regular hours are spaced so evenly—but these digital landmarks are, too. Exactly seventy-one minutes apart. It's just a longer hour. Then I started thinking about the analog-clock equivalents of these magic times where the digits are the same. Twelve noon, when the hands cross. Six thirty, too, though not exactly. It's more like 6:33, because the hour hand has already moved halfway past the six by 6:30. And what's the next one after that? Seven thirty-eight? Then 8:43? They have to be one hour and five minutes apart since each hour is spaced five minutes apart on the clock, but then what about 1:05? Isn't it really more like 1:06? Or 1:05 and twenty seconds?

I could tell I was going mildly insane, so I slipped out of bed at 5:55 to sneak up and preview Lauren's garden. The only way up was through Tyrone's room, so I crept in quietly but he wasn't sleeping either. He was talking to the little blue sculptures—whispering, really. Giving them secret orders with numbers and angles in them. "Latitude twenty-eight, zone three, time alpha one eight eight. Have you identified the target? Again!" He heard me come in and he stopped suddenly.

"I'm just going up to the roof," I told him. He didn't move, so I slowly and nonthreateningly approached the ladder and climbed all the way up. I noticed a set of ropes and pulleys that Lauren must have installed in order to hoist her materials up the shaftway and onto the roof. I swung open the trapdoor. The air was brisk and the sky had just begun the slow dissolve to morning.

Lauren's garden was beautiful. There were stone benches placed in a circle—well, not a perfect circle, but it felt like a circle. In the center, slightly off-center, was an arrangement of rocks with water dripping over them and a bonsai tree. Off to the other side, but still connected by a path of pebbles, sat an incomplete pagoda-gazebo. It had two red-lacquered boards as steps leading to a flat area with a little railing and the beginnings of a roof. I could hear the water trickling in the night silence.

The whole garden sat quite asymmetrically with respect to the building beneath it, but it looked just right. If it had been squared off, I thought, it would have just called attention to the awful contrast with the brick-and-tar nonaesthetic of the rest of the rooftop.

When did she have time to do all this?

I got inspired to practice the tai chi I had learned in college. I went to the middle of the bench arrangement, just next to the rocks, and faced due north the way the old Chinese man taught us to begin. So there I stood in my boxer shorts, doing my compromised version of the ancient Wu-style form, gently rotating eighth turns and quarter turns as the movements dictated. Hands like clouds. Carry tiger to mountain. Repulse monkey.

As I accomplished the more yang, masculine punches, I realized I was facing the tree. Then, as I softened to a yin deflection, my hand nearly touched the running water. Of course—both fêng shui and tai chi are based on the same I Ching hexagrams, the eight points on the compass, and elemental forces of nature. As the sun rose, perfectly from the east, the shadow of the pagoda slowly formed over the shadow of my moving body until there was a perfect black image on the white pebbled path of me, dancing beneath the pagoda roof.

She was speaking to me through her garden, and I was decoding her message with my tai chi motions. I understood her essence. The deep feminine knowledge that symmetry is deceptively reductionist. The points mean nothing without the circle. It's all slightly off-kilter, which makes it just right. The heartbeats in two syncopated gestures. Even the earth wobbles in its spin. The clock, its numbers, the digits, they mean nothing in the face of a sun going up. The inner world of Lauren's garden was infinite because it was tied to the greater motions of the world around us. This was the real launching pad. Imperfectly and absolutely right.

The brilliant solitude was broken by the sound of Kirsten and Duncan having a row downstairs. He had sent Lauren to Kinko's to run off the programs for the evening's play, without showing them to Kirsten first. On the back page was the complete set of Nine Goals of the Ecstasy Club, which Kirsten thought detracted from the style and meaning of her play.

By the time I made my way downstairs, it had gotten pretty ugly.

"But the play is about despair!" Kirsten pleaded. "Not that optimistic rave rant. It's real human suffering I'm talking about."

"You're presenting it at the PF, under the auspices of the Ecstasy Club." Duncan was very cool.

"Fine. Leave your own handouts on a table at the door. Not in my program."

"It's not your program. It's the club's. Isn't that right, Zach?" I was off-guard and still in my boxers. I hated having my allegiance tested this way. It seemed so cruel—but Duncan's point was to break down our neurotic personal obligations in favor of our pure collective relationships. If what she believed was truly out of line, then my taking her side would be dishonest codependence.

"Strictly speaking—," I began.

"Don't speak strictly," Duncan said calmly. "Just speak."

"The Ecstasy Club did pay for the programs," I said.

It's hard to convey how painful a simple moment like this can be. Through the back cover of a theater program, Duncan was making me crucify my own girlfriend. In theory, we would both be

stripped of our barriers to transformation in the process. Our social programming was getting dismantled, and it hurt. Duncan
may look like the villain in this, but Kirsten and I already knew our
relationship had ended—and over issues just like this. We simply
hadn't admitted it out loud. Here I was, thinking to defend her
from Duncan's cold logic, but why?

"So that's what matters?" Kirsten asked, blood filling her face.
"The money? Fine. I'll pay for it myself."

"You know that's not the point," Duncan said, as much to me as
to her. I was still hedging.

"Look, Kirsten," I tried to soften the situation. "All Duncan
means—"

"All *I* mean?" Duncan stopped me. He was right. I couldn't
blame this on him. I had to stand up for the club against Kirsten.

"The projects we do here are all part of a bigger project," I corrected myself. "It's not about you and your play. It's about group
transformation."

Kirsten was dumbfounded. She had bailed me out so many
times before, like when I renamed the club without Duncan's permission. But in a roundabout way I was doing her a favor. Sacri-
ficing whatever it was we had left to our clarity of purpose. If she
couldn't handle it, then she really didn't belong in the Ecstasy Club
to begin with. Or maybe I was hoping she'd leave so I wouldn't
have to keep living with an ex-girlfriend.

"What's happened to you?" she asked with contempt. Then she
started to cry.

"We can make a separate flyer next week, Kirsten," Duncan
said, suddenly relenting. That pissed me off more than anything
else. "These are already at the printers. I'm sorry. You should be in
charge of every element of your production."

Great. Duncan had let me hang myself defending club principles, then totally gave in.

"Thanks," Kirsten said to Duncan and most definitely not to
me. She threw another contemptuous look in my direction and
stomped out to her theater. Once she was out of earshot, Duncan
surprised me again.

"She really can be a bitch, can't she?" he whispered. "She's not going to make it." He put his hand on my shoulder. "You will, though. You're going all the way."

"She's not a bitch," I said.

"I know," Duncan said, then added without a trace of duplicity, "I was just testing your reaction. You can't be proud just because you know better than her." These were the kinds of tricks that the yogi plays on his students, or a shaman plays on the tribe.

"Come on," he said. "Pig and Peter are testing their visionquest program."

In Pig's loft, we found Nomie in the middle of the room seated on a pillow. Wires seemed to trail out from her body—stereo headphones on her ears, electronic goggles over her eyes, an old Nintendo VR glove on her hand, and little suction cups attached to her forehead and chest. Each of these devices had wires running into a patch bay in back of the giant computer on Pig's worktable. Peter and Pig made adjustments to a TV monitor while Nomie moved her gloved hand around and giggled. She looked like someone getting her dreams scanned on *The Prisoner.*

On the TV were colored swirls forming a loose representation of Nomie's head. There were two yellow depressions where her eyes would be and a glowing orb where her brain would be. On another monitor, lines of numbers scrolled by faster than anyone could possibly read.

"We've got it set up to do pure feedback," Pig said proudly. "She's looking at the output of her own electrocranial activity, and altering it with her thoughts and mood."

"It's like a feedback loop," explained Peter.

"It's precisely a feedback loop," Pig corrected him. "It's as if you pointed a video camera at its own output in the monitor."

"Except here," Peter said, pointing at the pulsing orb on the screen, "the camera is Nomie, whose own rhythms and perceptions change the picture. As she reacts to her own output, she changes it."

"At least it's a rough estimate," Pig said modestly. "We don't have it calibrated just right, and there's a few seconds' delay between what she does and what she sees."

Nomie didn't seem to mind. Her giggles turned to moans and oohs, then back to giggles again. She was pretending to get sexually excited by the apparatus. Or maybe she really was.

"What's it for?" I asked. Peter had already lost one friend to an experiment like this and I didn't want them taking pointless risks with anyone else.

"The theory is that by generating an almost instantaneous feedback loop," Peter explained, "we create an opening to another level. A higher order of complexity."

Pig was used to creating real-life metaphors for technological events. "If you look in a mirror with another one behind you, you know how you see an infinite number of mirrors? That's the opening we're talking about."

"But in a mirror," Duncan said, "you can't see all the way back. Your own image and point of view get in the way." Since that first party, Duncan himself was operating on more than one level at once, and everything he said took on metaphorical significance—at least for me. I marveled at his depth: *Of course it's the self that gets in the way. Ego is merely point of view. Break the self, and you see from everywhere at once. You break time and see through your own image.*

"We evade the paradox," Peter said, "because the image passes through Nomie. It is altered by her perceptions, but it flows right through her."

"So it's like a filter," I said. "Standing in front of a mirror as a clear, slightly colored piece of glass. You can see through yourself, again and again, millions of times."

"But the problem," Pig said, "is that the color darkens the image. It's not perfectly transparent. You can see through it many times, but eventually—no matter how pale the color is—if you try to pass light through it enough times, it will absorb the beam and you won't be able to see through it anymore. That accounts for the opacity of the image on the screen."

I loved these heady theoretical conversations—especially when we had real technology and drugs around to test them on.

"What we want to figure out how to do," Pig continued, "is amplify the signal each time it passes through Nomie. Boost it back to its original intensity so it can keep iterating to the computer and back to her without losing any signal."

"May I try it?" asked Duncan, knowing they'd be delighted for him to audition their work.

They disconnected Nomie and fitted Duncan with all the gear. Nomie just sat in a daze, giggling and touching her forehead. Her performance was a bit pushed, though. I knew she was merely trying to keep the focus on herself by faking a series of intense post-VR reactions.

As soon as Duncan put on the gear, the image on the monitor changed to an ordered series of tiny boxes. A graph paper of squares containing little colored balls, moving back and forth. I remember seeing something like that once when I was tripping.

Peter knew what it was. "The optical grids of the limbic neocortex," he announced. "Those are the building blocks of visual information."

Duncan seemed to be struggling, but then he smiled. On the monitor, the little colored balls dissolved into yin-yang symbols. We were all stunned. Duncan was controlling the image on the monitor with his mind! The yin-yangs faded into something that looked almost like swastikas, and then into yin-yangs again. Suddenly, Duncan sat up, ripping half the gear off his face as he did.

"I want to try something," he said.

Duncan took a small foil packet out of his shirt pocket and opened it up. There was white powder inside.

"It's ketamine." Duncan took out a small straw in order to snort the dissociative anesthetic, a molecular relative of PCP that he got from a guy in Santa Rosa who built isolation tanks. "You all want some?"

Far be it from any of us to refuse drugs. Snorting one small line had an instant effect. I expected a mild buzz, but this was a full-on psychedelic experience. An acidlike trance, but without all the speedy soul-searching. Just deep alteration. Generic trippiness.

As we all dazed into the K-holes we were digging for ourselves, Duncan got himself back into the gear.

No grids this time. Just shades of white and a vague outline of Duncan's head. Duncan looked confused, and then he laughed out loud. We all laughed with him. Then the monitor got very bright and suddenly blinked out.

Duncan screamed for a second, then threw off the goggles. We waited tensely for him to say something. Peter panicked and checked Duncan's wrist for a pulse, his desperate motions betraying the psychic scars of his trauma at JFK.

Duncan suddenly inhaled, gagging and coughing like a person pulled out of the ocean. Then he slowly sat up and moved his mouth around as if he were tasting his own saliva.

"Al-set," he said, then shook himself out of his zoned state of mind. He was back.

"All set?" Peter repeated, with meaningful concern.

"Al-set. Huh? Something tastes like electricity," Duncan said, before returning completely to normal.

Nomie started touching her face frantically. She was dipping into a bad trip, or putting on a convincing performance. I put my arm around her and stroked her shoulder. She leaned her head against me and began purring like a kitten.

"What did you mean by that?" Peter asked.

"By what?" Duncan said.

"Al-set. You said al-set."

"I did?" Duncan said, amused. "That's funny."

"What did you see?" Peter asked him.

"Just white. Bright white."

"That's what we saw, too," I said, "on the monitor."

"And then I thought I was traveling. Moving through time," Duncan said, as if reflecting on an experience he had had years ago, not just seconds before.

Pig broke the eerie stillness. "I'm going to give my friends at SRL a call," he said. "I think they can help us devise an amplification circuit."

Peter just stared off into space.

12.

By about four in the afternoon Kirsten's actors had arrived and, although there were only two of them, they were driving us crazy.

"Can someone please put this Band-Aid on me?" the guy kept shouting. "I have a boo-boo and it hurts."

"Powder. Powder. I forgot my powder!" the girl was saying as she picked at her curlers. She was impersonating a nervous actor—psyching herself up into some kind of panic.

I brought her a can of Gold Bond medicated powder. She looked like she spent so much energy being a professional ac-TOR that she didn't have any left to act with. She didn't take my powder, either. Fine. More for my feet. (Someone at the PF had athlete's foot, and it was spreading.)

I talked to the guy for a while as he applied makeup to a latex nose he held between his fingers. *Great, it's gonna be a show about a nose*. He got me pretty damn depressed. He was thirty-four and had been back and forth from LA to San Francisco for the past twelve years. He'd acted in tons of "equity waiver" shows (no pay) and once understudied Officer Krupke and a few other nonsinging roles in a Tel Aviv production of *West Side Story*. He had gotten picked to be on *Star Search* for the comedy-sketch competition, but they discontinued that feature of the show two weeks before his taping was supposed to take place. He had no agent, but, he said, "many of them know my work." *Maybe that's why they won't sign you.*

"Everything's coming together for me right now," he told me. "This is going to be a great year. Through Kirsten I met Dolores, the actress playing opposite me in tonight's performance." He sounded as if he were reading from a Playbill.

"Oh, really?" I said, distancing myself. Duncan did that habitually—"Oh, really?" Now I knew where it came from.

"I just started *The Way of the Artist*. It's *A Course in Miracles* for the artist."

"Oh, really?"

"It's been a wonderful experience so far. I do exercises, set goals, meet my goals, and experience a great deal of transformation." I sure hoped we didn't sound like this. Nah.

"So this course is helping you?" I asked, starting to rise. He pushed me back in my seat, with his hand and his voice.

"It. Has. Changed. My. Life," he said.

I smiled, holding back another "oh, really?"

"I see the world differently now," he said, "and the world has changed, too. The whole universe is assisting me. Like I was saying, I met Kirsten. I set that as a goal. To meet a director. Then I met Dolores. She was a goal, too, once I recognized it. I was focusing on getting an agent. I did the visualizations every day. And then, by 'coincidence,'" he made little quote marks with his fingers, "Dolores needs a scene partner. She's auditioning for a theatrical agent next month and needs to do a scene right in his office."

"But it's her audition, right? The agent's considering *her*."

"That's a negative worldview," he said, shaking his head. "Once I'm in the office, anything can happen, right? I'm in a space of possibility now. I'll conveniently have my head-shot and résumé with me. I'll bring many copies of both and slip them under each agent's door before I leave." Chinese-restaurant menus would probably be received with the same level of enthusiasm. "Now that I've redone the shots with my new hair, I'm sure I'll get calls. I can't even believe I sent out so many of the old photos."

He sat dreamily for a moment, then added, "That says a lot about what I thought of myself until very recently. How could I have expected someone else to want me in a play or film when, in the biggest sense, I wasn't ready to cast myself?"

Lauren rescued me from the depressing backstage saga.

"Can you drive me to Berkeley?" she asked, knowing I'd say yes. She had a brand-new stack of flyers for Saturday's big rave and needed to put them in the record stores.

Some of my best memories of the Ecstasy Club are the times when I got away, even for just a few hours. There was so much pressure at the PF to be "on" that I always looked for an excuse to do some chore in the real world and be "off." Evolution can be grueling.

It was starting to drizzle outside, which probably wouldn't help Kirsten's attendance any. I unlocked Lauren's door, and once she scooted under my arm into the car, I was out of my PF head.

I loved being Sir Lancelot to her Guinevere. The valiant young knave who she knew adored her from afar yet always maintained respect and distance. After that night with Kirsten, though, I had been avoiding Lauren. I feared I had sullied something pure, and that she would sense the difference. It had been so perfect when there was no real-world lust or possessiveness. She was like a sister. I was determined to return to that state of effortless intimacy, but her gentle, flirtatious gestures weren't making it any easier.

She sat next to me in the car, her eyes following the motion of the windshield wipers. Every time I drove on the freeway I was amazed by how the outside world reflected my inner state. The clouds in the sky, the squeak of the frayed rubber against the glass, the streaks of water distorting my vision—all mirrored my hazy confusion and the little voice inside me that wanted to get out. Was it really a good idea to shut all this out in the name of deprogramming? Wasn't the whole world just a big fractal? In its infinite complexity and self-similarity, didn't real life offer all the clues anyone should need?

I found a spot on Telegraph with time on the meter (major parking karma), so I got out with Lauren to place the flyers and chat up the record-store clerks about our events. Those clerks with the dyed black hair are the best possible word of mouth for anything because the clean-cut college kids going into the stores always ask them for advice about new CDs and hot parties—as if the colored hair makes them experts on everything cool and underground.

The counter was already packed with other flyers, mostly for other PF events. It was so inefficient. Someone made a separate trip to each store for each flyer. We couldn't get organized enough to bring them all at the same time, and whenever one of us would suggest this to Duncan, he'd just say that whichever flyer was ready should go out on the streets immediately. We were all expending so much effort for so little actual work. Sometimes I got the feeling that Duncan didn't care how much was accomplished—only that we kept struggling constantly so that lots of conflicts would keep arising, giving us the opportunity to drop more of our attachments to our own, personal ideas. Turbulence was the modus operandi.

Compared with all the others, though, this new flyer was definitely the coolest. The rave was named Phylogenic Foresight, and the handout was a round card with a picture of a giant-headed fetus in the center. Duncan was riffing on the ontogeny-recapitulates-phylogeny concept: how the fetus passes through all the stages of evolution before it gets born. It's a very fractal idea that plays to the old rave/rebirth crowd. It was a hint to the hardcore that this would be a spiritual party with music at the traditional 120 beats per minute—the pace of the fetal heart rate, and the beat that South American shamans use to draw tribespeople into a trance. We would project those tunneling, psychedelic videos that evoke the passage down the birth canal, and our vibe would be rebirth.

The fetus's head was bigger than normal because it represented the next stage in human development—a new mutation. Our evolutionary successor. The word *foresight* meant that we saw it coming. This was the main PF rave. The complexity of the graphic image and the expensive glossy stock on which it was printed communicated this.

After we dropped off the flyers at a few key shops and handed out hundreds more to the most likely suspects, Lauren and I ducked into an espresso bar next to Cody's books. It felt like we were doing something wrong. Like kids playing hooky, monks going to a whorehouse, or Hassids scoring some pork on Yom Kippur.

The rain was a great excuse. Anything not to go back into the harsh light of constant evolution—that monitored existence where

I had to attack people for not adhering to the Nine Goals. Zero tolerance was no fun.

I ordered a plain espresso, Spartan that I am, while Lauren opted for a big fancy almond concoction with a long spoon. When she licked the whipped cream off the end of the spoon I had to avert my eyes. I saw other couples in the coffee bar, college kids and grad students all paired off and in love. Leading their normal lives. I was so jealous of them. They didn't have the weight of the next dimension on their shoulders. They could just get married and have sex. While here I was with the most beautiful and clear-thinking girl on the planet—and, well, we just sat there.

"Duncan doesn't love me, you know," Lauren said out of the blue. Any response from me would have been a violation of one trust or another.

"Oh, really?" I said.

Lauren laughed. "Oh, really?!" We smiled. She knew.

"You love him, though," I said, like it was a fact.

"Sure," she said. "Of course I do. But not in that way anymore."

I sensed a story coming, but it didn't. We just sat drinking our coffees.

"You're from Cleveland, right?" I asked. We had been over this information before and she probably knew it, but it was safer ground.

"Yeah. My parents are there. It's not a bad town. I doubt Duncan will ever want to go."

"He will if there's a proper party," I said, imitating his accent.

She nodded. Then she looked down, sipping her coffee and squinting as if trying to decide whether to tell me something. She thought better of it, sighed, and looked out the window to the street. A girl ran by holding her knapsack over her head as a shield from the rain. I imagined Lauren wondering where she'd be if she hadn't left school.

So what if we never rose from the terrestrial into the timeless? Plain old earthly life looked like it had so much to offer.

She turned to me and smiled mischievously.

"I feel so naughty right now, don't you?" she asked.

"Totally," I said. "I've got this tremendous urge to talk about the most mundane things. And to gossip about people in the club."

"Me too!" she said, giggling, and touching my wrist.

We had a bond. It was real, even if it was based in nothing more than that we were both trusted and abused by Duncan in similar ways. We knew, eventually, it would all come down to us two. This is why we had to be strong. More or less. I let my doubt escape.

"Do you think Duncan will make it?" I asked.

"It doesn't really matter, does it?" Lauren was more mature about all this breaking-dimensions stuff than I was. "That's not why we should be doing this." She was right, in a Buddhist sense. It's not the goal but the path.

"I know, but how can you go through all this without hoping for the prize? The rush of breaking through?"

"I never really cared about that," she said. "Duncan is so delicate. More delicate than any of us. Sometimes he doesn't see anything but the big picture. He forgets about the people. I'm with him because without me, I don't know what would happen to him. I'm his only connection. He needs me."

"And what about you?" I asked, crossing the invisible boundary between self-doubt and doubt infliction. It's one thing to have a bad trip—it's another to impose your negative set on someone else.

"I think the rain is letting up," she said.

It wasn't. It was coming down harder. But it was time to go. I fucked it all up.

We got up and went outside. A flashing red hand told us to stand in the rain while people in their cars got to go. The noise of the traffic around us loosened something in my throat that came up and out as words.

"I'd give up all of it," I said. "Touching the next dimension and everything. I'd throw it all away to have a girl like you." Just taking the liberty to say this to her proved I was still in control.

The red hand changed to a green, walking man.

"Sometimes you're so sweet, you know that?" she said, taking my hand as we crossed the street.

13.

That so-called magical moment in the theater when the house-lights dim is not a magical moment at all—except for the actors about to go on, and maybe their parents. For the rest of us it's not magic, it's dread. We, the audience, remember the last time they made us sit in the dark and suffer and we pray to God they're not going to torture us as badly this time.

Such was my state of mind as I sat in the front row at Kirsten's play. I didn't want to be there. Theater seemed so contrary to everything we were doing. The artificial duality between actor and audience, the churchlike quality of the whole ritual, the Aristotelian moral structure, and the identification with a protagonist all seemed so ancient and obsolete for a club based on timeless truth and breaking static cultural templates. But maybe I just didn't want to be there.

Dolores had sent out little postcards to all the agents in town. Apparently it worked. Maybe twenty of the forty people who showed up wore suits or other yuppie outfits. Most of the others were in an entourage for a girl named Margot, whom Dolores knew from theater school. Margot, it turns out, had dropped out of their acting program to join the Los Angeles "cast" of MTV's *The Real World*, which had just finished taping.

Kirsten's play was surprisingly interesting. No one talked, which was an immediate plus, and it ran a mercifully short twelve minutes. As the lights went up, an old man (the guy in the latex nose) sat at a wooden table in front of an empty plate while an old lady (Dolores) worked in the kitchen behind him. They moved really slowly, as if in a dream. The old man repeatedly turned a fork over in his hand, waiting for the woman to cook him something to eat, while she methodically opened each of the empty cupboards, looking for food. This went on for about five minutes but wasn't really boring. I watched Kirsten part of the time. She was concentrating very intently and taking notes. Duncan yawned loudly but I don't think Kirsten heard him.

Eventually, the old lady took a big carving knife out of a drawer and approached the old man at the table. He looked up at her sadly as she took the fork from his hand and put it down on the table. Then she held onto his arm and began cutting his hand off at the wrist.

A few people in the audience gasped. It was an intense moment. The blade sliced through his hand but there was no blood (he must have replaced his hand with a fake rubber one when we weren't looking). I could hear Margot giggle a little bit, and some members of her entourage followed her cue. But the old lady kept slicing and the room got quiet again. She gently picked up his hand using both of hers, walked with it over to the stove, and placed it in a frying pan. The old man used his remaining hand to pull his shirt sleeve over his stump.

The old lady cooked the hand for a while, then brought the frying pan over to the table. She served the man some of the food from the frying pan. It looked like chopped meat. The man picked up the fork with his remaining hand and ate the food as the woman went to the sink and cleaned the pan. When the man was done he put down his fork and looked back up at the old woman, who was in her original position from the beginning of the play. It was a feedback loop.

I flashed on Pig and Peter's VR visionquest. Here in the play, every time the loop passed through the subject, something was taken from him. What had happened to Duncan in there? What did being in a feedback loop like that do to a person? Did they lose something? What was "al-set"?

The lights slowly came down. A slide was projected on the back wall with the name of the play, *Hand to Mouth,* and everybody applauded. When the lights came up the actors were gone. No curtain call.

After the play I went up to Kirsten and gave her a hug. A cluster of her theater friends were saying "very good work"—that noncommittal response of theater competitors. I wanted Kirsten to know the play had moved me and made me think.

"Wow," I said. "I didn't know a play could do that."

"Do what?" she asked. I was walking through a minefield.

"Put my head in that sort of space. I was tripping out on feed-back loops. On the dangers of self-reflection. I got kind of scared about what we're doing here." I thought my honesty and admis-sion of self-doubt would earn me back some of the points I'd lost by being such a righteous purist before. And Duncan was out of earshot.

"Be careful," she said with an uncharacteristic smirk, "or you'll have to ban my plays for violating the Nine Goals."

"It was really good, Kirsten. I mean that." I tried to make con-tact.

"I'm glad you liked it, Zach," she answered plainly. It sounded more like an I-told-you-so. She turned back to her theater friends.

There was a much larger crowd around Margot, asking about her stint on *The Real World*. Even Duncan was busy sucking up to the minor starlet.

"You've been under the looking glass in a very tangible way," he said to her. "I'd love for you to come to the PF and discuss it some-time soon." Duncan rarely, if ever, used the word *love*. It made me sick to watch him play to her ego. "We could sponsor a panel dis-cussion."

"I saw the article on you in the *Guardian*," Margot said. She was the kind of person who "saw" articles but probably never read them. The size of the photos and headlines was all she needed to know to judge a person or event's ranking in the media hierarchy.

Margot had been kicked out of *The Real World* house just three weeks in. The other fake real people "voted" her out because they couldn't get along with her anymore. According to Margot, this was because the camerapeople just couldn't keep their lenses off her, and everyone else was scared she was going to become the center of the whole show, like that male model did in the first New York season of the series. One of the girls in her entourage (who seemed more intent on bad-mouthing Margot than properly en-touraging) told me that Margot was also sleeping with the show's assistant director—strictly against the rules for both of them. He was fired, and they staged a "vote" to get rid of Margot within the context of the plot of the program.

Margot was a survivor, though, and the facility with which she worked Duncan was almost inspiring. By the end of the evening, we were all sitting on the stage smoking pot and determining which room would be hers. Since I hadn't used my studio yet, Brooks suggested she use that. The only reason I had for objecting was Kirsten's and my impending breakup, but this was still only subtext and Margot's steamroller was crushing all resistance in its path, so I quickly agreed.

Conveniently, she had brought her clothes and cosmetics from LA with her in the car, so on Duncan's instructions we helped her move in that night. At least she was a girl, which evened things out a bit.

By the time the rest of us went to bed, Duncan and Margot were alone in my former studio conducting an "orientation" and going over the Nine Goals. We all knew what was really happening in there. Lauren seemed the least disturbed of us all.

14.

I don't know for sure how long Duncan stayed with Margot. I do know that he never went up to his pyramid because he would have had to pass through my room, and Kirsten and I were up all night in there having a long, boring fight. She was relentless, and kept attacking me for my allegiance to Duncan and the Ecstasy Club. She just didn't get it.

She was naked the whole time, which made it much harder for me to argue my points because I still wanted to have sex with her. I'd mindlessly agree with whatever she was saying, but instead of accepting my conciliation she'd just advance further. I was sitting on the bed in my boxers while she paced around the room smoking cigarettes and waving her arms.

"A real spiritual path doesn't involve attacking people," she said. "You guys are all getting off on calling people on their shit— and thinking that you have the right to do it. It's a power trip."

"You think I like it?" I said. "It's a constant challenge. It's not supposed to be fun."

"Then why did you move in here in the first place?"

"This is an experiment," I told her. "We want to push the envelope. We've got equipment, determination, and the time is right."

"Can't you hear how silly you sound? 'The time is right.' Come on!"

"The time *is* right. We're approaching a historically high rate of novelty worldwide. Don't you understand how big this is?" I could hear myself sounding silly.

"And you kowtow to Duncan like he was your guru. You're his sidekick. Worse. You're a parrot on his shoulder."

"Hey," I stopped her, "a lot of what Duncan says is stuff *I* came up with. Just because I'm not ashamed to credit Duncan with what I get from him doesn't mean we're not equals in some ways."

"Some ways, maybe, but not many. You know he's practically your master. What kind of spirituality is that? You'll be bowing down to him before long."

"Just because you have a problem with Duncan doesn't mean I have to." I was trying to turn this into Kirsten's dilemma, and not mine.

"My problems with Duncan aren't the point. We're talking about my problems with you." Kirsten was nothing if not direct. But she was kind about it, too. "You're a whole person. A brilliant person with your own ideas. You don't need Duncan to get where you want to go."

"I'm not using Duncan to get anywhere. *You're* the one doing that." I shouldn't have said that.

"You're so fucked up to bring my plays into this. I could do my plays anywhere."

"Yeah, right," I said spitefully.

"You change the subject because you know I'm right," she said. She could see I was panicking and didn't take my attacks personally. Looking back on it, she was probably more mature than I gave her credit for.

"I'm not here to use Duncan. I'm here to help him, okay?"

"I'm glad you can at least admit it." She gestured for me to go on and explain myself. I went on in a whisper, half-embarrassed by my rationale.

"Duncan is closer than any of us. You should have seen him doing the VR visionquest. He actually got somewhere. It doesn't matter who breaks through it—if someone does, everything will change. Only one point in the system has to change for the rest of us to get it."

"Great," she said. "Trickle-down enlightenment. I thought you hated hierarchies."

"It's not a hierarchy. It's a fractal. If any one of us can tap into the beam, it'll mean all of us have. Then it will spread to everyone else, too. We're manipulating some powerful forces here."

"That's all fine," Kirsten said. "You just shouldn't have to become manipulative assholes to do it."

We went on like this for hours, with Kirsten slowly chipping away at my idealism. If I hadn't already been in so much doubt—largely precipitated by Duncan's conduct with Margot—I would have just squashed Kirsten with canned dogma.

After one of our long pauses, I asked her, "Do you think you're going to stay here much longer?"

"I doubt it," she said honestly, confident I wouldn't report her to the authorities. (It really had gotten pretty SS at the PF.) "I've got a few more plays I'd like to do, but not if it's going to be this intense around here."

We didn't even broach the topic of our relationship. It was so over that I was in that final stage of wondering if we'd ever have sex again before we parted company. I got my answer.

"I'm going to move my stuff into the second dressing room," Kirsten said gently, "until I figure out what I want to do."

"That's cool," I said. Then I tried to think of something profoundly kind to say, so that she'd regret dumping me for a long time. All I could think of was "I'm glad I got to know you."

"I'm sorry you never really did," Kirsten said, turning off the light and getting into the bed.

She was right.

I just lay awake until it got light. Once I heard people milling about downstairs, I got up and joined them.

We had a party to prepare for tonight and it already felt like a routine. Parrot would go to the bank to get stacks of fives and ones for change. Brooks would go into town and do some last-minute promotion. Peter and Pig would check the lights and sound, Lauren and Kirsten would put up decorations, Duncan would get on the phone and try to round up a few celebrities and guest DJs, and I would get some more gasoline for the generators and make another payoff to the cops.

My first big mistake of the day was to take Brooks along to Laruso's office. Brooks didn't misbehave, but the second Laruso opened his door and saw a stranger sitting there, he turned cold.

"Come on," he said, like a prison barber, "just you. Hurry up." I motioned for Brooks to stay on the couch and went into Laruso's office alone. I put an envelope containing two thousand dollars on his desk.

"So what's this I hear about you having parties every night?" Laruso said, eclipsing the small talk I had prepared.

"We did a little play and had a private affair for some gays," I said, working the male camaraderie thing as best I could. "I put in some extra for that. And we're paying early." He was quickly counting the money in the envelope.

"Two hundred? That's not extra. That's barely a tip."

Where was all that clever innuendo and the euphemisms? I changed the weight on my feet. He hadn't asked me to sit down and now I was afraid to.

"I hear you're running some generators over there, too. It's a fire hazard. I'll have to make some calls about that."

"I'm sure it's all up to code," I said, having no idea if it was, or what "code" really meant.

"You can't just shove a whole lot of crap up my ass, kid." He sounded like an *NYPD Blue* reject. I wondered if TV shows got their dialogue from cops or if the real cops were just copying what they saw on TV. "We're going to need at least another thousand for each night you let the public in there, and you'll have to deal with the fire department separately. They'll be in touch."

"I think you're entirely overestimating the size and extent of our organization," I told him, trying to sound like the treasurer of a nonprofit charity.

"I think you're entirely underestimating my ability to shut you down anytime I want to," he said. Without Parrot I felt defenseless. "You've got posters all over town. A lot of people are pissed off. There's a legitimate club south of Market that has an exclusive on Saturday nights. You're going to have to leave that night open from now on."

"What club? Plasma? That's just a promotional party . . ."

"I don't give a shit what you want to call it," he said. "Some of the folks at *Plugged* magazine have their money in it, and you're not going to compete for their crowd, is that clear?"

"We're not out to compete with Plasma, but—"

"Then you won't have a problem moving to Sunday." He put the envelope in his drawer. "And you can bring the rest of the money on Monday morning."

With that, he ushered me out. He had taken our money and closed our club. I was a complete failure, and not looking forward to going back.

In the car, Brooks tried to take my mind off my impotence by selling me on his new business idea: a meta-infomercial.

"It's the perfect moneymaker," Brooks said.

"I don't get what you're selling," I told him, my thoughts still totally consumed with how to break the news about Saturday nights to Duncan.

"We're selling a course in how to make infomercials! Don't you get it? We make an infomercial about how easy it is to make infomercials! We show our infomercial being made, bring in the fake audience and show how they are taught to react. We get celebrity investors to explain how they participate in the infomercial because they have a stake in the business. And these celebs will be telling the complete truth, because they'll have a stake in *our* infomercial business!" He was applying the PF principles of feedback, iteration, and bracketing to a pyramid scheme. A business based in reframing a marketing concept and then selling it as the new product.

"So what do we send to them if they call the 800 number at the end?" I asked to humor him.

"We send them instructions for how to make their own infomercial! Sample scripts, set plans, lighting instructions, casting companies for extras, a list of celebrities, telemarketing companies, production facilities—just paper. But the best part is that our cash flow doesn't stop there. All the companies we list in our kit have to agree to give us a kickback for any business we send them!"

"And you want to shoot this at the PF?" I asked.

"It'll make us more money than a hundred parties! If the PF invests, then the club can have a percentage of the money," he said.

"The other percentage going to you, of course."

"Well, it's my idea," Brooks said apologetically.

I suggested that today might not be the best day to pitch Duncan on a new business venture—not with the future of Phylogenic Foresight in jeopardy—and dropped him off in the City. I drove around for a few hours by myself, trying to find a way out of my jam other than telling Duncan. I thought of asking Lauren to tell Duncan—she was a notch higher in the order of things than I—but that would have been penny-wise and dollar-foolish. No reason to look like a wimp to Lauren just to avoid looking like a failure to Duncan.

I got back to the PF around dusk and decided to call a meeting. If everyone else was around when I made my admission, the group might serve to buffer Duncan's reaction. Everyone came except Pig, who was up in his loft with his smelly hacker friend working on that amplification circuit, and Tyrone, who usually didn't come out until well after dark. We gathered in Nomie's smart lounge. She had covered the entire floor with old mattresses wrapped in exotic, furry fabrics that Kirsten had pilfered for her from a Dumpster behind Cloth World. It was a cozy place to get reamed.

"The cops say we have to move Phylogenic Foresight to Sunday," I opened, getting right to point. I rip off Band-Aids quickly, too. "They've got some kind of deal with Plasma and say we can't compete."

"Plasma is a *Plugged* venture," Peter said. "Figures."

"They can't get away with this," Lauren said, "can they?"

"I should have been there with you, Zach," Parrot apologized egotistically.

"Fucking bullshit, that's what it is," Henry contributed.

Margot beamed at Duncan. "Isn't there something you can do?" She made us all sick.

Duncan was standing in his Doc Martens, his fingers on his chin. "It's simple," he said too matter-of-factly. "We do Phylogenic Foresight on Sunday." Duncan was being uncharacteristically cooperative, but I was glad to be off the hook.

"We're just going to give in?" Brooks asked. I wished he would shut up. It looked like I was getting away scot-free and I didn't want him to blow it.

"We're going to do precisely as we were instructed," Duncan said in schoolboy Brit. I knew there was something hidden in that word *precisely*. "We are going to open the doors for Phylogenic Foresight at 12:01 A.M. Sunday morning, in absolute compliance with Officer Laruso's request."

We slowly grinned at one another. It was brilliant!

We were all giddy with perverse delight at having outsmarted the cops. Even if they clobbered us in the end, we had beat them at their own game in the short term. We passed around a bong to celebrate while Adam and Andy treated us to nitrous balloons from a huge tank they had bought from a restaurant supply house and stowed behind the bar.

The whole atmosphere of the club changed with whatever drug was coming through that week. When we had good windowpane LSD, the vibe at the PF was intellectual. When that skunk pot was coming through, we walked around in a fuzzy stupor. After the brown super-E, we were convinced that the gods were directing our actions. Our group personality took on the qualities of our drug stash at any given moment.

The practically infinite new supply of nitrous threw us for a loop. We had all done whippits before—tiny one-hit canisters of nitrous used for making whipped cream. A whole package yields only eight balloons, and the work required to crack them open without freezing your hands as the gas condenses serves to limit one's intake. A full tank like the one Adam and Andy scored holds nearly a thousand balloons' worth of gas, and the long tube coming from the spigot allows you to dispense it like beer from a keg.

We each did dozens of balloons. It was great, and we were all laughing hysterically. It felt like one long collective orgasm. We were writhing around on the floor, congratulating one another on outsmarting Laruso, messing each other's hair, stroking one another. Everything was buzzing. There were sparkly twinkles floating in the air, and the room seemed to vibrate with sound.

Nomie put on some Indian raga music and began doing a strange dance. It was a variation on Persian belly dancing, with her arms swimming at her sides as she slowly went up and down on her knees. Nomie was unquestionably weird, but she was also undeniably sexy when she got animated. She started making the orgasm sound from her CD, as if to seduce us all into a sex trance. Between that, the pot, the NO_2, and the music, our giddy mood transformed itself into something entirely more erotic.

Not to be upstaged, Margot quickly joined Nomie, raising the stakes of the dance to a competitive sex-off. Dueling Kalis. Nomie's sinuous moves, erotic chanting, and sheer self-absorption had Margot beat by miles, so Margot began to peel off her clothes. Peter and Brooks nudged each other like junior high school locker-room voyeurs. Still, the undulating goddesses were truly a turn-on. Adam and Andy clapped in approval of their Mistress. Kirsten got up and started to dance, too, probably to break the mounting tension of the two-woman showdown, and Parrot joined the bacchanal, not to miss out on this supply-side sexual windfall.

Lauren sat cross-legged on the furry floor, doing her own, slightly tamer version of the sex-goddess movements. But she kept looking over at me while she did it. *She doesn't mean anything by it,* I told myself. I averted my eyes—it was too much to deal with.

Henry started chanting "Kali, Kali," and went off about the female goddess and how every woman on earth is just another face of the same irresistible force. "She's the destroyer. Your severed head is in her hands, but so is your heart. She's your entrance to life, but also the taker." I was staring at Lauren again. Her little body undulating. Her eyes fixed on me. Her lips just parted. *I can look.* We're in public. Everyone else's presence made my adoration acceptable. There's no shame when there's no secret. And the whole thing was just a game, right? Bracketed by ritual.

Nomie was in a trance by now, or doing a pretty good imitation of one. She started to take off her clothes and dance seductively with the now-topless Margot. Feeling the need to prove herself, Margot played along, matching each of Nomie's radically lesbian moves, much to our delight. The two girls pressed their chests against each other and shimmied up and down, licking at one another like snakes, hissing and spitting.

Parrot was holding himself against Kirsten's butt as she moved. I thought it looked quite lecherous. Then Kirsten wiggled over and took Peter's hand. She danced moving up and down in the style Nomie had introduced to us, with Parrot behind her and Peter in front. Then Kirsten and Peter started to strip each other, and the line between play and true heterosexual business was crossed. All hell broke loose. Duncan got up and tried to get in on Nomie and Margot's breast-fest. Adam and Andy slow-danced, kissing with big open mouths and holding each other's butts.

Henry, Lauren, and I were the only ones left on the floor. He started to edge toward Lauren but I stopped him, protecting my sweet little sister with one determined glare that sent him crawling over to Duncan and the Kalis. Peter and Kirsten were completely naked, rolling around on top of each other—almost like this wasn't the first time. I inhaled a giant balloon as I tried to ponder this, but every ounce of will in my mind and body was straining to keep myself from peeking over at Lauren. I knew her eyes were on me. I could feel her line of sight burning a hole in the sprinkles around my head.

When I finally turned to look, half the room seemed to follow my motion. I saw her face and my eyes zoomed in on her. I couldn't control the motion of the lens. Then I realized it wasn't my eyes zooming in at all. She was moving toward me, through the throbbing sparks. We were the only clothed people left in the room. We were kneeling, facing each other an inch apart. She was so beautiful. The life radiated from her pale skin. I could feel her breath on my chin. I almost had the courage to kiss her but she started to rise, taking her mouth out of reach. She made it a dance. *Harmless fun.* We both raised and lowered ourselves, breathing against each other's bodies. Then, something took hold of us and we started slowly unbuttoning each other's shirts as we moved up and down. Her head slowly made its way down my body and then she stopped. I stopped, too, because I knew what was about to happen.

She pulled down the zipper of my jeans, a tooth at a time, then fumbled to pull me out of my underwear without bending anything, though I don't know what could have diminished my excitement at that point.

I couldn't get over it. *Lauren is holding my cock in her hands.* She touched it to her cheek. So soft. Such a gentle person. So fully caring. A princess. Then, without pointless foreplay, she took me in her mouth.

My whole body vibrated. It was electric. These were sensations I had never felt before. I was light-headed and touched Lauren's hair for some grounding in reality. Everything was spinning.

That's when I saw him coming. Duncan. Naked. I couldn't stop. I wouldn't stop. Nomie and Margot were now in a groping clump with Peter and Parrot, and Duncan wanted some attention for himself. I felt an animal instinct take over. He wasn't going to get Lauren.

I held the back of Lauren's head so as not to fall out as I tackled Duncan to the ground. Lauren looked up a second but didn't stop what she was doing. I had to think fast so I grabbed Duncan's hips like I wanted him for myself and started to stroke his dick with my hand. *It's worth it. I'm getting Lauren.*

I was on my haunches as Lauren lay on her back beneath me, almost worshipfully sucking on me. But Duncan's dick was getting hard in my hands, and he wanted more. I didn't know what to do— he was starting to rise to get behind me in order to fuck one of us, so I pulled him toward me and started sucking on him while Lauren sucked on me. Maybe the humiliation he was inflicting on me would compensate for the earthshaking blow job I was getting from his girlfriend.

I remember inspecting Duncan's dick for herpes sores before I put it in my mouth. But once it was in I tried to keep my attention on Lauren and what she was doing to me rather than on Duncan and what *he* was doing to me. Mathematically speaking, it was like a flow-through equation. Lauren was giving a blow job and Duncan was getting one. I was just the medium.

I'm sure Lauren was granting me a much better set of sensations than I was granting Duncan. I had never had a penis in my mouth before. It tasted bitter and made me gag when it hit the back of my throat. I just set a pace, tried not to breathe and went on automatic so I wouldn't have to think about it. Lauren's movements were heavenly, though, and pumped enough endorphins into my blood to make Duncan almost tolerable. She could tell I didn't want to have to be sucking Duncan off, and moved faster and faster, trying to get me to climax sooner rather than later.

I could feel the tension building. I prayed that Duncan wasn't in the same state. I couldn't have taken that. Lauren was one with my body. Duncan was an intrusion.

She knew exactly where I was on the curve toward orgasm, and she moved her finger slowly behind me and just a bit up my butt. No one had done that before, either. Right away I started to come. It hit me like a convulsion—a perfect excuse to throw my head back and get Duncan out of my mouth. I tried not to think about that lingering taste as I came, and came, and continued to come into Lauren's accepting mouth. I was about to feel sorry for Lauren having to deal with so much come, but then I realized I had totally lost track of Duncan.

He was back there, all right, and I prayed he wasn't aiming for me. No, he was spreading Lauren's legs apart and preparing to go inside. I started to get myself off her, but she put her hands on my thighs to hold me in place. As Duncan pounded her from behind me, she looked into my eyes and put my hands on her breasts. She groaned with my movements, not his. I squeezed her breasts and stared into her beautiful face as it moved up and down from Duncan's thrusts. She stroked my chest and continued to respond to everything I did. Every touch I made, however subtle, registered on her face, just as if we were alone. Then she closed her eyes and came.

She came for me.

15.

I didn't see Lauren for the rest of the day. After everyone dispersed from Nomie's lounge to attend to their duties for the evening party, she went up to either Duncan's pyramid or her roof garden and didn't come down. I wanted to find her, but I wasn't sure what I would say if I did. I felt I should make it clear that this wouldn't happen again—that we could still be friends. But something didn't let me.

"Faith is such an endearing trait," Danielle the transvestite told me as I shared a drink with her at the main bar that night. "But it's so boring. And there's no room for decadence." We were talking about evolution, and what sexuality would be like once people—thanks to the Ecstasy Club's efforts—were empowered to direct their own mutation.

Our second gay party was in full swing and jam-packed. The word of mouth from our first party, combined with the addition of cult-star–drag-queen Mistress Nora as hostess, brought most of SF's glam-queer crowd out of the woodwork. There must have been close to eight hundred people. (I'll get to why we had no accurate head count in a minute.) The music was almost exclusively seventies disco with some good Detroit garage mixed in, just to keep it current. Duncan thought it would be nice to have it bright in the PF for a change, so we kept the sodium floodlights on the whole time and used everything else for effects.

Everyone was smiling—no edge, no attitude, except for that fun drag-queen stuff. Even Tyrone came out for this one. He had braided his hair and was wearing an orange jumpsuit that Kirsten had found for him. He looked like one of those Biospherians. He seemed to get along just fine with the transvestites; I'm not sure he knew they weren't girls. When Mistress Nora got up on the bar to sing Janis Joplin's "Me and Bobby McGee" with all the lyrics changed to "Me and Keanu Reeves," Tyrone stood right beneath her, applauding and trying to look up her skirt. But with his new outfit and hairdo, even Tyrone appeared absolutely non-threatening.

It may have been this congenial atmosphere that got me to pour my heart out to Danielle. Or maybe it was the shots of Bushmills. I felt relaxed, welcome, safe, and understood. However weird and bisexual my sex life had gotten, I was certain my experiences paled in comparison to Danielle's. She had understanding eyes and she nodded and "mmm'd" her sympathy with my plight. I told her everything—the club, the Nine Goals, self-directed rebirth, evolution, Duncan's special gifts, my talk with Lauren, the orgy.

"What does it all mean?" I asked her, ready for her to diagnose me as a latent Oedipal freak.

"You're in love, dear Zach," she said. "You're in love and it's one of the most beautiful things in all of this world. The fact that you would suck another man's dick just to be with her moves me so. You're a beautiful person, Zach. A beautiful person, and you deserve the very best things life has to offer."

Oddly, her vote of reassurance did wonders for me. It made perfect sense. I *was* in love. With Lauren. The world would just have to deal with that. Even Duncan would have to deal with that. I had spent the whole day avoiding Lauren. I thought it was because I was afraid and embarrassed by what had happened, but now I realized it wasn't that at all. I was afraid that Lauren, in the light of drugless day, would let common sense and her devotion to Duncan outweigh the possibility that she loved me too.

Once my therapy session was over, though, I was put in the role of counselor to Danielle's patient, and I didn't feel particularly qualified to help her with her dilemma.

"When I was born my parents assumed I was a boy," Danielle began. "My name was Daniel. I had a penis and testicles. It all looked normal. There was a little crack under my anus, but the pediatricians told my parents it was just a little crease from the womb and it would eventually heal over. But it didn't."

"Oh, really?" I said. My heart went out to her. I knew what was coming and felt her pain, but I couldn't relate.

"When I was fourteen I was jerking off in the shower thinking about Michael Buber—this boy from my gym class with straight brown hair and a huge chest—well, the specifics don't really matter, do they? Gosh, I wonder whatever happened to Michael! He's probably a halfback or something!"

I laughed politely.

"I was really getting going when my dad banged on the door and barged in. I pushed my penis down so the oaf wouldn't see what I was doing, and that's when it happened."

"What?"

"All this blood started coming out from under my balls. I thought I had broken something!" She laughed and rolled her head back. I was getting nauseous.

"What happened?" I asked, hoping to get it over with.

"What do you think? It was my period! I was on the rag! We went to all the specialists and found out that I wasn't a boy or a girl. I was both. My dad wanted to have me locked up but my mom still loved me, dear woman, so we went to a special counselor and were told the options: I could have my dick chopped off and take hormones to become a real woman, I could have my cunt sewn up and take hormones and become a man, or I could stay the way I was and deal with it. Which is what I decided to do."

"How? I mean, you grew tits, right?"

"Indeed I did. Big ones! Look!" They were pretty big. "I grew my hair out, transferred to another junior high school, and became Danielle. A doctor's note got me out of gym, and only the vice-principal knew the whole story."

"So you're still a hermaphrodite now?" I asked.

"Yes, I am. But it gets worse." She took a swig from my drink (I figured the alcohol would kill any disease she might have) and lit a cigarette. "By the time I was in high school I knew I was not going to be getting any dates. A few boys even asked me out but, like, I was going to make out with them in a car and let them see? I think not."

"What'd you do?"

"I got very good at masturbation. Too good, in fact. I used to decide whether I was going to masturbate as a boy or a girl, and then either find a carrot or some hand lotion and go for it. But then I realized I could do both at the same time. I'd jerk off with my right hand and stroke my pussy with the left. I got so good I could time it to have both my orgasms at the same time."

"Wow," I said. "Simultaneous orgasms in one person. The best of both worlds."

"And the worst," she said. "I started college last September. I'm a sophomore now. I went to a gay film festival on campus and saw this movie where a guy gave himself a half hard-on and then stuck his dick up his own butt and fucked himself up the ass. And that's when it hit me: I could fuck myself!"

"You mean—"

"Right. I get a half hard-on, then slip my dick back into my own vagina. Then I can let it get as hard as I want and it doesn't fall out."

"But—"

"I can show you, if you like . . ."

"I trust you," I said, finishing the drink.

"It has to do with the angle—I point sort of down. Well, anyway," she took a deep breath, "after I got through that awful hymen stuff, I started fucking myself almost every night. It felt great. I got the timing down cold. I started reading books on tantra so I could hold back my boy orgasm long enough for my girl orgasm to catch up. I got great at it. I rode the seven waves of ecstasy. Both of me could graduate from the Tao of Sex doctoral program."

"That's great," I said. "You found a way to be happy."

"Sure. But it never occurred to me that it might not be such a good idea to keep coming in my own vagina."

"No!"

"Yes. About ten weeks ago. I've missed two periods already, but I haven't gotten tested."

"And you never . . . with anyone else?"

"I'm a virgin, so to speak. A pregnant virgin."

"Gosh," I said, feeling more like Opie Taylor now than a cool rave guy, "it's going to be a clone of you, isn't it?"

"Not necessarily. It'll get some of my recessive traits, too. The egg and sperm only have half the chromosomes on each. There could be variations. But one thing is for sure, according to my genetics specialist."

"What?"

"If I carry to term and somehow deliver—we're not sure if my uterus is fully functional—my child will be a hermaphrodite, just like me."

"Jesus." Talk about feedback loops.

"Now there's a reason I'm telling you all this," she said, taking my hand. I got scared she was looking for a father for her mutant child.

"What's that?" I asked.

"I'm telling you this to show you something," she said, directly and sweetly. Almost like a mother.

"What?" I asked again.

"I want to show you that if you believed my whole story, you may be more naive than you think. Watch yourself, my darling. Watch yourself."

With that, she kissed me on the forehead and ran into the crowd. I watched her as she danced. Everyone welcomed her—whatever she was—into their little clusters. I didn't have time to consider what her story really had to do with my own plight. There was a commotion at the door, and Parrot was frantically waving me over.

Two uniformed cops—San Francisco police—were at the entrance, their bats drawn. Parrot was in a tug-of-war with one of them over the cash box.

"Let go. *Now!*" said the one with the mustache.

"You have no jurisdiction here," Parrot argued, tightening his grip on the box, his holy covenant.

The other cop was just about to choke-hold Parrot with his club when I stepped in. Badge number 881. I made a mental note for all the good it would do us.

"What seems to be the problem here?" I asked in my most authoritarian tone.

"This is an illegal gathering," barked 517. "We are confiscating your cash and records pending further investigation."

Duncan and Lauren made their way through the crowd toward us as many of the gay kids stopped dancing and gathered around.

"I've been in regular contact with Officer Laruso," I said, playing my only trump card. "I'm sure if you call him . . ."

"He called *us*, kid," answered mustache, finally yanking the box from Parrot and sticking it under his arm.

"This party is over," said 881, unplugging Parrot's computer and preparing to take it with him.

"No! You have no right!" screamed Parrot. His faith in the American Way had met the ultimate challenge. He was starting to cry.

"*You* have no rights, punk," said mustache as he lifted the PowerBook. "Now clear out this room or we'll do it for you."

Duncan just stood there. It was moments like these when he wished he had a green card so he could fight back without fear of deportation. Instead, it was all up to me.

"There's been a terrible misunderstanding," I pleaded.

"Well, you'll just have to straighten that out," mustache snapped back.

Out of nowhere, a flailing orange figure charged us all. It was Tyrone, and he was holding a big blue pistol.

The cops dropped their booty and pulled out their guns in an instant.

"FREEZE!" they shouted in unison.

Peter, Mistress Nora, and I tackled Tyrone. His gun was a hastily prepared clay model. I squished it demonstratively for the cops. The DJ finally saw the commotion and shut off the music.

"That's it!" said 881. "He's coming with us." They approached Tyrone with cuffs. He crouched and started grunting at them like an animal.

Then Duncan took action.

"How do you imagine it will feel?" he said, looking at both the cops, calmly, gently.

"Huh?" one grunted.

"When you remember this room. Right now. How will you remember yourself feeling?" Duncan was doing something to them with his words.

"What's your problem?" asked 881. They were both facing Duncan now. The kids on the dance floor pressed in around Tyrone, obscuring him from view.

Duncan touched the cop's shoulder. "When you're driving back in the squad car, you'll both look back on this moment and be glad you didn't take anyone with you." Textbook Eriksonian hypnosis, masterfully performed.

"Get the fuck out of my way," said 881. They took the cash box and the computer but seemed to forget entirely about Tyrone.

Later, in the squad car, they looked back on this moment and felt glad that they hadn't taken anyone with them.

16.

I have no doubt that Duncan possessed abilities the rest of us don't. I witnessed too many events with my own eyes to question at least that much.

Duncan had saved Tyrone but not our money or Parrot's laptop. He called a meeting the next morning to evaluate where we stood. We met in the kitchen, not in Nomie's smart lounge, and not a word was spoken about the orgy.

Lauren and I sat about as far from each other as possible. I wasn't sure which of us had initiated this distance. Kirsten was practically sitting in Peter's lap on the couch, and the two of them whispered to each other the whole time. I wasn't jealous. I was just suspicious about when that little coupling had germinated. Parrot sat at the table with a yellow marker, highlighting key phrases in a copy of the U.S. Constitution. Pig was in a lounge chair, his hands folded on his big stomach and his eyes closed as if to absorb the important data without distraction. Lauren had a little pad and a Tweetie Bird pen to take notes, and Nomie stayed on her feet, pouring everyone except Margot (who said she'd never do drugs again) cups of ephedra-spiked "supercoffee."

For some reason, a little black-and-white TV was on in the corner. It was tuned to a long infomercial for Cosmotology, the movie-star cult. Tad Steppling, a fallen gay TV star who joined the cult and got married before enjoying a tremendous comeback at the box office, was sitting in a huge wicker chair giving a testimonial to the cult's founder, the notorious E. T. Harman. Behind him, palm trees swayed in the wind. Margot stared at Steppling's image on the tube, discreetly mimicking his gestures.

Meanwhile, Henry stood by the microwave reducing something down to snortable heroin. Tonight was his Pandora's Fix party, so he probably wanted to take it easy and forgo his injections until later. To us, the sight of Henry snorting smack rather than shooting it was an encouraging omen of temperance.

All in all, this was the Ecstasy Club's version of domestic bliss.

"I just got off the phone with Renn A. Sanz," Duncan announced. "He'll be coming to tonight's party." Duncan sipped from his mug of supercoffee to allow for a moment of murmured approval.

Henry halted midsnort. "Bloody brilliant!" he exclaimed, laughing with glee as he finished his line.

"Renn also had some interesting suggestions to help us maintain focus," Duncan continued. This was going to be good. "The key, ultimately, is to counterbalance peripheral distractions with centering rituals." If Duncan was taking the time to build up to a suggested plan of action, it meant trouble. "We ran through a number of possibilities, all capable of reclaiming the psychic landscape for ourselves and confirming the immutability of our purpose." Here it came. "What I settled on," he said, strolling to Lauren and taking her pad from her, "was this."

He held up the pad. On it, in Lauren's Magic Marker style, was a colorful logo of a fetus with the words *Ecstasy Club* emerging from its navel as an umbilical cord. A new logo. No big deal. Or so I thought.

"What it will ultimately look like," he said, unbuttoning his shirt, "is this." On his chest, directly over his heart, was the Ecstasy Club logo, indelibly tattooed. The fresh ink was extraordinarily bright, and little puffy sores within the design oozed blood.

"You should keep that bandaged the first two days, mate," Henry, our human palette, advised.

Duncan gingerly buttoned up his shirt.

"Deliah from Body Parts has left the whole afternoon free to do the rest of you," he said, oblivious to our revulsion. "Lauren will schedule your appointments."

Jews aren't supposed to get tattoos. Many Holocaust victims get them removed just so they can feel better about being buried in Jewish cemeteries. Not that I cared about keeping a kosher epidermis, but I hated the idea of making any permanent mark on myself. My little sister had a nose job before her senior year of high school and I was still giving her shit about it. Besides, a tattoo seemed hypocritical for people who claimed to be constantly evolving. It was a full stop.

That was the brilliance of it, though. Were we really committed enough to the Ecstasy Club to state it so directly? How could we ever expect to break on through to the next dimension and shatter our illusions about the mundane reality if we couldn't make a simple declaration of allegiance to the journey? It wasn't that the tattoos would last forever, that we would have these marks on us when we were sixty. It was to demonstrate, in the present, that we were willing to brand ourselves forever. If our lives were really going to be about this, if we were truly more than dilettantes playing drug games, then this should have posed no problem.

As I sat in the chair at Body Parts enduring the ache and smell of my own scarring flesh (I had the honor of going first), I realized that this was about something else entirely. That's why the idea came from a cult leader and mind-control fanatic like Renn A. Sanz. I was engaged in an activity that defied my own judgment. I was acting against my own common sense. Was I finding my "true will," or merely having it broken?

The only way out of the trap was to accept that the Ecstasy Club must be an essentially worthy enterprise; otherwise, why would I be willing to put myself through this misery on its behalf? *Duncan must be right about my getting a tattoo because here I am getting one.* I retrofitted my logic to conform to my actions.

That's how rituals work. From the outside in. Just do it. *I get it.* The pain released so many endorphins into my bloodstream that I started to feel high before it was over, and the lingering buzz wiped away any lingering doubt.

I got the tattoo on my arm rather than my chest. I figured I might as well score a couple of macho-sailor points as long as I was at it. It didn't look so bad. Tons of people had tattoos, especially in San Francisco. It wasn't so radical anymore. I'd be fine, as long as my mom never saw it.

Lauren got hers on her hip—actually, just inside her pelvis where it would be hidden by her underwear (no doubt for the sake of her own parents). I sat with her while she got it done, which almost made the whole afternoon worthwhile. I still hadn't gotten to talk to her alone and, until this moment, I was convinced she was avoiding me.

But she asked me to come over and then held my hand tightly the whole time she was getting tattooed. She squeezed me harder during the most painful parts, and smiled at me through her grimaces. I kept wiping her brow with a cloth, and felt like I was assisting her in labor. Maybe this was Duncan's way of punishing us for the orgy.

"We should talk," I told my captive audience as the tattoo artist pushed the ink into Lauren's delicate flesh.

"Yeah," Lauren said, half-smiling through the pain. "But later, okay?"

As Peter, Lauren, Brooks, Pig, and I drove back from the parlor with our fresh tattoos still stinging, I felt more like I had just been certified as a Cub Scout than as an interdimensional warrior. Kirsten had refused to come. It was easier to call her on her abstinence in front of everyone now that she was fucking Peter instead of me, but I had a sneaking suspicion that she was holding onto her personhood with good cause. No, she wasn't demonstrating any willingness to drop her attachment to the dominant social set, but she wasn't about to cower to the one that Duncan was imposing on us, either. For better or for worse, she wasn't Ecstasy Club material. Parrot got out of it, too, claiming he had some mild variation of hemophilia and wouldn't clot properly. Nomie was going to apply her own tattoo using organic dyes, and Margot said she still had a sunburn from LA and would get hers next week, which Duncan chose to believe.

Henry already had so much body art that he decided to go for broke and get the E Club fetus tattooed directly onto his forehead. The face bleeds more than other body parts, so he insisted on wearing a bandage on his forehead for two days. I couldn't understand why he was so much more meticulous about his tattoo hygiene than his heroin injections. Everyone who met him at the entrance to Pandora's Fix that night kept asking him how he had gotten injured.

We had worked out a new security protocol to minimize the damage from any future police raids. Every hour, on the hour, Parrot would give me all the money he had collected and I would store it in a hiding place up behind Duncan's pyramid. Meanwhile, Brooks and Peter would take turns standing watch from the top of Tyrone's shaftway.

With the skylight open, you could stand on the highest rung of the ladder bolted to the wall and see out over the roof to the street in front as well as back to the alley behind the PF. Pig rigged up a switch at the top of the ladder connected to a red light at the DJ perch, where someone was always sure to be during a party. If the cops were coming in the front way, the watch would flash the light once. If they were coming in the back, he'd flash twice. If Duncan wasn't up on the perch, the DJ would call for him or me through the PA. This would give us a chance to hide whatever money and drugs were around, and instruct the crowd to storm out en masse and trample the invading force.

Looking back, I guess the advance warning system offered us nothing but a sense of control in a completely powerless situation. If you were tripping really hard, at least you didn't have to worry that there'd suddenly be cops in your face. We'd have a psychic jump on them.

It was fitting that we developed our war strategies on the opening of Pandora's Fix, the Ecstasy Club's obligatory nod to the Goth-Industrial scene that Henry came from. It was our only intentionally "darkside" party and naturally lent itself to endless thought exercises about escape routes, psychic warfare, and apocalypse scenarios.

Purists criticized us for combining two scenes they saw as distinct into one. Goth kids were dreamy romantics who followed the Cure, listened to depressing music, wrote poetry, and fetishized vampire activities. They'd wear big puffy shirts, capes, and whiteface makeup, and dance like ghosts. You could beat them up pretty easily. The Industrial kids, on the other hand, were themselves a mix of modern primitives and hardcore German-style skinheads. The primitives had piercings all over themselves, colored hair, dreadlocks, spiky mohawks, and artsy tattoos. The hardcore Industrials wore big scary rings and lots of leather; they pierced themselves, too, but with nuts, bolts, and other pieces of factory metal.

There were real distinctions between the two groups, and they resented being lumped together. The Goth kids were into the aesthetics of death and depression. They would listen to hardcore, head-banging factory sounds, but only as a way of proving that they could stay waifish and delicate while dancing to the most aggressive machine-age noise. Goth was definitely a bad, darkside trip, but it was aestheticized into a delicacy. By going into the darkness and deciding to stay in it, there was nowhere further to go. It was as if they had accepted their own deaths and had nothing left to fear.

The true Industrial folks were a much scarier bunch. Their movement had something to do with listening to as much violently mechanized sound as possible—their records sampled steel mills and assembly lines—as a way of learning to cope with the ambiance of our industrial age. Their mosh pit was beyond anything I could have survived, and whenever any dreamy Goth songs came on, they gathered around the bass speakers and repeatedly lifted and dropped them until the DJ put on something hard again.

To us soft and squishy rave-intellectuals, though, dark was dark, and these sad people only deserved one night of the week.

Thankfully, Renn A. Sanz's arrival gave us instant credibility with the Industrial faction, who were in the process of forming a human pyramid to climb up to the DJ's perch and take over. I enjoyed watching them break their tough-guy facades and gleefully whisper to one another that their hero was present.

Renn was much smaller and more soft-spoken than I had expected, given his reputation as a dangerous cultural provocateur. He was known for spitting and puking on his audience when he played and, most recently, for being kicked out of his native UK for making films of abortions and fetus-eating (art videos he says he faked). If it hadn't been for his entourage of S&M girls, he probably would have gotten lost in the crowd.

Well, maybe not. I ran to the entrance to greet him and it was only then that I could see the decades' worth of scarification, branding, and piercings under his black leather vest. His overly friendly cult-leader stare was equally unsettling. He spoke quite softly, but with a driving intensity and about the darkest of subjects.

"I've planned a pagan ritual for later, my darlings," he said, looking straight at me before he even knew who I was. "Attendance is mandatory."

I smiled politely and walked him into the club. He seemed generally approving of the crowd, even though it was mostly Goth kids dancing slowly in circles to a relatively obscure Nine Inch Nails track. They seemed to be mesmerized by their own black nail polish and didn't even notice Renn walking among them, nodding to them as if they were his subjects.

Before Renn was able to acknowledge his Industrial devotees, Duncan glad-handed him and walked him over to the mind gym for a private conclave with the main E Club members. Duncan had separately instructed me, Peter, Brooks, and Henry not to let anyone else in the room. Not knowing he had said the same thing to the others, I took this to mean that only Duncan, Renn, and I were allowed in. Henry, Brooks, and Peter came to identical conclusions about their own status at the meeting, which led to quite an uncomfortable moment as each of us tried to keep the others out. Duncan finally broke it up, criticizing us all for being so selfish. Divide and conquer.

We sat around on folding chairs doing lines of E (if it's really pure you can snort it for faster but shorter-lasting effect) and listening intently as Renn A. Sanz shared his insights with us. We were like grad students taking a seminar in cultural subversion, and Duncan was the TA.

I was sure that Renn would feel put upon, but he seized the opportunity to program a new audience. First, he took a moment to admire our tattoos. I got a little pissed when Lauren decided to pull up her skirt and show him hers. She should have known he would lick his lips and then bury his gray dreadlocked head between her legs and savagely suck on it.

"Nola has a tattoo of my totem on her vulva, you know," he told her, referring to his ex-wife. "Whose totem would you say this is?" he asked her with a grin, glancing over to Duncan.

"Well," Lauren said in that sweet, matter-of-fact way of hers, "Zach came up with the name, and I drew the picture . . ."

"Oh ho!" Renn exclaimed like a madman. "So it's *this* one at your ovum!" He stared at me with his acid-enriched eyeballs. "Do you understand the power she has bestowed on you, sir?"

Lauren tried to intercede. "It's really everybody's totem. The whole Ecstasy Club." But the moment had passed. Renn saw something and there was no hiding it.

Duncan quickly moved to correct this impression, but Renn's eyes stayed glued to me for a few more interminable seconds.

"I had them all get the tattoos," Duncan interjected, as if he were our school teacher, "to help them stay focused on the task at hand."

"And what might that be?" Renn asked patronizingly. As Duncan thought a moment, Renn crossed his effeminate legs to form a platform for his elbow, then propped his chin on his palm and waited, smiling blankly like a secretary taking dictation.

Lauren suppressed a giggle, and Renn's entourage smirked. This was a showdown between two social programmers, a hazing for Duncan, and a male-dominance ritual all rolled into one. I was glad to be just a sidekick on the sidelines.

But Duncan was good. "Why don't you explain it to him, Zach?" he said. Brilliant. Reinstate his dominance over me while ducking out of the question. If I got it right, Duncan would still get the credit for having me in his dominion. If I got it wrong, I'm just an incompetent underling, and I've given Duncan more time to figure out how to respond.

"The task at hand," I repeated, as if I had forgotten the question raised so long ago, "is nothing other . . . than to convince ourselves that what we're doing means something."

"And what does it mean?" Renn asked, purring at me like a cat, or some riddling villain out of *Batman*.

"It doesn't matter, does it?" I said, mirroring Renn's little animal gestures. "As long as we can project whatever we want into it. It's something we did to ourselves, and can continue to do to ourselves. We know we're in charge."

I was making this up as I went along but it sounded good. If I could just wrap it up somehow and make it circular, it would sound true.

"We're taking social space. It starts with our own skin and extends to our home, the city, the world, our whole universe. It just has to begin somewhere definite. That's the fetus in the middle. The conception of a new order. Rebirth. Renaissance."

"Yes, darling?" I had said his name. Everyone laughed. Renn A. Sanz seemed satisfied enough. He directed the rest of his insights and inquiries to me. Duncan's tactic had backfired.

"In the UK," Renn continued, embroidering his spin on British repression in a conspiratorial whisper, "piercing, scarification, and tattooing have been declared illegal. They call it 'grievous bodily harm,' and even if you do it to yourself, it's only one charge below manslaughter in the law books. It carries a seven-year minimum sentence. Why?"

We weren't sure if he wanted an answer or not. Henry couldn't stand the suspense.

"Because they know the power of the ritual!" he said.

"That they do. Did you ever wonder why they call a ring through a man's urethra a Prince Albert?" Renn asked, responding to Henry's British accent.

"It's named for Victoria's Prince Albert, who had one of his own. The rituals are as old as the stones in the Tower of London!" Henry said. We didn't let on that he always said this.

"Indeed they are," nodded Renn. "The Masonic traditions go back centuries." Henry was so proud of himself. If he could have patted himself on the back he would have. Dear Lauren did it for him.

"But the criminalization of countercultural rituals has a much more devious purpose," I said, remembering what I could from the Renn A. Sanz record jackets.

"Yes, it does," Renn finished for me. He didn't need me to prove myself at the expense of his rhetorical tour de force. "By making the activities of your enemy group illegal, you make the group into criminals, vulnerable to attack."

"Surely they won't arrest everyone who pierces their skin," Duncan interrupted, his common sense getting the better of him.

"Surely they won't," said Renn, imitating Duncan's schoolboy accent. "They'll just arrest anyone they want to."

He gave us time to absorb his message. If the governing body can turn the entire population into outlaws, then they can arrest anyone they want to, whenever they want to, for whatever reasons they may have. Even with all the E in our brains, the thought made us queasy.

"You do not own your own skin," Renn said. "*They* do. The real question for you, then, is who is 'they'?"

"The cops," Henry said.

"No."

"The government?" Brooks guessed.

"Could be . . ."

"No one. There's no one really out there," Lauren said. "They're just a projection of our fears."

"But can you be so sure of that, my darlings? This is psychic warfare. It has a long and proud history. The Babylonians, the Crusades, Jack the Ripper, the MI6, the CIA, Aleister Crowley, the British Empire, Cosmotology. There's lots of thems out there. And inside you right now. Among you. You say you want a revolution, baby? Well, you know. If you're really going to disengage from the dominant social set, you had better figure out who 'them' is."

It was the best and worst advice we were ever given.

17.

Sensing he was through (or responding to a cue I had missed), Renn's entourage of "S&M mistresses" attached chains to his metal collar and escorted him out onto the dance floor. Although he appeared to be dragged away against his will, when one of the chains snagged the collar of his vest he winced ever so slightly and the dominatrices immediately rushed to comfort him and loosen the collar. I couldn't tell who was the dog and who was the master.

Henry pumped our sound system as loud as it would go and put on an old Renn A. Sanz recording, "Znas A Nner." It was raw sound. Pure assaulting noise. The bass was so low and loud that I could feel my bones separating from the flesh around them. The only discernible rhythm in the lengthy track was the vibration of the PF building itself. The mass of sound created a palpable pressure against the skin. It had weight and an almost numbing effect, like being in an isolation tank.

Renn got hold of a wireless hand mike and started screaming over his old recording, wagging his tongue at his fans like a serpent. The gentle Goth kids all retreated outside or into Nomie's lounge while the Industrial guys took charge of the main space, slam dancing, climbing up beams and leaping off, and having a tug-of-war with Renn's chains. Renn pretended to enjoy the harsh yanks at his collar but kept turning to his dominatrices, wide-eyed and desperate for them to unleash him. He was getting flung all over the place. When the dominatrices grabbed hold of Renn's waist to keep him still, the tugs on the chains practically pulled his head off.

I couldn't watch.

Lauren was struggling to get up to the mezzanine but the mass of slam dancers was too much for her. I managed to make my way through to her just as one of the chains was about to cut her down. I took her by the waist and half-carried her over to Nomie's lounge.

We found a place on the stage amid the Goth kids, who were looking at one another's jewelry and preparing potions for themselves. Nomie was selling something she called "absinthinum," but no one believed that her beverage had anything to do with the psychedelic wormwood from which real absinthe is made, and they wouldn't drink any until she offered samples for free.

The sound from the main room was still too loud for us to have a real conversation. I smiled at Lauren, and she smiled back.

"I've been missing you," I shouted at her.

"Huh?" she asked.

I put my mouth next to her ear.

"I miss you!"

She just looked at me, either confused by what I had said or unable to make it out at all. Then she laughed. She laughed at the utter silliness. I laughed with her a long moment. I realized how our soap opera was so absurd. Here we were—great, deep, spiritual friends. Maybe we would have sex someday and be lovers, and maybe we wouldn't. A part of my body had been in her mouth. Period. The rest was a mental construction; power games, ego, competitiveness. Our connection was so much deeper than that, lifetimes long. Our current, momentary confusion barely amounted to a ripple in the surface. Or maybe this wasn't what she was laughing about at all.

I saw her expression suddenly change to horror. I followed her sight line to find out what had upset her so.

A few clusters of people away, two girls sat together holding what appeared to be scalpel blades. One girl had rolled up the other's sleeve and was gently making a long slice down the skin of her friend's forearm.

I felt the grip of Lauren's little hand tighten against my arm as the girls licked up the blood together and started to kiss.

18.

It was easy for me to sneak out the next morning. Kirsten was sleeping with Peter full-time, and as long as I didn't use my car, no one even noticed my departure. I took BART from Oakland to downtown SF, then the N-Judah out to the Barnows' house in the Inner Sunset.

Alex Barnow was the only student I had retained after Duncan told us to quit our jobs. I would have kept Melanie, too, but she had started wearing little more than skimpy T-shirts to our sessions and intentionally bending over her workbook so that I couldn't help but see every beautiful young thing she had to offer. When Kirsten became unavailable to me I didn't know how much longer I'd be able to hold out, and Melanie's parents looked like the sort who would press charges.

Alex was a good kid. He had already scored in the low six hundreds on both verbal and math, but his dad wanted him to get into Princeton, his own alma mater. Alex's dad was a Lebanese immigrant, and he worked himself through college when he was thirty. Now he owned three pharmacies in the Bay Area, and was determined for his son to continue his version of the American Dream. But Alex was into video games, basketball, and Beat literature. He wanted to go to Vassar or Sarah Lawrence because of the gender ratio and the likelihood of his getting on a varsity team. He had already been accepted early to one of them, but his dad was insisting on Princeton, and for that he'd need higher numbers.

So there we were, toiling away on analogy problems and reading comprehension in order to get higher test scores for a college application that Alex didn't even want to complete. We spent most of our time talking about all the pressure his dad put on him, and coming up with ways to convince Mr. Barnow that Vassar and Sarah Lawrence were good schools. It was an all too typical upper-middle-class nightmare.

We were deconstructing an analogy question from last spring's exam. It was my technique to show kids how the test was put together, so they'd feel more in control of their experience as they suffered through it for three hours on a sunny Saturday morning. The question went:

23. witch: coven
A. vampire: crucifix
B. ark: covenant
C. soldier: regiment
D. hive: bee

"Witches are to a coven," I said, reading from the exam book, "as . . ." I waited for his response. Nothing.

"Okay, let's say you don't know the word *coven*," I began.

"You'd be right. I don't," Alex answered in a monotone.

"Fine. Let's eliminate wrong answers. As a vampire is to a crucifix?"

"Sounds good. Witches, vampires . . ." He began to mark the choice.

"You fell into their trap," I told him. "It's a false family. They do that to confuse you."

"What?"

"Anytime you see an answer in an analogy question that comes from the same world as the example, you know it's wrong."

"How do you know that?"

"It's their mind game. If the example were 'television is to picture tube,' then you'd know that any answers with TV programs or antennae or anything to do with TV were wrong."

"So vampires is wrong because they're from the macabre, like witches?"

"Exactly," I said. (I was glad to hear the word *macabre*. It was on the vocabulary list I had given him the week before.)

"That's evil! They put it there just to fuck us up!"

"Exactly. That's all the Educational Testing Service is. An evil bunch of fucks trying to exasperate kids. There's only so much knowledge they can test you on, so they resort to the psyche-out.

They're not testing your knowledge—they're testing your ability to stay cool under pressure. And to do that, they put you under as much pressure as they can."

"Hmph," Alex said, looking at the problem again.

"You have to think of them as the enemy. Nerds who got teased in school and now want to make everyone else suffer. Who else would voluntarily take a job at ETS? The only way to win is to beat them at their own game and think like a nerd." I felt like Renn for a minute.

"That's why they make us use number two pencils," Alex said.

"Why?" I asked. He had lost me.

"To make us into little slaves. We can't just use our pens, or number three pencils. No. We've got to use these special ones. Number twos. When we go out and buy number two pencils, we've already lost. We're in the system. Once they get you to do one thing you don't really want to do, you may as well surrender."

"You're right, you know." He was. He returned to the problem with a vengeance.

"Ark to covenant is totally the family thing," he said. "It's a phonetic family, you know? The word *covenant* is a decoy for coven."

"Right."

"And hive to bee, that makes sense but it's the wrong way around," he said, zeroing in on the right answer. "A coven might be where a witch lives, but it's in the wrong order."

"Yup."

"So it's gotta be soldier–regiment. A witch is to a coven as a soldier is to a regiment."

"You got it." I patted him on the back.

"Those motherfuckers. And I don't even know what a fucking coven is."

Alex was well on his way to crashing the great conspiracy. Against my better judgment, I left him a flyer for that night's rave. He was a senior in high school, after all, a few years older than many of the kids who were already showing up. And tonight's rave was intended as a younger person's party. It wasn't going to be as intense as last night's Industrial riot or tomorrow night's

Phylogenic Foresight. It would be more of an introduction to rave for those who had missed out on the beginnings of the SF rave movement two years ago. A happy night about the music and the vibe, to bring people up-to-speed. Besides, he probably wouldn't come and it was nice to make him feel invited to something I was doing.

My ears popped as the BART train descended back under the Bay. The car I was riding was filled with homeboys from Oakland. From my book bag and whiteness they must have assumed I was a Berkeley student. They kept walking in front of me smoking cigarettes and waving their hands around in gangsta code, trying to intimidate me. I was looking forward to getting off at the West Oakland stop along with them, proving myself a member of the 'hood.

When the train stopped and I headed for the door, only a few older black folks got out with me. The rapper kids were staying on for the ride up to Berkeley. Then I noticed one of *them* had a Berkeley jersey. They stared in amazement as I got off the train and voluntarily forsook the safety of BART for the perils of Oakland. Turns out they were the suburban wanna-bes and I had the street cred.

But who was I really kidding? What was I doing in this neighborhood? I walked past the faded old houses of the residents. Teenagers sat in small groups around their parked cars, listening to music and checking out whoever drove by. Potential targets and potential threats. Another group of young men on a corner were leaning against a fence, walking up to idling cars and selling drugs to the occupants. Meanwhile, kids were playing in the street while their moms sat in the living rooms watching TV with the sound turned up so loud you could hear it from outside.

And here I was holding a master's degree and a promising future, walking to an even worse neighborhood where I was squatting in an abandoned warehouse. This is why it was so dangerous to leave the PF. It gave you perspective.

I snuck back in but no one noticed I had been missing. They were all excited about a high-security Internet site that Pig had cracked online.

He had been working with Peter for three days on the VR visionquest amplification circuit. They kept getting distortion whenever it cycled more than a few hundred times, so they decided to look around and see if anyone else had tackled the problem. (Pig's comrades at SRL refused to get involved in the project because, in their words, it was "all head and no metal.")

Back in the eighties Pig had been involved in Cosmotology, the infomercial cult. The actual program involves getting hooked up to biofeedback machines (called Orgonometers) and answering lots of questions. As the cult member got more relaxed about the questions (more programmed to respond a certain way), the Orgonometer would register smoother wave patterns. While he was a member, Pig had been approached by the San Francisco center's director to work on a prototype for a consumer version of the Orgonometer, but Harman's head office eventually nixed the project, fearing that people would buy the machines, use them at home, and stop paying for seminars.

The whole cult was based on keeping the way the machine worked a secret. Even the certified Cosmotology trainers knew only how to use the Orgonometer, not how it actually did what it did. Pig hated that the organization was such a cabal and split. Two weeks later, a dozen Uzi-carrying U.S. Secret Service agents were in his apartment arresting him on old, trumped-up phone-phreaking charges.

Pig believed that one of the controls on the original Orgonometer, called "phenogain," was very close in function to the amplification circuit that he and Peter wanted to build. It was a dial that allowed the programmer to increase the gain of the person's biofeedback responses. But instead of using a piece of software to cycle the responses through a microchip in a computer, the phenogain control passed them through a vacuum tube—like the kind in old radios. It was analog technology, and had a smoother response pattern.

When I got up to Pig's loft, everyone was gathered around him at the terminal. He was using an old back door in Cosmotology Corporation's computer system to hack into their purchase order records and find out the serial number of the phenogain vacuum tube so we could order one for ourselves.

His fingers moved nonstop on the keyboard as screens of text flew by. He hopped from one server to another, covering his tracks with tiny roving viruses that erased any signs of where he'd been. He'd break into a system, use it to hack into another, and then just hit Ctrl–J to drop the little coded smoke bomb behind him. By the time a savvy sysop figured out that security had been breached, Pig was gone and his entrance and exit completely sealed as if he'd never been there.

Peter, whose psych experiments with computers qualified him as an intermediate-level hacker in his own right, translated Pig's movements for the rest of us. Pig had already found the serial number of the tube and put it in the paste buffer. But the number wasn't a standard radio part at all. It had a double-E prefix, and neither Pig nor Peter had ever seen that before. It was distributed by a company called Electronics Transponders.

"I'm going to take a peek at the Electronics Transponders Company and see what they're into," Pig said, as he hopped from the Cosmotology computers to their supplier's.

"Electronics Transponders Company," Nomie giggled. "E.T.C. Et cetera!"

ETC operated a secure server, and it took Pig about fifteen minutes to get in. "This is military-level security," he said. "I'll go back to Cosmotology's server and start a packet sniff, then I can do an IP spoof to slip inside ETC."

Peter leaned into the monitor as Pig worked. Then his jaw dropped.

"Holy shit," Peter said. "Get out of there, now!"

"Nah," Pig shrugged him off. "They can't see me."

"What's happening?" Duncan asked. "Don't draw attention to yourselves." He was quite the pansy when it came to getting caught at something.

"Electronics Transponders Company isn't just secured like a military institution," Peter said. "It appears to be one."

"What do you mean?" asked Parrot. "It's either military or corporate. It can't be both."

"It's a company," Peter said. "At least it looks like a company."

"But it's selling military hardware," Pig added. "Obscure, old military hardware off a base in Arcata."

"That's where you're from, Kirsten," I said.

She looked uncomfortable. "I'm from Humboldt," she said. "It's nearby. But I don't know of any base up there."

"Well, can we order the parts from them?" I asked, ever practical.

"I don't see why not . . ." Pig replied, hitting a few more keys.

"Don't use our company name," I said. The Ecstasy Club DBA was registered to me, personally, after all.

Pig laughed. "Like they'd deliver the parts to a place called Ecstasy Club? The EE prefix means top-security-clearance distribution only, dig? Two levels below bomb-grade plutonium."

"What are you going to do?" asked Duncan.

"Cosmotology just opened a new center, my friends," he said, hitting a few keys. "And here it be. At this address."

We laughed. He had just made us an official franchise office of the Cosmotology cult.

"And they need two EE 136 PZ tubes rushed FedEx by tomorrow morning." Pig finished his keystrokes with a flourish.

"What about when they get the bill?" Lauren asked.

"That's the funny part," Pig said. "I don't think they will get a bill. From what I can tell, they don't pay for these things. They just order them and they're sent."

Peter hadn't said anything in a while. He looked weird. I motioned for him to follow me out to the stairs.

"What's the matter?" I asked him when we were out of earshot.

"I don't like this," he whispered. "I've heard of that base. It was part of a weather-tracking operation. The one that sent off all those balloons in the forties and fifties that people thought were UFOs."

"So, what?" I said. "The vacuum tubes are from weather balloons?" Duncan was hovering in close enough to hear.

"The old guys at JFK," Peter said, "you know, Sturgeon, Macey. The old acid casualties with all those paranoid theories? They used to tell me that the whole military weather-tracking operation was a cover-up for experiments in thought control. That they'd project sound waves or something to freak out the enemy troops."

"Those days are over now, Peter," Duncan said with confidence. "It's our game now."

Peter was unconvinced. I felt for him.

"It'll be okay," I said, putting my hand on his shoulder. "You're not alone this time. The group can handle it." Whatever dear Peter had been through, paranoid conspiracies were not going to get the better of me.

"Shit!" Pig yelled. Something was wrong. We went back in.

"Just throw out another one of those viruses!" Parrot said.

"I did. It just dissolved."

"Then get out!" Duncan ordered.

"I can't."

"What's going on?" I asked.

"They're onto us."

Peter hit the power switch on the modem. The cursor on the screen froze. We were all breathless.

"I could have gotten out, Peter!" Pig said, annoyed.

"They were tracing back. It wasn't worth it," Peter said.

"I was coming from an anonymous node. They never would have found me."

It was a judgment call the rest of us had no way of evaluating.

"Come on," said Duncan. "We've got a party in an hour."

19.

The kids shouted "CONTACT! CONTACT!" as they pumped their hands into the air in unison. It was a young crowd, just as we had expected for our Friday night trance-dance party, and they seemed quite willing to absorb whatever programming we had to offer.

Most of the projections on the walls depicted spaceships or little aliens, and the music we played early on was pure techno-bleep. No vocals or discernible instruments—just computer and video-game sounds dubbed over a 135-beat-per-minute click track. The bass was extremely loud, though, leading hordes of boys to cling to our bank of six-foot bass radiators like piglets absorbing nourishment from a sow. The most enthusiastic of the bass-heads held onto the tops of the huge speakers and just dangled there, vibrating passively with the sound. Dozens of others crowded their bodies in around them until there was a wall at least ten boys thick. They were in a mass, worshiping the bass as it pounded through their bodies.

Duncan had told us there was a possibility that Dr. Samuel Clearwater would show up, and when I spotted the old man at the door and corralled some E Club members to form a welcoming party, I was glad the E we'd all taken hadn't kicked in yet. I wanted to stay alert for at least a little longer, both to impress the great Dr. Clearwater with my own psychology theories and to deal with any trouble if it arose. I had been completely neglecting Officer Laruso ever since his cops busted our party earlier that week. I knew he wouldn't just go away, but I wasn't looking forward to standing in his office and getting chewed out or worse. If he was going to shut us down or kick us out of the PF completely, I wanted it to be with Duncan and everyone else right there. Maybe I was secretly hoping Laruso would close our whole operation before we got into any real trouble.

The wrinkled, white-haired old Clearwater half-staggered in and was immediately mesmerized by the sight of the bass-heads. What he lacked in physical stamina he made up for with a stream of enthusiastic superlatives. "Wowww!" he shouted. "Amazing! They eat it up like a drug and it leaves no trace in the bloodstream! It's good for them, too! The best thing they could do!" By the time we escorted Clearwater to the bar, he had run through at least five other subjects. "Those films!" he yelled over the din, "they're perfect! Beautiful! I wrote about space travel back in the sixties, you know. That was my idea. I just had it republished."

People of all stripes broke through the moving blockade we had formed around Clearwater's frail body to offer him advice, handshakes, books, pamphlets, and drugs. One admirer handed him a bottle of herbs that supposedly keep you young forever; another gave him a new prototype of a brain machine that uses electronic pulses instead of sound and light; and others just complimented him on his Web site, his latest *Dateline* appearance, and his rerelease of the book *Staying High*. He grimaced on every step, having just recovered from hip-replacement surgery ("I'm the bionic man!" he told us), but he still managed a high-five or thumbs-up for everybody.

Clearwater was a showman and had committed so intensely and so long ago to this public image of wily clown that he wasn't going to let a graphite joint negate years of hard-earned self-promotion. He was milking the last drops of fame and fortune from a city that had always been one of his ideological strongholds. There were still deals to be made, film options to be sold, and benefactors to schmooze before he crossed the finish line.

It turned out he hadn't come up to the Bay Area for our party at all but to attend *Plugged* magazine's Plasma rave on Saturday night. They were paying him to appear and covering his expenses, so he had stretched the trip a few days to take some meetings and scan the cultural horizon. We should have been honored that Clearwater thought we embodied that next wave and that he came to the PF at all, but Duncan felt betrayed that Clearwater would choose Plasma over tomorrow evening's Phylogenic Foresight, and his dismay was infectious. We were second best and, when push came to shove, Clearwater was on the other side.

We escorted the doctor to an empty stool next to Duncan at the bar, per Duncan's instructions, but the old psychologist sensed the little power game and would have nothing of it.

"I can't sit up on a stool!" he said, glaring into my eyes as if I should have known. "Don't you have a chair or something? With a cushion?" Lauren ran up to the kitchen for a chair while Clearwater held himself up against the bar. He was short of breath—exhausted from the walk.

"How are you, Samuel?" I asked.

"I'm not here to talk about how I feel. I'm here to forget it!"

Duncan spoke to Clearwater in a formal monotone. "Would you like a drink?"

"Two," Clearwater said. "White wine and a vodka."

Duncan nodded to one of the bartenders, who quickly filled the order.

Clearwater's drinks and chair arrived at the same moment, and he struggled to hold onto both glasses as he sat himself down. We all winced along with Clearwater as his artificial hip stabbed him. He closed his eyes and breathed a moment, then took a pill from his pocket and washed it down with the shot of vodka.

"I hate wine glasses. They have stems. Don't you have a tumbler?" he asked.

Duncan reached down from the stool to take Clearwater's glass and hand it off to a bartender for an exchange. In his lounge chair Clearwater was much lower to the ground than any of us. He took on the role of a king relaxing while everyone else danced for his pleasure.

"So this is great!" he said of the goings-on. "Beautiful!" Then he looked up to Duncan. "Tell me something about it."

"Well, Samuel," Duncan began, "as you can see—"

"As I can see?" Clearwater barked back. "Don't tell me what I can already see!" He made sure all of us got his meaning. "Fascinating expression, isn't it? 'As you can see'. . . You tell another person what he's seeing! Heh! Eriksonian hypnosis. You can't tell me what I see, can you? It's probably the only thing you can't say. What *I see*."

He wasn't being cruel, exactly, just "on," like the Yale professor I imagined he once was.

"Go on," he said to Duncan.

"What we're doing here—," Duncan began again.

"Now that's good. You can tell me what you're *doing*. Go on!"

Duncan hated this. "What we're doing is creating a space where social mutation can occur."

"Social mutation? What's that?" Clearwater looked like Duncan was speaking another language.

"Conscious evolution," Duncan continued, forcing himself to remain calm, "through the manipulation of external circum-stances." He used Clearwater's old "external circumstances" catch-phrase to gain acceptance through assimilation.

"Manipulation?" Clearwater played with the word in his mouth. "Manipulation. Do you notice how you moved your hands when you said that?" Clearwater imitated Duncan's gesture, fluttering his hands like a magician. "Manipulation. Ahh."

"It's just a series of choices about sensory stimulus," Duncan said. "Ones that we've found effective for detaching from consen-sus social templates and creating new ones. Ones that we hope to share with the kids who come here."

"That's beautiful," Clearwater said finally, looking back over the dance floor. "Sharing what works for you. That's all you can really ever do. Communicate your experiences to others in groups."

Duncan was pleased to have made contact and tried to get on a roll. "The ultimate purpose, of course, is to—"

"The ultimate purpose?" Clearwater interrupted again. "Ulti-mate? Ul-ti-mate? That's the kind of word used by a Hitler or a Stalin! Ultimate. The Ultimate Solution. It's reserved for people who think they hear the voice of God. Heh-heh. You understand what I'm saying?"

"All I mean is that the real point of what we're doing—"

"The 'point'?" Clearwater put his hands together into a point. "That's a military word, did you know that? The point! Point of attack!"

Duncan had all but given up. Clearwater didn't want dogma; he wanted sensation. Lauren had a much better grasp of this, and touched Samuel's bony shoulder.

"Look at the videos on the wall," she said gently but enthusiastically.

Clearwater readily responded to Lauren's sweet suggestion and stared up into the image on the wall. A flying saucer slowly rising from the White House lawn—a clip from some old sci-fi movie.

"Wow!" Clearwater exclaimed. *"Vvvvroom!"*

Duncan sipped on his smart drink, defeated. Then Clearwater, as if by instinct, switched gears.

"This is amazing what you've accomplished here, George." He looked into Duncan's eyes with genuine admiration. "Truly amazing. Hats off to you!" He toasted Duncan with his glass, and Duncan clicked his own against Clearwater's. The Ecstasy Club was officially approved, and just in time. The E we had all taken was finally taking hold.

"I invited some friends tonight," Clearwater told Lauren. "Colonel Edmund Brock, Renn A. Sanz, and Tad Steppling." I wondered where Margot was. She'd drop Duncan in a minute for a movie star like Steppling, even if he was a Cosmotology member and probably gay.

"Renn is a close friend of ours, too," Duncan bragged.

"Oh, really?" Clearwater said, utterly unimpressed. I glanced over at Lauren to see if she'd caught his use of Duncan's phrase.

"I'll make sure they get in and find you," Lauren said.

"Is there a little room where I can sit with them?" Clearwater asked.

"We'll arrange everything," Duncan responded, taking charge.

As we walked Clearwater up the stairs to the mezzanine, I noticed Alex Barnow crossing the dance floor with some of his high-school friends. They were wearing bright white MADD T-shirts and clean blue jeans. I peeled off to welcome them.

I shook Alex's hand and smiled, even though I was blinded by the light reflected off his stark white shirt. The ecstasy was coming on strong, and I worked to maintain my equilibrium in the presence of my young mentee, against my Rule of E.

"Those are some pretty bright shirts!" I said to the trio.

"Are you stoned?" Alex asked me, somewhat surprised. It must have been obvious.

"Not really," I lied. "I just took a hit off someone's joint."

"You look so different," Alex said. "So much . . . cooler."

"Thanks," I said. "Right?"

"Yeah. It's a good thing. I never saw you when you weren't tutoring."

Alex introduced me to his two friends. Cammie, a pretty girl with short red hair, was the president of their high school's chapter of Mothers Against Drunk Driving. She had lost her best friend to a DUI asshole. Scott, her boyfriend, was some kind of student government stud. The young couple had responsibility practically written across their foreheads. I wondered how the word *responsibility* would look if it were truly etched onto their foreheads like Henry's fetus tattoo.

They had just come from a Friday night MADD rally, and were so sweet and squeaky clean that they made me feel demonic. These were beautiful, innocent kids, or so the E told me, and should be shielded from the madness of the Ecstasy Club.

"Look, Alex, um," I said, trying to keep his face from turning into a cartoon character's, "Samuel Clearwater is upstairs and I better make sure everything's okay."

"Sure," Alex said. "Don't worry about us. We'll look around and find you later."

"Great!" I answered, way too jubilantly, in the manner of Clearwater himself.

Alex laughed at me, amused but disillusioned. His eyes spoke. His tutor was a druggie.

I sprinted away as if I were needed urgently elsewhere.

And so I was. At the door to the smart lounge, Tyrone was making a scene, jumping up and down in his orange jumpsuit like a Day-Glo bigfoot on speed. Facing him, a foot away, was a strange little old man, also in an orange jumpsuit, copying each of Tyrone's movements.

Tyrone screamed and waved his arms.

The little man screamed and waved his.

Tyrone panted and whacked his head.

The little man did the same.

A crowd of kids gathered round the spectacle. It climaxed with Tyrone pounding on his chest and pulling on his braids. The old man suddenly wrapped his arms around Tyrone's midsection and embraced him. It was Clearwater's old friend Colonel Edmund Brock—former U.S. intelligence officer, dolphin communicator, and famous psychedelic–out-of-body–interdimensional traveler. I wanted to let him know that Clearwater had arrived, but Brock was in a shared space with Tyrone and there was no reaching either of them.

They began to stroll together, arm-in-arm, in a big circle around the whole PF. I followed them on their tour to make sure nothing awful happened. They were conversing in a gibberish only they could understand. They nodded and laughed as if they really understood each other. Everyone probably thought they were putting on an act, but they weren't. I'm sure of it.

Tyrone walked Brock into his airshaft and began pointing at objects and explaining what they were.

"Abba tu baganash be yappa dey," Tyrone said.

"Ni gamma tu shappa?" Brock asked, and they both laughed.

Then Tyrone pointed up to Peter, who was manning the lookout post above.

He explained something to Brock, sadly and seriously. Brock nodded and smiled. They both stared up at Peter for a long while, then shrugged in unison. I figured they were lamenting our need for security measures. Then Brock turned to me and spoke in English.

"My penis feels like jelly," he said. "Where's Samuel? I have a present for him!" He clutched the small canvas purse hanging over his shoulder.

"Right this way," I said, escorting him out.

Tyrone saluted Colonel Brock and froze in that position, but Brock ignored the gesture. He finally returned the salute from what must have been thirty feet away, halfway up the stairs and long after he was out of Tyrone's direct line of sight. I peeked over the railing just in time to catch Tyrone ending his salute and about-facing back into his shaftway. *How did he know?*

"Have you met Tyrone before?" I asked.

"He's been around," Brock said, smiling. "But we don't speak of such things here in flesh-land, now do we?"

"What things?" I pressed.

"Call it the air force days," he said, as if he were making this up. "We served together. Yeah. That's it. How's that?" I assumed he was telling the utter truth because he was so obviously intent on making it sound like he was lying.

Up in the kitchen sitting on the couch next to a drunken, prone Clearwater was a battered Renn A. Sanz. He was wearing a huge neck brace and holding a cane. He looked awful, and only one of his mistresses was with him. The others must have been banished for losing control of their chains to the rowdy Industrial fans last night at Pandora's Fix.

"Hello, Colonel," Renn said, holding out his hand to shake. "You look well."

"Days and nights the same," Brock said. "Keeping it all in the bloodstream for future reference." *Huh?* Then he noticed Renn's sorry state. "What happened to you, Renn? Fall into a K-hole?"

"Those damn fucking kids," Renn bitterly cursed his core constituency. "I can't terrorize them into submission anymore."

"Looks like *they're* the ones terrorizing *you*, old man," Brock smirked.

"I was just inquiring about the possibility of Samuel here writing a letter on my behalf," Renn said. I found his obsequious tone more frightening than anything he had said or done last night.

"And that's what put Dr. Clearwater to sleep?" Brock asked, sarcastically.

Renn pandered on. "You see, I've got another immigration hearing next month. Mightn't you be willing to jot down a few words on my behalf, Colonel Brock . . . ?"

Clearwater suddenly pulled himself up to a sitting position.

"Colonel Brock? Whoahh! Edmund Brock! Edmund Brock! Hello! Hello!"

The colonel sat down next to Clearwater and the two embraced on the couch.

"You're in town for that Plasma party?" Clearwater asked.

"Yeah. They're paying pretty well and I wanted the chance to see you."

"What'd they give you?" Clearwater asked.

"Thirty-five hundred plus expenses," Brock answered.

"Hmph. My assistant got four grand out of 'em for me," Clearwater said. "You should have held out, Edmund! What'd *you* get, Renn?"

"Less," he replied, absolutely deadpan. The two older men laughed at him.

Were these our psychedelic forefathers or professional side-show performers? Or both?

They decided to go back to Clearwater's hotel room to inject some ketamine. (Actually, Clearwater and Brock were going to go alone but Renn begged them mercilessly and finally offered to pay for the cab if they'd let him tag along, too.)

"Thanks so much for coming," Lauren was saying, trying to stall them as Duncan hurried up the stairs, dispensing with what-ever dramatic entrance he had planned for himself.

"Colonel Brock! A pleasure to meet you," Duncan said.

They shook hands.

"I've been meaning to speak with you about our work here," Duncan said, trying to engage Brock, who was already in motion.

"I'd like to do that sometime soon," Brock said. "But we're just leaving. I've got to prepare for the big night tomorrow." He searched absentmindedly for his belongings and stuffed them into his orange jumpsuit. "Fluids fluids fluids."

"Excuse me?" Duncan was unaccustomed to Brock's random phrases.

"They say that Plasma is going to be 'the next big thing,'" Brock said. That stung. *We* were supposed to be the next big thing. "It should be an interesting evening. You must come. I'll secure some passes for you."

"I heard E. T. Harman's flying down for this one," Clearwater piped in.

"In his private air force–issue jet, no doubt!" Brock laughed.

"No doubt . . ." Renn echoed mischievously.

Duncan was floored. His own Phylogenic Foresight was so insignificant to the fathers of psychedelia that they weren't even acknowledging it. It seemed as though the entire world was conspiring to humiliate him.

"I'll give you a call next week," Duncan said, evading the issue, his voice practically breaking. He unconsciously clicked his Doc Marten heels while bowing his head ever so slightly, then walked straight out and up the next flight of stairs. He motioned for me to follow him up and I obeyed.

"They're all clowns," Duncan said angrily. "They saw the clear light and just lost it."

"Wait a minute," I said, running after him. "Their work set the foundations for everything we're doing." I was getting a little dizzy from chugging up the stairs on E. It felt good, though, and I felt good—up to challenging Duncan's arrogance. "We wouldn't even know about psychedelics if it weren't for those guys."

"Maybe. But they're on the other side now."

"They were fucking college professors, Duncan. In the fifties and sixties, no less. They broke through a hell of a lot of the crap." We passed through my room—where two kids were practically fucking on my bed, *under* my sheets—and continued on up the precarious ramp high over the dance floor toward Duncan's pyramid. "You're going to condemn them for falling short of making it the whole way? For being human?"

"No. I condemn them for running to the highest bidder. I condemn them for their inability to see light from dark."

"Don't you think you're waxing pretty Old Testament, Duncan?" I asked him frankly.

He stopped short on the narrow incline and turned around to face me. We were a good thirty feet above the crowd. "It sounds to me like their visit accomplished exactly what they were hoping it would, Zach," he said. "Listen to yourself."

"What? You think I'm being uppity or something?" I was getting a little mad, but I didn't like the idea of a confrontation on E, either, especially atop this rickety wooden plank.

"They came to undermine us. Didn't you hear the way they were talking? About Plasma? About me? They're on the other side, Zachary. They want us to question each other and ourselves."

"Come on, you think they did something to me? To us?" (They couldn't have, could they?)

But he didn't answer with words. He just swung his door open dramatically.

Peter was inside the pyramid, sitting on the floor with his head on his knees. He was crying.

"Peter had an experience I think we should talk about," Duncan said.

"What happened?" I asked, touching Peter's arm.

Peter raised his head and looked back and forth between Duncan and me.

"Are you okay?" I asked. The E made me totally empathetic. I was inside Peter, feeling his despair. But he was calm. Relaxed. Gentle. His heart was so warm.

"They came up and spoke with me," Peter said.

"Who?" I asked.

"Tyrone and the old man. I thought they had climbed the ladder, but they were just standing there in the air. Floating in space. Smiling sadly at me."

That moment in the shaftway. I warned myself not to freak out.

"They were speaking in gibberish," I said.

"No," Peter explained. "They were kind of hovering there next to me, watching as I looked out over the alleyway. I couldn't move or acknowledge them, but they spoke to me—well, not speaking exactly, but thinking at me."

"What did they say?" Duncan asked. "It's absolutely imperative you remember." (Absolutely imperative? Clearwater was right; Duncan was a tyrant. Or maybe Clearwater had injected this doubt intentionally.) My brain wouldn't stop.

"They knew about my experiments at JFK," Peter said, as if remembering a cloudy dream. "About my friend Steven—the one who died. They said they saw it happen, and that there was nothing

I could have done. That I shouldn't worry about him. He made a choice and he's fine."

"What did you take tonight?" I asked him.

"Just that E. And I smoked a little pot."

"What else did they say?" Duncan asked. Their participation in the Plasma party had him completely paranoid.

"Just that it was all okay. They wanted me to feel okay."

"And do you?" I asked. (Peter's well-being was more important to me than this little debriefing. I felt proud of that. And ashamed. Was I losing sight of our higher priorities? I had to stop questioning everything.)

"I do," he said. "I feel really good, I think. For now."

I could barely hear him. His voice was so doleful, and the voices in my head were so grating. And the noise from downstairs was reaching a peak. I looked down through the window in the floor.

Hundreds of kids were jumping up and down with their hands in the air, shouting "Contact! Contact!" Margot was close to the middle of the huge circle of bodies, her head tilted back and her long hair drenched in sweat. She was staring straight up, looking right through the window in the pyramid but not seeing us at all. She was looking through to something else.

She had dosed up on E tonight for the first time and was in total communion with the kids as they shouted up to the ceiling, calling for a UFO to land right on top of them. "Contact! Contact!" Although most mystics and psychedelics gurus considered the UFO to be a useful metaphor for something in the future—perhaps our own evolution, or the great attractor at the end of time, drawing us forward—these kids took it literally. They truly believed that their dancing, the drugs, and the group vibe could summon an alien craft. Amid the UFO worshipers now, Margot had found her true calling.

Her eyes were wild. She moved her hands, beckoning something or someone to come down to her from the sky. She opened her mouth and smiled in ecstasy.

20.

The next bright-gray-concrete-PF morning, Lauren and I sat alone at the kitchen table smoking cigarettes and not talking about anything in particular. We just wanted to be together in our post-E doldrums.

We were always the first to get up, and I think we both counted on it. We'd find each other at the kitchen table and pretend we were more hazy and hungover than we really were. It saved us the anguish of not being able to talk about our real feelings. We could just sit there together under the pretense of a laconic stupor, feigning exhaustion so that no one, especially not we, could possibly interpret our half-clad morning trysts as trysts. Which they weren't. Not really.

Sure, my mind would wander past the point where her beige camisole thwarted my eyes, but there's no harm in that. That's just thought. And maybe I'd come down to the table with most of my morning hard-on still pushing through my boxers, but that could be chalked up to a lack of awareness on my part. Or simple, biologically justifiable, overnight testosterone discharge. I could just pretend I was too lazy and too comfortable with Lauren as a friend to worry about it.

We were saying it without saying it. We couldn't say it. We weren't allowed to. Which is why we played this game in the morning, every morning, until someone else came in.

"Good coffee today," I said. I meant, *I feel so connected to you right now.*

"It's just from a can," she replied. *I like you, too, but get real.*

"Yeah, but I like that." *I mean it.*

"My parents always grind it fresh," she said, relenting. *My parents stayed in love their whole lives.*

"That's sweet." *That's sweet.*

Whenever subtext peeked up into text, we retreated into business.

"How was Duncan when he went to bed?" I asked.

"I wouldn't know," she grumbled into her coffee cup. Whoa. This meant he had slept with Margot again. I was going to ask how she felt about this, but I didn't want to press it. She trusted me not to. That's what had given her the freedom to say something real—to confide in me. This was our unspoken arrangement. We were required to bail each other out of personal digressions, even though we wanted nothing more than to share them. This way we could say meaningful things to each other without danger of the other returning in kind and breaking the surface.

"He thinks last night's multicelebrity snub was a concerted action," I said, returning to the matter at hand.

"Yeah," she said, looking back up, "he's convinced they were sent here to psyche us out."

"Well, we've got to get his mind back on the party tonight. Phylogenic Foresight is the main event, and if he's all weirded out, it'll never come off."

Our jobs as Duncan's keepers took precedence over any feelings we had for each other. (For the time being, I consoled myself.) Lauren was the head priest, I was the Levite steward, and poor Duncan was the sacrifice itself. I don't know how much we really believed in Duncan or what he saw as his potential to break through dimensional space, but we respected his unflinching commitment, and the fact that he was significantly farther along that path than we were. We accepted his paranoia and rage as symptoms of his stress, not expressions of his core being. Sometimes, we were proud that we had subverted our own desires and created a safe enough environment for Duncan to behave as foolishly as he needed to without repercussion. He was our child, and we were willing to give up a lot for him.

The whole PF and all of its parties and events were merely vehicles to help Duncan through a portal he would most likely enter alone. We were just creating a setting and bringing him the energy of thousands of bright-eyed young people for him to apply to his own journey. And we were still hooked on the idea of getting to go along for the ride. A shotgun seat on the joyride to the next dimension.

I was sitting there, talking with Lauren and wondering what would happen if I just broke the facade and admitted my doubts or my real feelings right then and there, when Brooks strolled into the kitchen, mischievously holding something behind his back.

"What have you got there, mister?" Lauren asked playfully. She was so resilient, able to shift instantly from one emotional moment to another. She spoke to him like the caring mother of a two-year-old, but without a trace of condescension.

"Guess!" Brooks responded.

"Come on, Brooks," I said, already fed up with the game. I wasn't as good at shifting gears or nearly as free with my reserve of good spirits as Lauren was.

"Abba gabba emsay!" Brooks said.

"Colonel Brock?" Lauren asked. "Something of his?"

Brooks smiled proudly and produced Brock's canvas bag from behind his back and placed it on the table.

"You stole his bag?" I asked.

"He left it . . ." Brooks said, "on the couch for much too long!"

"I can't believe you swiped it!" Lauren said as she began looking through it.

"What's in there?" I asked Brooks, knowing he already knew.

Brooks giggled as Lauren pulled out four labeled vials of pharmacy-fresh ketamine and a half-dozen syringes from the bag.

"They're going to come back for it, Brooks," I said firmly.

"So what?!" Brooks squeaked. "Gimme a break, man! My chain-letter business is in the tank and I've got a serious coke problem and a slipped disk. Besides: finders keepers! He lost it at a *club!* Anyone could have taken it!"

He gathered up the vials and put them back in the bag.

Lauren smiled at him. "You little devil."

Brooks trotted off to wake people up and show them his prize, singing the old Dead song "One More Saturday Night."

Lauren and I continued to sip our coffees and plan for the evening as lights and stereos went on throughout the giant wooden hive.

When a robed Duncan finally came down to the kitchen (from the stairs leading up to the studios and Margot's room), he didn't need any of the consolation or redirection Lauren and I were so determined to offer. He looked like he was already tripping—but he might have affected this disposition just to prevent either of us from questioning his sleeping arrangement.

"We have to talk," Duncan said, scratching his messy red hair and sitting down between us. I knew it. He was going to keep Lauren and me apart from now on and justify it with some big spiritual rationale.

"Where are you, honey?" Lauren asked him. We could smell Margot's perfume. Lauren casually pulled a long brown hair from Duncan's shoulder.

"Things are heating up," he said. "Many different energies are acting on us all at once. We have to be ready for anything."

"We are," I told him, trying to stave off whatever he was going to announce. "We're ready for anything. The club is united. Morale is good."

"It's more than that. We've got to keep ourselves directed toward our own goals and not let anything distract us. We've got to keep alert, and we have to shore up our vulnerabilities."

"Like what?" Lauren asked. We were both dreading his next words, although we had no idea what they would be.

"With *Plugged* and Plasma so intent on stealing the cultural moment from us—" Duncan stopped short as Kirsten and Tyrone came up to the kitchen from downstairs and poured themselves some coffee. We all nodded at one another in silence. Tyrone seemed more grounded than usual. Something in him had changed. Kirsten surmised they had walked in on a "top secret" conversation and took Tyrone back downstairs.

"With *Plugged*, Plasma, and Cosmotology so dead set against us," Duncan continued, "we have got to make ourselves impervious to their attack."

"They're just copying us," I said. "That's probably why they sent those guys over here. Don't worry. The kids still know what's real."

"They're co-opting our memes for a very different agenda," Duncan said. "It will happen just like it did in the sixties. That's why they're bringing in Clearwater and Brock and the others. They're attempting to reinvent rave, psychedelia, our whole movement and recontextualize it into a validation of their own cabal and a repudiation of our most deeply held beliefs."

"It's just business," I said. "They don't like competition." I was trying to take the desperate edge off Duncan's scenario.

"They are opposed to evolution!" Duncan shouted, emphatically banging his hands on the table. "You have to remember that I can see what's going on. I know what's happening. I can see these things."

We couldn't make light of his concerns. We trusted Duncan enough to believe that when he claimed to "see" something, it meant that he had really seen a pattern and it behooved us to hear him out, give him our opinions, and then move as he instructed. Duncan saw things the rest of us didn't. He held the map.

"We are the purest and most direct expression of the light they are dedicated to extinguishing," Duncan explained passionately. "I can't tell this to the others, but it's important that you hear me. They know I am at the center of this, and they would do anything to stop me. I am the most vulnerable person here, which is why I need to be protected."

"How?" I asked.

"The easiest thing for them to do is challenge my residency," he said. "My visa expired months ago. One phone call to the INS and they can have me deported."

"You think they'd do something like that?" Lauren asked. "Something so blatant? It would martyr you."

"But it would also get rid of me. An 'anonymous' call is all it would take." Duncan paused for effect. "That's why we have to get married, Lauren. As soon as possible. Zachary, I know you'll be glad to have handled the details on this. Find out how we get a license, and how my residency can be established."

I found myself just nodding slowly.

"It's very important for me personally as well," he said over my unvoiced objection. "Not just in terms of legality but for grounding. It's the right thing for us to do. I'm journeying farther out than ever before, and my connection to the earthly dimensional plane is waning."

Here was the fabricated spiritual rationale I had been waiting for, but somehow as he said it I accepted it as fact.

"We all have to make compromises," Duncan said to me, knowing exactly what I was thinking and feeling—or at least pretending that he knew. "I know you had an attraction. The both of you. But that was corporeal. Transitory. A temptation. This is your challenge. My connection with Lauren is too important to sacrifice to a mundane drive that would end as soon as it was consummated." He dismissed the great love of my life without as much as a blink.

"I hadn't really thought about marriage," Lauren said. "Not in a long time, anyway."

"It's your role, Lauren," Duncan said, taking her hand. "That's what the last two years have been about. You left school, you broke from your parents. You know we have a connection. This isn't a base, romantic relationship. You have to drop that programming. It's the Third Goal, Lauren: to drop the social mindset."

"And what about you and Margot?" I asked, much more boldly than I even intended.

"Oh, dear Zach," he said, as if he were deeply disappointed in me, "I thought you had the clarity to see that what I'm doing with Margot has nothing to do with me. It's all for her. It's the only way she understands how to relate to what we're doing. I'm not attracted to her in the least."

He wasn't even looking at me as he spoke. He was staring into Lauren's eyes—pacing her breath, drawing her in like Mesmer himself. Then he was onto something else.

"The other good news," he said, "is that I've convinced the *Rolling Stone* reporters to come to Phylogenic Foresight after they're done at Plasma. They'll do a two-part story pitting the old entrenched values against ours. The journalist understands exactly what's going on."

"That sounds great," I said, with barely a nuance of appreciation.

"It's all coming together, Zach," Duncan said. "Don't give up now. I know you've been having doubts, but you are essential to what we're doing here. I need you with me as much as I need Lauren. I hope you recognize that."

"I do, Duncan," I said. I thrived on the acknowledgment, but managed to muster some honesty. "I'm just a little uncomfortable, that's all. You shouldn't be taking all this on yourself. You don't have to turn into some kind of messiah. This is a team sport. We're all in this together."

"You're right," Duncan said. "That's why I need Lauren. So I never forget I'm just a human being. She's the only one who is willing to push back against me."

I imagined the two of them years later, married and unhappy. I hoped that the fighting spirit Duncan so admired in Lauren would give her the strength to break free and, ultimately, come to me. There. I said "ultimately." I guess I was hearing the voice of God.

21.

The rest of the day was a haze. All I could think about was how I was losing Lauren before I'd ever really had a chance to have her. Maybe all that subtext had just been in my head. Now I'd never know.

The FedEx man delivered the two vacuum tubes we had ordered, and Pig busied himself installing them into the VR visionquest system. Peter wanted nothing to do with the experiments anymore. After absorbing whatever it was that Brock and Tyrone had communicated to him—and I had no reason to believe that anything real had actually transpired among the three—Peter said he was content to leave the development of technovisionquest hardware to others. But when Pig threatened to conduct the rest of the experiments by himself, on himself, Peter agreed to monitor his work.

As I had suspected, Tyrone was a completely changed man. He had cleaned up the whole space by himself, stopping only to ask Kirsten about the location of supplies and where to stack the garbage bags. He was energetic, articulate, even cracking jokes. He asked me if he could be assigned to a shift at the watchtower from now on, and I could find no good reason to refuse him. He asked Kirsten to shave off most of his hair, which she did after washing it at the sink wearing rubber gloves.

Then he convinced Kirsten that the two of them should quit smoking together. They borrowed my car to go to the Berkeley Free Clinic for NicoDerm prescriptions. When they came back, each was wearing a little beige shoulder patch stamped "2 mg."

On Duncan's instructions, Parrot went around and handed each of us five hundred dollars in twenty-dollar bills—our individual takes for the past two nights. My tutoring days were definitely over. I would call Alex and explain. He probably didn't want to see me again, anyway.

I phoned Laruso's office at about 6:00 P.M.—early enough to look like I had tried to reach him but late enough to be sure he was gone. I hoped that a few cycles of voice-mail tag would give me plausible deniability for tonight's party. I could explain to him later that I was calling for permission.

We had the party-preparation drill down cold by now. The speakers were stacked up in the afternoon and all the video and projectors were wired up by early evening. Henry picked up our DJs and their equipment from the airport, and Brooks worked with Peter and Pig to assemble giant set pieces and an amusement-park ride. Although Phylogenic Foresight was going to be our biggest party yet, we had so much extra time to set up that there was almost no frenzy. Not inside the building, anyway.

By about five minutes before midnight a huge and impatient crowd had gathered outside the main doors. Not everyone knew that we were holding until 12:01 to comply nominally with the mandate from Laruso, and they were getting angry. There must have been close to five hundred people out there shouting for us to open up.

Parrot was hysterically enlisting people to help him process the imminent onslaught, and even though we had set up two alternate ticket stations, once the steel doors were parted the throngs just crashed the gates and ran out onto the floor. I saw a girl about to get trampled and ran over to save her but it was too late. By the time I got her bruised body off to the side, she just cried that she wanted to go home and pushed her way against the oncoming human traffic, clutching her bag to her chest like a young Vietnamese mother holding her baby in one of those newsreels about the last airlift from Saigon.

It was pandemonium. We finally managed to stop the flood of crashers, but then everyone else started complaining that if the people who had broken in didn't have to pay, why did they? Were we rewarding the crashers and punishing the compliant?

Just when I thought there was going to be a riot, Tyrone appeared out of nowhere with a megaphone he had fashioned out of rolled-up poster.

"Form a line to the left of the cashier table!" he ordered like a drill sergeant. The flattop haircut Kirsten had given him perfected the caricature. Everyone froze. "Now!"

The kids obeyed readily. They seemed relieved by Tyrone's authoritarian tone. Maybe people *like* established boundaries and hierarchical convention, I remember thinking. Even the kids who had stormed in found themselves walking quietly back out to the doors. Tyrone walked out into the crowd carrying a trash can filled with the foam-filled pantyhose legs from the herbal smart lounge. He placed them like traffic cones, as the sea of bodies parted and organized itself into neat lines.

One bald tough guy with a chain around his neck blocked Tyrone's path, but our enforcer wasn't having any of that.

"Do you have a hearing problem, young man?" Tyrone barked at him before tilting his head comically.

Several of the kids laughed until the bald guy went limp and fell in line. Tyrone was brilliant! He had diffused the situation completely with assertiveness and humor. His movements became more stylized and mock-military until everyone realized he was merely giving a performance. They were all participating in a playful ritual of dominance and subordination, and most important, the ritual was going to get everyone inside unhurt and properly processed. *And so went the Sixth Goal: to reframe and disengage through ritual.* It worked.

In spite of Tyrone's magnificent save, those first few moments of aggro chaos set the tone for the rest of the evening. We were all on edge about the cops, Plasma, Brock and Clearwater's visit, and Duncan's expectation that tonight would be the *really big night*. He had been building up to this evening for two weeks, telling us how it was supposed to launch an entire chapter of human history.

"We're going to touch it tonight," he kept saying whenever he'd see one of us. "You'll know why we're here. Tonight's the night we'll see the clear light. There will be a sign. Something will be conceived tonight. Stay focused. Don't hold back."

With instructions like that it's no wonder we all went a little crazy.

We had been hosting a party every night of the week. We had peaked so many times already that we could barely imagine pumping out another peak experience for ourselves or anyone else. What we needed was some R&R. What we were doing was pushing ourselves even harder. We had all done so much E over the past two weeks that we were practically immune to its effects. We decided to do "candy flips" instead—LSD with a hit of E to fill in the gaps. We also sucked on some dried leaves that Nomie had procured from a Mexican shaman in the Mission. They weren't psychedelic in themselves, but acted as an MAO-inhibitor, giving the LSD more opportunity to find receptors in the brain. It effectively tripled the doses we were taking, which were already pretty high.

Push, push, push. This is the big one.

The music was great. Duncan got DJs to fly in from all over the place. Masto came in from Amsterdam, Hal from LA, and the Nexus Twins from New York. We rented a whole new sound system with some trillion gigawatts of bass, industrial-quality laser lights, and three smoke machines. There was an amusement-park ride called "The Lasso" spinning around on one side of the space and a "Moonwalk" inflatable bouncing room on the other. We had video cameras rigged all over, and a CUSeeMe interface with the Internet projecting live pictures of people and parties in Japan, England, and Australia. We had leased six more generators to power everything—two of them just for the Lasso—and they made the entire back of the building vibrate. We were stretched to the max. Overload.

Maybe that's why, even with all the chemicals, people, and equipment we had packed in there, the vibe was so scattered. Energy was extremely high but bursting in all different directions. So many people came because they had heard this was going to be "the next big thing," yet they had no idea what to expect or what to do. A rave is nothing more than a composite of the intentions of the people attending. With all these people coming with no intention other than to be part of the next big thing, it's no wonder there was no unified field. It was raw, random expectation. Hype.

I was watching the whole mess from the DJ perch. Tons of people were dancing, in many different styles. The Nexus Twins were spinning with the amazing, synchronous finesse that made them legends in the dance-music world. Eight turntables, four arms, two heads, and one sound. The two identically skinny brothers wore headphones and never looked at each other as they passed records back and forth in movements more coordinated than a championship mahjong game. Sound over sound, beat over beat—sometimes all eight tables spinning at once. They knew their discs so well they could play a sample, flip off the volume, backtrack one and a third turns, flip the volume back on, and play the sample again by the next measure, all the while finding a cue in another song and modulating the EQ in rhythm with the main beat.

For all their unearthly synchronicity, the twins couldn't quite unify the crowd into a single organism. There was too much going on. The kids in line for the Lasso and Moonwalk kept getting shoved by dancers, and the bass-heads worshiping the speakers impeded the path to the smart bar and mind gym, which was being used as an ambient "chill-out" lounge. The noise was so loud from the main sound system, though, that the ambient DJ had to blast his amplifier just to be heard. No one could talk in there, much less chill out.

Peter and Tyrone took turns at the lookout. Tyrone was a model sentry. He walked back and forth on the roof scanning for police, and kept testing the signal to make sure it worked. The DJs started getting tired of his false alarms and "A-okay" Vietnam-vet hand gestures. Peter just sat up there during his shift, staring out at the horizon. I went up the ladder a couple of times to talk to him, but he remained as silent as a Zen monk.

As long as the candy flip hadn't kicked in, I wanted to check up on how everybody was doing—my final Levite duties. The acid was very strong and very pure, so I knew it would sneak up on me. Impurities like strychnine create a whole array of physical sensations you can use to gauge your progress in the trip. With extremely clean pharmaceutical-grade LSD, you simply realize all at once that your whole world has changed. It's an invisible transition and you don't know it's happened until it's well under way.

I went up to the loft, where Pig had been holed up since the vacuum tubes arrived. Brooks was up there too, trying to get Pig to buy a bottle of the ketamine he'd stolen from Colonel Brock.

"It's the perfect visionquest drug! That's why Duncan used it in there," he told Pig, holding up the bottle like a salesman. "Didn't you see *Altered States?*" Actually, in the movie they used an organic potion William Hurt got from a shaman, but I didn't have the heart to expose Brooks's scam. I figured karma would pay him back later. I should have been more diligent.

Pig finally dished out fifty bucks for the bottle, anxious to sample it on his next test run of the system. The new amplification circuit was working fine but the rig still had a few kinks. The solenoid in the tube appeared to be generating a voltage of its own once it was put in line, and Pig wanted to figure out where the line noise was coming from before he went in again. Pig was anxious to shoot up and dive in, but I made him promise to call me or Duncan before he attempted another full immersion.

Brooks and I went back down to the party so he could chat up some high-school girls he had spied earlier. "They're a delicacy," he told me, describing his strong preference for the youngest of females. "Clean and sweet, but terrifically dangerous." I wished he had kept the danger part in mind. He started dancing with them, using his vials of K as maracas.

"Put those in your pocket," I warned him. "We don't know who's here." He told me I was being paranoid and shrugged me off. The acid had definitely come on, so I got my head out of that mental space and my body out of the bombardment of sound and light.

I was making my way across the dance floor when I ran into a familiar face I couldn't place. It was a boy, smiling at me. I knew he was a friend.

"Zach?" he said.

It was Alex! He wasn't with those two friends from before and he wasn't wearing that white T-shirt. His pupils were huge. He was tripping on something and seemed to be having a good time. But I was suddenly flushed with guilt. He was a convert. He must have felt so cool. I should have been happy for him—it's what we were trying to do. But the sight of my student in a rave jersey tripping his brains out spun me the wrong way.

"Alex," I said, embracing him. "I'm glad you came back. Tonight's the big one, you know." The party line came off my lips in programmed perfection. I hated myself for it.

"Yeah! It's great!" he said. "What's gonna happen?"

"You'll see!" I said, playing the showman. I gave him a big Clearwater-style thumbs-up (now I knew where that came from) and kept moving. Searching for some silence.

The ambient room was useless. I sat and watched as people tried to shout over the music. There was a mound of beanbag chairs in a corner, and on top of them all sat Margot doing a variation on a mudra, with her legs crossed and her fingers splayed like a goddess in a Hindu sculpture. I stared at her awhile before I noticed that the *Rolling Stone* reporters were standing next to her, taking her picture and trying to get her to give them a quote. Maybe she was ignoring them for effect, I thought. A new publicity stunt.

Everyone else was writhing around on the floor, stoned out of their gourds. I was one of them. Too wasted to move, but too pummeled with sound to stay still. Their faces were all contorted in various stages of psychedelic bliss. Or was it? What would be the difference in the way they looked, I wondered, if they were in agony—their guts blown out in a nuclear holocaust? Wouldn't they be writhing around in just the same way? What if it were true? What if we were writhing around in our own blood? There could have been an accident. There might be shards of glass all over us. *Maybe they're all over me, too, but I just can't feel it.* I wanted to pull out of the trip for a second just to make sure everything was all right. That no one was in danger. I wanted my faculties back to be an objective Levite observer for just one second. I was the one who was supposed to watch out for disasters during the revelry, but I couldn't pull myself back to the real reality. And if I could, I was afraid of what I'd find out. The struggle made me nauseous. *It's just the drug.* I got out of there.

Back in the main room I checked my hands. No blood. I was okay. But the Lasso ride was waving its metallic arms at me. *Something could come loose and strike me.* I retreated through a door.

I found myself in the herbal lounge. Tyrone was on the stage, stacking up his little blue statues to form a giant metasculpture. He was trying to help us come together, I thought. It looked like one of those Hieronymus Bosch triptychs, with Ecstasy Club members' heads carefully placed within a network of goblins and fairies. I was going to talk to Tyrone, of all people, for grounding, but he was so involved in his task that I didn't want to break his trance and bring him down with my own bad trip.

That's what's happening. I'm having a bad trip! The truth was relieving and horrifying at the same time. Every time you drop acid you know it's Russian roulette. I tried to remind myself that Clearwater and his friends tripped thousands of times before anyone ever reported a bad trip. It was only after the CIA and the government wanted to crack down on all the casual LSD use that they published those false stories about kids freaking out and committing suicide. The propaganda changed our perception of the drug, creating an expectation of the occasional negative experience, and sure enough bad trips became a reality. Art Linkletter's daughter had actually been murdered, indirectly, by the CIA. But this spiral of reasoning made little difference to me at the moment. Who cared that the CIA was behind my bad trip? Bad trips were real, I was having a doozy, and I didn't know how much worse it was going to get.

I kept searching for quiet but couldn't find any. People were everywhere. Strangers. The "no one but residents upstairs" rule wasn't being heeded at all, and none of us was straight enough to stand on the staircase and keep people out. I pushed through the masses to get to my room only to find two kids at my desk taking my computer apart. They looked like they knew what they were doing and I didn't want to make a scene so I continued up to Duncan's pyramid. Maybe it would be empty.

Lauren was in there with Duncan, preparing him for the *Rolling Stone* interview. I nodded to them, then sat down in a corner and just breathed. *I've got to have faith.* What we're doing is real. It may look fucked up, but *something real is happening tonight.* I convinced myself that my negative experience was actually something good. A confirmation of the intensity of the evening. The disparate elements trying to come together. The sperm rushing toward the egg—competitive, desperate, confused, blind.

Gaining equilibrium, I opened my focus to include the rest of the room. There was a weird smell. Duncan had just thrown up into a trash can. Half a bowl of brown fluid sat in front of him. Ayahuasca—a hallucinogenic brew of rain-forest vines. The South American tribesmen drink it, throw it up, then see visions. It's powerful, life-changing stuff. Duncan was pushing it. How could he possibly give an interview while tripping on ayahuasca?

I moved the trash can out onto the steps. The stench was overwhelming. As I came back in I could see that Duncan had a cigarette in his mouth and Lauren was holding up a lighter. He kept drawing on the cigarette and getting a corner lit.

"It's not lit, Lauren!" he'd say, and then she'd hold up the lighter again.

Even after the cigarette was fully lit he'd just take it out of his mouth, unsatisfied with the rate at which it was burning, and ask for another light.

"It's not lit, Lauren! Come on!"

Instead of getting panicked, Lauren started laughing. She tried to suppress it but it wouldn't stop.

"Fuck it," Duncan said, throwing the cigarette on the floor.

Lauren continued to laugh. I started laughing, too. Duncan was so cute when he pouted. Like a baby throwing a temper tantrum.

He picked up the bowl of ayahuasca and, as if out of spite, drank down the rest of it and stormed out.

Lauren and I were laughing uncontrollably. It must have gone on for at least five minutes. My ribs started to ache from the convulsions but I couldn't stop. I kept thinking, *This is it? We are the next wave? We are the core group of advance scouts to the next dimension?*

But the bad-trip vibe had completely subsided, even if it was at Duncan's expense.

When I could finally see through my tears of laughter, I realized I was alone with Lauren in the pyramid, and we were both tripping as hard as we ever had. Somehow, the fact that she was getting married to Duncan—the futility of ever having her—gave me the permission I had been waiting for. I had admitted defeat. I had already lost the war, so I was free to win this battle without consequence. The E part of the candy flip was working on me now, and the LSD crucible made it impossible for me to repress what the ecstasy was urging my body to do. I believe I would have died had I done anything else.

Once I made the first move there was no turning back.

I knelt in front of her and kissed her on the lips. We hadn't kissed before. Not lips to lips. It was perfection. I needed nothing more. We were connected. Two fish, soft contact, moist interface. We fell slowly to the floor and kept kissing each other, still totally clothed. It was innocent. Love. I put my hand on the small round form pushing itself through the fabric of her sweater. Her breast expressed her whole self. Alive, its spirit dancing against the pull of gravity. I held it in my hand and felt it press its essence back at me. The shape, the give, the heartbeat within it. And it was Lauren's.

I welcomed her soft tongue into my mouth. Hers was a sweet inquisition, a test of new boundaries, an angel never incarnated touching solid flesh for the first time.

I watched as her body exposed itself to me by using its limbs to remove the fabrics that covered it. I hadn't remembered how beautiful she was. She was like a recurring dream of a special place that you remember only when you're in it. This was that special place. Our place. Heaven.

She lay back onto an Indian tapestry, and her body holding its form seemed a miracle to me. Arched, curved, white, so soft. This was real. I pressed myself against her skin. I felt its pressure against my own. Its gentle resistance. Resistance? *Am I raping her?* No, I told myself, there's another human being here. No resistance at all would mean no person was there. I looked at her face. No fear, no pain. Just openness.

We were fully naked together for the first time. I shivered—not nervous or cold but electrified. I had goose bumps and my hair stood on end. I felt my hand move down to the small of her back and pull her toward me by instinct. She was pulling me inside her at the same time. There was nothing we could do but follow along as our bodies mated.

This was union. I melted into her like wax until there was only one being. Pure love. No thrust or friction. Just a pulse, a charge, a vibrant perfection. The Garden of Eden. The world was whole.

Imperceptibly our shared being changed state. It was evolving. Forming something new. Creation. As we came the universe came with us. I could feel the flow from me to her. I was aware of my essence entering her and following through. Summoned by her womb. Pulled by the great attractor at the end of time toward a higher level of being. The future.

The egg opened to accept its chosen partner. I felt it happen. Duncan was right. Something magical was conceived that night. A fetus had materialized. A new generation.

Then we heard the explosion.

22.

At precisely 3:01 A.M. Pacific time, a galaxy named Corpus Exsasis, presumed to be among the first to spin off from the big bang at the beginning of time itself, exploded—or, rather, imploded.

The other explosion—the one we all heard—turned out to be the generators behind the building. We're not sure what caused what, but hundreds of boys had been hanging on to the bass towers, thrusting their bodies forward and back in unison. Then, suddenly, BOOM. One entire bass tower came crashing down on top of the boys and one of the leased generators exploded. Either the explosion outside knocked over the bass speakers, or the bass speakers crashing to the ground overloaded the generators. We had a way of rationalizing sabotage in either case.

It seems a lot happened during the same moment I was making love with Lauren. Serves me right for putting my Levite duties aside. Or maybe it serves everyone else right for having only one of me around. All I wanted to do was participate—not monitor and adjust—but participate fully in an experience. I paid dearly for granting myself this privilege.

Everyone else did, too. It all happened at once, and I only got the full story the next day. It began with Peter on watch. He was sitting up on the roof, scanning the horizon, when he saw them coming. Three police cars, lights off, cruising into the parking lot and surrounding the building. He was about to get up to push the alarm—one if by front, two if by back—but realized that there was no signal for cops from both front *and* back. He was tripping pretty hard, too, and almost got paralyzed by the indecision, like the mule who starved to death because he couldn't decide which pile of oats to eat. Peter broke the spell by deciding to push three times and hope that someone would get the idea. He managed to push the button twice, but then the generator blew and the whole alarm system was fried. A sustained electric shock (nothing was properly grounded) pinned him to the ladder. He couldn't pull his hands free, and if he did he'd fall fifty feet onto hard concrete.

While he vibrated up there at 59.97 hertz of alternating current, he had a bizarre vision: his dead friend Steven and our own hacker Pig were floating in the air next to him on the ladder, just as Brock and Tyrone had before. They smiled at him and slowly peeled his fingers from the ladder. Then, instead of falling to the ground, Peter was escorted down by the two benevolent presences. He just floated his way to the floor. He awoke later with bruises all over his body, indicating a more violent descent, but all he remembered was his gentle float down.

Pig wasn't so lucky. Once he got the rig working, he looked for Duncan and me as I had instructed. But Duncan was deep into his *Rolling Stone* interview and I was deep into Lauren, so he decided to give it a go by himself, with Henry as a monitor. As a safety precaution, he had installed a rheostat (a controllable buffer) in line with the amplification circuit, so that the intensity of the feedback could be attenuated manually. Its purpose was to pull the visionquester out of trance slowly, as if from deep underwater, to prevent a psychic equivalent of "the bends."

Pig said that it began perfectly. He saw a circular tunnel with a beam of light shining straight through it. He positioned himself on the line and then started to move, as if through time itself. He saw very bizarre things—women dancing, aliens, demons, machinery, and more that he couldn't remember. Henry saw it all on the monitor as it happened, but when they played back the videotape all that was visible was a beam of light. Pig had wanted to get off the beam and touch one of his visions, but he was stuck in constant motion and it disoriented him. On Pig's verbal instructions, Henry tried using the rheostat to decrease the amplification a bit, but then Pig just fell off the beam of light and was pulled out of the vision altogether.

Maybe the whole crisis stemmed from the fact that Pig shot himself up with a half cc of Brock's ketamine before he launched himself into the technovisionquest circuit again ten minutes later.

He told Henry that he thought the K might "put a little play in the steering wheel" and give him a chance to hop off the beam, which he had assumed was some sort of time line.

The second trip was very different from the first. No tunnel, no light. Just command code. Digits and ASCII text ran across the screen. Pig twitched uncontrollably during the whole ordeal. Henry watched amazed as the computer's modem software launched itself and dialed up a number that he had the rare presence of mind to jot down. A connection was made (57,600 baud, for what that matters) and then the visions started. Henry wasn't tripping, so I really believe he saw all this on the screen even though the videotape record shows nothing at all.

He said the screen displayed diamond-fractal textures jumbled into one another, but the textures formed the surfaces of objects in an alternate, hazy interpretation of the same visual data—like a room where the walls, furniture, and objects were covered in shimmering, psychedelic wallpaper. Henry couldn't make any of it out, though, and the videotape recording was just a mass of color. Until the last part. Just as Pig screamed and rolled back his huge bearded head, the monitor pulsed very rapidly. On later analysis, we determined the rate to be exactly 59.97 hertz. It corresponded with the frequency of the alternating current passing through Pig's body, and then stopped, along with Pig's heart, according to the respiration monitors, when the generator exploded.

While Henry performed what he could remember of CPR on the prone body, Pig experienced the weirdest part yet. He saw a piece of computer code flying at him from a distance. He recognized it as a self-modifying virus, but with no discernible function. He was floating in the ether, unable to move as the invading code spiraled into his brain and zapped his cortex. He suddenly twitched back to life, not knowing where or who he was.

Did Pig overload the circuit? Did the generator simply overload Pig? Did whatever or whoever it was they connected to by modem send something back through the computer that overloaded both? Did Pig visit Peter while he was on his visionquest, or after his heart stopped, or was this just a bizarre coincidence?

Or was it the aliens? It turns out that while I was watching everyone in the ambient lounge squirm around on their bean-bags, they weren't just writhing in bliss after all. At least Margot wasn't. She got abducted by a UFO—the one she had summoned with the rest of the kids the night before, she said. But her experience wasn't fun at all. She claimed (I guess I shouldn't doubt the legitimacy of her experience—just the legitimacy of her interpretation) that she was doing some yoga up on the mound of bags and reeling from the candy flip. Suddenly, there were flashes of light (the *Rolling Stone* photographer would be a logical but far less romantic explanation for those). She was completely paralyzed. She could see the other people in the room, the reporter, the photographer, even me, but she couldn't respond. This sensation lasted for many minutes, until she heard the explosion.

At that moment, she said (and related to the *Rolling Stone* reporters during the later melee), time stopped. She saw everything and everyone except herself just freeze in place, like on *Bewitched*, while she was carried up a bright beam of light into a spaceship. There, she waited for a while in an elevator with some other paralyzed people until she was teleported to an operating table. Some ETs with big black eyes and long fingers started poking at her with long, shiny steel straws. They took samples from under her knee-caps, and inserted an even bigger metal tube with a blue light on the end of it up her vagina and planted something on her cervix.

Then she found herself in a room made of flesh. She thought she might have been transported to her own womb somehow. While she was groping around in there, the ETs communicated to her telepathically. First, they told her that the abortion she had undergone as a teenager may have caused her irreparable psychic damage. Then they told her that human beings are destroying planet Earth, and that if we don't do something to stop the pollution, the human race will end. They promised that they would be visiting her again.

Before she knew it, Margot was back in the PF sitting on the pile of beanbags, and everyone else was in motion responding to the explosion and the raid. She grabbed one of the *Rolling Stone* people to tell him how the aliens had violated her privates and to pose for some more pictures, but they were more interested in document-ing the raid. Go figure. She had a small scar on her knee as proof of her ordeal and showed it to everyone who would look, but the cops were too busy having fun filling up their squad cars with drug of-fenders to pay much attention to a stoned MTV diva abductee.

Brooks proved an easy target for them. Like an idiot, he kept dancing with those little vials of K in his hands even after the po-lice had stormed in. He was so high he thought the cops were gay guys dressed in police costumes, like the Village People. He offered them K, willingly shared with them how he had dosed up the two high-school girls with whom he was dancing, and even laughed along as they cuffed him until he realized what was happening. If I had been downstairs I might have been able to prevent at least some of this.

I had heard the DJ announce something over the PA, but Lauren and I were at that ramp-up moment toward the end of lovemaking when nothing else matters. After the three earlier false alarms, I wasn't about to let some recursion of Paul Revere halt the sexual union of all time. But the explosion shortly afterward was far too loud to ignore. I was still holding Lauren in my arms—I had just climaxed and we were still fully linked—when our whole world shook. The pyramid vibrated at first, then began to swing back and forth like a pendulum. With a long, loud snapping sound the pyra-mid detached from the wooden ramp connecting us to the rest of the PF substructure. I didn't care about falling. My only instinct was to prevent that motion from making me lose hold of Lauren. I man-aged to keep myself inside her until the swinging stopped—and took this as a good omen. We were dangling from a single bolt hitching the pyramid to the roof beam, but we were together.

But then all the screams from downstairs and a fire in the herbal smart lounge yanked the rest of me from my trance and summoned the Levite within. There was blood to clean up. I threw on my shorts and worked on getting out into the fray.

I had to leap a good five or six feet from the pyramid to the rail-ing. My sneaker touched but just missed the other side, and as I slipped Lauren screamed. I thought about how it was going to feel to hit the concrete thirty feet down, and whether Lauren's scream would lower in frequency due to the Doppler effect, but my hands managed to find a sturdy plank in the splintering section of ramp still dangling from the main frame. I paused there a moment, hanging from the plank to feel my heartbeat. I was still peaking on the candy flip. I had almost forgotten. I envisioned myself as a rat-creature, and this made my rapid scurry up the ramp almost effortless.

Seeing Lauren across the great divide with only a sheet wrapped around her returned me instantly to my human form. I detached a lighting cable and threw it over to her. She tied it to the door frame and I pulled my end, bringing the pyramid close enough for her to make it to the railing. She put on some clothes from my room—I loved how Lauren looked in my flannel shirt—and made it downstairs in time to catch most of the action.

Only the emergency lights were on—thank God I had had the presence of mind to install a couple of those in case the generators failed. It was still pretty dark, though, which didn't help anything except maybe the hiding of drugs. Cops were everywhere and the kids were all running around screaming. It was not a well-organized raid.

Alex Barnow ran right into me. He was thrilled and panting in a delighted ecstasy rush.

"This is so cool!" he said. The E high was still such a new feeling for him that nothing could bum him out. "Totally cool! I better run away!" and then he was off.

I saw the cops cuffing Brooks but decided that the smoke coming from the herbal lounge demanded my attention first.

Tyrone was in there, on the stage, dousing his already flaming blue-clay monument with gasoline. All the little figures were burning and bubbling. Some were melting. The pantyhose legs dangling from the ceiling were beginning to catch, too. I grabbed some pitchers of juice from behind the bar (Adam screamed at me not to waste them) and extinguished the fire.

"No!" Tyrone shouted at me. "It must burn!"

The acid in my brain allowed me to communicate effectively with Tyrone.

"It's finished!" I told him. "You did well. It's completely done! It's freezing time!"

Tyrone smiled as I used the juice to put out most of the fire. I saw him pull a tiny blue statue out of his pocket. He had spared the little bust of Kirsten.

"We did it," he said to the figurine. "Mission accomplished."

The cops pushed their way into the herbal lounge and made a diligent and destructive search of the bar for illegal drugs. They didn't lift a finger to help me put out the fire. They kept opening the jars of prepackaged smart powders and putting their fingers in to taste samples, like they'd really know a drug if they ate one. But Nomie's powders were all flavored like whiskey-sour mix and iced tea, so I think they realized they had hit a dead end. Maybe the potions made them a drop smarter.

Once I got the fire out, I went back to the generators to see what was happening. A few dozen bums were gathered around staring. There was no fire, but one of the newly leased Hondas was charred completely black. The metal gas tank was crushed into a ball, as if it had imploded. The other generators were just sitting idle, undamaged.

"A fairy came and hit it with light," one of the bums said.

"A fairy?" I asked.

"We had nothing to do with it, boss," another bum said. They started to get suspicious of me and backed off into the darkness. I started up one of the downed generators—the one that powered the kitchen and house lights—and it kicked over easily.

When I went back inside, everything was getting a little quieter.

Peter was walking around in a daze, blood staining his Christ-like forehead, saying "It's not my fault." He had rung the alarm, after all.

The cop with the mustache from the other night walked up to me and smiled. I wanted to hit him. *Fuck you. Don't give me your shit. We didn't cause this mess. You did.*

"I think we'll just get your statement in the morning, Mr. Levi," he said. "When you've had time to think all this over." What was that supposed to mean? Was he giving us time to construct alibis, or simply to absorb the fact that he and his soldiers had complete control over us?

The police eventually left, along with the remaining partyers, at about 5:00 A.M. The cops were as beat as we were, but an obscure regulation forced them to stay and wait with the kids who didn't have cars until their parents picked them up. Two vans with HOME SAFE painted on them and driven by some do-gooders from UC Berkeley packed in a bunch of kids, too. I heard another group discussing whether to drive back into the City to see if Plasma was still cooking. Talk about loyalty.

Once everyone was gone, Lauren, Parrot, Peter, and I made a futile first effort to clean up some of the mess. It wasn't the way I would have chosen to come down off a candy flip. There was broken glass everywhere, cables, wooden planks, huge puddles of beer and water. *Welcome home.* The Moonwalk had deflated down to a heap of smelly plastic, thanks to a fallen lighting instrument that had pierced its roof. One of the sheets onto which we had been projecting our movies lay over a huge clump in the middle of the dance floor. Lauren and I lifted it up together as if we were folding laundry.

Beneath it we found Duncan, sitting cross-legged in a pile of rubble. We knelt down in front of him. His eyes were wide open and he was grinning. He looked at us with big black watery pupils, smiled, and said,

"Brilliant."

23.

It was about one the next afternoon. The place was still an absolute mess, but Pig was already up and walking around, and I had bailed Brooks out of jail with some of the money Parrot and I had hidden before the raid, so Duncan held an emergency meeting to "debrief" us on what had happened the night before. He said he had been watching it all "as it unfolded." I anxiously waited for the bomb to drop, convinced that he would blame it all on me for having sex with Lauren instead of attending to my duties.

We sat on chairs and cushions strewed around the main dance floor—all of us except Kirsten, whom no one had seen since the party began the night before. It was a strange and scattered way to hold a meeting. I wondered what he was going to address first: Pig's seizure and viral infection, Brooks having to go to jail, Margot's abduction experience, Peter's guilt over the whole raid, or, God forbid, Lauren and me. Maybe Duncan would just talk about himself, and having witnessed the clear light of infinity.

When he finally spoke, he walked around the room as if at a lecture, his voice echoing everywhere. He didn't begin with any of our individual experiences. I suppose that would have been too obvious. That's why I wasn't in charge. I don't think like a cult leader. Instead, almost as non sequitur, Duncan read to us the entire front-page article in the *Examiner* about the imploded galaxy.

Astronomers in Guam reported this morning that the galaxy Corpus Exsasis, believed to be among the first to spin off from the big bang, imploded at 6:01 A.M. Eastern Standard Time. It was the most distant light ever known to have reached the earth. Astronomers at the Berkeley Observatory said that the particulate matter in the galaxy condensed so rapidly that its entire mass was converted into pure energy.

"Wow," Margot sighed.

"Don't you get it?" Duncan shouted, throwing down the paper. "This event itself occurred millions of years ago. It's simply the light of the explosion that's reaching the earth right now. The oldest matter in the universe is transforming into something else. We have already seen the oldest stars we are ever going to see, and now those are dying off. As far as those of us on earth are concerned, this moment—last night at one minute after three—was the beginning of the end."

As he spoke, each of us naturally made associations between our own experiences of the evening and the greater cosmic event. It was a brilliant opening, in retrospect. It depersonalized our individual sagas and began the process of knitting them together into a unified whole.

Even the magnitude of my tryst with Lauren was reduced, at least temporarily, by Duncan's reportage to a single expression of a much greater astronomical event. There was a moment in time— a moment of extreme novelty for us in the Ecstasy Club—that coincided precisely with the moment that earth experienced its first sign of the great universal shift of matter into energy. Historical time itself, defined as beginning with the big bang, was now concluding. We had passed over the event horizon of the great attractor at the end of time. Corpus Exsasis—body of Ecstasy. The Ecstasy Club. Our whole universe was being sucked in—and the Ecstasy Club was the focal point. In the cosmic fractal uniting matter, energy, life, death, entropy, and evolution, the Ecstasy Club was a crossover point. Just as randomly tossed coins correspond to an I Ching hexagram that can be extrapolated to the movements of a person's whole life, the tiny moments we had each experienced last night could be unfolded into an interpretation—a map of the evolution of time and space. And luckily, we had Duncan to read that map.

"The police raid, the explosion, Pig's death, Brooks's arrest, Margot's abduction, and the experiences each of you had at precisely 3:01 this morning," Duncan said, looking at Lauren and me too purposefully, "I saw it all as it happened from far above. It's important for you to understand that these were not coincidences.

Nor were they part of a linear cause-and-effect, action-reaction chain of events."

He paced around the room for a minute, not saying anything. "How can I explain it to them?" he asked himself, as if he needed to download information of a magnitude too complex for our tiny, human minds. "Let me put it this way," he finally said, like a schoolteacher talking to children. "We entered a space together. I penetrated a boundary last night, and the entire club was drawn into the vortex."

Duncan stood motionless in the middle of the room, his back to half of us, as he recounted his tale. "I drank the second bowl of ayahuasca and went downstairs to talk to the *Rolling Stone* people. They were quite intelligent about our whole situation. They understood completely about the efforts of Plasma and others to impede our progress. I want us to stay in touch with them, Zach," he said, as if I should be taking notes. I just nodded. "They're very bright, and they might be able to help us in the future."

"After the interview," Duncan continued, "I felt the visions coming on and moved instinctively to the middle of the dance floor. The fixed energy of the crowd around me and Lauren in the pyramid directly above me created an axis by which I could travel, so I sat down and closed my eyes." Duncan sat down in the center of the dance floor and closed his eyes in a pantomimed re-creation of the event.

"Then it happened. I disappeared. I became completely porous. I literally vanished. People were dancing right through where my body was sitting. It wasn't a psychedelic trip where the room looked different to *me*. It was an interdimensional journey where *I* looked different to the *room*." Wow, invisibility. If it really happened—and it very well may have—Duncan was onto something big.

"As I sat there, invisible, objects in this reality became invisible to me, too. Walls, ceilings, certain bodies. Eventually, the only other things I could see around me were all of you." He looked up at us and smiled, like a loving grandfather on his deathbed. Then he looked back at Lauren. "I saw you all."

I didn't believe him. If he had really seen us or what we were doing, he would have included Lauren and me in his list of the events he knew about. Pig, Brooks, Peter, Margot had all related their stories, which is why Duncan could weave them in his magical vision. But he really didn't know whether Lauren and I had made love. He had his suspicions, but sought confirmation by suggesting things and seeing how we reacted. Lauren and I were well aware of his reconnaissance tactics and stayed cool.

"I saw Pig leaving his body and getting attacked by the virus. I saw Peter watching paralyzed as the police surrounded the building. I saw Tyrone setting his fire. I saw the boys pulling down the speaker. I saw Margot and the aliens. I even saw you, Henry, frantically trying to revive Pig with your bare hands."

As Duncan went through the list, everyone he mentioned smiled. Their experiences were real because Duncan acknowledged them as such. It was brilliant. If they wanted confirmation of their own outrageous journeys, they would have to accept Duncan's, too.

"I realized we had generated a moment of absolute novelty. A space where anything could happen. Pure potential. The cosmos itself had pushed the clutch pedal, and if any of us were conscious and willful, we could slip reality itself into any gear we wanted. My mind was clear, time itself had stopped, and there was an infinite possibility of directions. I experienced the totality of creation. I was at the very center of the big bang. It was fully accessible to me. My will, conducted through nothing more than my awareness, could direct the flow of matter, energy, and time. It wouldn't have happened if I hadn't been completely detached from my ego and personal will. This had nothing to do with George Duncan, yet there I was at the center of it."

"So why didn't you protect me from the virus?" Pig asked, breaking the spell. Good question. His face was twitching—a symptom of the code that he believed had infected his brain.

"I couldn't interfere, don't you see?" Good answer. "Whatever I wanted personally had to be ignored. I wasn't even in the space of wanting to save you, however much I care about you. That was simply something that was happening. I didn't move to save the starving in Rwanda or the bleeding in Bosnia, either. Infinite compassion means not to do anything to change the great dance. That's what a bodhisattva is all about. Appreciating the unfolding in all its manifestations, however painful on the temporal plane. The pain and suffering is part of the illusion. It's the game. It's no more real than mundane joy or happiness. In the clear light I experienced this. And now that's within me above all else." I held my tongue. It sounded like he was about to announce himself as the next messiah.

"So you saw that everything is just perfect?" Peter asked.

"Yes," he said, "and no." Another paradox. Great. Then came the kicker. "Now I don't want to frighten you, but there was another presence in the space with me."

"Who?" asked Margot. "The aliens? I knew they would be!"

"No," he answered quietly. "This was on a higher plane entirely." Of course it was. It was Duncan's plane, not Margot's or some ET's. "But there was another force there. A dark force. A force connected to the beings that took you, Margot; connected to whoever attacked Pig in the visionquest; responsible for the generators exploding, the police raid, Kirsten's disappearance . . ."

Kirsten's disappearance? No one had called it that until now, and Duncan waited for this repositioning of the event to settle in.

"I'm not saying she's working against us, necessarily, but there are connections we can't ignore any longer. If she were here, I'd have no problem confronting her directly. But she's not. Odd, isn't it?"

"What would you confront her about?" I asked, quite surprised that I came so quickly to Kirsten's defense. It should have been Peter's job now.

"I know it's hard, Zach, considering how you must still feel about her," Duncan said. He knew I didn't still have those feelings, and underscored that fact by pretending I did. I sensed this was for Lauren's benefit—to raise doubt about the longevity of my affections. "But we have to look at the connections objectively," he continued without missing a beat, pushing a myriad of agendas with every sentence. "Where is Kirsten from? Humboldt. Where is the air force base supplying the vacuum tubes? Where is the 707 area code of the number the computer spontaneously called on the visionquest? Northern California. Arcata. Humboldt. What is the connection between Malthus, eugenics, and Kirsten's Grateful Dead? Her play *Hand to Mouth* equating feedback loops with cannibalism and limited resources? How does that relate to Margot's aliens, their environmental doomsday message, and the genetics experiments they are apparently carrying out in her womb?"

Damn, he was good. It was like three seasons of *The X-Files* in less than a minute.

"How are they connected?" Henry asked, desperate for an answer. I had never seen him so cowered into submission. He was utterly dependent on Duncan to make sense of things.

"I'm not omniscient," Duncan said, half smiling. "I don't see everything." His admission of human imperfection made him seem all the more supernatural. "But I do know there's a force dead set on stopping us. They know we're onto the very engines of creation. We are raising the overall level of novelty, and this is diametrically opposed to their intentions."

The phone ringing made us all jump.

Lauren picked it up.

"It's for you, Zach," she said uneasily, holding her hand over the mouthpiece. "I think it's Kirsten."

"Be careful, Zach," Duncan told me. "Speak naturally. Act concerned. Tell her we all care about her. But find out where she is."

I took the phone. This was going to be tough.

It wasn't Kirsten at all. It was Laruso's secretary.

24.

With everyone standing around expecting me to do brilliant damage control, I couldn't refuse the call no matter how much I wanted to. I took the phone and before I had a chance to say hello, Laruso's angry voiced boomed through the receiver. The drugs from the night before had parched my brain of every last drop of serotonin, so there wasn't any way for me to dilute my emotional response to his attack. I just took it, down to the core of my being.

"I could put you in jail right now, kid, you know that?" he barked.

"Yes, sir, I'm sure you could."

"You're mine, Levi, you got that?" He loved having a spoiled, overeducated Jewish kid at the end of a string. His dialogue reverted back past *Hill Street Blues, CHiPS*, and even *Dragnet* to the Jimmy Cagney era.

"I'm sure we can work something out." My dry throat cracked pathetically.

"We're not working anything out, you little prick," he said. "You're just doing everything I say from now on. Exactly like I say it."

"Yes, sir, I understand." I wanted him to hang up so I wouldn't have to look like such a wimp to everyone around me. I'd figure out what to do later.

"I don't think you *do* understand, Levi," he said. "I think I need to explain this to you. In person."

"I could schedule a meeting . . ."

"Just get your ass down here now or I'm sending some boys up there for you."

"I'll be there as soon as I can, Officer."

"Don't 'officer' me, you shitcase." Then he hung up.

Everyone was staring at me. I couldn't tell if they were feeling sorry for me or agonizing over my ineptness. Laruso had shouted so loud that everyone in the room must have heard every insulting word he said. My psychedelic hangover had left me so depleted I couldn't even look up at them. By coming to my rescue, Duncan should have earned a friend for life.

"You were brilliant, Zach," he said. At first I thought he was being sarcastic. But he wasn't. "Did everybody notice Zach's technique? How he drew the man in, let him hear the sound of his own inanity?"

Henry nodded approvingly, the little fetus tattooed to his forehead bobbing up and down as he did.

"Calling him 'officer' was a stroke of genius, Zach," he went on. "You used his own position to intimidate him. If he indeed held every card, then why would he need to assault you like that? By demonstrating to him his own outrageously disproportionate effort, you revealed him as powerless. That's why he had to hang up."

Brooks smiled, and Henry patted me on the back. Others murmured their approval. Duncan had convinced even me that I had performed well. It felt better to believe him, so I did. I was immensely grateful.

Duncan and I decided that I should see Laruso that afternoon. I begged him to let me take Parrot with me, and he finally relented. He wanted me to go alone as a sign of strength, but we both knew I had no cards to play at this point. At least Parrot could speak Laruso's language.

It felt as though I hadn't been out of the PF for ages. Parrot and I drove to the Mission to grab some lunch at a burrito stand before we went downtown. It was well out of the way, which suited me just fine. While we searched for a parking spot, I noticed that the streets were filled with the Mexican American immigrants who lived there, and the artsy folks who live on the fringes of the Castro and shop at the Mexican groceries for cheap beans and rice.

"Who do you think are the real immigrants here, Parrot?" I asked.

"You mean that because this is now a Mexican neighborhood it's the whites who are the immigrants? Cute, but it doesn't make sense. It's American land and most of these folks are illegals."

"How can you say that?" I asked. "The Mexicans are more indigenous to California than the Anglos. This whole neighborhood is called the Mission because the first mission was built here centuries ago. And it wasn't even a spiritual enterprise—it was just a way of coercing the local Indians into submission to the western European system of gods and hierarchies before we took over."

"But we did take over, Zach," he said as if it should be obvious to a three-year-old. "This is America now. Mexicans are immigrants by definition."

I was going to tell him he was making a purely semantic argument, but I spied a parking spot across the street and it took my full powers of concentration to make a U-turn in the middle of the street without running over any of the Mexican men pushing their shopping carts filled with cans.

As soon as I pulled into the spot, a large, dark, and extremely thin bum approached my car and opened the door for me. He was holding a rusty old crowbar.

"A dollar and I'll watch your car," he said, smiling.

"Huh?" I asked.

"There's crooks here," he said. "A dollar and I'll make sure nothing happens to the car. It's a nice car."

Parrot was incensed. "This is extortion. Go away."

"How long you be away from the car?" the bum asked, fingering the crowbar.

"We'll call the police," Parrot threatened.

"It's okay," I said, producing some change. "There's at least a dollar here. Take it, okay?"

"I don't know . . ." the bum said, like he was going to raise the price.

"Come on, I'm sorry," I pleaded. "It's at least a dollar, all right?"

The bum took the money and walked off.

We got a seat right in the window of the burrito place, where the car was in plain sight. Strangely, I felt it was in more danger now that I had paid someone to protect it. We ate in silence for a while. I assumed Parrot was mad at me for succumbing to blackmail, but when he finally spoke it was about something else entirely.

"We've lost our competitive advantage, Zach," he said sadly.

"We'll get it back," I reassured him, not exactly sure what a competitive advantage really was.

"It's not something you get back, Zach," he explained. "You either have it or you don't. And I don't think we do."

"Things will get better. This is just a rough spot," I said, nudging his elbow across the table.

"This isn't a question of morale, Zach. It's a business consideration. The Ecstasy Club is not a good investment anymore. The police are against us, the established competitors are against us, our customers aren't loyal to us, our product is flawed if not absolutely misrepresented, and our CEO is a paranoid." He was right.

"You're wrong," I told him. "We're just meeting up with resistance. Like Bill Gates did against IBM, and Sega did against Nintendo. We'll replace them soon enough. That's what they're scared of, and they're using whatever they have against us."

"But what do we have to use against them? Teen spirit? Come on, Zach, we're shooting blanks."

"The Nine Goals work, Parrot," I said, practically pulling rank.

"And how many have we broken already? How have we deprogrammed the social set? By having an orgy? Is Duncan reframing his mundane attachments by screwing Margot behind Lauren's back? Does a tattoo of a baby constitute rebirth as pure consciousness? It's all symbolic and it's all empty. There's no product. No service."

"What if it's an idea we're selling, Parrot?" I tried a tactical retreat. "What if the only product is the idea that people can be happy by thinking about things differently?"

"Are we happy, Zach?" He took a long pause. "Do you like living in a big concrete room and hosting parties that get busted? Do you like that someone gave himself brain damage doing drugs while frying his nervous system with a computer? Do you like knowing that the biggest, baddest thought-control organizations in the world—organizations like Cosmotology—might actually know who you are?"

"Is that what's really bothering you?" I asked. The last technique I knew was to help Parrot see that his fears were projections of some inner doubt. I wanted to tell him to run away now while he still could—but I held it in.

"I have an economics degree, Zach. I could be making serious money by now. I don't need to get arrested or blacklisted or Lord knows what."

"I thought you were an atheist," I jabbed playfully. He cracked the tiniest smile. "Everything has an opportunity cost. Don't fall into that trap. Where's the Parrot I met that first day? You were invincible. Don't let this shit freak you out. Those *Plugged* guys are lame, you know that. And you handle Laruso like he was your pet dog. We've got the edge, Parrot. We understand the market better than anyone. This demographic belongs to us. We get thousands of kids coming to our parties. These old assholes are the ones who need *us*."

"You're right, Zach," he finally said, eating a bit more heartily. "I can always go and start a business after this. Infamy is the best publicity, anyway."

"Sure," I pumped him. "Even if this whole thing fails, which it won't, you'll be remembered as the guy who stood up to the establishment and worked their vulnerabilities to your advantage. Shit, guys like Laruso shiver when you walk into their office. The PF is just the first mission, Parrot. By the time this thing is franchised, we'll own the nation."

Perhaps I went a bit too far. When we got to Laruso's office, Parrot was back to his overconfident, libertarian self, and utterly unprepared for what was about to happen.

We were expecting the customary wait on the big couch, but before we had time to sit down Laruso's secretary told us to let ourselves into his office. We went in and then, out of nowhere, Laruso came in behind us and closed the door.

"You brought your junior businessman along this time, eh?" Laruso said. He was wearing a gray sweatsuit with the San Francisco Police Department logo on his chest. He looked a little overweight, but dangerously strong.

"Glad to see you again, too," Parrot said, unfazed. He held out his white hand but Laruso ignored it.

"I'm so sorry about that confusion the other night," Laruso said, much too emphatically. He was almost maniacally sarcastic, but Parrot took it at face value.

"These things happen," Parrot said. "I hope we can communicate better in the future."

"Me too," Laruso said, staring into Parrot's red spectacles. "Me too."

"The important thing is for us to keep the PBA well supported," Parrot said. "I hope the contributions we've been making have been of some help in that regard."

Laruso looked at me inquisitively for a moment, as if he were giving me a chance to distance myself from Parrot before he shot him.

"You know?" Laruso practically shouted with glee. "I'd like you boys to see for yourselves. Just so you feel *really good* about all this."

"Thanks," I said, "but you don't have to—"

"It's no trouble at all!" Laruso assured me, slapping one of his huge fat hands on each of our shoulders. He could have crushed our clavicles if he had wanted to. "Ms. Hansen," he said, taking a pair of what looked like infrared binoculars off a hook and opening the door, "I'm taking the boys down to the box."

The box? What was this, *Homicide?* Was he taking us to the little room where the cops badger suspects into confessing?

"I get worried when people misunderstand the police," Laruso lectured us with inflated sincerity as he walked us down a long metal stairwell. Parrot's worried glance told me that he was finally catching on to the fact that Laruso's amiability was less than genuine.

"We really didn't mean any harm," Parrot cowered.

"Harm? Why would I think you meant any harm? You don't mean me any harm, do you, Levi?"

"Of course not, Officer," I said.

"No, no," he laughed. "I know that. You're just learning how to play the game, right?"

"Sure," I laughed with him.

"And I'm trying to teach you to play it well, that's all."

He took us through a winding series of dark corridors.

"You see," he told us, "the PBA Youth Athletic League is in dire financial straits. Everyone pledges huge amounts of money, we hire contractors to build facilities, and then the pledges dematerialize."

"That's awful," Parrot said. "They're probably taking the deductions on their taxes, you know."

"Why, thank you!" Laruso said. "I should check into that."

He opened a metal door at the end of a corridor and motioned for us to go into a completely darkened room.

"Right in there, boys." I wasn't sure whether to be relieved or panicked that he followed us in before sealing the door. "This is how your money's being used."

"What is it?" I asked, my voice cracking.

"It's a racquetball court, Levi. Haven't you ever seen one before?"

"Sure, but it's kind of dark."

"Yes, it is, isn't it? That's why I need these infrared specs in here. We had enough money to build the court, but we still need two thousand dollars for the lighting system."

"That's all?" Parrot's scared voice penetrated the darkness. "We could generate that in a single good party."

Laruso didn't say anything. I was thinking he might have left us alone in there to die when I heard the sound of a ball hitting a wall. *Thwack!* Hard. I couldn't tell where it was coming from.

"Racquetball's a great game," Laruso's voice boomed from a good distance. He hit the ball again. *Thwack!* Then it ricocheted on the wall behind me. *Btack!* "But it sure is hard to play it in the dark." *Thwack!* "You just can't tell what you're hitting." *Btack!* That was close. I felt the wind of the ball against my cheek and instinctively ducked.

"Oh, now, don't you move, Levi. You wouldn't want to get hurt now, would you? I can't see a thing in here, remember?" Then how did he know I moved, I wondered. *Thwack! Btack!* That one was a bit farther away. Closer to Parrot, probably.

"What makes racquetball such a good game for kids is that the rules are so clear." *Thwack!* "Inbounds, out-of-bounds, serves, and returns." *Btack!* That one was meant for me. "Business, people, zoning laws, dates, and times. They're trickier." *Btack! Btack!*

"We really could pledge a fund for the lights—," Parrot whined.

"Now I made a rule, remember?" Laruso said. *Thwack! POOF!* The ball hit me square in the abdomen, knocking the wind out of me. I doubled over. "Oops!" he apologized, "just toss it back!"

I scrounged for it on the floor and rolled it gently toward Laruso's voice.

"My rule was that you were not to have a party on Saturday night. Remember? But you boys found a way around that rule." *Thwack!* "You waited until 12:01 the next morning. That was smart. College smart." *Thwack! Btack!*

"But we—" Parrot tried to interrupt but was silenced by another *thwack!*

"Now I just want to show you I can play, too. I'll just make another rule for you. You're going to be shut down for four weeks. You're not allowed to make a move without speaking to me first, is that clear?" *Btack!* "If there's as much as a peep out of you boys. One flyer. One secret event." *Thwack!* "I'll come in there and shut you down for good."

Btack! Thwack! Btack! Thwack!

"People like rules, boys," he said. "They like to be led. Told what to do. Rules make people feel safe."

Btack!

"Don't break them. Don't bend them. I'll bend them right back."

Thwack!

Then silence.

"Do you boys understand me?" He was moving closer now. I was scared to say anything. We stood there, petrified, as Laruso slowly bounced the ball. He was getting closer. Closer. His breathing sounded like a giant reptile's.

Then I heard something else. A crackling sound—no, dripping. And then the smell.

Parrot had pissed down his own leg.

"We're going to need some money to paint the floor, too," Laruso said, finally opening the door. "I'll be in touch."

He escorted us down the hall to a fire door and let us out into the daylight, firmly patting my shoulder one more time.

25.

Laruso's concrete threats to our physical well-being earned us little sympathy at home. Parrot and I had been the victims of a pedestrian, grassy knoll–size conspiracy at best. The horror of getting attacked with a rubber ball just didn't translate effectively to people who believed there was a cosmic force working consciously against them.

The immediate problem after fixing Duncan's pyramid, of course, was Pig and the computers. Both our network and its chief operator appeared to be infected with some sort of virus. The computers kept switching off as if a screensaver had been activated, then throwing weird hexagonal patterns onto the monitors. Every time it happened, we would lose any unsaved changes on the machine affected and have to reboot the entire network. It started with just the Sun workstation in Pig's loft but spread by the afternoon to every PC on the network, even the ones that weren't being used. By nightfall, the network was crashing every fifteen minutes. None of the virus-checking software could detect a problem, but there was definitely something very wrong, and it originated on the visionquest machine.

Pig's ailment was a little trickier to diagnose. I first noticed it when he was trying to explain the phantom computer virus to us that night.

"I've isolated the origin of the virus to this computer," he told Duncan, Lauren, and me as we sat on the floor listening attentively. "It either came through the modem when I was in the visionquest or was generated from our vacuum tube, the EE 136 PZ."

That's when it happened. As soon as he finished saying the serial number his face went blank.

"Pig?" Lauren took his arm. "Pig, are you all right?"

He stared into space, then twitched for a moment.

"Al-set," he mumbled. Then he was back with us. He looked around, panicked and confused. "What are you all doing here?"

This bizarre sequence kept repeating, and Pig was getting more frustrated and frightened each time it did. We sat up with him all night up in Duncan's pyramid, taking notes and trying to determine if there was a pattern to his blackouts. Several keywords always activated this weird loop in Pig's brain. It happened whenever he said "Ecstasy Club," "Tyrone," or "Duncan." Peter struggled to find some mathematical, etymological, or phonetic commonality among these phrases, but couldn't. It happened at other times, too, but by isolating these four triggers we were able to get information from him about what was going on without setting him off too frequently.

By morning, his twitch had become chronic—like the twitch people got from that batch of bad ecstasy in Texas, where they squinched their foreheads and blinked a lot.

Duncan had gone to bed hours earlier, but Lauren and I stayed up trying to comfort Pig as he pleaded for help.

"I haven't slept since this happened!" he cried. "You have to find out what's wrong with me! I might never sleep again."

"We'll get you better," Lauren said. "I promise."

"Don't you understand? I've been infected with a virus. It's a mutating computer virus that's managed to lodge itself in my biological circuitry."

"That can't happen, Pig," I assured him. "It's probably just a side effect of the electric shock."

"No, it's a virus. It's erasing whole sectors. In a few days my brain will be completely reformatted!"

Duncan finally rolled awake, saw that Pig was still in the room, and sat up.

"Don't worry, Pig," he said smiling. "Let me touch you a moment."

Pig sat in front of Duncan expectantly.

Duncan just touched him on the shoulder and said, "Don't worry. I can see what's happening to you. I can see it's only temporary." He stared into Pig's eyes. "You'll drink some water, and then you'll start to feel better."

"Really?" Pig twitched.

"Really."

Pig left the room to find a glass of water and enact his programmed cure.

Later that morning, though, as we sat on my bed talking and eating some oatmeal Lauren had made for us, Duncan confided in me that he thought Pig was in grave danger.

"We've got to isolate the memetic structure of the thought virus surging through Pig's nervous system," he told me, "before it infects the rest of us."

"If we just stay out of the visionquest machine we should be okay," I said, just as selfishly self-protective as he. Hell, Duncan was the one who had tried that thing, not me. "By the way, have you thought about what *al-set* might mean? Remember how you said it when you came out?" I think I was being a little cruel.

"No, Zach," he said as if he hadn't a care in the world. "Why don't you work on it with Peter?" Peter had already made an appointment with Marcus Sturgeon, one of our old teachers at JFK who had been involved in mind-control and radar-evasion experiments (time travel, Philadelphia Experiment stuff) at the Department of Defense in the fifties and sixties. He was a casualty of the thought wars, but we hoped he might be able to shed some light on what was going on. With this suggestion, Duncan patted my knee with affectionate condescension and headed back up to his room to meditate.

I was about to go downstairs to find Peter when I heard Duncan and Lauren yelling at each other up in the pyramid.

"Don't adopt that bloody attitude with me, Lauren," I heard Duncan say.

Then Lauren started to cry, shouting something like "You're evil!"

"Just because you fantasize about fucking Zach, you need to see me as evil?" So Duncan really didn't know about what happened. "Go ahead and fuck him if you like! You think I care? It'll last six weeks, then he'll find out what kind of girl you really are and run scared." Did he really know something horrible about her or was he just being mean?

"I hate you!" Lauren yelled at him. I heard a loud slam. Did he hit her? Then something fell to the floor. I was worried she was hurt. I was about to run up the ramp to Duncan's pyramid when Lauren came running into my room and flopped down on the bed, crying.

"He's such a fuck sometimes," she said.

"Yeah. I heard."

"All of it?" she asked.

"Enough." I would have liked to have heard more, actually. "Did he hit you?"

Lauren didn't say anything. I got paranoid for a second that this was a film noir setup. She'd tell me he beat her and then ask me to help her kill him. Maybe I just wanted an excuse to do so.

"Stay here with me, okay?" she asked. She rolled over onto her back and looked up at me.

I sat next to her and wiped away her tears with my hand. How could I have suspected her, even for a second, of some plot? The PF's paranoid atmosphere was getting the better of me. I lifted the locks of hair that were pasted to her temples by drying tears. She wiped her little nose and sighed.

"What's Duncan doing?" I asked, keeping myself from falling into the spell. The sheer perfection of the moment.

"He's doing his vision thing," she said. "Don't worry."

That was enough for me. I was all over her.

When Duncan walked in we still had most of our clothes on, but it was obvious what was going on. I didn't change my position for quite a while. I wasn't going to hide anything anymore.

None of us spoke. We just stayed there, frozen for a minute, Duncan taking in the scene. I'm not sure if he was trying to think of something profound or guilt-provoking to say, or if he was waiting for us to start begging for his forgiveness. It was a standoff. Then Duncan just turned and continued down the stairs.

We both remained motionless for a moment. I kissed her and ran my hand back up her leg but she stopped me.

"I've got to talk to him," she said, picking up some clothing from the floor.

"It's okay," I told her, taking her by the shoulders and trying to kiss her again. "He knows, and it's okay. Let him say something if it's not."

"I've got to talk to him," she said again.

My lizard brain didn't understand the interruption. She wanted me, I wanted her, and nothing else should have mattered.

26.

Over the next few days we made basic repairs to the building and talked about how we were going to spend our four-week embargo. Duncan wanted us to use the time to get a better handle on the forces working against us and come up with an overall plan of attack. This meant that intense psychedelic sessions were in order. Duncan had scored a huge load of DMT (a superstrong psychedelic) from a Hawaiian psychopharmacologist but thought we should work on creating physical and psychic security before we embarked on the all-important group trip. All this accepted, it was still hard not to see the video surveillance cameras as an invasion of privacy.

Maybe the sight of Lauren and me making out had pushed Duncan over an edge. Even in its best light, I'd have to agree that our affair was, as Duncan put it, "a peripheral distraction" from the effort to achieve a one-pointed focus at the Ecstasy Club. He never explicitly told us to stop loving each other—only that what we were feeling wasn't real. We were caught in "the game" and violating the Third, Fifth, and Sixth Goals. Our attraction was just an attack and contaminated the entire field with physical-plane, mundane, frictional concerns. We should remain focused on our higher purpose: cultural and species evolution in the face of tremendously antagonistic forces. We were the last holdouts in a world that was resisting novelty and aching toward apocalypse. As renegades, we were in constant danger, both from human opposition and from our own, internal demons.

This is why, Duncan said, he had decided that we should all do DMT together as a group. None of us had tried the substance Samuel Clearwater called "the hell-ride of the psychedelic family" except for Henry, and his account of the gremlins he met during his five-minute trip, who viciously taunted him to prove he had any identity at all, was small comfort.

Twisting the rules of set and setting to an all-time low, Duncan insisted that we needed to establish a sense of safety at the expense of everything else. He spent our last several thousand bucks on equipment, and got Pig to rig up video cameras inside and outside the building, with four monitors in the kitchen that switched automatically among the various camera angles. The idea of putting the monitors in the kitchen instead of Duncan's room was mine. One-pointedness is one thing; Command Central up in the pyramid felt Gestapo. Duncan accepted my logic that the Ecstasy Club would be less likely to object to a more democratic application of surveillance technology.

Parrot complained that we were using media as Big Brother would, but (thanks to my modifications to his master plan) Duncan was free to explain that we weren't being monitored by a separate governing body—we were simply monitoring ourselves and our own activities. If the Ecstasy Club was one organism, Duncan improvised, then all the cameras and monitors simply served as a multifaceted mirror. Remembering what it was like to jerk off as much as Parrot did, though, I understood his concern.

Nomie took it completely differently. She loved the idea and used it as an excuse to move into the herbal lounge full-time and make an art project out of the whole thing. Whenever she was in her room, she made sure she was naked. Adam and Andy frequently took the camera off its rigging and improvised handheld sex videos. Nomie danced erotically in front of her camera constantly, and I caught Parrot sitting in the kitchen in the dark with his hands in his lap under the table on more than one occasion.

Despite his lapses in memory and constant twitching, Pig also managed to install electronic locks on the main doors. By pushing in a secret code (there's no harm now in telling you it was 8181), members could gain access. Three wrong tries and an alarm went off. It's no big deal in a city like Oakland to have locks on your doors, but the sudden implementation of security measures felt less appropriately vigilant than it did Branch Davidian.

As we all assembled in our newly fortified bunker for the group DMT session, Duncan took Lauren and me aside to discuss what had occurred the afternoon before. We were in Nomie's room, and Duncan sat down on the edge of the small stage that now served as her sleeping den, while Lauren and I stood above him.

"I want you two to spend a lot of time together," he said. "You shouldn't let Lauren out of your sight, Zach." I suspected he had concocted some kind of aversion therapy. He was trying to accelerate the inevitable decline of our relationship. It was a challenge, but I was in love and took the bait.

"I'd be glad to," I said. "Thanks."

Lauren wasn't ready to let Duncan simply give her away like that. I don't know if it was because she still had feelings for him, or if she just didn't like being treated like a possession with a title that could be so easily transferred.

"So is our engagement off," she said, "or what?"

"No. Everything will proceed as we've arranged it." Duncan had it all worked out. "I'm not available to Lauren as human being anymore. I'm not a suitable companion. You can do that, Zach."

He was making me feel like a lower-order creature for being able to make Lauren happy. I was only capable of normal, human relationships. Duncan was pursuing supershamanism.

"Lauren and I have an open relationship," Duncan said. "We'll all be the best of friends." In some weird permutation of the Oedipal triangle, I would be child to Lauren and Duncan's mom and dad, but in my case, the fact that I was sleeping with mom only attested to my compromised spiritual prowess. *Paint it however you like. I'm the one who got her, right?* But we never said such things at the PF.

Lauren rose and went over to where everyone else was sitting. Duncan took a final moment to shake what I'm sure he saw as my victory stance.

"Still, Zach," he warned, "be aware that your attraction to Lauren could be something else entirely."

He left me standing there worrying as he went to sit with the others in a big circle on the floor. Those weren't the nicest words to leave me with immediately before I embarked on a psychedelic trip. I found a place between Brooks and Parrot and watched as

Henry fumbled with a brown paper bag and removed a plain glass crack pipe he'd bought on Market Street. As our most experienced junkie, Henry was entrusted with preparing and dividing the doses, and he made the occasion as dignified as a Japanese tea ceremony.

He carefully divided the pale orange powder into about a dozen identical lines. Then he deftly used his razor blade to scoop up one of the lines and deposit it onto a fine screen within the bowl of the clear glass pipe, before handing it off to Nomie.

"Now be sure to smoke all of it, Nomie," he said as he pulled his long hair back into a ponytail and picked up a tiny, butane-powered blowtorch lighter. "Don't be afraid of the taste. It's meant to be like that."

Nomie held the pipe to her lips as Henry gently heated the powder from the bottom of the bowl. He told us that fire can't be directly applied to DMT because it ruins the chemical. Within a few seconds, though, the heat from the torch coaxed the orange powder to sizzle and then smoke.

"Breathe it in now, Nomie!" Henry said, concerned about wasting any drug. As she drew in, the stream of smoke rising out of the pipe pulled itself back down, like a movie going in reverse. "Exhale and again!"

Nomie rolled her eyes as if this were a silly exercise class, but complied with Henry's instructions. She inhaled a second time, then coughed it out, making an awful face.

"Yuck!" she said, half-gagging at the taste.

"Again, Nomie!" Henry insisted. Nomie began to inhale once more, but then stopped suddenly. Her eyes rolled back a bit into her head, her mouth opened, and she hunched over into a stupor.

"Right, then," Henry said, filling the bowl again and turning to a nervous Parrot.

He inhaled his full dose and looked completely unchanged—just waiting for something to happen. Then he raised his arm and said, "Worse than that." He kept doing this, every ten seconds or so, but he didn't look like he was too uncomfortable. Nomie just wriggled around with her eyes wide open but not seeing anything. Adam or Andy sat behind her to make sure she didn't injure herself.

"Come on, mate, you can't stay up in the stalls," Henry prodded me, holding the readied pipe in my face. I couldn't help but wipe Parrot's spit off the end of the stem. Lauren laughed at me, which felt good. I was neurotic, but at least it was real-life neurosis.

The stuff tasted like plastic. I had to force myself to take the second hit—I didn't want to get only halfway up and then feel stuck in some kind of limbo with evil elves telling me I didn't exist.

"That's good, Zach," Henry said. "Smooth in, hold it, and smooth out. A regular pro."

I appreciated his encouragement. On this level, Laruso was right. I liked being led.

I saw Henry's face coming awfully close to mine. He was smiling and taking the pipe from me. I couldn't say anything to him. I just saw the fetus on his forehead. It slowly turned into a yin-yang and then into an @-sign. That's when everything else disappeared and my entire range of vision was occupied by an @-sign/fetus mandala.

The @-sign! Of course! The fetus, the Internet address, the DNA strand viewed from above. It was the cosmic spiral. The journey of the soul through time and space. We alter the DNA frequency by taking a drug, travel through the artificially constructed DNA networks online, or just do it the old-fashioned way and mix genes to make a baby.

Then I saw them. And they weren't elves. I was in the middle of a story, but it wasn't like one of those dreams where you're onstage and don't know what's going on. I had been on this world for a whole lifetime.

I had materialized in the suburbs, on a well-manicured lawn. I knew that the story had something to do with those men in the white cars. There were two cars and at least six guys, wearing black suits and sunglasses. Vintage conspiracy theory. I laughed, until I remembered that this was for real and saw that they had lizard heads and foamed at the mouth—and that they were coming to get me.

Just then, an @-sign on the sun began to revolve, spinning out flaming debris that fell all around me and seemed to impede the lizards' pursuit. I laughed. This meant I wouldn't have to pulverize them with the ray gun I had so cleverly hidden beneath my lapel. It would be a long night. A long night, indeed, and I might as well keep a few tricks up my sleeve for them, too.

This was intense. Life or death. Then I realized once again that the whole thing was just a game. They could have killed me if they had really wanted to. They should have, if they had any sense. But they didn't because they like me. I'm what they live for. Where would Dr. No and the Joker be without James Bond and Batman? It's as much making love as it is a battle. I saw the timeline of history unfold as a ritualized, erotic power war. Tiny icons representing the Masons, the Crusaders, Malthus, the Media Center, and Cosmotology scrolled by from left to right, as if chiseled on an Egyptian frieze.

But the marching troops didn't look truly hostile. They were just parts of the collective human being, making love to itself the only way it knew how, over time. You just choose up sides—it doesn't matter which. The good guys and the bad guys are the girl and the boy. We like to think that we're the good girl, but they probably think they're the good girl, too.

When we get together, who really is the naughty rapist? The cop conspiracy chiefs with their guns and money and attaché cases? Mr. Macho Gordon Liddy pushing our VW off the road so that Oliver North can lead the troops to victory? Or is it us? The Jimmy Dean Electric Kool-Aid Nigger junkie freaks from whom any thought or deed can emerge without a moment's notice? Or are the Christians right and it's really the girl who's the evil one in all this?

I realized they were all in on it, and it felt good. The world was just a bunch of freaks trying to get laid. And the @-sign was what connected us all. Our DNA. Our fetuses. Our addresses on the Net. Was it really zachlevi@authority.com, or authority.com@zachlevi? Whose domain were we in, and does the @-sign care? Of course not. It's just the yin-yang, providing an interface for us to meet. Pure revolution. It's not an aggressive upheaval, it's just a circle. That's what makes life go. The eternal revolution. It's all circular once you break the illusion of linear time.

I was already coming out of it when I had my moment with Duncan. He must have dosed just minutes after I did. Everyone in the room was deep in the trance. Duncan and I just looked at each other and knew what the other was thinking. These weren't thoughts, exactly, but conclusions. We understood together what this war was about. The war between the two of us, and the war between the Ecstasy Club and the people behind the Cosmotology tube. We were playing a game. *Thwack!* It was all just a game. We both knew that we wouldn't be able to hold onto this perception once the DMT wore off—that we'd return to the realistically depicted, time-based, dualistic fiction called life and, with full knowledge of its status as theater, still engage in it as if the stakes were real.

That's when Duncan made the secret gesture. It was just a little hand signal. Three fingers crossed over the thumb, the pinkie separate and pointing straight ahead. He signed it twice. I did it back to him. A secret Masonesque ritual. But it marked the moment. It proved we had been there together. It validated our bond. I knew at once that this signal, done anywhere, at any time, by anyone, would demand immediate attention. It would forever signify the place beyond our mundane illusion of conflict. Only a person who had seen exactly what we had just seen would ever be shown it— because only those of us who had seen this deep truth could possibly be entitled to refer to it.

As I came down even further I began to question the whole thing. Had Duncan really seen what I was seeing, or had he just exploited my vulnerable rapture to program me with a signal? He knew I was in a profound space. What better opportunity would he ever have of inserting himself into my psyche? That most sacred of spaces would always have something to do with him. He could call on it whenever he wanted. He had bound me to him in a way I would never be able to undo. We were blood brothers in the deepest sense.

Then Peter bolted up, gasping for breath.

"I've got it! I've got it!" he shouted.

Margot was by his side. "Peter, are you okay?"

"It's not al-set at all!" he cried euphorically. "It's *Tesla!*"

27.

We waited for everyone else to emerge from their trips before Peter explained what he had seen.

Margot came out shouting about another full-on alien encounter, but this time she said they just danced around and congratulated her for having remembered what happened to her, and for telling the rest of us their important message about saving the planet. They gave her a warning, though, that if she didn't keep spreading their words of environmental wisdom we'd all be in a lot of trouble.

The weirdest emergence was Henry's. He had been staring at Duncan throughout his trip. While Duncan was making his secret hand gesture to me, Henry experienced it as a gesture made directly to him. Then, just as Peter shouted "Tesla," Henry threw himself onto the floor, completely prostrate before Duncan like a Muslim facing Mecca.

"Take me with you," he pleaded from the floor, his hair flung all the way out in front of him.

Duncan looked down at Henry for a long while, smiling benevolently. I expected him to tell Henry that he should get up. He was being foolish. He was breaking the Seventh Goal: *no one more important than any other.* Instead, Duncan put his hands on the back of Henry's head as if he were a priest blessing him.

"I will be your doorway," he said.

I glanced over at Lauren. She was probably disgusted, but she was disciplined enough to keep a completely straight face. *What a trouper.* I wanted desperately to exchange eye rolls, but she was having none of it.

But when I looked back at Duncan, *he* was the one rolling his eyes! Just for a brief second, he deliberately rolled his eyes at me as if to say "what a joke!" He wasn't letting Henry in on it, that's for certain. He just held Henry's head tightly in his hands, saying, "I will be your doorway. Open me. Come through me."

Parrot was the last person to come to, and as he pulled himself up off the floor, he noticed Henry still bowing to Duncan. He looked confused for a moment, and then he started to laugh—not cruelly or patronizingly, just long and loud. He couldn't stop himself, and soon the rest of us were laughing too. Some of us were laughing at Henry, I suppose, while others of us were laughing in delight at the messianic proportion of our little clan. I couldn't tell who was being ironic and who wasn't. Duncan seemed to ride on a line between the two. To me, his expression said "wink-wink-nudge, I know this is just a game" but to others, especially Henry, I imagine Duncan was expressing some infinite transpersonal truth. The half-smile of the Buddha himself.

That was the whole point—but it was also the whole problem. If you were caught in the game and playing the stakes like they were for real, then Duncan appeared to be supernatural because he rose above the game. But if you were aware of the game and the closed little world in which it was played, then you saw yourself as a great pal of Duncan's. You shared in the secret knowledge and the arrogance of being superior to the others—but then you were breaking the Seventh Goal. It was a no-win situation.

Duncan listened intently as Peter finally explained what he had seen on DMT. He said he flashed back to the whole experience he had with his friend and martyred test pilot Steven at JFK.

"We were using a technique based on the Philadelphia Experiment," Peter said. "Professor Sturgeon outlined it for us but left the details hazy. They had been working on a radar-evasion technology for the navy so that ships could move around undetected. They used some intense radar beams to shift the whole resonant frequency of the ship—the resonance of its matter, Sturgeon said. They used a theoretical property of phase states and constructed a giant radar beacon and focused on the ship. They ended up moving it hundreds of miles away."

"They discovered a crude form of time travel, you mean," Duncan said. Either he understood Peter fully or he had simply seen the movie.

"Right," Peter continued, delighted at being understood. "By shifting the resonance of the ship, they accidentally moved the

USS *Philadelphia* forward in time. It disappeared from their radar screens for a few hours, then reappeared in another place. It completely left our dimension and then came back hundreds of miles away. The horrible part is that everyone on the ship died in transit. Except for one sailor, who they say went completely crazy."

"They're telling everyone that to keep the story quiet," Brooks added, engrossed.

"The whole project was scrapped and then the Korean and Vietnam wars came and got everybody busy doing other stuff. But later, in the seventies and eighties, out on some secret air force base, they started up the experiments again, using weather balloons and radar dishes to work out the same time-travel theories."

"What's that got to do with you and your friend Steven?" Lauren asked, gently steering Peter back toward something more relevant. She looked nauseated. I assumed this talk of interdimensional travel made her uneasy.

"Well," Peter continued, "they concluded that the reason the whole Philadelphia thing got screwed up was because there was no link for the sailors between the two time zones. Their consciousness couldn't tolerate the gaps. Their matter made it, but their minds didn't. Sturgeon says he was involved in developing an answer—creating a link between the two time zones using human psychics and amplifying what they theorized was a carrier wave between the two times. They built something like the visionquest circuit we made upstairs, but instead of amplifying the signal back to the user, they projected it toward other times."

"Did it work?" Parrot asked, still laughing from before. In his head he was already packing his bags.

"I don't know," Peter said dreamily. "Sturgeon never told us more than that. We got the story from him when he was stoned with us at our house, but later he denied the whole thing and said it was all just a joke. I believed him, though, and started working on a time line myself. My friend Steven was into telepathy, writing a dissertation proving the statistical legitimacy of ESP in guessing games. We started doing simple thought-projection exercises using the school's computer and a refitted radar dish."

"Is that how he died?" I ventured.

"He didn't really die, at first," Peter said, drifting into an eerie space. "Steven was far better at thought projection than I was. When I went out alone, I just saw weird sparkles and got high. When I went out with Steven, we were like ghosts wandering around in people's homes. These were either great, shared hallucinations or we had actually achieved remote viewing."

"This is amazing, Peter," Duncan said. "I've always seen a special quality in you." *What the fuck is that about,* I wondered. Why did he have to fold everything into himself?

"Well, it was more amazing than I realized," Peter said, condemning himself. "Steven was so much more of a daredevil than me. One time we had been out for a long while—twenty minutes or so. We were floating around at an old-age home, looking for someone to die so we could see them leave their body. Suddenly, another beam passed right through us. It was like a beam of light. I assumed it was an alien, or a spirit of some kind, traveling fast and leaving a wake. I resisted the beam but Steven pounced right on top of it. It's hard to describe. It's like choosing which wave to surf, except you just do it with your thoughts, you know? Like a lucid dream."

We were all quiet now. None of us had any reason to question Peter's experience. To us, it sounded like fact.

"I could see Steven looking back at me disappointed, then zipping through a long round corridor of starry stuff. At the other end was a big laboratory with lots of electrical equipment sparking and humming. This old guy with large eyes saw Steven approaching and smiled really big, then the corridor collapsed into itself and I woke up. Steven was in a coma. I waited with him for two days, then called the hospital. His parents wanted to bring me up on charges."

"But I thought he died," Brooks said.

"He did eventually," Peter answered. "I kept going back in to find him. The whole thing was my fault, in a way. I couldn't make any progress without Steven though. I just kept getting lost in the void. I wasn't getting any work done anymore, and Sturgeon told me to forgive myself and forget about it. Things like this happen;

he'd seen it before. But I felt too guilty. I took a bunch of LSD and went in alone for the last time. I was out of my mind, I admit, but I found him, or more likely he found me. He looked all fuzzy—the outlines of his body were undefined, but I could make out his face and his eyes and his smile. We communicated without words, but I know we were really communicating. He wanted to know why I had hung back. He thought I had left him for only a couple of seconds, but I told him it had been close to two months. He was surprised, but undisturbed. I tried to convince him that it was time to come back, but he thought I was crazy. Why go back, he asked me, when we could go anywhere? I told him he was in a coma back in a hospital in Palo Alto and that he could die if he didn't come back now, but he didn't care."

"So what happened?" Margot asked. She was entranced, as we all were.

"We said our good-byes, and then I saw him make his choice. He smiled at me and kind of lit up. He got really, really bright, his edges buzzing and glowing until he just expanded out and exploded. It was intense—like an exploding sun. Then I was back in the computer lab. I got a phone call that night from Steven's mom. He had died in his hospital bed."

A tear rolled down Lauren's cheek. Margot put her arm over Peter's shoulders. I kept my mind from lingering on how effectively Peter's story was seducing every girl in the room.

"In a sense," Duncan consoled strategically, "Steven found precisely what he was looking for."

"Did you ever see him again?" Adam or Andy asked. One of them was crying too.

"Just now," Peter said, "I did. I saw him during the DMT trip. I didn't see him, but I could feel him. Like a hand on my shoulder. More like a hand coming off my shoulder. It's as if he had been holding his hand on my shoulder all this time and just then took it off. I felt so glad he had been with me, but so sad that he was now finally going to leave me."

I remembered Steven from the halls of JFK. Pretty wild, but a good guy. Okay, I was starting to get moved by all this, too.

"But just before I stopped feeling him altogether," Peter added in a new, determined tone, "he told me, well, communicated or revealed to me two things. The first was a number: 188. It means something. It's like an index or an address. A reference point. An @-sign. And the other thing was about that man in the laboratory. It was from back in time, so everything was reversed. Al-set means Tesla. That's who we had seen back there. And he had seen us, too."

28.

I'm just going to stick to the facts from now on and let you judge for yourself whether there's anything to all this, or if that even matters. I know Peter wasn't lying, and that's enough for me. Whether it's just a fantastic myth he had experienced or stone-cold reality is less important than the way his story was pursued and played out by the rest of us. The thinking made it so.

We fooled around for a while with Steven's 188 number, making numerological analyses of every name we could think of. The Ecstasy Club didn't fit, but the galaxy that exploded, Corpus Exsasis—itself a tremendous and improbable congruity—fit perfectly. The values of the letters, C=3, O=15, R=18, and so on, added up to 188 exactly. So did Cosmotology chief E. T. Harman's name: Earl Tyrone Harman adds up to 188. Tyrone liked that a lot and claimed it meant he himself was connected in ways none of us could understand. The cop that busted us the first night—his badge was 881. Not 188 exactly, but a perfect reversal and obviously more than coincidence. On a whim, Peter added up the values of the letters and numbers in the vacuum tube we had ordered from the Arcata base, EE 136 PZ. 5 + 5 + 136 + 16 + 26 = 188. There was something going on.

In real life, or back in the game—depending on your point of view—Lauren had started sleeping in my room. We didn't tell anyone else in the club, yet, so they wouldn't get confused by what we were doing. I repositioned the camera so that it didn't show my bed. Nominally, Lauren and Duncan remained a unit and point of reference for everyone, and I could see why that was important right then. I was confident enough of my relationship with Lauren to let the plans for the marriage continue on course, too. That was just a legal formality and had nothing to do with us. A game within the game. I started fantasizing about Lauren and me leaving the PF and having a baby and a real life together somewhere normal.

Aside from my candy flip–enhanced perceptions on that fateful night, I had no reason to believe Lauren was pregnant until the morning she started throwing up. She thought she was sick from some hash brownies Nomie had made for us all the night before, but I suspected differently. Believe it or not, I hoped differently. A pregnancy was about the last thing any of us needed right then. We were trying, in theory, to detach from the mundane reality, not get further encumbered by it. What more mundane material-world concern could possibly strike than a fetus? Something real growing inside you.

Lauren finally finished puking and plopped down on my bed. She was green. I put a washcloth on her head, and felt my own stomach turning over in sympathy. I was sitting on the edge of the bed next to her holding her hand and suggesting she go to a doctor when Duncan came down from the pyramid.

"I need your help," he said. He looked scared.

"Lauren's pretty sick," I told him.

"Yes. But she'll be fine," he said, anxious to return to his own crisis.

Lauren sat up as best she could to listen to Duncan's problem, hopefully solve it, and go throw up some more.

"What is it, George?" she asked. I hadn't heard anyone use his first name in a long time.

"I'm hearing things," Duncan whispered. "I can't sleep through the voices. There are too many people looking at me. Depending on me." I hadn't seen him act this vulnerable in a while. I was suspicious of being drawn into something and didn't offer any consolation. Lauren motioned for Duncan to sit down next to her on the bed. My bed. It was a strange moment: my girlfriend comforting her fiancé on my bed while I stood by and watched.

"You don't have to feel responsible, George," she told him, taking his hand.

"I'm not some awakened being," he pleaded. "I'm just like you."

"We know that, honey," Lauren soothed him with her voice. I couldn't help but try to make some headway.

"If you don't want to feel like a guru," I said, "then you have to stop acting like one."

"You don't understand," Duncan said.

"I do, Duncan," I pushed. I was on firm ground. "That business with Henry. Why did you tell him you were the fucking doorway?"

"I didn't tell him that—it's the way he saw me," Duncan whined like a little boy. "He wants a way through. A point of focus. He could have picked anything—even a tree. But he picked me. It wasn't an act of ego for me to accept his devotion. It would have been an act of ego to reject it."

"But you told him 'I'll be your doorway.'"

"Yes. I will be his doorway if that's what he wants. I have to. I have to be all things to all people. Let them play out their games as long as they need to."

"You're going to make yourself crazy, George," Lauren said. "Stop doing this to yourself. We can still throw great parties. You can still lead everyone through to whatever it is we're looking for."

"Duncan," I tried, "being all things to all people is a messianic trip. If you want to go that way you're going to have to bear some discomfort." I tried to lighten things up a little. "Didn't you see *The Last Temptation?* Willem Dafoe kept freaking out and Harvey Keitel kept having to hold him together."

He started to cry. It didn't look real. There weren't any tears at first, and when he finally mustered one he showed it to us way too dramatically.

"Please don't lose faith in me," he pleaded. "I need you both. I know this is hard, and I'm looking very strange to you, but you can't lose faith in me. In what I'm doing."

He was right. I had lost a great deal of faith in what he was doing. I felt sorry for him now. But something in his weakness, however artificially wrought, moved me enough to let him know I would be there for him. I was the Levite after all. I raised my right hand in the secret gesture—as if to tell him that his pain, his act, and his very solicitation to us were all part of the game. We were linked on a level beyond all that.

He kissed Lauren.

"I miss you terribly," he said. "I don't know if I can live without you." He looked down to his feet and bit his bottom lip like he was going to cry again. "But I know you need a man who can love you in a way that I no longer can." *Damn him.* He was trying to win her back.

I pulled my trump card: real life. "Look, Duncan, we think Lauren might be pregnant. We've got to get to the doctor to find out." That shut him up.

He watched us as Lauren got dressed and I packed a little knapsack to take with us. We moved with the slow, methodical motions of people leaving for a funeral or an operation. But it was also such a dear moment. Quiet, caring, genuine. If it was true, I thought, if Lauren was pregnant, it meant there was a ticking bomb inside her. A real, incontestably linear event. Something with undeniable repercussions. Here we were, dealing with authentic, organic fallout. I was in my element, and I knew it.

"I'm so jealous of you right now," Duncan admitted to me. "You're taking her to the doctor. Caring for her." He started to weep again in that same melodramatic way. Lauren put her hand on Duncan's head.

"Do you want to come, too?" she asked.

"No," he said. "It's better for you two to go. It's only that sometimes this is so hard for me. You need to know that."

"Just take it easy, okay?" she said. "I love you very much, George."

"There's not a baby in your future," he said to both of us. "I can see that. You won't be having a baby, but you'll be happy about that. It will be okay."

I escorted my girlfriend out of the room.

What did Duncan mean by that? I wondered, as we drove to the clinic. Was it his honest premonition of how the pregnancy test would come out? Or was he trying to program our reaction to the pregnancy if it happened? He did use that Eriksonian future tense.

Though Lauren wasn't an active student anymore, her health care at Berkeley was still carried over from last semester. We rode in sober silence, but I have to admit I felt wonderful to be with her, taking care of something so tangible. It was the first time we had been alone together outside the PF since our coffees in the rain. It was so good to be doing something real. Something with traction, consequences, lab results. People, doorways, cash, insurance forms. They were all footholds. The pleasure of the steering wheel and the traffic lights. Order, cooperation, conflict, dented fenders. It was paradise.

Lauren threw up again in the parking lot as soon as I stopped the car. Once I got her inside, the rest was a formality. They asked her some questions, took some blood, and told us to sit in the waiting room. All around us were students. They looked so young in their Berkeley sweatshirts, holding ice packs on lacrosse injuries and reading from Calculus 2 textbooks as they waited. Their lives were so normal. So innocent compared to ours. I reminded myself that they were the ones trapped in the workaday fiction, but the more I watched them, the more I wanted to be one of them again. An Asian girl spoke in an Asian language to her friend. I imagined how hard she must have worked to get to the United States and attend college.

The nurse called for Lauren and asked her if she wanted me to go along with her to hear the results. Lauren said I could come if I wanted to, but I got the feeling that she would rather have gone in alone. I went with her, anyway, determined to prove my steadfastness.

She took the news without emotion. She just nodded as the hook-nosed doctor sitting safely behind his huge metal desk said the test registered positive and that she should either enroll in prenatal care or consider her options. He gave her a few pamphlets that she put in the knapsack, and then we left.

"You want to get something to eat?" I asked, hoping to extend our shore leave.

"I feel pretty sick," she said, getting into my car. "I'd rather just get home."

Home. For a brief moment I thought she was talking about Ohio. Back to her parents, a real house, and a real town. She meant the PF. Our concrete barracks and time-travel station.

"Sure," I said, starting the car and gently pulling out so as not to jostle her. I was holding back a smile. I was mortified by the confirmation of Lauren's pregnancy, but unexplainably giddy about it, too. It was my baby in there. I knew it.

Lauren cried softly as I drove her back to the PF. Each tear held light, I swear it. They glistened like little stars as they rolled down her face. Her crying made me realize the magnitude of what was happening. How could we ever hope to have a baby at the PF? We weren't hippies. I wasn't going to raise a child with all those drugs around. And how would she still get married to Duncan? How would we ever push through those Nine Goals with something as grounded, socially fixed, and mundane as a baby? I assumed she was crying because she had decided to have an abortion. It was the only way out.

I pulled up behind the PF and put on the parking brake. Lauren fixed her face with some colorful cosmetics and zipped up her shiny plastic purse.

"So what do you think I should do?" she asked me.

Marry me. Let's run away and have our baby. I'll get a job and take care of you.

"It's your decision," came out of me. "I'll be here to support you in any way you want."

She looked away, disappointed. Did she want me to tell her to keep it?

"I love you, Lauren," I said. "You know that, don't you?"

"I do, my sweetheart," she said. "I'm just so scared of hurting you. Of disappointing you."

Disappointing me? Impossible.

"It's mine, isn't it? From that night?" I asked her.

"Would it matter?"

"No. Not really, I guess." Of course it would matter. "I just wanted to know. I'm just—"

"It's yours, Zach. Yours and mine."

I walked up to the side door, punched in the security code—8181 (hmm . . .)—and let Lauren in. She went straight upstairs and I would have followed her if Alex Barnow hadn't been sitting at the kitchen table. He was wearing one of our "Phylogenic Foresight" jerseys and had a big duffel bag next to him.

"Hey, Zach!" he said, taking my hand. "I'm here!"

He had run away from home and wanted to join the Ecstasy Club.

29.

So now I had two kids—one in the oven and one in the kitchen.

I should have been happy about Alex. He was a believer. He was the intended product of everything we were doing. I should have been delighted by his exuberance.

"This isn't fun," I warned him.

"I know it's work." He would have pulled out his résumé if he had one.

"You have to graduate high school. You have to go to college."

"I've deprogrammed that social set, Zach. Just by coming here."

"It's not as easy as that. You don't even have a social set yet."

"How can you say that? You know my dad, my family. And you have no right, Zach. You can't judge me. No one more important than any other, remember?"

I had created a monster.

"It's not just that, Alex. It's dangerous, too." I thought fear might work. "One person almost died already. Physical death, Alex. Now he's got some kind of brain damage from the computer. Another guy shoots up. I don't think this is a good place for you."

"It's the only place for me, Zach. You know I'm right."

"Alex, honestly, it sucks here in many, many ways—" I cut myself off when I saw Duncan coming up the stairs. My words were traitorous. Blasphemy. I'm sure he read it in my face.

"Who's your friend, Zach?" he asked me in typical double entendre, putting his hand on Alex's shoulder.

"His name is Alex. He was one of my SAT students." I thought the association with my tutoring life would turn Duncan off.

"Well, he doesn't look like an SAT student now."

Alex beamed and pumped up his chest to display the PF jersey.

"I wanted to join, but Zach was saying how—"

"How it's harder than it looks to be a live-in, full-time member," I interrupted.

"Oh, that's what you were telling him, Zach?"

"Yeah." I nodded for Alex to play along, but he didn't understand my situation.

"And he said how someone almost died here, but I'm not scared. Really. I can handle it."

I gave up on pretense.

"Look, Duncan, he's still in high school. You don't want to—"

"I'll be eighteen next month." Alex wasn't making this any easier. Neither was Duncan.

"Men have joined the army at younger ages." Duncan knew that the word *men* would win over Alex completely.

"So are you at least going to finish high school?" I asked.

"I can do it from here. I'm already accepted to college—if I choose to go someday. I just need to pass my finals. I can even count the Ecstasy Club as an independent study. And, you know my dad's a pharmacist."

With that, Alex was in. Our official Ecstasy Club trainee and prescription-drug source.

Suddenly, Tyrone fell from the sky and landed on his feet next to us. My heart jumped. I hadn't realized that the whole time we were speaking he had been sitting up on the refrigerator listening.

"Can you get me some more patches?" he asked, his bottom lip quivering. He was wearing a muscle T-shirt and had three patches on his arms.

"You might be overdosing on those, Tyrone," I offered.

"I'm quitting for Kirsten, too," he said, scratching his scalp compulsively.

"I can get you more," Alex said gleefully. "No problem. I've got a car and everything. I'll steal some from my dad tomorrow." Great. Enthusiasm, a car, drugs, and poor judgment. Alex was not going to make my job at the PF any easier.

"A car and a pharmacy, eh?" Duncan sounded like Vincent Price. "We must speak, Alex. We must speak."

"Cool! I'll be here. Where can I put my stuff?"

"Zach will attend to you. I've got to talk to Nomie about some business." He started out, then turned back for emphasis. "Thanks for bringing Alex here, Zach. It's a great exercise in commitment."

I gave Alex the mind gym. We weren't having any events for the time being, and it was a lot easier than building another room. I dropped him off in there, apologized for discouraging him, and said he should make himself at home. I was anxious to see what Duncan and Nomie were meeting about. With no parties on the horizon and thousands invested in security and cameras, we were desperate for money. I still had two thousand in a savings account and didn't want things to get so bad that people found out about it.

Duncan was going to hit up Nomie for some cash. Her parents were rich—filthy rich, actually—and although they kept Nomie on a monthly allowance, Duncan thought they might be willing to invest in a PF smart drugs pyramid-distribution scheme. By the time I found them up in Duncan's room, he had convinced her to get a few of us invited to brunch at her parents' estate in San Rafael. Parrot and I were to work on a business plan, and Duncan would casually spring it on her dad as a concrete professional opportunity for their otherwise flighty daughter.

Lauren's nausea spells passed that next night, and I launched a campaign for our personal happiness. I bought new linen and matching curtains for the railing. I bought her all sorts of bath oils and a complete set of prenatal vitamins, just in case she decided to keep the baby. I wanted to convince her how great we were together. She already knew that, though. She was committed to me, if not to our unborn child, and I figured I'd end up with her one way or another—even if as the third partner in an unconventional marriage.

Pig was getting noticeably worse. It turned out that most of the words that set him off had something to do with the number 188. But almost anything can be turned around to equal 188 or some multiple, and the more widespread our awareness of the 188 syndrome became, the more easily Pig would twitch, crash, and reset. He could hardly speak anymore.

The computers were down almost all the time. Then the security system, which was hooked up to the computers, started to act up, too. The code kept changing itself and setting off the alarm whenever one of us wanted to get in.

Margot said the aliens had come back several times and scolded her for not getting the message out better. Why hadn't we put out a press release or something? She was supposed to do a *Real World* reunion in a couple of days (the prodigal daughter returns) and was determined to do her alien buddies proud. I think she was scared that if she didn't, they would inflict another alien Pap smear on her.

Duncan took another big DMT trip by himself and saw that we were in a special period of time that would end on December 19—less than a month away. That would be the night of the cosmic showdown. It added up to 188, in a way. Even though December is month 12, the letters add up to 55. The year 1995, if you add it up as 19 and 95, equals 114. Then the nineteenth is 19. So 55 + 114 + 19 = 188. There was even a bump on Taggert McDoogal's Zero-Wave fractal based on the I Ching corresponding to that date. Extreme novelty. But it was a window that would close as quickly as it opened. Before it did, we had to determine who or what was working against us. If we didn't figure out by the nineteenth how to reverse what we or our adversaries had set into motion, we would never be able to do it.

That's when Duncan asked me to start writing this book. So we'd have a journal of what had happened—especially if it turned out to be something awful. He wanted me to be the official Ecstasy Club archivist. I remember tripping out on the word *archivist*. Did it come from ark of the covenant? Were the first archivists the Levites who carried the Torah through the desert? Had I traveled so far just to be right back where my ancestors started five thousand years ago? I decided I'd make the book a pure work—uncorrupted by all the personal problems I was going through. But clearly that isn't the way it turned out.

Meanwhile, Peter made an appointment for us to go see Marcus Sturgeon. Maybe he would appreciate everything we had endured and tell us something he had refused to tell Peter before. We even put in a call to Colonel Brock to see if he could tell us something more about the air force and Arcata, or whether the ketamine we "found" had something strange in it, but his assistants wouldn't let us talk to him. Brooks was sure there was some mean-ing in the fact that his name was so close to Brock's, and that he was the one who had stolen the chemical. Was it planted? We also e-mailed Taggert McDoogal in Hawaii for advice about how to ex-ploit the novelty curve of the I Ching, but he didn't send anything back. We were on our own. Uncharted turf.

The world seemed to be collapsing around Lauren and me, but there was something growing between us—in her, actually. The trick was not to let ourselves believe that we had caused the whole catastrophe. In one of his angry fits, Duncan suggested that Kirsten used "sex magic" on me and that I unknowingly contami-nated Lauren with the spell. It's true, my attraction to Kirsten was predominantly sexual, especially in contrast to what I had with Lauren. And her disappearance followed immediately after Lauren and I had consummated our relationship. But it was a stretch. Still, Arcata, the Dead, her play, her connection with Tyrone . . .

When I was in Lauren's arms, all this doubt and paranoia seemed to fade away. Maybe that's part of what made our attrac-tion so strong. The pressure of the maelstrom around us made us cling to each other. Duncan said we were clinging to all we had left of the game: the illusion of romantic love. It felt more like we were clinging to all we had left of real life. Duncan told her to make her appointment for an abortion soon. He called it "an exercise" she had to complete. All I knew was that the longer I could keep Lauren clinging to the so-called illusion, the longer our baby would be alive.

We had a lot less straight sex and a lot more holding and caress-ing. It was quite tantric, really. Sometimes I'd even be inside her, not moving. Whenever we had the chance and the privacy, we would just lie together like this for hours at a time, talking about the tiniest stuff—mundane, nostalgic "distractions." She told me about her three older sisters and how they'd throw plastic fruit at their dad and then run and hide in the closet. And the summer she went to a sleep-away camp and made out with a counselor, then came home with head lice. Or about her mom and dad, still together, and how they always sit together late at night and talk about their day.

We were deep into a moment like this when Duncan's voice came in over the loudspeaker.

"Zach, Parrot, and Brooks," it blared. "I need you."

The moment was torture. Here I was, physically inside Lauren, being called to task by her fiancé, my superior. A guy she loved but hated.

"You better go," she said.

"Look—"

"Just go, okay?" She was so hard to read.

We met Duncan up in the DJ booth. Without the turntables it looked pretty sad. Just a bunch of wires and two stools. Duncan had a copy of the new *Rolling Stone* with the article about Phylogenic Foresight. It was bad.

Duncan told us not to read it. He officially decreed the article off-limits. It would only serve to elicit an "attack." Just the desire to look at it indicated a need to hear bad things about Duncan, our work, and our beliefs. It wasn't that we were to be afraid of the piece—only disciplined enough to realize that the temptation to look at such negative views was a distraction straight from Mara (the Evil One). If we were strong, we would not read or ever talk about the article again.

Of course I read the piece. After about three thousand words on the magnificent Plasma event, they got around to the Ecstasy Club:

As if to prove *Plugged*'s place at the top of the cybersocial hierarchy, a cultlike group of psychedelic squatters calling themselves The Ecstasy Club staged a protest event at their run-down warehouse space in Oakland. Their leader and spokesman, British expatriate George Duncan, apparently holds Michael Mackey and his magazine responsible for everything from the Kennedy assassination to the nuclear fallout at Chernobyl.

"It goes beyond mere social engineering to downright thought control," Mr. Duncan contended, sipping on a cocktail he claimed enhanced his neural functioning. "If we seem paranoid, consider this: The International Business Society and Massachusetts Media Center share many of the same key personnel."

To be fair, Mr. Duncan's event did offer forms of entertainment that the *Plugged* gathering lacked: the thrill of watching a banished member of *The Real World* cast, hallucinating on psychedelics, pantomime her own abduction and dissection by environmentally responsible aliens.

The only pictures from the PF were two nearly identical photos of Margot sitting on the beanbag mound, before and after the abduction. The caption read: "Back from the Real World." I wasn't sure what they meant, but it stung.

Duncan was convinced that *Rolling Stone* was merely a pawn in the *Plugged* conspiracy. By painting us as their adversary (he admitted that the article went this far), they were actually declaring their war against us. Except they weren't doing it directly. They were afraid to face us head-on. (The problem with Duncan's logic, though, was that he was referring to *Rolling Stone* and *Plugged* as the same "they.")

Duncan's plan was for us to go to the offices of *Plugged* magazine and tell them we were onto them (whoever "them" was). They could either leave us alone or face the consequences.

Duncan wanted Parrot, Brooks, and me to go and make this declaration. He would stay behind.

"It will be a good exercise for you," Duncan explained. "And I can't go myself. It wouldn't look right. They need to see you can defend and attack on your own." I think he was so embarrassed by his treatment in the article that he was afraid to be seen in public for a while.

"Aren't you being indirect, though," I asked a bit too pointedly, "just like you're accusing them of being?"

"You're not afraid to go, are you, Zach?"

"Why don't we draw straws?" Alex suggested.

Duncan knew I wanted to protect the kid.

"That's a great idea, Alex," he said.

"No," I relented, "you were right to begin with. I'll go with Brooks and Parrot."

It was a pattern I never should have let get started.

So the three of us piled into my car and set off across the Bay Bridge for *Plugged*'s South of Market offices. I felt like such a fool—but Pig was sick, the computers were out of control, and Duncan was going crazy. It was worth a try.

We got in and asked for Norbert, a kid in the art department who had worked on a rave flyer for one of Duncan's parties last year. He was our only real connection to the magazine. Norbert took us back to his cubicle. *Plugged* was a huge operation. They had three floors in a big, funky building on Second Street, with hundreds of computers, wires everywhere, and lots of windows. The people working there seemed to be having fun. There was a bulletin board with listings for jobs and I would probably have applied for one if I hadn't already sworn allegiance to the belief that the *Plugged* organization was the twenty-first century's primary locus of evil.

Norbert told us that Michael Mackey was in the Netherlands at a marketing conference and that Delmonico Dante was back at the Media Center. The only big shot around was a senior editor, but he was only about thirty years old and probably unconnected with any longtime conspiracy. Besides, he was in a meeting. Just so the mission was not a total waste, I told Norbert about how fucked up his employers were and how he was contributing to the suppression of novelty and human evolution.

Norbert got a little shaken up. He confessed that he was uncomfortable with the fact that Michael Mackey was a devout Christian. Norbert didn't feel right sabotaging the magazine, though, or even helping us crack into the private records to see what they were thinking about us or doing to us. He did agree to put a note on Mackey's desk when no one was looking.

Brooks wrote the note: "We are watching you watching us. EC." I liked it. It was an outright lie—we had no idea if they were really watching us at all, and certainly no way of monitoring them, but if they *were* watching us, this might spook them a little.

We didn't exactly lie to Duncan when we got back. We just told him that the mission was accomplished. Soon it would become very clear that *Plugged* wasn't the real enemy, anyway. They were just the PR firm.

I don't know if it had anything to do with the note he wrote, but when we got back to the PF, just as he was entering the 8181 code into the security touch pad, Brooks caught the twitch.

30.

If we hadn't been so determined to generate just the right hype for ourselves, and equally determined to counteract everyone else's negative spin about us, we would probably never have gotten into so much trouble.

On the morning of her *Real World* reunion, and against Duncan's explicit instructions, Margot couldn't resist reading the *Rolling Stone* piece in its entirety. I guess something primal took over; from that moment on, her need to do spin control far outweighed her fear of anything the aliens might do to her for ignoring their environmental mandate.

Nomie and Lauren went along with Margot to the SF *Real World* house for moral support (and to spy) and returned later that day, without her, to report on what had happened. The MTV producers had the whole cast sit around on couches in the *Real World* house. Spando, an up-and-coming rapper who had been one of Margot's main adversaries during her brief residence, pulled out the *Rolling Stone* piece and started reading aloud about Margot's abduction, turning the words of the piece into a rap song. Everybody else started to laugh, and they pulled a handheld camera right up to Margot's face. I guess it was just too much for her. She totally turned on us.

Margot told her ex-housemates, the camera, and the entire MTV audience on the other end that she had been brainwashed by a sex-and-drug cult: the Ecstasy Club. We forced her to take ecstasy, LSD, and DMT, put video cameras in her room (hardly a crime in *Real World* ethics), and made her submit to group sex. Somehow she knew about Lauren's pregnancy—or had guessed from the morning sickness—and said we were planning to do the abortion ourselves and eat the fetus in a ritual. I'm sure it made for great television.

Needless to say, Margot wasn't coming back. She got the assistant director she had been sleeping with to take her back to his condo and protect her from us if we tried to kidnap her again.

While Margot was authoring what would amount to our most lasting legacy on videotape, Duncan, Peter, and I went to see Professor Marcus Sturgeon at his home office near Santa Cruz. After Peter had related our entire saga to him over the phone, Sturgeon agreed to see us at his house, a place that had taken on mythic significance among us students of JFK. We had all heard about his ramshackle compound, its secret bomb shelters and half-assembled spaceship prototypes, but none of us had actually seen it before, or knew where it was. Peter said that Steven had once tried to find Sturgeon's home by tailing him on a motorcycle after he left his lab at school, but that Sturgeon kept driving his old Volvo in circles and then just vanished into thin air.

Following Sturgeon's circuitous directions, we eventually found the little gray house on a nondescript block in Watsonville. It was the NASA equivalent of white trash. Giant solenoids mounted on cinder blocks, copper tubing everywhere, rusty satellite dishes and parts from weather balloons composed a high-tech-trash sculpture garden on Sturgeon's lawn. A little dog yapped at us from behind a screen door, and Sturgeon came out to greet us. I hadn't seen him since graduation the summer before and he was looking a lot older than I remembered him.

We introduced ourselves but Sturgeon didn't say anything. He just smiled and shook our hands. Then he pulled a metal cylinder out of his pocket—about the size of a flashlight—and held it up to his neck.

"I am Marcus Sturgeon," said the computerized device. It was a voice synthesizer. It sounded like an electric razor with some extra reverb.

"What happened?" I asked him. "Did you get cancer?"

"No," he responded in transistorized monotone. "I have my reasons."

He raised his eyebrows provocatively at almost everything he said. His face was extremely expressive, in stark contrast to his machine voice. He never told us why he spoke through that thing. Either he was embarrassed about some medical condition or he was using it purely out of paranoia. Maybe "they" couldn't hear what he was saying when he spoke through it. Who knows? It didn't add to his credibility, that's for sure.

Sturgeon led us back to his little office—an only partially converted garage with weeds growing all over the roof. He was a small man, and completely bald, but his huge bushy eyebrows more than compensated for any lack of hair. He hunched from the shoulders up, making his whole head jut forward.

"Don't touch anything," he buzzed as he opened the door and let us in. There were hundreds of little wooden drawers with wires and tubes sticking out of them. Old stereo equipment, military-surplus metal boxes, headphones, and what looked like ham radio equipment were piled up everywhere. Sturgeon had a little stool on which he sat. The rest of us had to stand.

"So you found the EE 135?" he asked. We stood silently, not knowing what to do. "That's why you're here, right? You found the tube?"

"Actually," Peter said, "it was an EE 136."

"Really?!" Sturgeon was surprised. His computerized voice didn't modulate but his eyes were wide open. "I haven't seen one of those since—" He stopped himself. "A long time ago. Was it a PR or a PZ?"

"PZ," Peter said.

"Close the door."

Sturgeon removed a set of blueprints from a cabinet with huge, flat drawers. He unrolled them onto a messy worktable, and the paper buckled wherever tools, tubes, and other junk pressed from beneath.

"I was already off the project when they developed the 136 prototypes," Sturgeon said, clumsily holding the voice synthesizer to his throat as he attempted to keep the blueprint unrolled. Peter and I each held on to an end of the blue paper to free Sturgeon's hands, but for whatever reason he didn't let go, so all three of us held on to it together. "But I found one later in a downed weather balloon I bought at a garage sale in Phoenix, and drew up these plans after I took it apart."

"Impressive," Duncan said, kissing Sturgeon's ass.

"The EE series had many functions," Sturgeon explained, "but few of them were advertised in the military literature. Officially, it was a temperature and barometric gauge, but only two of the forty components inside had anything to do with atmospheric readings."

"The rest of it is some sort of amplification circuit, right?" Peter asked.

"Yes, indeed," Sturgeon said. "But a very particular kind." He pointed to a squiggly line on the blueprint. "This is a frequency generator. It can be modulated by remote control. The odd thing about it is that the entire frequency range is higher than any radio crystal can detect. The only thing that can perceive it is the brain."

"An ESP device," Duncan concluded confidently.

"More than that," said Sturgeon, fingering his metal cylinder mysteriously. "It doesn't simply read thoughts—it *programs* them. It's a carrier wave very close to the resonant frequency of the brain—the sustaining waveform of consciousness. The wave that gives us the illusion of continuity from one moment to the next. By generating a carrier wave very similar to the organic frequency of the brain, we were able to induce a sympathetic reaction."

"The wavelength of the subject's brain would conform to the wavelength you generated?" Peter was ahead of us on this stuff.

"Yes. If it was focused properly and amplified enough to reach him." Sturgeon saw that the rest of us were confused. "Have you told them about the Philadelphia tests?"

"Yeah, kind of . . ." Peter admitted.

"That's fine. That's fine," Sturgeon said. "After the navy experiments failed, we developed the EE tubes to broadcast a carrier frequency that would hold subjects in an artificially generated continuity. So they could move between time phases without losing consciousness."

"Thus, the tube." Duncan was trying to hurry Sturgeon along. He didn't like to endure primers of any sort.

"But there were two opposing views about what should be done with the technology once we developed it," Sturgeon continued. "The private entities funding the research were interested in dimensional research. The military branch housing our operations saw it as an opportunity to develop methods of mind control and psychological warfare. Put some of these tubes in a weather balloon over the enemy troops, generate a sympathetic tone, and then move it, along with the enemy's state of mind, wherever we wanted to."

"That wouldn't really work, would it?" I asked.

"Why do you think the Iraqis came running to the American troops and begged to be rescued when they could just as easily have sat in their bunkers for months?"

I'd have to research that one later.

"What about the other group? The private sector?" Duncan asked. "Who were they?"

"I'm sure you already know," Sturgeon said. "That was E. T. Harman."

"And all he got out of it was the Cosmotology cult?" I asked. This was implausible.

"Oh no," Sturgeon corrected me almost angrily. "It was much, much more than that. He got the Electronics Transponders Company."

Okay. We were buying this. His story connected too many dots for us to discount it.

"Now I know this will be hard to accept," Sturgeon began, as if everything else he had told us was easy to swallow, "but Harman used the tube to conduct time travel. He got access through his military connections to an old air force base near Arcata—you know, up by Humboldt Bay?"

From our faces he could see that we knew. He smiled. Fellow paranoids.

"We would put people who already exhibited some psychic talents through an intensive program where they could harness their energies. Usually they were old fighter pilots. Much of the roots of neurolinguistic programming comes from this research, by the way. Once the subject was able to generate and maintain a psychic connection with another time zone, we would put him in line with the EE tube to amplify and stabilize his beam. Then, anyone else could plug himself into the system—often with the help of some ketamine courtesy of Colonel Edmund Brock's isolation-tank experiments, which we also happened to be funding—and travel to whatever point in the time continuum the psychic had located. It was precarious, but it worked."

I smelled a fire. A real fire.

The blueprints were burning. I pulled them off the table. They had been sitting on top of a soldering iron. Peter stamped out the fire and I unplugged the iron.

"I wonder how long that's been on," Sturgeon mused out loud. "The electric bill has been awfully high lately."

"But about the time-travel experiments . . ." Duncan none too gently steered Sturgeon back on track.

"I've told you too much already." He was clamming up. The soldering fire was probably just an excuse. He wasn't as dottering as he pretended to be.

"Tell us about Tesla," Peter said. He was so direct and calm. His friend had died. He wouldn't be refused.

"Now you didn't hear this from me," Sturgeon began, "but the entire ET Company's stature is based on a cleverly exploited feedback loop. It might have been because so many of the transistor components were from the ET Company to begin with, but on one of our first psychics—a young man named Tyrone something—"

Oh shit. Duncan, Peter, and I looked at one another but didn't say a word.

"—he kept projecting right into Tesla's laboratory. Without fail. Well, Harman saw an opportunity there. At the time, Tesla was still little known. He had done some experiments in static electricity, but that was about all."

"What are you trying to say?" I asked. "Tesla was a time traveler?"

"No, no—not at all," Sturgeon laughed. "Harman used most of the money he had to buy shares in the ET Company, which was started by the men who had invested in Tesla's patents while he was alive. Once Harman had a controlling interest in ET, he used the beam to go back to Tesla's lab and give him hints on his projects. He gave Tesla equations that hadn't been worked out in his own time—and modern principles of electronics. Each time he did, the invention would trickle back up through time and the ET Company would have the patents on more devices. No one knew what they were for until Harman pulled them from the archives. He became incredibly powerful."

"But the ET Company has always had the patents on these things," I said.

"Don't you see?" Sturgeon pleaded through his machine. "They didn't always. It's all we can remember because it came back up through time that way!"

"Tesla always said his ideas came from aliens," Peter added.

"No doubt," Sturgeon said. "That's who Harman told him he was. That's why he got Tesla to call it the ET Company. And it was Harman's proof to the rest of us that the company was really his. It was the marker he put back in time to prove he had been there."

I had to step in. "But couldn't this all be a giant prank? A masterful public relations scheme? Couldn't Harman have bought an interest in the ET Company just because it had his initials? Isn't it possible that all Tesla's inventions were there from the beginning, and Harman is just trying to take credit for them now? That he convinced all of you that all this was going on?"

To the others in the garage, *I* sounded like the crazy one.

"Why would Harman have left that work to begin Cosmotology?" Duncan asked.

"Good question," Sturgeon answered. It was as if no one had even heard my tirade. "First off, the boy with the link got less predictable. Our psychics had only ten or fifteen good trips in them before they wore out."

"What, exactly, does it mean when you wear out?" Peter asked.

"Why, it means you've lost your mind," Sturgeon said plainly. "There were a tremendous number of casualties. At least a hundred, maybe more. Harman just let them out to walk the streets.

They're considered schizophrenics. They always go on about how their minds are being controlled by radar—that sort of thing. Funny, eh? It's actually true!"

"So," Duncan was getting impatient, "after Tyrone left, they couldn't get back to Tesla?"

"They could. They could," Sturgeon said. "Once you go to a particular time repeatedly, it makes a little impression in the continuum. Like a score in a piece of sheet metal. It becomes hard *not* to go there."

I started to think about all the drugs we had been taking. Did acid have a particular frequency? And ecstasy? Were we indelibly scoring our psyches with these little notches?

"That's why Steven ended up in that old lab . . ." Peter drifted off.

"Yes. And it's why Harman has been sealing off everything he can ever since. After a point, there's a diminishing return. The predictability of his manipulations is compensated for by the exponential increase in associated novelty."

"What do you mean?" Duncan asked, intrigued by this addition to his own theoretical outlook on reality. "The time-travel experiments had an effect on cultural predictability?"

"Yes." Sturgeon looked like he wasn't going to say anything else, but then couldn't help himself. He had kept it all bottled up for so long. "He had created a feedback loop between Tesla's time and our own, and kept going back with the newest technologies to see how they would move up through time. But once things got so advanced—computers, microchips, television—he had less control over their application. They were no longer simply bizarre, esoteric devices, and people were figuring out and exploiting the technologies before his control of the ET Company began. He found that all this pervasive technology decreased his ability to monopolize it."

"So what'd he do?" Peter asked.

"He sabotaged his own company. He went back to the time shortly before Tesla had his first encounter with the time travelers. He couldn't undo what he had done—short of killing the scientist altogether—so he debilitated him just enough to make his later choices of how to apply and document his discoveries a little less sound."

"That's why he tried to light up the eastern seaboard using static electricity," Peter added. He was back in school.

"But they saw someone else in there, too." Sturgeon's voice synthesizer seemed to be speaking at a lower pitch. We were getting scared. He touched Peter's shoulder. "That was you, twenty years later, tapping onto the same waveform we had created. It's like a scored area in the spectrum—you couldn't help but roll into the nook. It was all the more reason to shut things down before the technology got loose."

Peter's jaw dropped. I knew he was thinking about Tyrone and Brock—how they'd recognized him on the ladder.

"But why Cosmotology?" Duncan wanted to know. "What reason did he have for going into all that?"

"Cosmotology?" Sturgeon's voice suddenly sounded lower and more electronic. His battery was running out. He pulled a spare out of a drawer and changed it while we waited. His voice began very high-pitched. He adjusted his synthesizer and continued. "Cosmotology is the science of mind control. It's the pure programming application of the EE tube technology. Those machines are brainwashing devices."

"And he's been attempting to brainwash our culture in order to restrict the novelty he had already set in motion." Duncan saw the light. At least his light.

"He realized that if he can limit a population's mindset, he can limit reality."

The bald old man nodded ominously, then switched off his voice synthesizer and hastily showed us out. We left Marcus Sturgeon's with a new understanding of the battle in which we were already engaged. Or maybe we were just falling further under E. T. Harman's spell.

31.

Why were we given that ketamine? Did Colonel Brock really leave it behind accidentally, or had he subtly programmed Brooks to take his bag? And why was Brooks now affected by the twitch-reset syndrome? He hadn't even used the visionquest rig. Had the ketamine been tainted with another chemical? Was Tyrone a plant? Kirsten? Would others start twitching soon? Would I?

Amazingly, Duncan seemed more concerned about enacting a preemptive counterspin to the airing of Margot's *Real World* reunion than with evaluating Sturgeon's story. Maybe the threat of being labeled baby-eaters on national TV bothered him more, at least in the immediate sense, than an attack by time-traveling novelty-dampeners. Or maybe Margot was simply a more tangible enemy. Duncan was about to choose between two members' suggestions—Henry proposed "I Hate Margot" bumper stickers while Brooks thought we should release a computer worm that splashed her face on people's screens—when Nomie showed us the paper.

There had been a fire near Santa Cruz last night, consuming what police identified as an "illegal speed lab." Dr. Marcus Sturgeon was dead. To Duncan, this meant war.

I couldn't help but reject the assumption that "they" were really out to get us. It was preposterous. Besides, Sturgeon's house was a firetrap. It was more likely that he had left another soldering iron smoldering somewhere. Maybe our visit shook him up and he got careless.

"If they know so much about us," I asked, "why would they kill Sturgeon *after* he told us the whole story? It doesn't make any sense."

"This was meant as a warning," Duncan said, "for us to back off."

"Maybe we should," Peter said.

Pig and Brooks objected in autistic unison.

"B-b-but . . ." Then they twitched and reset. We got the point. We couldn't back off now and leave them to twitch out the rest of their lives in misery. And we had an obligation to the rest of the world, too. Harman was attempting to change the rate of novelty universally. (So were we, actually, but he was doing it the wrong way.) He wanted to increase predictability, and even redefine it where he could, for his personal gain.

As we paced around the mezzanine, all I could think about was the gentle ambient CDs Lauren was playing through the main speakers to relieve her morning nausea. The soundtrack was so incompatible with our dialogue.

Henry was the only one of us sitting down. His hands were in his lap and he stared up worshipfully at Duncan. As penance to his new master, he had given up heroin, cold turkey. He loved having an in-house messiah. People like leaders, Laruso had told us. Or maybe it was a British thing. Honor your king, know your enemies. Same difference.

"What is it you want us to do?" Henry asked, sounding like a biblical character. He made me sick.

"We have to find Harman," Duncan said. "And quickly. He's at the center of all this—"

"Maybe," Parrot interrupted gently. He entered these kinds of conversations rarely, so when he did everyone turned to listen. It was a technique he'd probably picked up from E.F. Hutton commercials. "Or maybe that's his whole point."

"You think it's all propaganda?" I asked him.

"Harman was one of the main financial contributors to the communications department at Penn," Parrot continued, luxuriously inflecting his voice. "Guys like Harman don't dish out that sort of money for nothing. They control communications studies because with it, they can control our perception of media and communication."

"This isn't perception, Parrot," Pig interrupted. "Look at me!" He had a point. To a point.

"I understand that, Pig," Parrot said in a tone like that of a dentist about to perform a painful procedure. "All I'm saying is that, historically speaking, communications has been a science of empire maintenance. Central, top-down control of populations. And the key to maintaining that control is to maintain the illusion of the emperor's centrality."

He was making a "meta" point. I think only Duncan and I got it.

"So," he continued, deciding to pick up the intellectual stragglers later, "by dominating communications research and education, you can control, to some extent, the prevailing view of how media and communications technologies function."

"If you want people to think that propaganda works, teach them that it does." I tried to wrap up his soliloquy so we could get on with the matter at hand.

"It's much more pervasive than that," he said, trying to scare us.

As he spoke, though, I got the sense that Parrot was somehow removed from everything he was saying. Something had been different about him ever since the racquetball interrogation with Laruso. Parrot was extremely eager to talk about worst-case scenarios, but he did so with a wanton disregard for the impact of any of this on our lives. It was as if he felt immune to any consequences, or as though he saw our whole plight as delusional. A game. I suspected he considered our fears to be fictional. But more likely, he was so afraid for his personal safety that he had constructed a defense mechanism of superiority and immunity. Painting horrific scenarios kept him in control of the game. Or maybe, in the midst of such chaos, it just felt good to be sadistic.

"Take milk cartons. Now you've all heard the real explanation for those pictures of missing children they keep putting on the sides of milk cartons?"

It drew a blank.

"I'm surprised," he said, genuinely surprised. "They were put on there to make us feel less safe. To make us believe that children are getting abducted by devil worshipers all the time. Why?"

"So that we are afraid of the devil?" Brooks asked. He was engrossed.

"Not exactly," Parrot said, grateful for a captive, if less than worthy, audience. "It was so that in a few years, those of us brought up with missing children on milk cartons will more readily accept the idea of embedding location transponder chips in our children's teeth in order to find them if they are ever lost or kidnapped. The obvious side effect being that the government, or whoever, could locate us at any time, too. The satellites for the system are already up and working."

Brooks turned green. He covered his mouth with his hand and ran to the bathroom.

"It's even more insidious than that, though," Parrot accelerated toward his finale. "What I've been wondering is what if the whole thing is a sham? What if they released this little urban legend themselves, just to try to convince us that this sort of propaganda works?"

"But most people never think about it that far," I argued.

"That's fine," Parrot said. "They'll get programmed on that first level and simply implant the chips in their children's teeth out of fear. But those of us who do comprehend the bigger picture, we stand the risk of getting programmed on a second level. The game wrapped around the game. We can't help but believe that if they're expending the energy to perpetrate such a scheme, then these communications technologies must be valid. Our belief in their efficacy makes them real."

"Right," I said, hopefully. "What if Harman's whole time-travel and mind-control experimentation was just elaborate theater? He made the military and corporate establishment believe he could do this stuff—he could have made them believe he was responsible for the ET Company's inventions even though he wasn't connected to them at all."

"It doesn't matter," Duncan said, stamping out our little thought revolt. "In either case, Harman is using technologies at his disposal to direct consensus reality. And, right now, he's directing it against us. We don't have much time left."

There was a scream from the bathroom. Lauren stood there, holding the door open in horror.

"I was just making sure he was all right . . ." she managed to utter. No one moved. Except for me. It was my job to deal with whatever had happened.

Inside the bathroom, Brooks sat on the toilet holding a bloody pair of pliers. At his feet, in a red puddle, lay four of his teeth.

32.

I might have taken a stand or dropped out of the whole thing right then if I hadn't felt so needed, or if I had thought Lauren would go with me. I believed what was happening to us was real—I think I still do. But I didn't see any need to martyr ourselves to powers so much bigger and meaner than we were. Perhaps I stuck around because I wanted to find out what was going to happen. I didn't want to miss the fireworks.

Brooks came back from the emergency dental clinic with big swollen cheeks and a black eye. They managed to get one of the teeth back in but had to stitch up the other three sockets. He could get bridgework later if he wanted to. He didn't tell them that his injuries were self-inflicted—only that he'd had an "accident."

Alex Barnow had become our chief gofer. He ripped off some good stuff, too. The dentists had only given Brooks a bunch of Motrin for the pain, but Alex smuggled out a bottle of expired Percodans for him from his dad's pharmacy. He got so many of them that even after we all grabbed a couple there were still more than enough for Brooks. Alex was young and unfocused, but I sensed he had the same responsible streak about domestic affairs that I did. He was decidedly more enthusiastic about the Ecstasy Club than I was by then and even more eager to please than I had been at my worst.

Alex appropriated a full case of nicotine patches for Tyrone, who began wearing them six at a time and walking around with his shirt off, proudly displaying his creative configurations of the little circles. Tyrone got more charged up than ever before. He kept imitating Tony the Tiger telling us how "Grrrrreat!!" it feels to quit smoking. His manic stares and sudden whoops were enough to frighten Nomie into putting a lens cap on the video camera in her room and locking the door at night. Duncan promised Nomie he would talk to Tyrone. He treated her like a valued client—which she was. We were supposed to be visiting her parents the next day, and Duncan didn't want anything to get between himself and their money, least of all a frightened girl. Until the check was in his hands, he would do anything she said.

When I saw the way Duncan closed the door behind him on entering Nomie's room, I realized that he was having sex with her, too. Adam and Andy standing guard outside their mistress's threshold confirmed it. I was going to tattle on him to Lauren, but then wondered what really would be the point. To make her feel worse about him than she already did?

By the time Duncan came out it was pretty late.

"How was she?" I asked, not subtly.

"She's afraid of Tyrone. It gives me a good excuse to confront him." Duncan had been fixated on Tyrone ever since his name came up at Sturgeon's.

"It also gives you a good excuse to comfort her, eh?"

Duncan acted shocked. He took my arm, pretty firmly, and dragged me into Alex's room. Alex was already on his bedroll trying to sleep.

"Get out!" Duncan told him. The boy obeyed. Once we were alone, he released my arm and began pacing around the room. "You think I *want* to sleep with her?"

"She's pretty, and she's exciting. I'm not saying there's anything wrong with it, Duncan."

"She's disgusting, Zach. She's not going to last here much longer. I just have to keep her happy until we can get to her father."

"What? So, you're like a prostitute then? Selling your body to her for her dad's money?"

Duncan pinched the bridge of his nose between his thumb and forefinger, very tightly.

"You should never have started with Lauren, Zach. It has confused everything."

"What has it confused? You said it was a great thing. That she needed someone." He was using Lauren to take the focus off himself, but I took the bait anyway.

"Somehow it's changed you, Zach." *Yeah, for the better,* I thought. "It's put you back into a lower state. Changed your priorities."

"I'm still here for you, Duncan. That's all I'm saying." Why was I telling him this? Was it even true?

"I hope so, Zach. I don't want to have to go through it alone. I want you to be there."

He looked into my eyes in a very strange way. I think he was expressing a version of love. Then he opened the door and went up to the kitchen. I reassured Alex that everything was okay and tucked him back in.

Duncan instructed Henry to microwave some of the remaining liquid ketamine down into a powder. Duncan assumed that the sense memory of the K trance might help Tyrone recall, or help him want to recall, some details of what had occurred in his yesteryears with Marcus Sturgeon and E. T. Harman. After they dosed up, Duncan and Tyrone sat together over by Tyrone's melted blue mound, whispering to one another for hours. It was one of the few places in the club out of range of our surveillance cameras. Parrot, Henry, Peter, and I watched them for a while from the railing, but eventually we all decided to go to sleep.

No matter how internally divided or farcically paranoid the PF got, the hour we all went to bed was almost always strangely warm and domestic. Sometimes we even shouted "'night Mary Ellen" to one another across the cavernous space.

The "turning in" moment had become tricky for Lauren and me, though, because no one officially knew that we were sleeping together. I mean, maybe everybody knew, but it wasn't something any of us talked about out in the open.

We were in my room getting undressed. I was looking in the mirror at my body—at how thin I had gotten. Where were my muscles?

"They'll grow back," Lauren said, stroking my back. How did she know?

"You think I'm vain, don't you?"

"I think you're cute."

Lauren looked at her naked reflection next to mine. Her breasts had gotten larger. She stood sideways and regarded her profile.

"Don't worry, it's not showing yet," I said.

"You mean it's small enough to forget about?"

"Huh?"

"To nip in the bud? Is that what you meant?" I couldn't tell if she was joking. She turned away from the mirror and sat down on the bed. "I'm sorry, Zach. I just feel like I may have spoiled everything for you."

"How could you say that?"

"You used to have such fun here. You and Duncan talked about breaking dimensions and creating global communities. Now you just worry about me."

"That's not true." I saw my opportunity and took it. "I'm in love with you, Lauren. I want us to be together. I want you to keep the baby. That's what I really want."

"But don't you see, Zach, that's what I do to people. I'm a chronic homebody. You should see what I built up on the roof. I can't help myself."

"That's not a bad thing, Lauren. It's a beautiful thing. I love you for it."

"But maybe Duncan's right. You're never going to make it if you're with me."

"He's not right. He's going crazy. And if he is right, I don't care. I don't want to 'make it' anymore, whatever that means. I just want to be with you."

She started to cry. She used the new bedsheets to wipe her eyes.

"I'm sorry, Lauren, but it's the truth. I'm not a hero. I just want a regular life. I'm not really into all this. I mean I am, but not this way. I get pumped about it and all; I think there's more to life than meets the eye, but . . ." I trailed off. I wasn't making any sense.

"It's funny," she said. "I like you this way."

"What way?"

"Normal, Zach. Sensible, sad, responsible Zach."

"I don't have what Duncan had, though, do I? Those visions of utopia. I'm just a Connecticut Jew in King Duncan's Court."

She laughed and started kissing me all over.

"I love *you*, Zach. Connecticut Zach, Jewish Zach, unvisionary Zach, pumped-up Zach, checking-his-puny-little-muscles-in-the-mirror Zach . . ."

"Hey!" I tackled her to the bed.

After we made love, I suggested my plan. We would all go up to Nomie's parents' house tomorrow in two cars. We would do what we could to help Duncan get his money, and then we would just split together in my car. We'd tell everyone we were driving back down to the PF but just cut out.

"What about our stuff?" she asked.

"We can't let them know. We can put a few things in the hatch, but—"

"Why do we have to leave like that, Zach? Why don't we just leave when we have somewhere to go. In a truck, with our stuff, like real human beings?"

"I'm scared we won't be able to—"

I stopped speaking when I heard Brooks climbing up from the kitchen. He came in and sat down on the floor next to the bed. He was trained well enough by this point to sit right on the plastic runner. He must have thought I was alone.

"I'm going to die," he said bleakly. "Aren't I?"

"Eventually," I said, trying to joke. Lauren nudged me. "Not for a long time I don't think."

"What's w-w-wrong with me?"

"We'll figure it out. Don't worry."

"I don't want to not worry. I think the worrying is keeping me alive. If I just give in to it, I'll disappear. It's been happening. I've gotten lost a lot lately. Like I have no identity. I haven't been to the mailbox in a week. That's not like me."

"They'll hold on to the mail. You'll be fine."

"I know they'll keep the mail. I don't know if I'll be around to get it."

"You're in an existential dilemma," I told him. "It happens to everyone at times. It's part of the trip." I used the hyped lingo because I had no true words of wisdom.

"Does everyone yank out their own teeth?" he asked.

He was scared to go to bed alone. I'd never felt so adult before—like someone's dad. He felt safe sitting in my room. There must have been something reassuring about me, or me and Lauren if he knew she was in there. Yet all I wanted was for him to go so I could be alone with her. Premonitions of fatherhood.

"Look, um," I said, "I better get some sleep. You should, too."

He got up sadly. "You're coming back tomorrow, right?" How did everyone know what I was thinking?

"Yes," I said. "I promise. We're coming out the other end. No problem."

"O-o-o-kay." He shuffled out.

Lauren and I lay in silence for a while, staring up at the ceiling. It wasn't just our ceiling—none of the rooms had ceilings, only walls. The roof above us housed everybody. We could sense them all in their beds, or watching TV, or brushing their teeth. All of us in the same open structure. A family. Lauren and I were both thinking the same thing. We couldn't just leave. We had to see this through.

Then things got violent.

33.

I thought only the LA Police Department had tanks, but at about two in the morning, I learned that the Oakland police have them too.

We heard a thunderous crash. I thought it was an earthquake at first, but the localized quality of the sound and the walkie-talkie squawks that followed immediately afterward made it clear that something else was going on. Everyone got out of their beds and to the railings in time to see the bulletproof-vested policemen charge like storm troopers through the hole they had made in the side of the building. There was cement dust everywhere.

They pointed their rifles at us and shouted conflicting commands we could barely make out.

"Get down!" "Hands up!" "On the floor!" "Hands on the railing!" "Get downstairs!" "Freeze!" "Move it!" I speak English pretty well yet stood a good chance of getting shot for not following directions.

I ran downstairs in my boxer shorts, holding my hands up as nonthreateningly as possible.

One of the helmeted cops—he couldn't have been any older than I was—pushed his metal gun barrel against my chest and told me to move back. "Now!"

I found myself bowing to him like a Calcuttan begging for mercy as Laruso strolled in through the gaping hole in the side of our building.

"Line 'em up against that wall," he directed his troops. All of us, even Tyrone, complied with Laruso's command. It would have been a lot easier if his young cops hadn't been herding us so haphazardly with their rifles. As we all stood there, half-naked, I felt a defensive posture come over me. Our women weren't even dressed. My tribe was being threatened and humiliated.

Laruso must have read my indignant stance. He walked up to me and, without warning, smashed his fist into my gut. He couldn't have moved his arm more than a foot, but in an instant I was doubled over, gasping for breath.

"Anybody else have something to say?" *I hadn't said anything!* Laruso stood there waiting. "Good, then. If you're through, I'll talk to you."

He loved playing this scene. I imagined Laruso checking his hair in the rearview mirror before getting out of the car. My brain always takes me to places like that when my body is in trouble.

"You know I could book three of you right now on suspicion of murder. Your prints are all over the crime scene."

I was about to speak, but when I saw Laruso's elbow coil up ever so slightly, I thought better of it.

"Who's Peter Lanborn?" Laruso asked, continuing his stroll.

Peter was standing behind Nomie, who was holding onto Duncan's arm. Peter slowly raised his hand.

"Good," Laruso said, smiling. "That wasn't so hard now, was it?" He walked over toward Peter. Duncan and Nomie moved aside to clear a path. "A lot of people have been dying around you, son, haven't they?"

Peter's lip quivered. I couldn't tell if he was thinking back on Steven and Sturgeon, or if he was simply afraid to be punched.

"We were only—" Peter cut himself off as Laruso tilted his head.

"It's okay, Peter," Laruso said gently. "You were only what?"

"We visited him. He was my teacher at JFK. We just wanted to ask him some questions. About time travel."

Laruso laughed out loud. Peter flinched like a frightened rabbit as Laruso raised his arm and put it on the boy's shoulder.

"Time travel? Is that new street lingo for amphetamines? Take that down, Lloyd," he said to one of the cops, who just chuckled with his boss.

"Look, kids." He adopted his *Dragnet* voice. "It doesn't matter whether you torched Sturgeon's place and stole his drugs or not. What does matter is that I can pin it on you and make it stick."

"But, sir—" I couldn't help myself. Laruso's huge frame took three fast steps toward me, his heels clicking against the concrete before one of them planted itself firmly in my groin. I didn't feel anything at first. I just crumpled into a heap on the floor. I heard Lauren scream, then I saw white as the heat rose. Then came the pain.

"But I want to make this easy for us." He noticed Parrot and smiled. "Hi." Parrot tried to smile back. "I'm your friend, kids. There are people who are very upset with you. Important people. They'd like to see your little operation closed down. That's what I came here to do. Between your connection to Sturgeon's death and that confession on MTV it would be easy. But then I thought to myself, Why close them down like that? They're good kids. They're just misguided. And what would the illegal Brit do for a job? Forge an immigration form? I couldn't let him do that! No, I realized I should take you all under my wing. As a project. Community outreach."

"We appreciate that, sir," Duncan's gentle voice answered back. Was our alpha male rising to the challenge?

"I'm so glad you do, son. Really I am. So as my first favor, my first act of kind guidance to you misguided young people, I'm going to help you throw your next party. My contribution will be to give you a date. Your contribution will be to organize the party, publicize it, and then turn over all the receipts to me. If it works, if you prove you can do that much, we'll talk about cutting you in on a percentage of the profit."

"But, sir, surely the expenses for the party—," Duncan tried to negotiate.

"Will be a noted and appreciated compensation for what you've cost my department already."

"Yes, sir," Duncan replied, defeated.

Laruso pulled a pad out of his shirt pocket. "Now they gave me a date . . . let me see . . . ah yes. December 19. That's it."

Though we were already silent, a palpable hush came over us. *December 19?* That was the day Duncan had told us about. And who were "they"?

"I've even gotten you a listing in *Plugged* magazine," Laruso said, putting his hand out for me to take. I carefully reached up to him, and he effortlessly hoisted me to a standing position. "For free. They were happy to oblige. See how nicely everyone can work together when we all cooperate?"

He put his hand on my cheek. He could have crushed my face. Instead, he pulled my head toward him and whispered into my ear.

"You work for *me* now. Understand?"

I nodded as he waved his arm for the troops to pull out.

Once they were gone, we all wandered around the dusty space for a while, stunned. There was a huge hole in the wall, exposing us to the cold night air. I noticed Alex wasn't with us. I went into the mind gym to look for him. There he was, lying in the fetal position in his bed with his eyes closed, just as I had left him.

Alex had slept through the whole thing.

34.

We stayed up most of the night taping black plastic bags to the hole in the wall. There was no one to bill for the damage, and the building wasn't even truly ours to repair. None of us said anything about what had transpired. We were all too confused, and afraid to interpret how Laruso's raid fit into the big picture until Duncan officially debriefed us. We just talked about whether to use duct or masking tape, and how we might be able to find some drywall for a more permanent fix.

Shortly before dawn, Duncan told me to climb with him up to the roof for a talk.

"I knew this was coming, Zach."

We were standing in Lauren's fêng shui garden. It was finally complete. The waterfall had been extended to a little pool between the benches, and the top of the pagoda was lacquered red.

"Lauren's idea of art," Duncan said, picking up one of her carefully placed stones and tossing it off the roof. "A cheap imitation of the bonsai garden in Golden Gate Park."

"I think it's beautiful, Duncan. She's an amazing person, you know."

"Oh good. Male protective instinct. At least you're mammalian."

"I'm a human being, Duncan. What are you?"

"If you can take your mind off nesting and fornicating for even a minute, Zach, we need to develop a plan of attack."

I sat down on one of the benches. Lauren's garden gave me strength. Especially because Duncan seemed uncomfortable in it.

"Maybe we should just lay low for a while, Duncan, and do as we're told. We're still getting to throw our party."

"On their terms."

"It's the date you would have chosen, anyway. The nineteenth. Eight days from now."

"Precisely my point, Zach. They're taking control of the ritual. It's the same reason the Catholics built their cathedrals over the pagan power spots. They're co-opting us."

"It's not a conspiracy, Duncan. It's just about the money. You know, 'render unto Caesar' and all that."

"You're so naive. She's really gotten to you."

"This isn't about Lauren."

"Oh no?" Duncan crossed in front of me. He wanted me to look up in his eyes but I didn't. "You two think you can just go back to your bourgeois fantasy life? Set up a little house with a white posted fence?"

"Picket fence, Duncan."

"She's not keeping the baby, Zach. You may as well know that right now. I can see it. Even if you could convince her for a time. It's not fated to be. It's not at all in her character."

"What do you know about her character, Duncan? She can do as she wants. We talked about it. We're keeping it."

There was a muffled sound from a corner of the roof. We both froze. We heard it again. Duncan moved cautiously toward the noise. It was just a pigeon, resting on a ledge in Lauren's pagoda.

"I spoke with Tyrone," Duncan said. "He remembered a lot."

"Did he?"

"Are you even interested anymore?"

"Sure I am."

Duncan didn't say anything else. I guess I was no longer to be fully trusted.

35.

Laruso couldn't have timed his little visit any better. The very next morning, December 12, waiting in the fax machine was the galley proof of our free ad in the next issue of *Plugged:*

Phylogenic Foresight, 19/december/19/95.
This is the big one. The Ecstasy Club.

"This is the big one?" Duncan repeated several times as he paced the kitchen, crunching the offending thermal paper in his hand. "The 'big one'? How dare they!"

"It's not so bad, Duncan," I tried to console him. "It's just hype."

"It's *their* hype. It's antihype. They have no intention of helping us. There's no information in that. They're attempting to make us look like silly kids. 'The big one.' They know perfectly well how that comes off. And the name! The Ecstasy Club. It should be just Ecstasy Club." (Electronics Transponders Company, The Ecstasy Club, ETC, TEC. I didn't broach the subject.)

"They used our graphic," I said. They had. Lauren's Phylogenic Foresight logo was in the center of the panel, in full color. She had made the pages of *Plugged.* I was proud of her.

"That just gives it false legitimacy, Zachary. They've appropriated our logo in order to discredit us."

"We've infiltrated, too, can't you see it that way?"

"No, Zach, I can't." He was shouting at me for everyone to hear. "Why send us a galley proof when the issue is slated to hit the stands today? It was already in there! They must have scheduled our party a month ago! And look at the Web site address!"

At the bottom of the ad was a pointer to our Web site, except now it was mirrored on *Plugged*'s own server as http://www. plugged.com/theecstasyclub.

Brooks came into the kitchen, looked at the fax, and went into an instant twitch-reset. The numbers were perfectly sequenced to total 188: 19, december, 19, 95. How did they know? Poor Brooks sat there with his jaw dropped, completely disoriented.

"Are we still going up to Nomie's today?" I asked Duncan, trying to get us at least marginally on schedule. An activity—any activity—would do us some good. Engagement in mundane affairs, however transitory, is restorative. Not that I would have told Duncan this.

"Yes, we should leave immediately. It's just a matter of who is to go."

As Duncan considered the guest list, everyone in the building literally emerged from the woodwork. Peter and Pig's heads peeked out over the upper railing, Nomie casually came out of the bathroom drying her head with a towel, Henry looked up from his cooking at the stove, Brooks popped out of twitch-reset, Parrot strolled in with a freshly bound business plan under his arm, Alex suspended himself upside down from the DJ perch, and Adam and Andy, more direct than the rest, ran up to Duncan like Yorkshire terriers begging, "Pick me! Pick me!"

"Okay, then, let's just take everyone," Duncan said, knowing that Nomie would be forced to object. She moved through the kitchen, considering exactly how to react, then sat down in a chair next to Lauren.

"Gee, Duncan," she said, "there's nothing I'd like more, but I think my parents are preparing a brunch for four or five."

"If you have to limit it to five, whom do you plan to exclude?"

"I don't know, Duncan—the whole point is for your business, you know."

"*My* business? You're doing this for *me?*"

Lauren's and my eyes met. We almost broke into laughter over Duncan's typically roundabout way of getting his way.

"I didn't mean it like that, Duncan," Nomie said sheepishly. "I just want this to work out like you said."

"Well, then, Nomie, who do think will represent you best?"

"I don't know. You, Lauren, and Zach would be good, right?"

"If you think so, sure."

"And maybe Brooks?"

"You want Brooks, Nomie?" Brooks looked up hopefully.

"He does lots of business things."

"It's your decision."

"Would Parrot be better?"

"That would make six, but he did write the business plan . . ."

"You want Parrot instead of Brooks, then?" This was clearly what Duncan wanted.

"Maybe we can fit six, right, Zach?" We were using my Escort because Nomie's Fantasy Ride could never make the trip.

Lauren tried to settle it. "I really don't need to go. I'm feeling funny today."

"No," Duncan broke in. "You're going. We need you."

"Zach? Would you be upset?" Nomie asked me gently.

I hadn't ever considered being left out of something before. I didn't think I would mind, but I did.

"I don't feel comfortable with someone else driving my car."

Brooks knew he was about to get axed. He looked up at Nomie, in perfect pathos. She couldn't stand it. He had been suffering so and could use some relaxation at a beautiful estate.

"We can use the van, too," I suggested.

"Then I'm going along, eh?" Henry lit up.

And then there were seven.

Two hours later, our motley caravan pulled into the Wards' long driveway. I opened my car window to push in the security code at the gate and looked to Nomie for directions.

"Eight-one-one," she said. Brooks went into a full-on twitch-reset. "It's my little brother's birthday, that's all. August 11. Really."

Other unsettling "coincidences" followed.

First of all, Nomie's parents weren't home. There was only a note in the kitchen, pinned to a huge platter of poached salmon, stuffed grape leaves, and Chinese chicken salad. They had left to meet some friends "at the club" for a round of golf. We were invited to make ourselves at home, and warned not to leave the Jacuzzi on because the automatic timer was broken.

We stood around the giant butcher-block table leaving the feast that had been prepared for us untouched for about half an hour while Duncan berated Nomie for not making the intention of our visit clearer to her father. He told her that she was unconsciously sabotaging the Ecstasy Club, that she was embarrassed by her life path.

We still knew how to make the best of a bad situation, and having free rein at a multimillion-dollar estate for an afternoon wasn't the worst of situations to be in. Before long, we were scattered throughout the Mexican-style villa and its well-manicured grounds, exploring.

The house was immense—at least twice the size of the PF, complete with acres of landscaped gardens, an orange grove, a jungle of exotic trees, a pool, tennis courts, a putting green, and a Jacuzzi. Inside were a sauna, two exercise rooms, at least a dozen bedrooms, each with its own bath (and medicine cabinet), a giant study, and a kitchen big enough to service a restaurant.

It was hard to keep track of where everyone was, which suited me just fine. Lauren and I wandered along the jungle paths and found a small clearing with a stone gazebo. It was still quite warm during the day and much of the jungle was in bloom. Hummingbirds buzzed around us. They were as small and nimble as insects.

"Imagine what you have to do to own a place like this," I said, thinking about the evils Mr. Ward must have perpetrated on humankind in order to pay for his palace.

"Everyone finds their own balance, I guess," Lauren said.

"But think of how many people you could feed on the landscaping budget alone."

"Think of how many people you could feed on the cost of your NIKE high-tops alone."

"Maybe I shouldn't own them."

"Maybe you should enjoy this place while you're here," Lauren said, putting her hands around my waist and closing her eyes for a kiss. Part of my brain wanted to put her in the role of temptress of the garden—but she was right and I was wrong. I wasn't a socialist. It was all about balance. I had been kissing her for a long time, forgetting about whether I had the right to this pleasure, when music began blaring from the trees. I searched for the source of the sound and eventually located two rocks with speakers cleverly hidden inside. The whole estate was rigged for sound and who knows what else.

We made our way back to the pool and patio area. Brooks had put on an old Public Enemy CD, with hard-ass ghetto lyrics about fucking up cops and bleeding in the street. It was blasting for miles, I'm sure, reverberating onto the neighboring estates. Nomie was in the pool with Duncan, teaching him how to swim (all was forgiven for now), and Henry sat on a wooden deck with Parrot, cutting up some blotter acid.

It was an ideal place to trip, on the surface. You just had to ignore the social implications of a bunch of educated white kids lounging around on a multimillion-dollar estate dancing to gangsta rap. Kids who should know better. But we felt ironic enough about our situation to give it a go, and in about an hour, we were all sprawled out around the pool and its waterfalls, naked, and vegging out to the music. Every once in a while someone would go into the house and bring out something he or she thought would be fun or useful. Food, drinks, bottles of liquor, cartons of cigarettes, towels, blankets, chairs, tables, a TV set, candelabra, a basketball, suntan lotion, massage oils, books, magazines, newspapers. Then people began bringing out statues, paintings, chess pieces, and other icons.

We didn't notice, or didn't care to notice, when it started to drizzle. Most of us had crowded into the Jacuzzi by then, and the tiny droplets of water against our heads felt good. The acid wasn't too pure—it was quite speedy, in fact, which accounted for why we had gotten so compulsive about bringing all that stuff outside. But the true, edgy nature of the blotter didn't make itself apparent to us until Lauren screamed.

A Mexican family was standing on a path opening to the patio. They were dressed in their Sunday best, and the woman was holding a Bible. They must have come from church. They were horrified.

The rain was coming down pretty hard, and they quickly went into action carrying the furniture and artwork back inside. We got out of the Jacuzzi and tried to help, but they just kept apologizing for barging in on us and asked us to ignore them.

"Please go inside now," the man told us. "We are sorry. We will take care of this."

Nomie had gotten out of the Jacuzzi and was explaining to us something about how these people were the caretakers of the property, and that whenever it rained they came and covered up the lawn furniture—but something about Nomie had changed. Her hair. The rain was turning it white.

"¡Dios mío!" cried the Mexican woman as she looked into the Jacuzzi. The water was bubbling black. Nomie's hair dye had dissolved into the hot chlorinated soup. The rain was now giving her hair a final rinse. She looked old all of a sudden. Black dye streamed down her naked body, which seemed to sag and puff all over. Parrot stared at her, terrified, as the object of his many fantasies suddenly gained decades of age, like the succubus at the end of a horror movie. He screamed and ran into the woods.

Lauren took a towel from around herself, covered Nomie's hair, and walked her into the house. Henry gathered up his drug paraphernalia, trying to hide it from the caretakers' view. Brooks was back in the house attempting to turn off the stereo, but all he managed to do was blast the music from different locations alternatively. We heard it coming from deep in the jungle, then under the waterfalls, then in the house, then from the orange grove. Each time the sound changed sources we heard a loud POP! after which the sound would turn garbled and buzzy. Brooks succeeded in blowing all but three of Mr. Ward's forty-six Bose speakers before we pried him from the stereo controls and pulled out the plug. He kept trying to yank the knobs off the amplifiers even after the system was off, so Duncan just shouted "188" and Brooks froze. (The twitch-reset syndrome had its uses.)

Nomie, Lauren, and I helped the caretakers as best we could. Our skin was bright red and starting to burn. We hadn't remembered that the Jacuzzi's thermostat was broken and we scalded ourselves pretty badly. We helped rescue what we could from the rain, but the Mexican woman kept telling us to get indoors and put aloe on our skin. I tried to converse with her in Spanish, but she would only speak broken English back to me.

"Inside. Please go inside," she kept saying. Her damage-control skills far surpassed my best Levite instincts. Surely the caretakers had seen worse before, I consoled myself as I sought refuge in the den with my fellow pillagers. Through the sliding glass doors we watched the caretakers efficiently reassemble their masters' home. Their clothes were soaked through, but they kept working, directing their children to rescue smaller items as the adults carried the bigger pieces.

Henry rolled a joint while the rest of us carefully pulled our clothes on over our raw skin. Eventually Parrot came back inside and sat quietly in a corner reading *The Wall Street Journal*. Brooks emerged from twitch-reset and began rummaging through the house, opening drawers and medicine cabinets.

The pot soothed us a bit. We were over the peak of the acid, but this only made the strychnine and other impurities in the cheap blotter that much more pronounced. It wasn't a nice way to come down.

After the Mexicans had restored as much order as they could, they instructed us to please not take anything else outside even if the rain stopped. Then they left us alone again.

We were all sitting silently in the den, recovering from the trauma and trying not to gnash our teeth too much (another strychnine side effect), when Brooks came in, his hands filled with plastic prescription bottles. He dumped them on a coffee table for us to see. Valium, Librium, pentobarbital, Darvon, Dalmane, Halcion, Nembutal, and Percocet, all "dispensed as written"—no generic substitutes. And all downers. The Wards must have been tense people. We each popped a couple to take the harsh corners off the toxic tail of the acid trip. I expected Nomie to react to Brooks's scavenger hunt, but she just swallowed a Valium and tightened the towel around her hair.

"I saw something you might wanna know about," Brooks told us as we ate our pills. Nomie's eyes became a little shifty, but she didn't object as Brooks led the rest of us down a long corridor to

Mr. Ward's library. On the wall were dozens of pictures of Nomie's distinguished sixty-something-year-old father with George Bush, Malcolm Forbes, Robert Redford, . . . and E. T. Harman.

They were standing together in front of a sprawling modern office building, holding a silver shovel. The framed photo was signed in black felt-tip: "Dean—Thanks for making this work possible. Once your teacher, now your pal, Earl."

The worst time to get a dose of paranoia is when you're coming off a dose of harsh psychedelics.

36.

After the third degree that Duncan inflicted on poor, gray-haired Nomie, I didn't expect her to come back with us. I suppose Duncan didn't want her in the club anymore, but Nomie persevered. When she climbed into the Escort in disgrace, her long gray hair hanging down over her shoulders, I respected her more than anyone else in the club.

I drove the car with Duncan riding shotgun and Lauren and Nomie in the back. Duncan spoke only about the most trivial, surface matters. This was because Nomie was no longer to be trusted. Her dad had been a member of the Cosmotology movement for eight years and was the chief patron of their new Eureka, California, research center (one town away from Arcata), yet Nomie had never divulged this to the Ecstasy Club. She cried real tears as she explained that she had meant to tell us from the beginning, but then as Cosmotology developed into such an archrival she became scared of how we would react. Well, now she knew.

Lauren held her hand, using the nonverbal language of women to communicate that everything would be all right. This, too, shall pass.

"We can stop somewhere for a bite when it gets dark," Duncan said, much too casually.

"I wanted you to find out, Duncan," Nomie said, cutting through his conversational armor. "That's why I invited you up. I knew it would come out if you met my dad."

"Oh, really?"

"Yes, Duncan. I thought it might help you rest a little easier if you saw that the Cosmotology people aren't all out to get you."

"Do you agree with her, Zach?" Duncan knew better than to use me this way at this late stage of the game. I was a looser cannon than Nomie, by far.

"I think Nomie has more than demonstrated her dedication to the club, Duncan. She should have told us, yes. But it's not a capital crime."

"Well, we aren't the ones imposing death penalties, Zach, now are we? As far as I know, only her dad's friends do that."

"We don't know that Cosmotology was responsible, Duncan," I said. "Maybe we shouldn't have ordered that tube to begin with."

"But you didn't answer my question, Zach. Do you think Nomie's right? That I should rest easier now? That I've deluded myself into recasting the harmless and well-meaning E. T. Harman as our antagonist?"

"We don't really know who he is, Duncan."

"Precisely." He glared into the rearview mirror at Nomie. "We don't really know who anyone is anymore, do we?" And with that he declared the conversation a victory.

We were on Highway 1, just getting into Mill Valley, when I saw a 7–Eleven. I put on my directional signal early for Henry to follow me into the parking lot in his van, but he was too stoned to notice and drove right past. We decided to get out, anyway, and hope they'd figure it out. It was another mistake.

"Michael Mackey lives right around here," Nomie said as we walked on the gravel toward the store.

"And how do you know that?" Duncan asked her accusatorily. He held the door open for her in spite of himself. (Good manners die hard.)

Lauren and I stayed outside under the pretense of letting me smoke a cigarette. We wanted some relief from their Spy vs. Spy match. We were alone for all of ten seconds before Duncan came running out waving a copy of *Plugged* magazine.

"He's on the cover! Is this proof enough? He's on the cover!"

There he was. E. T. Harman, founder of Cosmotology, photographed in eerie red light with a bold yellow headline, THE CYBERNETICS OF PERSONALITY.

It wouldn't have been so bad if this weren't the same issue in which the predetermined listing for our predetermined party appeared.

"This is more than coincidence, isn't it, Nomie?" He shoved the magazine in her face.

"I don't know, Duncan. I don't know. It's not my fault."

He was livid. The worst I had ever seen him. He grabbed her by the shirt and pushed her against a big ice machine.

"Did they plant you here from the beginning? Is that it? Have you been reporting back to them the whole time? Is this how they know our every move? Why did you seduce me, Nomie? To get more information?"

I was about to pull him off her (honestly I was) when an Asian man came out of the 7–Eleven asking for money.

"You did not pay! You did not pay!" he shouted at Duncan.

Duncan tore the cover off the magazine and threw it at the man's feet.

"You broke it, you pay!"

"Fuck off!" Duncan told him.

Nomie used the distraction to escape. She and Lauren headed back for my car as I tried to effect a conflict resolution.

"We're sorry," I said to the storekeeper. "He's just upset. How much is it?"

"Fuck if we're paying for that!" Duncan kicked the magazine and a fair amount of gravel at the man.

"No, fuck *you!*" said the man, returning to the store, frightened, but gaining confidence as he stepped into the safety of his threshold. "I'm calling the police!"

"How much do you pay them? Eh?" Duncan shouted after the man. Then he started banging on a Ms. Pac-Man game just outside the door. "How much do you pay for this?" Reverting to an earlier, punk version of himself, he began kicking the arcade game. His face was red and he spit as he spoke. He picked up a trash can and started slamming it against the machine. I had no idea how to approach the situation.

"Come on, Zach!" Lauren shouted from the car. "Let's just go! Leave him!"

I was about to do as she said—just get into the car with Nomie and Lauren and simply drive away—but I was rescued by Henry, who finally pulled his van into the parking lot. He had a dazed, happy expression on his face. He rolled down his window.

"Hey, mates! I thought we'd lost you for sure!" On recognizing Duncan's Sid Vicious routine, Henry jumped out of the van. He knew exactly what to do—maybe he and Duncan had been through similar scenes together in the East End.

"Come on, Dunc, time to go. You got 'em, boy, you did." He went behind Duncan, put one hand firmly on each of his arms, and escorted him to his van. "They'll pay, they will. We'll see to it."

I stood there stunned a moment, waiting for Henry to instruct me.

"I got him, Zach, don't you worry. Just lead us back, all righty?"

I picked up the remains of the magazine (no need to let it go to waste) and ran to my car.

Nomie, Lauren, and I drove back to the PF while Henry followed in the van. We stayed pretty quiet. I think we were all feeling like traitors. Lauren, for wanting to ditch Duncan; me, for refusing to back him up against Nomie; and Nomie, for being the daughter of a Cosmotologist and a decade older than she pretended to be.

We couldn't guess what was going on in the van. We would find out soon enough.

37.

The decision was made without me. As soon as we got back to the PF, Duncan called a meeting to brief us all on the mission he had planned.

Seven of us—Duncan, Henry, Brooks, Parrot, Peter, Tyrone, and I—would drive in two vehicles up to Harman's Eureka offices to confront him directly on his interference with PF business, his involvement in Steven and Sturgeon's deaths and Pig and Brooks's brain virus, and his manipulation of the space-time continuum. If for any reason we were denied access to Harman, we would break into the Eureka Cosmotology Center, learn whatever we could, and disable as much of their equipment as possible. To this end, Duncan had us gather ropes, chains, power tools, spray paint, flashlights, and anything else that might be of use on the expedition.

He had called Pig from the road, using Parrot's cellular phone, and instructed him to build two "tasers" capable of paralyzing anyone who tried to stop or capture us. The completed weapons weighed ten pounds each, required that the user wear a battery belt, and took nine seconds to recharge after being used. Still, they had a range of three feet and delivered a jolt of three hundred volts, so hopefully they would have to be used only once if a combat situation arose.

The "Ecstasy Militia" was born.

By midnight, we were in the lot in front of the PF, loading our supplies into the van and checking a map for the best route to Eureka. This would be my last chance to duck out, and I still hadn't thought of a reasonable excuse. Duncan was in hypermode and showed no signs of letting up, so I took him aside and gave it my best shot.

"I'm concerned about both of us being gone at the same time, Duncan."

He regarded me coldly—as coldly as he did the newly traitorous Nomie. Maybe everyone who had traveled back from San Rafael in my car instead of the van was a persona non grata.

"I understand, Zach. That's fine. Just give your keys to Henry and he'll drive."

He knew me too well. If my car went with them, I had no way of knowing whether it would make it back. And whatever they did using my vehicle would be traced back to me through the tags.

"But Lauren isn't feeling well. I really should have a way to take her to the doctor."

"Fine, then." He regarded the crowd loading the van. "Alex?"

The boy ran up to us, an obedient and enthusiastic private in the newly formed army.

"Yes, Duncan?"

"We need another vehicle and driver. Want to come with us?"

"Sure!"

Why did I feel so responsible for this kid?

"He's underage, Duncan. You can't take him."

"Why not?" Alex argued against his own best interests. "I can do stuff the rest of you can't because I'm a minor. They can't prosecute me."

"He's right, Zach," Duncan said calmly. "He'll make a better addition than you. Thanks for understanding."

"Can't you just take his car?" I asked. "You don't need him to go along."

"My car's a stick," Alex warned.

"It is?" Duncan asked, feigning alarm. "I don't drive stick." He shouted to the others at the van. "None of you drive stick, now, do you?" He intoned his words in a way that communicated, "Say no."

They all shook their heads, following his implicit order.

"I guess you'll have to come, then, Alex."

I couldn't let the boy go in my stead. I gave in.

"It's okay, Duncan. You win."

"What do you mean?"

"I'll go, okay?"

"No, no—Alex will be better."

"I said I'll go. I'm going to Eureka with you."

"I don't know . . ."

"Please, okay?"

"Whatever you want, Zach. Whatever you want." Duncan put his hands up, "defeated," and went back to the van. Alex stared at me, fuming.

"Fuck you, Zach. You're never going to let me in the club, are you? You're scared of me—that they won't need you anymore with me around. I don't know why I ever respected you. You're totally lame." He marched back into the building, tears welling up in his eyes.

I suppose both of us had lost our role models. Some small part of me hoped I was misunderstanding Duncan's greater intentions as much as Alex was misreading mine.

I went inside to say good-bye to Lauren but didn't receive the *Casablanca* farewell I was hoping for. She was up in my room, standing in the middle of the floor.

"Let's just leave now," she said firmly.

"I can't, Lauren. I'll just go along and make sure no one gets into any trouble."

"Right." She was unconvinced.

"Maybe if we find Harman, Duncan will see that he's blown the whole thing up out of proportion."

"But what if he's right, Zach? Ever think of that? What if these people are murderers?"

"Then we should find out what they want and get it over with."

"It's only going to get worse, Zach. The longer we stay, the harder it's going to be."

"I'll go with them, I'll come back, and then we'll leave, okay?"

She wouldn't say anything. I felt like a little boy. And she was a woman.

"I promise, Lauren. We'll pack and leave as soon as I'm back. Alex can stay if he wants. We'll just leave no matter what."

"I don't believe you. I don't want to have a baby here, Zach. I don't even want to be pregnant here. I'm not going through with it if we're here."

"Don't talk like that, Lauren. We're going to be okay."

I kissed her on the cheek and left before she made any hard threats, and before she could prove to me how much of a fool I was being.

38.

Leaving for a commando raid at one in the morning is never a good idea. But the nineteenth was just seven days away, and we had a lot to get into place by then.

The whole trip was only five or six hundred miles, but Henry's van had a top speed of about forty-five miles an hour, and even less uphill. I drove with Brooks and Peter. Everyone else went in the van. There were almost as many of us in the car as in the van, but for some reason it felt like they were "everyone" and we were the outsiders. Whenever we stopped for gas or food we'd ask Duncan, Parrot, and Henry what they had talked about during the last stretch. They would tell us more details of the plan, new things that Tyrone had remembered about Harman, and any insights that had occurred to Duncan about Cosmotology's intentions.

We drove right through the next day until late in the afternoon. Peter sat in the back and read an old Cosmotology book about mind control, while Brooks and I snorted frequent, short lines of coke to stay awake and keep conversing. Each bump of coke was a microcosm of my entire Ecstasy Club experience. I felt great for about half an hour: Here I was on a mission with my best friends in the world. We were going up against the baddest bad guy on earth—taking him down in a cosmic battle to the finish. We were young, powerful, virile, and smart. The next generation. Brooks was such a cool guy when I was high on coke. He coaxed me to drive recklessly, hang in the passing lane, force the car into lower gears for maximum power, and play the radio loud.

Then the coke would get a little speedy. I still felt young and powerful but needed to prove it every few minutes by hollering out the window or going along with one of Brooks's more outlandish suggestions. After that, we'd both get tweaked out. We'd start wondering why, if we were indeed such cool guys, weren't we up in the van with Duncan? Did Duncan associate Brooks with me and discriminate against him because of it? Or vice versa? Or did he have something against Peter? And why wasn't Peter saying anything? Was he awake? Could he hear our conversation?

Then we'd do another line and feel great again—but not as completely great as when we'd done the previous line.

At dusk, we followed Henry as he pulled his van off the road into a campground. We strung up a tarp between the hatch of my Escort and the sliding door on the side of the van. I was hoping the rift between our two groups was only imaginary, but each posse stayed close to its own vehicle, and we shared food only with the members of our individual factions.

Henry and Duncan had bonded deeply, and there was no way to insinuate myself into their relationship. Parrot had become their sadistic sidekick, egging them on to new levels of military fanaticism, and Tyrone was their nonsensically sage mascot.

We built a fire and cooked some turkey franks on the ends of sticks. It was almost quaint. After we ate, we stared into the fire and thought about the mission ahead. As if on a cue from Duncan, Henry produced a plastic bag from his vest pocket. It contained a few hits of orange DMT powder.

"Let's focus together," Duncan said. Then he looked at me. "It will help unify the group."

I was feeling so worn out from all the coke and desperate for any high at all that I gladly took hold of the pipe and received my dose. It was smaller than the last time, but in a few seconds it came on.

I closed my eyes and flashed on my father. He was treasurer of our temple in Westport, Connecticut, when I was growing up. I remembered how I used to sit at his feet at the dining-room table as he added up the membership checks and holiday contributions. Once, after a Purim carnival, we went to the bank together to deposit the thousands of quarters they had collected from the carnival games. The bank had a big machine that counted the change, and the man behind the desk let me pour in the bags of quarters and watch them get stacked into neatly wrapped rolls stamped with the bank's insignia.

"It's fun, isn't it?" my father asked me. I wanted to say yes, but for some reason I couldn't.

That's when I saw them again. The lizard men in the white sedans. I was still six years old, playing with a toy spaceship. They just pulled up to the curb and watched me. I was too young for them to attack. They only needed to monitor me. Check on my progress.

I realized who they were. The past. The lizard brain. Evolutionary history. The backward pull—almost equal and opposite to the great attractor at the end of time. The antagonists to progress. The keepers of the status quo. The enemy.

One of them reached into his jacket. I thought he was drawing a weapon, but he wasn't. It was a wrapped roll of quarters stamped with a Jewish star. He lowered his window and smiled. It was E. T. Harman.

"It was fun, wasn't it?" he asked.

Then I saw Duncan. His giant face like a film over the whole scene.

"You see the enemy now, don't you? You see him?"

I nodded.

"Do you know what to do?" he asked. "Do you know what to do?"

My eyes were open. I was back at the campsite. Duncan was now sitting face-to-face with Henry, whispering at him.

"Would you, Henry? Would you know what to do?"

Henry nodded.

"Would you do anything for me, Henry?"

"I would, Duncan. I would."

Duncan moved away from Henry, then knelt before Brooks the same way.

"Do you see him, Brooks? Do you know what to do?"

Peter sat cross-legged by himself. He was staring into space.

39.

We didn't get up and leave the campsite until afternoon. I was surprised yet oddly relieved when Duncan said we should change cars. He and Tyrone rode with me, and everyone else went in the van. Now "everyone else" took on a completely different meaning for me.

Eureka, our target, was still two or three hours away, but Duncan had a lot he wanted to share with me. After the evening's DMT brainwashing ritual, Duncan felt more comfortable with me. In spite of myself, I also felt more dedicated to him and our common purpose.

It was like old times.

"Tyrone remembered a lot more about the Arcata Project," Duncan said. "Didn't you, Tyrone?"

"That's right. Yup," Tyrone affirmed from the backseat. "Brock, Sturgeon, Harman. All of 'em. Taking the kids. Everything."

"He told us they employed him as a psychic link, just as Sturgeon described. But instead of using soldiers to do the actual time travel, they took children."

"They kidnapped them?"

"Yes. The abducted-children-on-milk-cartons conspiracy that Parrot told us about, where parents are induced to permit transponder implants in their children's teeth, was the cover story—the decoy conspiracy over the real one. Children were being abducted to work as time travelers."

"Why?"

Tyrone answered. "They were more open to the shifts in resonance. More resilient."

"Well, maybe interdimensional travel is an adaptive ability. Something in the DNA that new-type, evolved children already have."

"I suppose it's possible," Duncan said. "But it probably has a lot more to do with principles of brain development in children."

"And they didn't put up as much of a struggle," Tyrone explained matter-of-factly.

We went on like this for the rest of the trip, theorizing on the historical significance of Harman's work, whatever his intentions, and discussing how we were going to release all this information to the press—the good press, not *Plugged* or *Rolling Stone*—once we had physical proof of Harman's work, or a confession from Harman himself. This was the moment we had been waiting for.

"Once the time-travel information is released to the general public," Duncan excitedly explained, "the rate of novelty will suddenly explode. The limits of linear time will cease to exist, conceptually and practically."

"And fortunately, those of us who have been preparing for this will be equipped to navigate," I added confidently. I felt as high as I had from the coke a day before, and made about as much sense.

"Correct. The psychedelic space is the practice run—not for death as Clearwater speculated or as the Malthusians insisted, but for the rebirth into timelessness. Only those who have been able to let go of the mundane will make it. Those who can transcend the consensus social set and the static frequency of linear time and matter itself."

"And those who can't?" I thought of my parents back in Connecticut. My little sister in her first year of law school.

"I guess we'll find out on December 19, Zach."

We were there. It was 5:30 P.M. and cars were leaving the parking lot. The structure was a multitiered complex of geometric glass. There were satellite dishes and other large contraptions on the roof. Brooks snapped pictures of everything. The entire property was protected by a tall security fence with two guard booths.

Duncan was feeling bold and instructed me to pull up to the front guard station.

The uniformed man held a clipboard and wore mirrored glasses.

"Who are you here to see?"

Duncan leaned over me to speak with the guard.

"Dr. Harman is expecting us."

"Oh, really?"

"Yes. You might remember him mentioning us to you, personally, when you find our name on the bottom of the list."

"Might I?" Duncan's technique wasn't working. The guard was hip to Erikson. He must have been a Cosmotology member. They all were. "And what might you do when I call Security?"

"Let's call him on the cell phone, Duncan," I think I said.

"I'll be sure to let Dr. Harman know about this," Duncan said, motioning for me to turn the car around.

"You do that, Duncan," the guard said, sarcastically waving good-bye.

"How did he know my name?" Duncan asked, panic-stricken once we were out of earshot.

"I think I said it, Duncan."

"No, you didn't. I would have specifically remembered."

"I think Zach said it, Duncan," Tyrone chimed in.

"No, he didn't. The guard knew. He knew somehow."

We drove around the perimeter of the complex with Henry still following, and noticed several other gates without guards. There was a small touch pad next to each one. We pulled up to the gate at the far end of the compound and pressed 188, 881, 1818, and 12191995, but nothing happened. Our numerological theories were dumped on the same useless heap as our hypnotic-suggestion techniques.

Henry told us to pull to the side. He had an idea. We waited there as Peter and Duncan struggled with numeric sequences. Eventually, a car came out of the parking lot. The driver put a card in a slot, the gate swung open, and he drove out. In a flash, Henry had pulled his van through the opening before the gate closed. He motioned for me to follow. I hit the gas but before I was all the way through, the gate closed onto the side of my car. I was stuck.

"Just push through!" shouted Duncan.

I edged the car slightly forward. The sound of the metal posts digging into the unscathed finish of my Escort was too much for me. Every instinct in my body resisted destroying my door panels.

"Now, Zach! Just drive!"

I edged forward again, and the high-pitched squeal of abrading Ford nearly sent me into convulsions. I had paid for this car with the graduation money my grandfather had willed to me.

"Go!" Duncan ordered, stepping on my foot with his Doc Marten and flooring the accelerator pedal.

In a second it was over. The car was pierced through on both sides, and a detached wheel rim shimmied noisily on the pavement behind us. Then the gate slammed shut, trapping the orphaned chrome trim.

I glanced angrily over at Duncan, who glared back. *How dare you,* we were both saying.

We pulled into two numbered spots near the edge of the parking lot and debated what to do. Employees (cult members) were pouring out now. I realized I could have saved my car by simply waiting until the next time the fence opened. Every car that passed through the open gate reminded me of the permanent damage to my Escort.

Most of the employees were coming out two main doors in front of the building, but the better-dressed executives appeared to be exiting from a set of stairs off one of the side wings. Duncan guessed that this was where we'd find Harman.

When things quieted down a bit, Tyrone, Henry, Brooks, Duncan, and I headed for the stairway in question while Peter and Parrot waited with the cars. As we ascended, we could see through the glass windows into the building. There were lots of video-editing suites and offices equipped with what looked like dentist's chairs. Each landing opened to a terrace with sliding glass doors leading to another office.

Tyrone took charge. He made those Vietnam-vet gestures of his, spreading us out onto different terraces. He was wearing a taser and battery belt. Brooks took more pictures.

One of the sliding glass doors opened and a man came out, holding a briefcase. We tried to act casual as he looked us over. Tyrone took his taser out of the holster.

"No!" I shouted, alarming the businessman, but Tyrone pretended the gun was a measuring device of some kind and marked out imaginary spaces on one of the window frames.

"We'll need another yard of Duropane, 188 gauge," Tyrone said to Duncan, who pretended to look for a pen.

The man shook his head and headed down the stairs.

Why did Tyrone have to say "188 gauge"? Brooks stood frozen with the camera held to his face. We tried to shake him out of his twitch-reset but he wouldn't budge. We hardly noticed as another businessman came down the steps. The man made it all the way past us, then suddenly turned around.

"Tyrone?" It was E. T. Harman. He had recognized Tyrone.

Tyrone, panicked, pointed the taser toward his former tormentor. Harman pivoted and began to run. I followed after him, grabbing his jacket.

"Wait!" I said. "I'm Zach Levi. We're here from the Ecstasy Club—"

Harman yanked himself free but dropped his briefcase in the process, then tripped over it. We all watched as E. T. Harman slowly tumbled down two flights of concrete stairs, then lay at a landing in a pin-striped clump. He didn't move.

Tyrone ran down to him, pushing his taser into Harman's prone body and pulling the trigger. Harman's limbs vibrated violently for about ten seconds, then stopped.

"What did you do that for?" I asked. "He was unconscious."

Tyrone didn't say anything. We all just stood around the body for a minute, not knowing what to do. Then Duncan nodded to Henry, who pulled a large black plastic bag out of his shoulder pack.

"What are you doing?" I asked Duncan. Had they planned this during the drive yesterday?

"Plan B. There's no other choice," he said. "You told him your name. *Our* name."

Tyrone and Henry clumsily wrapped Harman in the plastic and carried him toward the cars. I had to lead the still-frozen Brooks down the stairs.

Parrot opened the van door and we dumped Harman inside. I could feel him struggling to breathe from within the bag, so I opened the top for him to get some air. Then the door closed behind me and the van started to move.

Duncan looked back from the passenger seat.

"Zach! Your keys!"

I had no other choice. I handed them over, and he tossed them out to Parrot. We drove in wild circles as Henry desperately searched for an exit. Harman was moaning from inside the bag.

"Keep him quiet!" Duncan shouted at me as Henry careened out of control.

Tyrone went for his taser.

"No!" I said, handing Tyrone a piece of cloth. "Just stick this in his mouth, okay?"

Tyrone fashioned a gag around the frightened Harman's mouth. The old man looked at me with terrified but information-gathering eyes. I looked away, afraid of what he would see. Tyrone covered Harman's face with plastic, relieving us all.

Suddenly, *BANG!* Henry had hit something with the van.

"Fucking Christ!" he said, pulling back.

"Just get in!" I heard Duncan shout out his window.

The back door of the van opened and in hopped Parrot, Brooks, and Peter.

"What happened?" I asked as we peeled out with the tailgate still wide open. No one responded.

As Henry made another sharp turn toward an open exit, I saw the remains of my totaled Escort.

40.

As far as I was concerned, our abduction of E. T. Harman was a complete accident. I doubt that he saw it that way. In fact, he would have had us believe he manipulated the whole event.

Once we were an hour or so away from the scene of the crime, Duncan joined us in the back of the van and instructed Tyrone to remove Harman's shroud and gag. Harman's face was dripping with sweat—it must have been hot in that bag.

"Let's get you out of there, eh?" Duncan said in his friendliest, most nurturing voice.

Harman remained silent as Parrot and I removed the bag from his body. He stared at Brooks, who refused to make eye contact.

"How long has he shown the symptoms?" Harman asked us.

"You should know, mate," Henry said, angrily.

"It doesn't look to me like he has much time left," Harman said sadly. Brooks looked up at him, pathetic, frightened, desperate for compassion. "You might want to tell them to let me go, so your problem can go away too."

"Let him go, Duncan!" Brooks pleaded, responding to Harman's hypnotic suggestion.

"Sit in the front," Duncan ordered. Brooks complied.

"You can't make them all sit in the front, Duncan," Harman said calmly.

"We know about you," Duncan said. "What you've been doing to us."

"Then you know I'm the only one who can make it stop."

"You killed two people."

"I don't interfere, Duncan. People do what they do. I can see you understand me. You're the same. A conscious mind directs an unconscious mind, just as the unconscious mind directs the conscious mind. Except there are some things the conscious mind knows that the unconscious minds don't. And other things the unconscious mind knows that the conscious mind doesn't. But when the unconscious mind—"

Tyrone suddenly zapped Harman with the taser. Harman convulsed a few seconds and passed out. That's when I saw that Duncan had been completely hypnotized.

"Duncan! Duncan!" Tyrone shook George awake. "Don't let him do that to you, boy. He's good."

"Huh?"

"He had you going, kid."

"I'm amazed I fell for it. Linguistic presupposition, associative linkage, then simple confusion. I *know* these techniques."

We put the gag in Harman's mouth for the rest of the trip. We should have put the bag back on his head, too.

We stopped only for gas. It was a long ride home, and we were all crowded in the back like illegal immigrants. I kept thinking about my car with its traceable license plates, the guard who saw us, the businessman on the stairs, Lauren and our child visiting me in jail. I was done for. I wanted to run away.

Peter was the only one of us who would look at Harman directly in the eyes after the episode with Duncan. It was as if Peter recognized him from his visionquest experiences. He hated him. Harman was blinking an awful lot, as if he was tired or had something in his eyes. Then I noticed a pattern. He was blinking in some kind of code. It would get faster, then slower. Peter was transfixed by it.

"Stop!" I shouted. Henry stopped the van. "Harman's doing something to Peter. He's blinking at him in some kind of rhythm."

"It's an induction technique, Peter," Duncan shouted. "Don't look at him. He's alternating the frequency of his blinks to bring you into trance."

Peter wouldn't look away, so Tyrone covered Harman's head with the bag.

"I need some air," Peter said, crawling over us and opening the door. He lowered himself out of the van and then suddenly darted off the road toward the woods.

"Peter!" I jumped out of the van. It was pitch-black. I could hear him running down the embankment. "Peter! Come back!" He was gone.

When I got back to the van I could hear Harman humming from inside the bag. I took Tyrone's taser from his belt, plunged it into the bag, and felt my teeth clench as I pulled the trigger.

Harman didn't make a sound for the rest of the trip.

41.

We got back to the PF the next afternoon. It was strangely quiet.

Parrot, Henry, and Duncan carried Harman's limp form to Tyrone's shaftway as I went up to find Lauren. She was in my bed, asleep.

"Lauren?" I sat on the bed. She stirred. "Things are getting really fucked up."

I switched on my lamp. Lauren looked pale. She opened her eyes.

"Zach. I don't feel well. Something's wrong."

"What is it?" I asked, sitting her up to give her a hug. She clutched her abdomen.

I pulled back the covers and there was blood all over the sheets.

"What's wrong? What's happening?" she cried.

I got some sanitary pads from Nomie and then dressed Lauren as quickly as I could. She just cried.

"We lost it, didn't we?" she kept saying. "Duncan was right."

"Don't talk like that." It was the only thing I could think to say. "Don't talk like that."

I was going to tell Duncan where we were going, but he and the others were occupied with Harman so I just got Alex to drive us to the clinic. He kept asking questions about what had happened with Harman and what was wrong with Lauren, but I told him to keep quiet and drive. Every time he shifted gears, Lauren grimaced in pain. Once we got to the clinic, I helped Lauren out of the car and instructed Alex to go back home. I think he was scared by the intensity of what was occurring. He had never dealt with real-life problems before. Come to think of it, neither had I.

I was amazed by how long they made us wait. When the nurse finally called Lauren's name, she told me I couldn't go in with her until after the doctor had finished his examination, and then "only if she wants you to. It's up to her."

I squeezed Lauren's hand but she didn't squeeze back. She had already admitted defeat.

She was in there for quite a while. I didn't know what I was supposed to be thinking about—Lauren miscarrying our baby or the guys back home with the kidnapped Harman. Which was the bigger catastrophe? A baby is a real thing. A whole human being. But we could get thrown in a real jail for what we had done to Harman, however accidentally and innocently.

Harman started the whole thing, I tried to tell myself. He was the murderer, not us. We hadn't provoked him—we were just going about our business of breaking through to the next dimension. What right did he have to stop us? My brain couldn't take it anymore. I picked up a copy of *Newsweek* from the chair next to me. There was a big article about the Unabomber, excerpting parts of his manifesto. Paragraph number twenty caught my eye.

> Notice the masochistic tendency of leftist tactics. Leftists protest by lying down in front of vehicles, they intentionally provoke police or racists to abuse them, etc. These tactics may often be effective, but many leftists use them not as a means to an end but because they PREFER masochistic tactics.

Were we the masochists, begging for abuse to confirm our own suspicions? Were the lizard men right? Were we just looking for some big scary authorities to fuck us up?

The nurse said I could go in. I went down the hallway to the office of the hook-nosed doctor. Lauren sat in a chair by his desk in a green hospital gown stamped "Property of Berkeley Clinic." She was crying and had a box of tissues on her lap. I braced myself for the worst.

"The sonogram shows that the fetus is fine," the doctor said. "I can give her something for the cramps. The spotting should stop in a few weeks, but it's nothing to worry about if it doesn't."

I realized Lauren had been crying with relief. I put my hand on her shoulder.

The doctor pulled a small dark fax from Lauren's folder and smiled. He seemed less evil now, but I still didn't trust him.

"You can keep this if you like."

He handed Lauren the thermal paper and we both looked at it. It was a radar sweep of an @-sign. *What did he know?* Who was this man?

"What is it?" I asked, suspicious.

Lauren laughed.

"It's the baby."

42.

We took BART back to the PF.

It was getting dark early. A couple of people had Christmas presents with them, and many houses were flashing with colored lights. I had forgotten about Christmas.

We were going in the opposite direction of rush hour, so the only people on the train were maids and university workers on their way home to Oakland. I remembered the last time we were coming back from the clinic. In my car I had felt so much safer and in control. Now we were unprotected. It was as if I were in a Beckett play and my few props were slowly disappearing. The only thing I had left to cling to was Lauren. My thoughts must have floated over to her.

"What happened to your car?" Lauren asked tentatively.

I wasn't sure what to tell her about the kidnapping. I thought if I kept her in the dark she might be able to claim plausible deniability. I was already playing out the courtroom proceedings in my head. Then I realized she would have plausible deniability whether I told her or not, so I burdened her with the whole gruesome saga. She listened with a straight face. I couldn't read her at all. Since she got pregnant, since she accepted the idea of keeping the baby, Lauren had become much more grounded. Practical. Real. Adult.

When I was through with the whole story, she just said, "We can't stay there anymore."

"We can't leave either, Lauren. We don't know what they'll do. What if they kill him?"

"Then we should be as far from them as possible."

"My car is up in that parking lot right now. I'm the only lead they'll have to go on."

"Then you should go to the police right now before it gets any worse. Tell them that you were on drugs."

"Go to who? Laruso?"

"Go to someone else."

"And do what? Turn Duncan in? What do you think he'll say? It will all come back to me. There's got to be a way out of this."

She wouldn't agree.

"Let's just wait until the party, okay? Maybe something really will happen. Duncan's been right about everything else. Maybe, if we can just hang on until then—"

The train stopped to let some passengers off and others on. A young black couple came in and sat across from us. The girl was very pregnant. She looked a little scared and self-conscious. The boy held her hand. We looked at them and they looked at us. Lauren was holding her hand over her lap the same way the other girl was. And I was holding her free hand the same way the boy was holding his girlfriend's. I smiled, and the boy in the mirror smiled too.

I had an epiphany. But then the train doors opened at our stop and I forgot it.

43.

The final Phylogenic Foresight was just four days away. I wondered if anyone had done the flyers. We couldn't forget the little chores. The record stores. The coffee bars.

Parrot was standing guard by Tyrone's door. He eyed me suspiciously.

"Alex said you went to the doctor?"

"Yeah. Lauren was sick. We had to."

"Duncan wasn't sure where you'd gone."

"It's cool, okay? Christ."

"Harman admitted to everything, you know," Parrot said, as if to justify our leader's actions.

"He's smart, Parrot. He'd say he's responsible even if he wasn't. It gives him something to play."

"Well, he's playing it."

"Are we still doing the '188' party on Tuesday night?" I asked.

"He says so." "He" meant Duncan. I wondered if we were supposed to capitalize the word from now on when referring to him.

"With our hostage on the premises?" I felt my sarcasm building. "This should be great."

"This is no time to be wising off," Parrot scolded me. *Wising off?* Where were we, junior high?

"Can I go in there?"

"I'll see."

Parrot knocked on the door. Twice, then once, then once again. A new code.

A voice, Henry's, asked who it was. After a moment of debate, the door opened and then closed again after I went in.

Harman was suspended about ten feet in the air, tied to the metal ladder. His wrists were bound to two supports holding the ladder to the wall. He looked like Christ being crucified, but he was pretty old—about my dad's age. Duncan sat on top of an

A-frame ladder directly in front of him, holding a tape recorder. He was trying to elicit some kind of confession. Duncan was quite frustrated.

Harman, much to my surprise, was smiling broadly. He couldn't move an inch, but he acted like he was in complete control of the situation. I imagined he must have been tortured back in World War II. We were mere amateurs. Henry and Tyrone stood with me at ground level, looking up at the thought-warring titans.

"What about Kirsten?" Duncan asked him uncertainly. "Was she a plant?"

"Your worst suspicions are true, son."

"I'm not your son."

"It's a matter of time."

"What do you mean by that?"

"This has all happened already—"

"Stop that. Did you approve our acquisition of the double-E tube?"

"I've been approving of you since the beginning."

They went on and on like this, with Duncan giving away information while deflecting Harman's attempts to manipulate him, and with Harman continually suggesting that he was somehow responsible for everything that was going on.

Eventually, Duncan signaled to Henry, who obediently picked up a bucket and started up the metal ladder toward Harman. Before he made it all the way up, I heard Harman laughing loudly. Drops of water fell on my head.

It wasn't water. Harman had refused our hospitality and was pissing all over himself and me.

44.

I tried not to go back in there except when Duncan specifically asked for me. I didn't want to have any more to do with this awful business than absolutely necessary.

Three more days until maximum novelty and, amazingly, life at the PF went on pretty much as usual—whatever that means—except for the sounds we all heard from behind Tyrone's door. Duncan spent all his time in there, so I was responsible for making sure the party went off properly. Alex, Parrot, and Nomie helped me get it all together. Alex was smart enough to know that whatever was going on in the shaftway was something he didn't want to know about. None of us spoke about it. No one knew how much anyone else knew. We became as apprehensive of one another as we used to be of Harman, Laruso, *Plugged,* and the aliens.

The stench in there got pretty bad. Harman refused to cooperate in any way. (He did eat the cut-up Power Bars that Henry put in his mouth.) He just stared straight ahead at whoever was up on the ladder across from him, and peed and shit on himself several times a day. His left hand was turning blue from the bindings. Duncan offered to clean him up if he'd just tell us one small thing, anything at all—how to cure Brooks and Pig, or how to fix the computers, or how the EE tube worked, or if aliens were involved in this, or if he knew Kirsten, or what he did to Peter to make him flee, or if he had really achieved time travel, or the nature of his connection with the *Plugged* people. By the second morning, with just two days left before the nineteenth, Duncan had revealed just about everything we knew or suspected. Harman revealed nothing. Only that he was in complete control.

Neither the TV nor the newspapers reported anything about Harman's abduction. The Cosmotologists had to know. They must have been afraid of negative publicity. Or maybe they knew exactly where he was the whole time. Maybe he had really planned it all.

After a long series of failed attempts to wrest a confession from Harman, Duncan decided we'd have to go all out to brainwash him into submission. On the third night, he called Parrot and me into the shaftway to observe as he and Henry pulled off Harman's shirt and Tyrone applied a dozen nicotine patches to the man's gray chest. It was a potentially lethal dose of the drug and I would have objected, but Harman seemed so pleased by everything going on that I really did want to see him suffer a bit.

Tyrone growled vindictively as he peeled and applied the patches to his old boss's bare skin.

"The gremlins are still haunting you, eh, Corporal?" Harman taunted him.

Moments after the patches were affixed to Harman's skin, he began to shake and sweat. Though he tried to hide it, the nicotine was making him jittery. His breathing got faster and labored. He grunted with each exhale but struggled to make it sound like he was laughing.

Duncan motioned for Henry to stand guard and the rest of us to go outside and receive his instructions. As he swung the door open, Alex, Pig, and Brooks, who must have been eavesdropping, scattered in different directions.

"I want us to sit with him in two-hour shifts," Duncan commanded. "Keep him off-guard. The patches will make him quite nervous."

"If they don't kill him first," I cracked.

"That's not our problem, or our objective, Zach."

"And what, precisely, is our objective?" I didn't mean to sound quite as sarcastic as this came out—just about three-quarters as sarcastic.

"Ideally, a way to reverse the damage he's caused us. At the very least, a confession with corroborating details."

Parrot and Tyrone nodded—Tyrone seriously and Parrot in that new, hyperenthusiastic way of his.

"Zach, you should do the first shift," Duncan said.

Luckily, I wouldn't have to. Just as Duncan was finishing his briefing, Henry opened the door.

"I . . . I . . . don't know what happened . . ."

"What?" Duncan asked a bewildered Henry.

"He's gone. He's gone."

We crowded into the shaftway and, sure enough, Harman had vanished. The trapdoor at the top of the shaft was open.

I specifically recall that his bindings had vanished along with him, but Duncan and Henry later insisted that they were still hanging from the ladder when we climbed up. Also, for reasons that later became clear to me but no one else, we all climbed to the top of the freestanding A-frame ladder and then jumped over to the metal ladder attached to the wall before making our way up onto the roof.

Once the five of us were up there, we searched for any signs of Harman's escape route. There was nothing. I ran to the edge of the roof and looked down to the back lot. A dark form was running from the building. I knew I'd lose him if I went back down the ladder and through the building, so I looked for a way down— Harman's way down.

The only possibility was a drainpipe descending from a corner of the building. If it had held Harman's weight, I figured, it would be able to hold mine.

"Zach, no!" Duncan screamed as I climbed over the roof ledge and took hold of the pipe. I remember thinking about that—about Duncan's heartfelt warning, his instinctual plea for me not to risk my life—as the pipe slowly detached from the building. I assumed I was having a dream when the pipe folded over like a plastic straw, its corroded mounting bolts popping out one by one. I would wake up before I hit the ground. I saw Henry and Duncan leaning over the roof above me, their faces frozen in terror as I descended toward the pavement. I was still gripping the pipe with my arms and legs. I held onto it with my whole body, pressing my cheek against it like an infant at its mother's breast.

The pipe finally reached the end of its arc. My head was below my feet. My heart was racing—I didn't really know which way gravity wanted to pull me, so I just let go of the pipe and fell. But I didn't hit the ground. I was already there. The pipe had lowered me all the way to the pavement and set me down so gently that I didn't realize I had landed safely.

I could still see the moving form at the edge of the lot so I took off after it. He moved slowly for a man with a dozen nicotine patches, letting me quickly catch up and tackle him to the ground. He smelled even worse than I expected a man who had been shitting on himself for two days to smell.

"No! No, man, please!" he shouted in a fake African American accent as I grabbed his collar and pulled him to his feet. I was about to punch Harman when I realized his accent wasn't fake at all. It was one of our generator-mooching bums, scared to death of me.

I apologized and brushed him off, at which point he spit at me boldly and gave me the finger.

I looked back up to the roof but they weren't watching me anymore. As I walked back around the building, I found myself wondering what kind of jail they were going to put me in. Would I be in a big penitentiary and just get raped to death, or would they put an educated but misguided white kid like me in one of those tax-evasion prisons? The Menendez brothers killed their parents but they don't get raped in jail, do they?

I made my way back to the shaftway, where I saw Duncan, Henry, and the others gathered at the door. They were all looking up. I pushed through them to see.

Harman was back on the ladder, tied as he was before, shirt off, nicotine patches on. And laughing demonically.

"Now do you get it, boys? Do you get it?!"

His voice was spine-chilling. Desperate, manic, and utterly mad.

"I'm not the prisoner, kids. *You* are!"

45.

I contend that Harman never really escaped at all, but somehow hypnotized us into thinking he had. That's why we took the strange route up the ladders, and why I saw the bindings and the others didn't—we each imagined Harman gone in a different way. But everyone else still says Harman really escaped and then came right back in order to prove to us that he was at the Ecstasy Club by choice. As it turns out, this difference in perception hardly matters. Or maybe it's the whole point.

Duncan stayed with Harman in the shaftway a few more hours and learned why the old man felt he could call us his prisoners. He claimed he was the original owner of the PF building before he took a tax deduction by donating it to the city, and as proof told us that if we looked up the history of the plot in the City Hall archives, we would find it was land parcel number 376 (twice 188). He told Duncan that Tyrone had been planted at the PF back in 1985 after the Arcata base was closed, and, on schedule, he became our host exactly ten years later. Harman said his whole scheme was proceeding according to plan, but he wouldn't tell Duncan what the scheme was.

Before we went to bed, an unsettled Duncan separated the guys into two squads—those who would guard Harman round the clock and those who would attend to the party. Luckily, I was in the latter squad.

Lauren and I hadn't made love since we had kidnapped Harman (or he had kidnapped us, depending on your point of view), and tonight didn't look any different. She refused to let me tell her anything about what was going on in the shaftway until the whole calamity was over or until I agreed we were going to leave immediately. I wasn't sure how much longer I would be able to hold onto her under these conditions.

It was a week before Christmas. This, combined with the trauma of being pregnant and the felony-rich atmosphere of the PF, had Lauren longing for the safety and familiarity of home. When we heard Nomie coming up to our room with the portable phone saying "It's for you, it's your parents," I saw Lauren perk up hopefully. Then Nomie entered and handed the phone to me. Lauren sank back down.

"Hello?" I tried to sound normal. I hadn't spoken to my parents in weeks. I had almost forgotten they existed.

"What the hell is going on there?" It was my dad. What did he know? Had the story been on the news?

"Um, hi, Dad. What's the matter?"

"We saw it all on TV, Zach," he said—not so much angry as disappointed.

"Speak softly, Norman, you're hurting my ear." It was my mom. They always called together from different extensions in the house, and she always complained that he spoke too loud. She even made my dad buy a special volume control for her receiver, but she couldn't adjust it properly to hear me and attenuate my dad at the same time.

"What did you see, Dad?" I was already mentally packing my bags and fleeing.

"Denise saw it first," my mom corrected him.

"Yeah, well, we saw it too. On that MTV channel." He knew to call it MTV, not "that MTV channel," but he liked to fake ignorance of newfangled youth media. "The Margot character said you abducted her and that you're planning to eat babies." I was so relieved. I had to suppress a laugh that my dad saw Margot as a character, not a human being. I suppose his perception was correct, at that.

"Oh, Dad," I said, "she's a nutcase. She was here for, like, two nights and she took some drugs and freaked out."

"You do drugs there?" my mom asked, squelching a shriek. I could tell she was pulling at her hair.

"*She* did, Mom, not us. She's crazy. Everyone knows it. They even kicked her off that show, you know." (Too bad we forgot about those bumper stickers.)

"Ask him why Tad Steppling proposed to her, then!" my little sister interrupted from yet another extension. She must have been on break from law school, but it didn't account for her reversion to a twelve-year-old.

"She's marrying Tad Steppling, the actor?" I asked. Margot sure worked fast.

"Quiet, Denise," my mom said. "Hang up the phone." My sister clicked off, her damage done.

"Look, Dad, Mom, that's all just TV nonsense. Margot's looking for publicity."

"Well, Zach, she's getting a lot of it at your organization's expense," my dad said, appealing to my business sense.

"Is it a cult, honey? You can tell us." My mom was more on target than she knew.

"Besides, I thought Tad Steppling was gay," my dad said, distancing himself from my mom's hysteria. She was probably the one who had made him call in the first place.

"He *is* gay," I said, following him off the main subject. "That Cosmotology cult arranges marriages for all its gay movie-star members."

"So that must mean the Margot character is now a Cosmotology member, too."

He was right. That's what it must have meant.

46.

19 December 1995.

The 188 party looked as though it would be our best yet. I was better at organizing a club by myself, without a cult leader involved. We even got faxes from the editorial staff at *Plugged* requesting passes. I hired young, little-known DJs to play. I liked the idea of giving a chance to some new talent, and there wasn't any money around to pay for the headliners.

By the time the doors opened at 10:00 P.M. on Tuesday night, I realized why so many people wanted to come to our club. We were the freaks. We had been exposed as a sex-and-death cult on national TV by a *Real World* starlet. Everyone wanted to experience our genuine piece of Bay Area neopsychedelic insanity before we were gone. We were the most famous circus sideshow since Mondo 2000 and, by this stage, even more paranoid.

A pack of Japanese businessmen in Italian suits ran to the back of the club to find Nomie and her herbal smart bar. They kept asking her for "real" drugs instead of the powdered over-the-counter drinks. We had to disappoint them. Hordes of high-school kids crowded into the ambient lounge looking for an orgy. Every once in a while a girl would expose one of her breasts for half a second, but there was no sex to be had. A gang of high-school boys went from bass speaker to bass speaker, hanging on them until they fell over, but they couldn't cause an explosion. Parrot carded them and kicked them out. A group of girls, all dressed exactly like Margot in her *Rolling Stone* pictures, piled on top of one another and stared at the ceiling, trying to get abducted.

Almost everything that had ever happened at the Ecstasy Club had been reduced to asinine folklore. The *Plugged* editors strolled around observing the spectacle with the cool distance of Malthusian social scientists preparing a report on a soon-to-be colonized South Pacific island culture.

If they'd only known what was going on in Tyrone's shaftway. Then they would have known just how significant, or pathetic, we really were.

Margot herself eventually showed up, with her fiancé Tad Steppling on one arm and Officer Laruso on the other. I hate to admit it but she looked really good. She was wearing a designer sheath dress, her hair was done up with lots of wispy strands sticking out around her face, and she had a professionally smooth makeup job. I think Tad had a professional makeup job, too.

As I approached the threesome and Laruso put out his hand for me to shake, I felt my testicles instinctively shrink. I knew he wouldn't hit me in public, and I knew he had no reason to be violent (unless, of course, he knew about our prisoner), but I couldn't hold back my fight-or-flight response on encountering a man who had so casually pummeled me before.

"See how easily everything can work when we coordinate our efforts?" Laruso congratulated me.

"Yes, sir, I do. Thanks so much for coming."

"You know Margot and Tad, don't you?"

"Yeah. Hi, Margot." I had nothing to say to her. "You look good."

"Thanks, Zach," she said condescendingly. "Isn't it funny to think I actually lived here?"

"Yeah, Margot," I couldn't restrain myself. "Almost as funny as the *Real World* house."

Tad laughed. Margot nudged him.

"It was a good launching pad," she said, as if she was onto better things.

"So I guess you'll be moving into one of those Cosmotology communes soon, eh?"

"Oh, heavens no, Zach. We visit the Hollywood Villa and work personally with E. T. Harman."

"Oh, really?"

"Why yes, we're in constant touch with Earl."

"And how is he?"

"We just spoke with him last night, didn't we, Tad?"

"Um, yeah," the movie star lied. "Just last night."

Some photographers moved in on the star and would-be star, so I took it as an excuse to cut out. Laruso grabbed my hand as if to shake it, then closed his steel grip and pulled me into his face.

"I know what you're doing, Levi," he spoke through his teeth. "You think you've got this all figured out but you don't. You're just part of the machine now."

"I don't know what you mean, sir."

"Don't play prep-boy with me. I know about your little field trip. The place is surrounded. I know everything." If he knew everything, he would have said what everything was. Probably.

Brooks rescued me from the interrogation.

"Duncan needs you," he told me, before noticing Laruso and cowering away.

I smiled at Laruso and took off before he could stop me. I saw that he was following me with his eyes, so I ducked into the herbal lounge, then snuck over to Tyrone's door and knocked the code.

"Who is it?" I heard Henry's voice from inside.

"It's Zach. Open up." In the time it took for Henry to let me in, Laruso spotted me again and headed toward one of his men.

"Damn it!" I said as Henry closed the door behind me. "Why did you take so long? They saw me coming in."

Tyrone placed a large steel bar into some brackets on the door frame.

"No one's getting in or out," he said.

Then Henry explained to me what was going on.

Alex had stolen some Thorazine from the pharmacy, which had stabilized Pig enough for him to operate the visionquest computer. Duncan's master plan for 188 night was to brainwash Harman using Harman's own technology: the EE 136 PZ amplification circuit. This was the last night of enhanced novelty before the window closed for another two years, and Duncan was determined to have it out now or never.

While the well-attended fiasco raged on in the main room and Laruso's boys circled the building, Pig was in the shaftway wiring

Harman and Duncan into the virtual visionquest gear. He modified it to allow for three sets of goggles, headphones, and gloves to be used at once.

"Three?" I asked.

"Yeah, mate," Henry said. "Duncan wants you there to back him up—and to bear witness to whatever happens. For your book."

Duncan was suspended from a harness attached to Lauren's pulley ropes going straight up to the grate on top of the shaftway. He and Harman were already patched into the system—one of Harman's arms was freed from its bindings so that he could operate his glove controller. Pig set up a monitor down at ground level for others to watch the showdown as it happened. They positioned me halfway up the stairs with a headphone and goggles, but didn't hook me up to any of the biofeedback circuitry. A Levite to the end, I was to view the proceedings but not take part. If they found Canaan, I mused, I'd be like Moses—seeing the promised land but never going in. If they killed each other in there, though, I'd be physiologically isolated from the carnage. I wouldn't have wanted it any other way.

I think everyone, Harman included, was looking for a way out of this mess, and the EE tube seemed about as good a solution as any. We were all willing to accept the basic premise that the tube had the ability to perform time shifting and psychic linking—Harman had based his career on it—and the belief alone would have probably been enough to permit a resolution on the rationale that "the tube made me do it."

So when Pig switched on the amplification circuit and the haze of color revved up on my goggles, I knew that something significant was going to take place, one way or the other. I just prayed it would be over before Laruso and his boys figured out what was going on, pounded down the door, and carted us off to prison.

Through my goggles I saw two clusters of sparkles, and assumed the spiky blue one on the left was Harman, because the pink-orange one on the right was composed of the same little yin-yangs that Duncan projected the last time he was in there. The background slowly shifted from pale blue to white and appeared to breathe. I also heard two buzzing sounds, not coordinated with the positions of the clusters but moving randomly from my left ear to my right.

What followed was something like a conversation. It wasn't in words, exactly, though the buzzing sounds were plainly Duncan's and Harman's voices. But I sensed it more as a conversation of racing thoughts—like a shared stream of consciousness.

It began as a thumb-wrestling match, with each voice trying to show the other that it was on top. They were attempting to narrate a history together but had differing opinions of whose history it was, or if it was a history at all rather than a future. Somehow, it felt as if the stakes of the story they were writing were those of the human story itself.

Harman's figure kept wrapping itself around Duncan's. It looked both violent and sexual. He was telling Duncan not to be afraid—that he had been expecting him for a long time. This was his destiny. But Duncan didn't want to go along. He kept allowing himself to get almost completely surrounded by the spiky blue form, then pushing a pseudopod of his own form through an opening at the last second.

For all I know, they may have just been playing an elaborate, thought-controlled video game courtesy of Pig's computer and the EE tube, but after a few minutes of these pixel wars I heard Duncan scream.

I freed one eye from my goggles to see what was happening up there.

Duncan shrieked and convulsed while Harman twitched along with him, gently laughing. Then Duncan's screaming turned to words.

"But you're wrong! I'm not really one of you!"

"You are," Harman shouted back confidently. "One eighty-eight."

"Earl Tyrone Harman is 188!" Duncan said. "Not George Thomas Duncan. I'm 190."

Harman laughed. At first it sounded demonic, but then almost paternal.

"But your father was named George, too," he said. "You're George the second. Minus two. One eighty-eight."

Duncan froze in place. He looked up in Harman's direction, but forgot that he couldn't see anything through the goggles. He was blind. Confused. I was pondering why one should think to subtract two for George the Second, instead of adding two, when the next wave hit.

They both convulsed again. Harman reached with his free arm toward Duncan, who seemed to be fighting him off. They were flailing about in midair, wrestling without touching each other.

I could hear pounding on the metal door beneath me. The police.

Even though Duncan told me afterward what happened, my recollection is that I understood what they were communicating to each other in the visionquest circuit while it happened. I was going through my own trip in there, I know, and worrying about the police, but my thought process followed along exactly the same lines as their argument.

They both wanted to come together—Harman admitted that he needed Duncan, which was why he had concocted everything up until now: to franchise Duncan's work. We were the ones who voluntarily established the Ecstasy Club as an official Cosmotology franchise back when we ordered the EE tube. But Duncan wanted assurance that he wouldn't simply be absorbed. The Ecstasy Club still had a mission that couldn't be sacrificed to the convenience of the moment.

Down below, Tyrone was pressing himself against the metal door. The pounding of the police clubs against it matched the rhythm of the rave music.

Then Duncan had a weird insight—I felt it, too. We saw that we could change history itself, and even the future, by seeing it differently. History itself is spin. Events are only real in the present tense—before they happen they're hype, and after they happen they're spin. The real substance of an event—if there even is any such thing—is inconsequential without pre-promotion and post-reportage. A rave is more about the flyers and the folklore than it is about the party; and the human condition is more about future expectations and historical interpretation than anything else. Human evolution is just the give-and-take between hype and spin. Propaganda and consciousness are the same thing.

That's the same logic that Duncan and Harman applied to their impasse, and it worked—though I only later understood exactly how. Both their bodies went tense for a moment, vibrating with a pulse that seemed to come from the computer or the EE tube inside it, or the banging on the door, or the pounding of the bass. As the police crashed through the metal slab, taking Tyrone down with it, both the bodies above me went limp. Duncan hung in space suspended by his harness, swinging peacefully like a baby in a cradle, while Harman stroked Duncan's hair with his free hand.

"What the Sam Hill?. . ." I heard Laruso exclaim from below. I remember wondering who Sam Hill was.

"It's okay, Phil," Harman said calmly. "We were just doing a little experiment together. Isn't that right, son?"

Duncan slowly looked up at Harman. He pulled off his goggles and then gently removed his elder's. They stared at each other, eye to eye, just inches apart. Then they both smiled. It was like they were in love.

"The fire marshal said this door should be kept open," an embarrassed Laruso spun his faux pas.

47.

The two opposing views of culture, evolution, society, control, technology, and time itself—they boiled down to Duncan's hype and Harman's spin. Two time travelers with different points of view—one rewriting the past and the other scripting the future. It was a perfect fit.

Like Stanley and Blanche, Duncan and Harman had their date from the beginning. They had been dancing this dance for centuries. All they wanted to do was make love, and they finally got to do it.

The yin the yang, the right the left, the man the woman, Apollo and Dionysus finally duke it out and learn what people on the sitcoms always find out: the one who bugs you the most is the one you really want to make love to. They'd have done it long ago if they could just have figured out who it was that should fuck whom. A semantic formality, but it mattered to these guys.

By dawn Harman had left, agreeing to make the Ecstasy Club an officially licensed but self-governing franchise of the Cosmotology organization. Duncan would go on the payroll as Cosmotology's Director of Youth Activities. He called an early morning meeting on the rooftop to tell us of our new beginning.

Lauren and I had agreed to hear Duncan out and then inform him of our plan to leave. He was in a good mood, our legal troubles were over, and we were sure he wouldn't want a baby around to cramp his newfound style.

We all sat on the stone benches in Lauren's beautiful Zen garden while Duncan lectured from the pagoda as if it were a stage, with Henry and Parrot flanking him like Farrakhan's bodyguards.

"We've finally been given an opportunity to infiltrate and redirect the whole Cosmotology effort—from the inside. I've had Parrot draw up the papers signing over our business to Harman. In return, he'll be putting us all on salaries higher than anything we could make on parties and granting us a ten-year lease on the building for free."

I wasn't sure how Harman could grant us a lease on a building he had already surrendered to the city, but I wasn't about to quibble. Duncan ceremoniously handed me a pen and I signed away the DBA of the Ecstasy Club—perhaps the greatest albatross I'll ever know—to "Cosmotology, 6, Inc." (add it up).

"So are we becoming an evil cult now?" Nomie sensibly asked. "My dad's in this thing, you know."

"That's what you have to get over, Nomie," Duncan tried to explain patiently through his unbridled enthusiasm. "The Cosmotologists are end-state propaganda. That's why they need us." Duncan put his hands on his hips and started to pace around the rooftop—awkwardly, like a scientist appearing in a PBS documentary for the first time.

"The mind-control propaganda machine of the historically evil Malthusian empire has gotten so effective that it is now working against its own controlling agenda. They have done so much test marketing, surveillance, and deconstruction of the group mind in order to manipulate it that their own techniques have ended up serving to enhance rather than stifle the will of the people they were hoping to dominate."

This was Duncan's new spin on the folks he used to hate. He could still hate their intentions, but now he was free to participate alongside them.

"The perfected EE tube was so carefully matched to the collective frequency of our cultural consciousness that it served as an amplification of our most natural, uninhibited will. This is the way the conspiracy has worked throughout history—and it was my own ego and stubbornness that prevented me from seeing it."

"Amazing grace," Lauren whispered sarcastically to me. I didn't react. We weren't yet in the clear.

"Propaganda is a good thing," Duncan continued, "because it forces the programmer to match his agenda to the underlying wants of his audience. That's why Harman had to incorporate my views—our views—in order to get what he wanted from us. That's why Christianity absorbed the pagan gods, solstice trees, communion ritual, candles, and altars. The religion was paganized, as it were, and thus made more populist as it mutated in order to assimilate the beliefs of indigenous peoples. Propaganda turned back on them. They became their own hype."

"Sounds like that's what happening to us," Alex said. Of all people, it was my protégé who had the nerve to protest.

"That's the final rebirth of the Ninth Goal," Duncan responded joyfully. "You separate from the mundane by lifting yourself completely into the realm of thought: prediction and recall."

"You mean spin and hype," I said, recalling the way the words came to me in the visionquest.

"Exactly, Zach. The entire episode with Harman was predicted by the goals you and I wrote. Disconnect, reframe, synchronize, increase, and rebirth. I synchronized with Harman, we went to a new frequency, and liberated from mundane events into pure re-contextualization. We rewrote the story."

"I don't get it," Lauren said. "Who won?"

"Harman thinks he did," Duncan said, walking up to her and taking her hands (why did she have to say anything?). "But that's how we know we did." I took this as my cue.

"I'm glad it worked the way you wanted it, Duncan," I said.

"The way *we* wanted it," he corrected me, suspiciously.

"Maybe so, but now that it's over—"

"It's not over, Zach. It's just beginning. You can't leave now." He knew.

"We are, Duncan," I said. I slowly rose, taking Lauren's hand. "You don't want us here."

"You aren't seeing things clearly, Zach," he said, motioning for Parrot and Henry to move in toward us. He had seen this coming all along.

I backed away from Duncan and his henchmen. There was still a chance we could make a run for the trapdoor, get through it, and then lock it behind us. Lauren followed my lead and edged backward with me.

"Don't be foolish, Zach. You don't want to throw all this away for an illusion. You weren't born for that. Don't you see? We broke through it all."

"I want the illusion, okay? I want the substance. Spin it or hype it however you want."

We were almost at the opening in the roof.

"You're not thinking clearly, Zach. Just take it easy."

"You can't force it down our throats, Duncan. We have our own true will."

"You do, but you're not in touch with it."

"Duncan," Lauren said tentatively. "You don't love me. Not really. Just let us go."

"Lauren, if you look at me you'll see I love you in a way no one else can."

Lauren looked down. She was afraid of his suggestion somehow hypnotizing her.

"Zach," Duncan pleaded. "All the work, all the risk. You are right now so close to the thing you really want."

"I'm holding her hand, Duncan." I was a smart-ass to the end.

"Once we go into the visionquest together, I'm sure you'll understand everything."

Duncan, Parrot, and Henry closed in on us. Lauren and I spontaneously lunged backward but were stopped by sharp metal being pressed into our backs. Pig and Brooks were playing stickup with the tasers.

"Listen to me, Zach. You can't have done everything you did if what I'm saying isn't true."

He was still trying to perform an induction. That's when I realized that two can play at this game.

"You're right, Duncan." I turned to face Pig and Brooks. "One eight eight."

They both twitched and reset as they believed they should. We took the tasers from their frozen hands and continued to back up slowly.

"I see that you'll regret this your whole life, Zach."

"I'm willing to do that, Duncan," I said, looking back at him one last time. It was a mistake. He was making the secret gesture at me—the one from the DMT trip. I let it zone me out. Suddenly everyone else was gone and it was just Duncan and me on the roof, staring at each other. On some level, somehow, I knew I was turning my back on something by leaving. There was a greater dimension. There was a place of infinite possibility—where reality itself could be altered by choice. Duncan and I smiled at each other—it was a divine feeling.

Then I felt something sharp in my hand. Lauren had seen what was happening to me and dug her nails into my palm. As she did—and I hate to admit this—I perceived it as an unwanted intrusion, but it was enough to pull me out.

I knew Duncan was as vulnerable as I was, so I turned his own induction against him.

"Duncan," I said softly, "when you think back on the way you let Lauren and me walk safely out of this building, you'll feel so glad knowing everything worked out just the way you wanted it to."

Duncan's faith in the power of hype obligated him to let my suggestion work.

48.

So it turned out to be a love story. Not just Lauren and me. That's the easy, *Reader's Digest* way to understand it. We left all our worldly possessions at the PF and bought two bus tickets to Ohio using the money I got for junking my Ford Escort. In the end, it's the part of the story that's most important to me—my personal moral, I suppose—but it has nothing to do with the club so it has no place here.

The real love story was between Harman and Duncan. To this day they are working side-by-side, each thinking he outsmarted the other, and allowing the other to think so too. The lizard and the hippie get out of a bind by letting their war go "meta."

Looking back on it all, but resisting the temptation to spin it, I can see there are not a lot of cold, hard facts to prove that any of this took place. I list them here as a way of fulfilling my obligation to the Ecstasy Club and completing my role as the archivist of these events.

1. There is an air force base twelve miles east of Arcata, California, that was closed in 1985 yet maintains a warehouse of weather-balloon supplies. Curiously, over fifty armed security guards patrol the base around the clock, and local residents report constant activity, the movement of heavy machinery, and strange buzzing sounds emanating from the installation late at night.

2. Electronics Transponders Company is a listed security on the American Stock Exchange, with E. T. Harman as chairman of its board of directors. According to their prospectus and annual reports, the original company was founded by an anonymous consortium of businessmen who regularly purchased the patents on Nikola Tesla's inventions, as well as those of Wilhelm Reich and other contemporaries.

3. Military experts are still unable to explain what led to the massive surrenders of Iraqi desert troops during the Gulf War, and

have never documented the purpose of the six 8-ton generators that were airlifted to the region two days before the invasion.

4. E. T. Harman has a prosthetic extension on the pinkie finger of his left hand, visible only in photographs taken after his abduction by the Ecstasy Club, when the circulation was cut off for three days.

5. Marcus Sturgeon died in a fire at his home outside Santa Cruz, California, six hours after we left him alone. According to State Farm Insurance investigators, the cause of the fire was never determined and Sturgeon's heirs were fully reimbursed for the value of the house.

6. The Corpus Exsasis galaxy imploded on the same night as the first Phylogenic Foresight rave, six minutes before the Oakland Police Department logged its raid on an illegal gathering in the warehouse district.

7. There is a concrete patch, eight feet in diameter, on the east wall of the warehouse on parcel 376 in Oakland, California. The city tax on the property is currently paid by Cosmotology 6, Inc.

8. A man named Tyrone Marshall, whose physical description matches that of the man we found living in the PF, was honorably discharged from the U.S. Air Force Special Services in 1985.

9. Margot and Tad Steppling were married by E. T. Harman at the Cosmotology Villa on Paradise Island, the Bahamas, in the spring of 1996. According to *Entertainment Tonight,* the couple is planning to adopt a Croatian baby girl.

10. E. T. Harman is a dues-paying Mason.

I've tried to keep up with the other members of the Ecstasy Club through Brooks, who still sends me e-mail proposals for pyramid schemes.

Henry, Duncan's first and still truest disciple, followed his guru into Cosmotology. At least he's off heroin. Brooks joined Cosmotology, too, in the hope of curing his twitch-reset, but no matter how long he worked on the Orgonometer, the symptoms persisted. When he ran out of money but refused to work in their bookstore, they kicked him out. Pig, in the true spirit of computer programmers, transformed his bug into a "feature." He exploited his reset function and associated memory loss to look at programming problems from a fresh perspective every time. He got a job troubleshooting command code at Oracle. Nomie tenaciously stuck to Duncan's side until her father and Harman had a falling out. Her dad gave her seed money to start a business for herself, and she has made three million dollars so far selling "Organic Ecstasy—Nature's Legal High."

Parrot was put to work in Cosmotology's Foreign Holdings division, where he approved the underwriting of a Singapore mining expedition that later turned out to be a cover for an international money-laundering ring. Cosmotology's board of directors learned of the investment's true nature only after Parrot had left the country. His parents told me that the letters they get from him are postmarked Jakarta. Alex stayed on with Duncan through the summer, but enrolled at Vassar on schedule and became a starting forward on the basketball team in his freshman year.

I finally heard from Peter last month. He wrote to me at my parents' address in Westport. He is getting his Ph.D. from William and Mary Theological Seminary and plans to become a Jesuit priest. He said he believes Brock, Sturgeon, and Tyrone were the ones who had set us up all along, using us as pawns in an elaborate revenge scheme against Harman for his past sins. I guess it failed. He claims he ran out of the van and into the woods that night not because Harman had hypnotized him but because he was looking for an excuse to get away. I suppose it doesn't matter which is true.

Tyrone disappeared that last night, just after the police busted down the door. I like to think he migrated up to Humboldt to find Kirsten. I still don't know what happened to her.

For his part, Harman believed the whole ordeal had been worth it. Just a good week's work. He now had a real inroad to that pesky 18–28 demographic that had been eluding him so successfully, plus a young man as dedicated to him as he could want.

The only proof that Duncan may have come out ahead in the deal was the amputation of Harman's fingertip. We had kept him tied up for so long that he developed gangrene. But I'm sure Harman brushed it off as a small price to pay for converting a bright, young, and influential man like Duncan to Cosmotology. How else could he spin it?

Lauren is bugging me to end this book with something about us so I will, but only insofar as it applies to the legacy of the club.

I was watching *Die Hard 2* on TV with Lauren last night when it all began to make perverse sense. The lizards and the rave kids are playing an extended game of cops-and-robbers, but no one wants to be pegged as the bad guy. Movies like this stopped working because they could only play with the permutations of good guy and bad guy, or good-guy-as-bad-guy-deep-down and bad-guy-as-good-guy-deep-down for so long. In the end, the bad guy is still the bad guy, or the good guy turns out to be the bad guy. The only way out is for there to be no bad guy at all.

You can't even play it like Gandhi and King did—that passive-aggressive stance merely forces the oppressor to accept his own dominating posture. Martyrdom proves rape. No, if you can't beat 'em, make them think you've joined 'em, but hold onto the faith that they've really joined you.

Which is why, for me, Lauren ended up being the perfect fit. She's a woman. The otherness is built in. If you want to evolve the species, just pick a person with whom you'd like to mix genes and try to get along with her. All the boys and their toys and their wars and their propaganda were built to play this thing out on a societal level. Making love as individuals just wasn't enough. They had to believe their multimillennial investment in the ideological war was worth something, so they orchestrated their big fuck at the end of time. The hype meisters and the spin doctors together work to hallucinate a world where this can happen.

Duncan and Harman think they've really done it, but my guess is the battle will go on forever in one form or another. The counter-culture can never truly win, or it won't be the counterculture any-more, will it?

So I guess I was just selfish in the end. I wanted to experience the whole universe, and I finally found a way to do it. Marriage, a kid, a house, and a job. I guess everyone else is going to have to look after themselves from now on. This Levite has retired.

And if real life is just an illusory trance like the Nine Goals say? Tough shit. It's a pretty convincing illusion and I like it just fine. I don't get the thrill of hype anymore, but I can't be spun by anybody else, either. I suppose this means I've abandoned the cause.

How Lauren put up with me through the whole PF experience I'll never know. I was convinced I had been protecting her the whole time, when it was actually she who was repeatedly saving me from my own fanatical idealism. If she hadn't let me fall in love with her, I don't know if I ever would have gotten out of there.

It was only after escaping from the "metasociety" we were creating with Duncan that I saw just how rigidly conventional our value system there really was. Honestly, I found a hell of a lot less novelty in the ether than I have living in a one-bedroom apartment with Lauren, whom I married last March. I still think she's nature's greatest gift to the cosmos. She says I have to get over that.

We've had a few bumps, to be sure, but they were mostly my fault and, luckily, Lauren sees something in me worth waiting for. We both went back to school at the University of Cincinnati, she to complete a degree in architecture and me to get my doctorate in psych. I work a few evenings and weekends at a youth center downtown, and Lauren designs Web pages for an online travel service.

Lauren had the baby in a hospital in Cincinnati. Her mother drove in from Cleveland to help out. It was just like the birth of any baby, I guess. Lauren panted like they showed us, and it was a whole lot of work until the baby's shoulders pushed through her birth canal, which expanded tenfold to release our evolutionary successor.

And as Lauren's mom held our tiny infant in her loving arms, I couldn't help but notice that his head was bigger than normal.

Douglas Rushkoff is the author of *Cyberia, Media Virus,* and *Playing the Future.* He writes a weekly column about technology and culture for the *New York Times Syndicate* and is a frequent contributor to *Esquire, Details,* and *Paper.* He lives in New York City. This is his first novel.